THE FINAL GUARDIAN

THE FINAL GUARDIAN

D. M. DECKER

decker
PUBLISHING

Decker Publishing
Text copyright © 2024 by D. M. Decker

Decker Publishing

The Final Guardian : a novel / by D. M. Decker. - 1st ed.

Book design by D. M. Decker

ISBN 9979-8-9906593-1-5 (paperback)

www.dmdecker.com

To my husband, Ryan, my three amazing kids, and my parents, who, without their love, support, and encouragement, this story would never have been published. Thank you for inspiring me every day.

Gratitude to my FMCA Cohort who opened my eyes to thinking outside the box and taking that final leap.

To all the relentless cheerleaders out there, may you always find someone who believes in you as fervently as you believe in others.

TABLE OF CONTENTS

I. The Beginning

Sword in hand, she ran. The medieval handle rubbing raw the open sores on her sweaty palms, while the stone on the hilt continued to burn bright blue. It was an unwanted beacon leading her further into the oppressive humidity. Gaining her bearings, she frantically scanned the moss-covered trees, hiding any clues to her location. Sweat burned her eyes as she tried to push through the thick brush carrying the heavy burden. The woodland had become her own personal maze to nowhere. Even her gown was a lavish design intended to weigh her down. The multitude of petticoats, laces, layers, and jewels becoming a magnet for the decaying rot on the forest floor. Hunted like a doe, her rapid heartbeat told her the end was near. Screech owls continued to send their alarm from above, covering the only light offered by the full moon. Snakes streamed through the bright white roses springing up on the dank, moist path. Her panic rose. She couldn't breathe.

Beep, Beep, Beep

"Evie, wake up! Your alarm's been going off for the past five minutes," called her father, his voice piercing through the the haze of the nightmare.

Evie started her first day of Sophomore year to the blinding sun streaming through her bedroom window, not to mention her father's irritatingly cheery morning voice. As she yanked the covers back over her head, a loud screech jolted her out of her dark cocoon.

"Sorry, Sheba," Evie yawned, rubbing her eyes. She reached over the queen-sized bed to pet the bright orange cat, already nudging its way underneath. "Wish I could spend the day under my bed," she added, glancing over at her dad and attempting a morning smile. Judging his expression, it left a lot to be desired.

"Already starting the day like a true student," her father said as he walked out her bedroom door. "Come on, kiddo. I have to get going. Your mom's in the shower and getting ready to leave. She has to open the store because Becca's sick, which means you won't have a car."

As she watched her father's starched navy blue pants disappear around the corner, she groaned and threw the covers back over her head.

"Get up, Evie!"

"Yes, sir!" She pulled the worn maroon bedspread back and gave a mock salute, then immediately dropped her hand as the Lieutenant Colonel stuck his head back in the doorway.

"Oh, and love you. Have a good first day." Winking, his salt and pepper hair disappeared, and Evie could hear the shiny black shoes clicking their way down the hardwood stairs.

"Love you too, Dad," she whispered.

It was a typical start to a normal day, well, minus the sweat-soaked-induced nightmare. Evie smiled at the poster of half the solar system hanging beside her closet. The poster had made it through every move since she was five, except for half the system being torn by her kitty cat clock haphazardly shoved into one of the moving boxes. It was the only decoration inhabiting the plain white walls. With a frown, she realized it looked like she still hadn't unpacked; already a year into the new assignment, and she continued to feel like a nomad. Taking stock, she took another look around. A bed, Grandma's old dresser, a matching nightstand, and a cheap pressed board computer desk her Mom found at a garage sale, all set in place for a sufficient and easy getaway. With her brown hair matted to her face, she pulled her favorite gray Air Force T-shirt from her chest. Evie had to admit she was pretty excited to spend another year at Hillstead High. In most of the places she lived, she couldn't wait until the new destination orders would arrive. However, Hillstead was different. Being a military brat had its pluses and minuses, especially when you wanted to get out of dodge. She just hoped Dad could make this assignment last through senior year. Perhaps she should think about painting the bedroom walls this time. Dropping her head into her hands, she rubbed her eyes as her cell phone rang. She already knew who it was before she even picked it up.

"Hey, Lana," Evie said as she answered the phone.

"Hey! Are you awake?" came the excited voice on the other end.

"I answered the phone, right?"

"That means nothing. I know how you operate. You're late for everything, including meeting your best friend. If I would've waited for you to say something to me on the bus last year, hell would've froze over."

"So you've told me a million times."

"You're gonna wear that outfit we picked out, right? No more boring T-shirts this year. Remember what we talked about. We're no longer freshmen, so we need to act like it. Oh, and please make sure you're here by 7:45. I don't wanna pink slip on the first day."

According to Lana, Evie had been her best friend for sixteen years. It was just that Evie had been late in getting to her. Lana was always one to march to a different drummer. She had lived in the small town of Hillstead her entire life and strived to be different, even at a young age. It was instant soul mates when Lana first sat down beside Evie on the bus last year. They bonded over old 90s episodes of *My So-Called Life* and stale Halloween candy. Lana loved the show and believed it was ahead of its time, much like herself. Mid-year, Lana started dressing like the character Rayanne and never looked back. To Evie, Lana was everything she wasn't. While Evie was short, Lana was tall. Where Evie had plain brown unruly hair, Lana had sleek raven black, minus the random colors she liked to thread through it.

"Oh, crap!" exclaimed Evie. "I wasn't thinking. I can't drive today. Mom has to open the store this morning." Evie's mom had always moved from job to job along with her dad. However, Hillstead had been her mom's hometown, and with her grandparents gone, they lived in the same house where her mom had grown up. Evie knew her mom liked the excitement of moving, but she seemed even happier now, taking part ownership in an antique store with an old friend.

"Couldn't Ms. Manser pick her up? Doesn't your mom understand how wheels will only improve our social status? I mean, being held back a year has to have some perks for you, right?"

"Becca's sick. Look, I don't see why it's such a big deal. We can just ride the bus," looking at the clock, she rolled her eyes, "Oh, scratch that. Can't Blake take us?" Evie could hear the huge sigh over the phone.

"I hate asking Blake for a ride."

"I get it, but at this point, we don't have any other options." As Lana's good-looking older brother, Evie was always a bit tongue-tied around Blake or any cute guy for that matter. Dark like Lana, he seemed to fit the bill when it came to his intense brooding. But that worked for Evie since he never said two words to her anyway.

"Fine! We'll pick you up in fifteen minutes. Don't you dare think about wearing your usual stuff! If I see you in another gray T-shirt and jeans, I swear I will scream!" Not bothering to move the phone away from her mouth, she yelled for Blake. "Loser!!! We have to pick up Evie. Oh, shut up. See you in fifteen, Evie."

Dropping her cell phone on the bed, Evie walked to the bathroom to assess her appearance. Every year, she thought something miraculous would happen. But all she ever saw was the same old Evie: brown curly hair, plain brown eyes without even a hint of green, and freckles that continued their lazy meander across her nose. During the summer, they practically overtook her entire face. All in all, she knew she was forgettable. She ran out of the bathroom, quickly pulled her unruly curls back into a small clip, and put on her usual T-shirt and jeans, opting for dark blue instead of grey; she hoped Lana would approve. She rushed down the stairs and entered the kitchen to grab a banana from the fruit bowl. On the way out, she noticed the note.

Have a great 1st day! Text me if you need anything. I put money in your account for lunch.   Love you, Mom!

Fifteen minutes later, Evie was still waiting on the porch swing, racking her brain for the details of her nightmare. She stared at the garden gnome sitting on the front step, frozen in a perpetual state of pulling his pants up. She wondered what her mother saw in the creepy decorative companions. Just as a glimpse of a white rose flashed into her consciousness, the strings of an electric guitar came blaring down the street with a screech of the car wheels. Evie grabbed her book bag and ran towards the orange GTO's passenger door.

"Evie, how could you?!" Lana pleaded, jumping out of the front seat to let Evie in the back.

"Hey! You don't have to yell at me! I was in a hurry, and it's like I told you when you bought the shirt: red and low cut is not my style." Noticing that Blake was busy adjusting the stereo controls, Evie hovered her hands over her chest. "Besides, it makes me uncomfortable."

"Are you talking about your boobs again?" Lana asked.

The blood rushed to Evie's face.

"Turn the music down, will ya!" Lana continued, glaring at her brother.

"Lana!!!" stammered Evie as she nailed Lana with a balled-up piece of paper from the back seat.

"He doesn't care," she said, nodding towards Blake. Ignoring his frown, she turned the music off. "He doesn't care about anything these days, do ya?" She pulled the passenger seat visor down to fix the thick black eyeliner already smudging underneath her dark brown eyes.

"Shut up. I could just drop you off right here," Blake warned before turning the music back on.

"Whatever," Lana said, catching Evie's gaze in the mirror and raising her voice to a near shout. "I don't know why you cover those things with a sports bra! You look great, and your boobs are fantastic! You should start showing other people how beautiful you are."

"Thanks, but I don't need a pep talk right now." As she watched Lana pinch color into her cheeks, she couldn't help but envy Lana's carefree attitude towards life. It seemed like nothing could dampen her spirits. "Did you seriously think I would wear that low cut thing?"

"No...yes...oh, I don't know," Lana said, shoving the visor back up and staring out the front windshield.

"Leave her alone, Lana," Blake commented, meeting Evie's eyes through the rear-view mirror."She looks fine."

Evie felt sick. Her words stuck in her throat, as Blake averted his gaze back to the road. Dropping her head down, she knew her face was a blotchy red.

The remainder of the car ride was silent except for the lead singer moaning about saving himself and losing his addictions on life. Evie gave in to the music and let her mind wander. She fixated on a cloud shaped like a snake, its fangs emerging with the strings of the electric guitar finishing its break. Just as the snake consumed a neighboring cloud, the word "forgiveness" echoed in her ears. Suddenly, the music stopped, and the driver-side door slammed shut. Startled out of her reverie, Evie pulled herself out of the car.

"Blake," Lana yelled. "Try to stay in school for at least one day this year!"

"Go to hell!" Blake exclaimed, hitting the automatic lock for the car.

"You ok?" Evie asked, lightly touching Lana's shoulder.

With a tight smile, Lana shrugged off Evie's hand. "I'm fine. It's just that Blake keeps pushing us apart. The longer Mom's been gone, the worse it gets."

"That can be normal, right? Maybe he just needs more time."

"Evie, it's been three years! At some point, he needs to move on. He just needs to realize that Dad's not the right person to-" Just as Lana was getting ready to finally tell her about her elusive father, a boy with a goofy grin, matching his little boy exterior, bumped into Evie, throwing her into Lana.

"Hey, Evie!"

"Hey, Seth," Evie said, rolling her eyes at Lana before turning back to Seth. "How was your summer?"

"Fine," he responded. "Had to spend it with my Dad in Seattle. But it wasn't all that bad since he ended up getting me the best gaming laptop on the market. Some perks to having a divorced dad in Sales, right? You aren't gonna believe the graphics." Seth was the brother she never had. Standing at her height with wavy brown hair, he followed her same relaxed dress code on life.

"Let's not start this already..." Lana whined.

Seth frowned at Lana and pulled on his red T-shirt that was a size too big.

Lana grasped Evie's shoulders and locked eyes with her. "Please promise me no more online gaming. Understand?"

"Understand," responded Evie in her best soldier impression.

"I'm being serious. No more."

"I agree with you—no more. Besides, I had this really weird dream last night, and I think it had something to do with it. Very graphic."

"Okay, I'm trusting you. I also wanna hear about this dream at lunch." Turning to Seth, Lana gave him a once-over. "Seriously Seth, didn't you wear that same outfit on the last day of school? You really need to drop the Clark Kent look. It's not working for you."

"Aw, how sweet!! You remembered what I wore!"

"Only because you freaking wear it every day. Why do I bother?" Making their way into the front door of the school, Lana turned back to Evie. "You really should think about choosing some better friends. See ya later. I'm off to homeroom. And remember, no more gaming."

"Yes, ma'am," Evie responded with a salute. She playfully bumped into the side of Seth. "She'd make a great General."

"I don't know how she's your best friend. You're so different. Are you really not gonna play anymore?"

"Well, sort of. I need a break. Time to start thinking about more important things," she laughed, hitting Seth on the shoulder. "I'm a sophomore, you know."

"Nice," he frowned as he turned to look at a redhead in a short mini-skirt struggling to open a bottom locker.

"Now who's thinking about more important things?" Evie smiled.

"What?" Seth asked, confused.

"Nothing. Who's your homeroom with?" Evie asked.

"Mr. Foster. You?"

"Ms. Lancaster," Evie said, stifling a giggle.

"What's so funny?"

"I guess you and Lana will get a lot of bonding time this year."

"Perfect." With a nod of his head, he turned down the hall.

The morning flew by with a brief orientation and locker assignments. Evie didn't even get the chance to see Lana or Seth. For as much as everyone wanted to change and look different, everyone stayed the same. With brand-new outfits and hairstyles, the interior rarely changed. Even the teachers hardly deviated from the norm. As she walked down the halls, she had to admire the perky kids that had already decorated with the usual gaudy bright-colored posters, urging every passerby to join their club. She had found out long ago that she wasn't well-equipped to be a joiner. With moving every two years, who could blame her? Though she had to give the school credit. Her parents had been ecstatic when they found out her grandparents' small house resided in the influential estate district of town; their house sparred the pricey renovations that were so popular. Either way, it meant Evie could attend the highly accredited Hillstead High.

She walked through the double doors with her lunch tray, feeling elated to have finally made it to her favorite period of the day. The long rows of tables were already filled with the usual groups one finds in every grade school cafeteria. It was always the same, whether in street clothes or uniforms. With a spring in her step, she could barely remember the extreme anxiety that used to have her running for the bathroom. The lunch room was the ultimate segregation of the masses. It was for catching up with friends, and when one didn't have friends, it was much easier to find a project that needed to be completed. Lana had changed all that. Yes, Hillstead was much better. Giving a prayer of thanks, she took a deep breath and scanned the crowd.

To the left of her were the cheerleaders and jocks, sitting at a table with their tray lunches, already punching each other in the shoulder and congratulating themselves on their coolness. Or at least, if you weren't in that group, that is how one saw it. To the right sat the lost students, as she liked to call them: the ones nobody ever bothered to remember and who always brought their bag lunches from home. And, of course, you had every other possible social network shoved into each section of the packed room.

"Evie, over here!" Lana called, waving her brightly colored nails.

"Decide it was time to make the dean's list?" Evie asked, glancing briefly at the school ambassador crowd sitting at the table to their right. She then set her tray down and smiled.

"Something like that," murmured Lana. "Oh, fries. Can I have one?" She grabbed the cold fry and bit into it.

Evie pointed to the small plate in front of Lana and stuck out her tongue. "Salad? Really?"

"I have to get into shape for my new crush."

"Crush? What are you talking about? Besides, you're already a bean pole."

"Aren't you gonna ask me who it is?"

"Who what is?"

"My new crush, silly," she whispered.

"What?" Evie asked, straining to hear over the boys sitting at the next table.

"Damek Adams."

Dropping her fry onto the tray, Evie gave Lana her best dumb stare.

"What? He would be perfect!" Lana huffed.

"Sure, he would. If you were the head cheerleader. Come on, Lana. You have to be joking. Besides he's already dating the actual head cheerleader."

"I never said that I didn't like a challenge."

"Yes, but you're just setting yourself up to get hurt again. Why do you continue to play this stupid game? Don't you remember what happened last year?"

"Last year's in the past. And I got over 'you know who' within three months."

"That was the entire freaking summer! I don't wanna go through this again."

"Hey! You're supposed to be my best friend."

"And I am. Which is why I'm not playing this game with you anymore," Evie declared, picking up one of her fries and throwing it at Lana. The summer had been a complete bust with Lana's constant moping. They had missed out on every freshmen party for fear they would run into Lana's last failed crush. Evie was determined not to let that happen again. Her complaints fell on deaf ears.

"Giving me the silent treatment now?" Evie asked. While waiting for Lana to respond, she looked over her shoulder toward the jocks. Damek Adams wasn't there yet, but Evie didn't need to see him to remember what he looked like. Last year, she had passed him in the hall one time and couldn't help taking a second glance. It was almost as if she could feel his presence. Being the most popular and good-looking guy in school assured her that everyone probably felt the same way. He was at least a foot taller than her, with sandy blond hair styled in a trendy, unkempt style, crystal blue eyes, and one of the most outgoing personalities she had ever seen. He was perfect. Even the tiny smattering of freckles covering his cheeks was irresistible. What was a blemish on her only added to his charm. Even his name was straight from one of her mother's romance novels. Remembering her mom, Evie pulled her thumbnail out of her mouth.

"You know," Evie added, picking up her tray, "I could just go over and sit with Seth's group."

Lana crossed her arms over her chest and leaned back. "I've made up my mind."

"Fine," Evie exclaimed. "But I'm not helping this time." She dropped her tray back onto the table for effect and looked to the ceiling for patience.

"Oh, come on! I only need your help one more time. It'll be simple. All I need you to do is to go to the fencing club orientation with me today after school."

"What??!!" Evie cried.

"You don't have to sound like I asked you to bite the head off a snake or something!"

"Lana! We don't know anything about fencing!"

"It's just the first orientation class," pleaded Lana, folding her hands in prayer. "That's all I ask. Damek's the student lead, not to mention the star. It's the only way. You know, building common interest?"

"But fencing?" Evie asked.

"Didn't you say one of the things you loved most about me was that I forced you to try new things?"

Before Evie could respond, Seth plopped down next to her. Bending his head low, he shoved his elbows onto the table. "What are you guys talking about so intently?"

"Damek Adams," Evie answered.

"Evie, shush!" Lana whispered, reaching over the table to cover Evie's mouth.

Seth shook his shoulders and mimicked a high-pitched voice, "Ooh, Damek Adams. He's so cute."

"Shut up," Lana said. "You're just jealous."

"Hmmm...maybe," Seth allowed. "The dude can use a sword. Did you see him last year win the district competition? Amazing!" He leaned back from the table and took a swig of his soda.

Evie wiggled her eyebrows. "Lana wants to date him," she said. Seth burst out laughing and then started choking on the soda coming out of his nose.

"Evie!" Lana yelled as Evie began hitting Seth on the back.

"Sorry! I need someone to help me talk you out of this ridiculous scheme."

Lana shrugged. "Not happening, and especially not with him as your stupid sidekick. Isn't it enough that I have to suffer through homeroom with him?"

"Sweet! I've never been a sidekick before," Seth said, winking at Evie. "So, Damek, huh?" he turned back to Lana.

"Like you care?" Lana clipped.

"I don't, but I always enjoy a good show."

"Screw you!" Lana exclaimed as she stood up and grabbed her lunch tray. She glared at Seth and then turned to Evie. "Meet me at my locker after school. I need to talk to Blake before next period." With that, Lana stormed out of the cafeteria.

Evie knew she was upset. Lana hadn't even bothered to glance at the jock table to see if Damek had made an appearance. However, Evie did; still no sign of him. While slowly scanning the room, she caught Seth's stare.

"So? Are you gonna tell me the plan or what?" he urged.

"She wants to join the fencing club," Evie said. "And don't laugh," she added. But before she could finish the sentence, soda was already coming out of his nose again. "That's so gross. You seriously need to get that looked at."

After the final bell of the day, Evie shuffled her feet from her locker to Lana's. Despite being the first day of Spanish class, they had already started on subjunctives. She had seriously contemplated being sick. She let out a few faint coughs, but even Ms. Reyes, who hardly spoke good English, could tell she was faking.

Lana slammed her locker shut and turned to Evie. "Are you ready?" she asked.

"I guess," Evie pouted. "You sure you wouldn't rather come over to my house and ogle Jordon Catalano? I'll even let you watch Angela and Jordon's first kiss for like the 20th time." Evie smiled and tugged on one of Lana's many necklaces. "I'll make chocolate chip cookies..."

"Don't even think about hiding behind *My So Called Life*," Lana responded. "And if you're making the cookies, then it's a definite no. Now stop stalling, and let's go." Grabbing Evie by the arm, Lana dragged her the rest of the way to the gym.

Just as Lana opened the gym's heavy double doors, a blast of cold air hit Evie in the face. Goosebumps broke out across her arms as her eyesight started to waver. Suddenly, complete blackness encompassed her vision on all sides, blocking out the entire gym. She felt an urgent tug on her upper arm as a hazy blue light shined bright in the distance, her only clear view at the end of a fully formed black tunnel.

"Evie..." Lana called, her voice breaking through the haze as the pull on Evie's arm strengthened. With each annoying tug, the blue light emitted bright orange sparks, the edges crackling with intense heat. "Evie, open your eyes. Are you ok?"

With one last brilliant spark, the blue light shrank down to a small ball, sucking in the black tunnel with it until nothing remained. The illusion was gone, and Evie's eyesight returned. She gazed at the image left behind by the vision - a boy standing in the middle of the gym, explaining the parts of a sword to an eager admirer. It was Lana's new crush, Damek Adams.

"Evie, can you see me?" Lana asked as she grabbed Evie's shoulders and moved into her line of sight, blocking any clear view Evie had of Hillstead High's reigning heartthrob.

"Um, yeah," Evie hesitated. "I'm fine." She pushed Lana aside and frowned at her arms. The goosebumps were gone.

"What happened?" Lana asked. "You kinda checked out for a minute."

"I don't know," Evie responded. "Did you feel that breeze when we walked in?"

With a glare, Lana tugged on Evie's hand. "I know what you're doing, and it isn't gonna work. You're staying. Come on, let's get a seat."

Evie nervously bit her lower lip and scanned the room. The first three rows of bleachers were already filled with students gossiping about the first day. The gymnasium boasted a regulation-sized basketball court, and the coach's office had three large windows overlooking the entire court. Fencing had become one of the more popular sports at Hillstead High since the fencing team had become district champions. With Damek Adams on the team, it was destined to be great. It was almost as popular as the championship basketball team that had earned the school the latest up-to-date renovations.

Lana found an empty spot on the third row and pulled Evie down next to her. Evie couldn't help but glance at her arms and feel the chill start to spread again. She lifted her gaze to the center of the court and found herself staring at the blond Adonis. She pictured him as a politician, laughing with a group of guys, and smiled at the comical image. However, the cold rapidly trickled into her back and swept down to her feet, causing her to freeze. Suddenly, she noticed that Damek's deep blue eyes were fixed on her. The cold breeze that had swept through her body was now replaced by a warm presence, which lingered in its wake. Evie froze in suspense as she was held captive by his assessing gaze until an urgent tug on her shirt broke the intimate connection.

"Evie," Lana whispered. "He looked right at me! Did you see that?"

Evie blushed and stared at a piece of gum stuck to the floor. "I didn't see anything."

"He looked right at me! I knew this was gonna work!"

Suppressing the butterflies swirling in the pit of her stomach, Evie kept her head bent low but covertly let her eyes drift back up. Damek had resumed his conversation with his friends, and while testing the strange emotions, she stared intently into Damek's back. Despite the rapid spasms contracting her insides, she forced herself to relax.

Damek stepped in front of the bleachers and introduced himself, "For those of you that don't know me, I'm Damek Adams." He turned to quiet down the smirks from the boys in the front row and continued, "I'm the group's student leader. Professor Mike is the instructor, but he's running late. He should be here any second. In the meantime, please raise your hand if this is your first time. I'd like to pass out the beginner's booklet."

Raising her hand, Evie looked at the giggling group of new students interested in fencing, noticing that most were female. "Are you sure you wanna do this, Lana? Look around...I don't think you're the only one interested in common activities."

"What are you talking about? Fencing is a pretty trendy sport right now."

"Yeah, I'm sure that's it," Evie said as she rolled her eyes toward Damek and dropped her hand.

Lana yanked Evie's arm back up, smiling at Damek. "A little more faith, please," she said. Evie tugged harder.

"Faith in what?" asked a male voice.

The cold was back. Evie shivered, confused by the unusual emotions stirring within her; the most beautiful pair of blue eyes only inches away. Had he said something?

"I was just explaining to my friend here that fencing is a very prestigious sport," Lana said, twisting the ends of one of her bright red hair extensions; her face flushing to a perfect match. "She's fairly new to Hillstead."

"I don't know if I would say prestigious, but we do pretty well," he responded. Turning to Evie, he extended his hand. "Hi, I'm Damek."

Evie swallowed against the lump in her throat. Her annoying habit of silence around cute boys continued its reign as a simmering heat enveloped her chest.

"This is Evie," stammered Lana, putting her hand out, "and I'm Lana."As an afterthought, she quickly added, "We're sophomores."

"Great," he said, handing the pamphlets to Lana. "Hope to see you at the first practice." He ignored Evie's blank stare and continued to the next raised hand.

"What the hell was that all about?!" hissed Lana.

Finding her voice, Evie rubbed her temples. "I don't know! What's with me? Any cute guy and I become a mute."

"Do you like Damek?" Lana asked.

"What? No! It happens with any cute guy. You know that!"

"So, you don't think your sidekick Seth's good-looking?"

Evie smiled and asked, "Do you?"

"Funny," Lana commented, "anyway, I'm sure Damek has that effect on lots of girls. He's probably used to it. Did you see how cool I was, though? It will be per-" Lana stopped mid-sentence as a new voice interrupted everyone's excited chatter.

"Welcome!" the teacher said. "I am so happy to see a bunch of new faces."

Evie looked up at the teacher with an overwhelming feeling of familiarity. "Have we seen him before?" she whispered to Lana.

"I don't think so," Lana responded as she glanced down at the booklet on her lap. She leaned closer to Evie and added, "According to this, he teaches AP World History, and we both know how you are in history." She gave Evie a thumbs down and then turned back to the teacher.

"My name is Professor Michael Senoy, but the team just calls me Professor Mike. I look forward to working with all of you as you progress in the sport of fencing. To the chagrin of my more advanced students, I always like to begin every orientation with the words of Sir Richard F. Burton, a 19th-century fencer. "The history of the sword is the history of mankind.""

The rest of the orientation was a blur. Evie ignored the drone of unfamiliar terms and continued to stare at the professor. She estimated his age to be in his mid-sixties, possibly even older, but he was in perfect shape. If fencing was responsible for his physique, count her in. The professor's comforting voice and golden hair, now turned wheat with age, along with his once-bright blue eyes, hiding none of the enthusiasm they still carried, were mesmerizing. Standing just over six feet tall, Evie felt sure she had met him before—his resemblance to Damek a bit uncanny.

"Well, that was boring," Lana muttered, interrupting Evie's thoughts. "I thought it would never end."

"It's over already?" Evie asked, tearing her gaze away from the professor. She pushed a loose strand of hair behind her ear.

"Already? I didn't think he would shut up. The Italian school, the French school, half jackets, blah, blah, blah." Frantically searching the crowd, Lana's face lit up with a smile. "Great, there's Damek. You stay here. I'll be right back." Jumping up from the bleachers, Lana pushed through the growing group of girls surrounding Damek.

Evie pulled her book bag onto her lap and opened the front flap to pull out her worn copy of *The Hitchhikers Guide to the Universe*. Suddenly, a flash of light caught her attention. She glanced at Lana's empty bleacher seat and took a double take. There was a book lying next to her, but not just any book. Evie stared at the front cover of the small publication and examined the worn cracks etched into its soft brown leather. A solid grey stone nestled itself into the center, weighing down the entire small print. The deep grooves chiseled into the stone's core made her fingers itch to caress it. The crude imprint of a star housing a circle in its center reminded her of the simple sketches left by the early cavemen. Wavy lines radiated in between each of the star's four spokes. It was familiar.

Evie carefully rubbed the stone for fear it would fall off and looked around for the owner, but the only commotion was that of the giggling entourage surrounding Damek below. Startled by a shout of laughter, she set the book back on the bleachers and spied Lana's black and red hair, keeping reign with the leader of the pack. With a flash of heat to the side of her cheek, Evie turned back to the book. She looked up for any signs of a window to explain the brief reflection of light, but there was nothing but large grey ductwork. Not even one small skylight decorated the highly rounded ceiling.

With a deep breath, Evie picked up the book again and pulled the leather strap from its loose bow on the side. Gazing at the first page, she saw gold lettering hovering in front of her and reached for the raised words. She read them aloud.

"Evelyn's Diary 1893 - Beware of Lilitu."

The sound of a violin's strings hummed in her ear, its sustained notes capturing the glittering text in a melancholic melody. She felt a strong sense of belonging as she listened. At the end of the last glittering word, a single white rose bloomed, its soft petals opening to encompass the word 'Lilitu.'

"Evie, are you ready to go?" Lana interrupted, her insistent voice erasing all signs of the brief illusion. "Evie, can you hear me?"

Evie's heart was beating frantically. She tried to recall the image that had just flashed in her mind, but it was gone. Seeing Lana's frown, she quickly flipped the book over to clear her head. She took a deep breath, and her adrenaline kicked in. "Sorry, I'm coming!" she exclaimed. Without thinking, she stuffed the book into her bag and hopped down the bleachers one by one.

"Are you ok?" asked Lana.

"Yeah, I just...well, I thought I saw...Oh, forget it. Too many French fries at lunch, I guess." Jumping to the gym floor, she landed next to Lana.

"Well, it pains me to admit this, but you were right," Lana muttered. She fumbled with her layered necklaces and lowered her gaze to Evie's shoes.

Evie forgot all about the book. "What did you say?"

"You heard me!" Lana exclaimed as she turned around to leave the gym.

Evie gazed at Lana's back momentarily before hurrying to catch up. She dashed towards the double doors, beating Lana to them. With a smug expression, she turned around and used her back to push against the exit.

"Hey, watch it!" came an irritated voice from the outside hall. Evie turned to see the redhead in the short miniskirt that Seth had been staring at earlier.

"I can't wait until they're done renovating the orchestra room," said the redhead to a tall girl wearing jeans that were an inch too short. "These acoustics are unbearable!" She adjusted her violin case over her shoulder and shot Evie a nasty look.

"I'm sorry!" Evie said, raising her hands.

The tall girl nervously tugged on her jeans while slightly smiling at Evie. "Chloe, I think it's that depressing melody you keep playing," she said.

Evie gazed at the violin case as the gym's double doors closed behind her, feeling a fluttering of butterflies in her stomach.

"Earth to Evie," Lana hummed, waving her hand before Evie's face. "You look like you haven't seen a violin before."

"Sorry," she mumbled. "I must be tired." Evie stared at the back of the redhead. "I can be so stupid sometimes."

"Stupid? What are you talking about?" asked Lana.

"Nothing. I need to stop gaming. It's playing with my head."

"I could've told you that."

Evie shifted her attention back to Lana, realizing that the violin's music had not been a part of her strange mirage. "So, how did it go with Damek?"

"I guess the stereotype is true when it comes to the most popular guy in school. All he wanted to do was talk about himself. No wonder he has a cheerleader for a girlfriend. She can't have much in her head, if you know what I mean."

"Weren't you a cheerleader back in middle school?" Evie asked, trying to keep the grin off her face.

"Spirit Team, Evie. It was the Spirit Team," Lana laughed, showing Evie her jazz hands. "Wanna head over to your house and come up with my next victim?"

"I think that's your problem, Lana. Why don't you just let it happen?"

"If I waited for everything to happen, I would be fifty years old and still living with my dad. Let's go."

Pushing through the school doors, Lana headed towards the parking lot.

Evie felt like she was balancing twenty tons in her book bag. She was in the midst of an internal battle with her conscience and contemplated returning to the gym to put the book back. However, as soon as she caught sight of Blake leaning against his car, her mind went quiet. Even with his scowl, Evie admired his rebellious attitude. Blake wouldn't be afraid of stealing a book. Her bag bit into her shoulder.

"Actually, Lana, I have some things I need to get done before my mom gets home." Nodding towards Blake, Evie cringed. "He doesn't look too happy."

"He's never happy," Lana whined. "Are you sure you can't hang out? What am I gonna do?"

"I've a lot to get done. I promise we can hang out tomorrow-"

"God, Lana," Blake interrupted, "I didn't know you were gonna be this long. Let's go."

Evie slid into the back seat and slumped down to avoid Blake's line of vision.

"Tomorrow, you guys are gonna have to find a ride," Blake said as he thrust the keys into the ignition. He pushed himself higher in his seat and looked at Evie through the rear-view mirror. Satisfied with what he saw, he swung his arm onto the back of Lana's seat and pulled out of the parking spot.

"Oh, come on! It's not like you didn't have business to take care of after school," Lana hissed. "I saw you talking to that blond before I headed to the gym."

"Stay out of it," Blake exclaimed. Squealing out of the busy lot, Blake shot the finger at a student patrol trying to yell something.

"Blake-" Lana interjected.

"I don't wanna hear it. I won't be here tomorrow."

"Why not?"

"Don't worry about it."

"Have you told Dad?" Lana stared at his stony expression and continued, "I don't know why you encourage him. Please say something!"

Blake blared the music and continued to concentrate on the traffic ahead. Evie noticed the tension between the siblings and tried to think of a way to ease it. Their father was always a touchy subject. One that even she was afraid to broach with her best friend. As she fiddled with the zipper on her book bag, her fingers began to tingle, and her eyes shifted to the bag's front flap. Suddenly, she felt a static jolt.

Blake screeched to a halt in Evie's driveway. Lana hopped out of the car to let Evie out, but as soon as she got back in, Blake was already speeding away with her hanging out the front window. Not understanding a word her best friend was yelling, Evie made her way to the front door carrying her heavy burden.

2. The Diary

Evie rushed up the front porch steps, passing by the lawn guy hacking at her mother's favorite bush, and fumbled with her keys. She flung open the front door and continued her rapid pace up the stairs, paying no attention to the empty house around her. She slammed her bedroom door and gently placed her book bag on the bed, methodically rubbing her hands on the front of her jeans. She hadn't been this excited since the day she met Lana. Dropping down onto her bed, a hiss sounded from underneath. Sheba promptly jumped onto the bed arching her back.

"Sorry, Sheba," Evie said. "You aren't gonna believe what I did today. I actually stole something." Letting the confession out, if only to her beloved cat, gave her the courage to pull the book out. She couldn't help running her hand over the cool, crudely etched stone on the front cover. Not sure if it was out of approval or frustration, Sheba lightly pawed at the top of Evie's hand. "I knew you would understand." Evie took a deep breath and opened the book to the first page. "Okay, here we go," she whispered.

Waiting for the magic to start, she tried opening and closing her eyes a few times, expecting to see the words floating before her. However, no matter how much she willed the words to move, in the end, they were just plain black text. She knew she was now just a common run-of-the-mill thief with no excuse for magic. Perhaps Principle Filch would give her lenience. After all, she had never committed a crime before. Slowly closing the book, a tingling sensation tickled the tips of her fingers. With a quick lick to the end of Evie's middle finger, Sheba jumped from the bed, squeezing herself back underneath. Before Evie could let the doubt overwhelm her again, she opened the book to the first page. The words were still plain black text, yet they seemed to call out to her, a strange itch pushing her forward as if an adventure was about to begin. Without any hesitation, she started reading the first page.

"Evelyn's Diary 1893 - Beware of Lilitu"

April 28, 1893
My name is Miss Evelyn March. I am eighteen years old. This is the first time I have ever written in a diary. I always thought diaries were for those insipid giggling girls who spent their days pining after their prince in shining armor and filling the pages with love poems doodled with those tiny annoying hearts. Alas, I have changed my mind, which seems to be happening often these days. I believe this journal may end up being the key to my survival. However, before I jump too far ahead, let us start at the very beginning.

Today was rather frustrating. Master Senoy is starting to sound like Father. I swear that sometimes all Senoy cares about is making sure nothing happens to the future of the March Estates. I do not understand why it is so important that I marry. Nab has already confided that once he finds his future Duchess, he will then provide me with a home of my own. At least my brother understands me. If only I would have been born at another time. I truly hope women win the right to inherit their own estates without having to be widowed to do so. Father's idea is absolutely barbaric! Of all people from a loveless marriage, how could he assume it would be the best for me? Besides, any man who sets his sights on me only sees a wealthy dowry and not the beauty of my overly rounded nose. Believe me, I am not being humble. My cousin Gertrude once likened me to one of those cute pot-bellied pigs. Even at six years old, I knew I was not destined to be a beauty. At least at that age, I did not tower over all the other debutants. Though the weight has finally settled in all the right places, averaging five foot eight, most men 'accidentally' forget to sign my dance card. I must not blame them, for who wants to dance with a giant that smells like a lemon? I used to spend most of my time hiding my freckles behind a fan until Mother introduced me to her wonderful sour mixture. However, I digress. Let us move along to the more important details, shall we? First, I shall introduce our Master of Arms, Senoy.

"Evelyn, get your head out of the clouds," Senoy yelled, striking the inside of my arm with his sword. "You will never win the fencing competition if you do not concentrate."

"This competition is positively out of the dark ages. How could Father create this ruse? Using our family sword as a prize when all he means to do is find me a husband? I can not help that men are afraid of me." Swinging my sword into a quick arc, I lunged into Senoy's chest, hitting my mark. "He acts like I will shrivel up into an old maid. It is ridiculous. What about love, Senoy?"

"It does not matter what I think. And is it so bad to have a husband who can protect you and perhaps even grow to love you?"

"Hog Wash! I think we have made sure I can protect myself." Lunging towards Senoy's side, he scooted further back, deflecting my point. "What I do not understand is how Father could just give the March Family sword away?"

"Your father has always been uncomfortable with the sword. He knows nothing about its history, nor does your mother, quite frankly. Beyond the fact that she is in the bloodline to protect it, she has never wanted to understand its true meaning. Why should your father? It was not his burden to carry."

"Burden?" I asked with surprise. "I thought it was our gift!" I smiled and swung to my left, lunging into Senoy's other side. "Besides, she never wants to *understand anything unless it has laces and bows tied to it."*

With a twist of his wrist, he deflected my point with a dull clack. "Now give her some credit, Evelyn."

"What for? It is true, is it not?"

"Yes, but perhaps there is a reason behind it. Do not pretend to understand how your mother feels."

"Well, regardless, I will not let it happen," I said, stepping off the fencing strip. With a salute to Senoy, I removed my mask from my face. I flipped my dull, brown waist-length ponytail off my shoulder and grimaced. "I should just cut this blasted nuisance. I hear the French are making it quite chic."

"I will disregard that self-indulgent remark," Senoy responded, laying his sword on the table flanking the side of the long gymnasium. He looked back at me with a slight frown, wrinkling his unnaturally smooth forehead. "Is your outfit ready for the tournament?"

"Yes, and it is truly a work of art! Nab gave it to me last night, though he disagrees with my actions. He informed me that he would ruin my cover should I be hurt. Older brothers can be ever so annoying. I told him, thee of little faith." Watching the concern on Senoy's face, I dropped my sword on the table by his. "These men will not know what hit them. Imagine me dressed as a young Lord! I swear I shall be the most beautiful boy in the match. Once I have won this competition and the sword, Father will truly see me as the warrior I am."

"Be careful," he warned me. "Your courage is starting to border on arrogance." He picked up my sword and wiped the blade clean before turning towards the only window in the large open studio overlooking the garden below. From there, one could see every statue in the rose-filled oasis, which were my mother's signature flowers. On warm, balmy nights, one could even smell the scent of tea wafting from the large bushes and filling every crevice of the grand manor.

As for Master Senoy, he has been with me since my mother bore me, kicking and screaming into this world. My grandmother made my mother promise that Senoy would be responsible for overseeing my entire education. From what I have been told, he has been faithful to all the women in my mother's family line, starting with my great-great-grandmother. He is beginning to show his age, though I do not know how old he is. Even his strength, still apparent in his agility with a sword, belies his true generation. It is a discredit that the young men of today have given in to the leisure money can provide. Standing a mere few inches taller than me, I can almost picture what his silver hair used to look like. His blue eyes still held the vitality from his youth.

I often wonder why he never married. He has always been a favorite among the ladies. Though even with his charm and sophistication, it is his grace with the sword that amazes me the most. He has taught me everything there is to know about the sword and has *become more than just my mentor-he has truly become more like a father. My favorite sound is the clashing of our steel and our heavy breathing as the sophisticated dance becomes second nature. The prejudices of the world disappear. I cannot believe the time has finally come. In just four days, I shall be entering the 1st Annual March May Day Fencing Competition as Sir Moore from Asbury. The house is already bustling with preparations for the extravagant event. I will win the sword and prove to my father that I can take care of myself, along with keeping this sacred piece of history for the generations of women to come after me.*

Here we are at the end of my very first journal entry. I look forward to our growing friendship.

Addendum May 4, 1893: To the girl in white-Words do not begin to encompass my eternal gratitude. I can only hope this will aid you on your journey.

****

"Evie, open your eyes." Surprised by a female voice whispering in her ear, Evie did exactly as she was told. She couldn't even remember closing them.

She found herself staring into complete darkness. As she reached out to discover her location or the nearest light switch, she felt a tightness descend upon her chest, making it hard for her to breathe. She struggled to gasp for air while the sounds of waves crashing around her made her wonder if she was dreaming. Remembering the journal, she felt around her for the worn leather only to find nothing, not even a solid surface to keep her afloat.

Irate male voices yelled through the thunderous surf, hitting up against something hard. "If you do not obey his command," bellowed a strong baritone, "you shall be drowned in the sea!"

A flash of white light blinded Evie, and fear took over as she tried to wipe the grogginess from her eyes.

She heard a woman's voice beg in response to the angry voices commanding from above. "Leave me be! I have taken Father's punishment. I shall be cursed for all eternity!"

Suddenly, the bright light disappeared with a loud clap of thunder.

Evie struggled to see through the pitch black as the scent of roses invaded her senses, indicating that the woman was close. Her presence engulfed Evie in warmth and unexplainable contentment, leaving her mind racing through possible scenarios for her current dream. The waves slowly drifted away, taking the scent of flowers with them. Suddenly, a pinhole light appeared in the distance, and Evie's mind reached out for the small glow. As she gazed at the blurry edges, they began to turn bright red before the entire thing shook and exploded into a million tiny sparks, causing Evie to cover her head. After the explosion, silence engulfed her once again.

She opened one eye and saw her reflection staring back at her from the dresser mirror. Her face was scrunched up, with only one brown eye peering back. Blinking, she realized that she was sitting cross-legged on her bed, the stolen book still sitting open in her lap. When she looked down at the open page, a heavy ball of orange fur jumped right on top of it, causing Evie to lean back in surprise. Demanding attention, Sheba pushed her head underneath Evie's shaking hand.

"Oh! I'm sorry, baby. Did I scare you?" Evie cooed, scratching the back of the cat's right ear. "I think I scared myself. I don't think this is just any diary. It was like I was there, Sheba...watching...and then there was this darkness." Shaking her head, she unconsciously rubbed Sheba's ear harder. "I must be going insane! I mean, that's the second nightmare this week!" With a hiss, Sheba clawed at Evie's insistent hand. "Ouch!" Evie yelled as the cat leaped off the bed.

A metallic screech echoed from the garage door below. "Crap, Mom's home!" She quickly grabbed the diary and placed it on her desk. She rushed down the stairs, sliding onto the kitchen's wooden floor with her socks, and opened the freezer door. She grabbed a package of hamburger and quickly dumped it into a large pot just as her mom walked in, juggling a heap of fabrics.

Dinner at the Bennett house was a rushed process these days. With her mother now responsible for her own store and her father trying to make the next military rank, they hardly had time for their usual family sit-downs. Evie was already finishing up her spaghetti when her dad walked in the front door.

"Hey, kiddo! How was your first day?" he asked as he placed his laptop bag on the floor. He then bent over the kitchen counter to kiss her mom. Dinner was now destined for the bar stools surrounding the large kitchen island rather than the old dinner table abandoned in the small alcove. Its sturdy old legs, marked with the nicks from each family move.

"Same old. You?" She wiped her mouth with a napkin before glancing at her plate to find a star doodled in the last bits of tomato sauce.

"About the same." He reached behind the counter and turned on the Bluetooth speaker. Frank Sinatra's habitual deep voice filled the kitchen as Evie picked up her plate from the table and dropped it into the sink.

"I'll let you guys catch up. I already have homework to do," she said with a roll of her eyes as she slipped past her mom and headed towards the stairs.

"Really? Man, they keep you guys on your toes these days. When I was your age," he paused, winking at her mom before continuing, "Well, never mind. I always did my homework." He pulled a bar stool to the counter and piled noodles onto his plate.

"Sure you did, Dad." Evie heard her parents' laughter fade into the background as she made her way up the stairs. All she could think about during dinner was the journal. She didn't even notice when Sheba swiped a piece of bread from the counter, landing her paw in her mother's spaghetti. Just as she closed her bedroom door, her cell phone started ringing. With a sigh, she picked it up and sat on the bed.

"Hey, Lana," Evie answered.

"Hey! Get your errands done?"

"Sort of. Sorry about this afternoon. I was a little out of it."

"It's alright. You sure you're okay?" Lana asked.

"Yeah," Evie responded before pausing. She tried to think of the best way to tell Lana about the diary. "Hey, have you ever stolen anything?"

"You mean like a candy bar or something?"

"Um, sure," Evie said.

"Yeah, I guess so. I once stole a Snickers on a dare. Why? Did you steal something? Not you! Not Ms. Goody Two-Shoes," Lana said teasingly, causing Evie to reach for the diary instinctively.

"No, I was just asking," Evie lied, unsure why she felt the need to. "I'm taking one of those stupid online quizzes."

"I love those. Text it to me. By the way, what did ya have for dinner?"

"Spaghetti," Evie replied. She never entirely understood why Lana was always so interested in what they had for dinner, but it had become routine at this point.

"Yum! So, Rick Meyer tomorrow."

"Rick Meyer?"

"My new crush."

"Rick Meyer?" Evie moaned, flopping back on the bed and clutching the journal closer to her chest. "The freaking quarterback of the football team? Seriously? Yeah, Damek was a much stellar idea."

"Nah, he's in the past." Lana's voice sounded muffled over the phone. Evie waited for her to continue but suddenly heard a yell before Lana spoke again. "Oh wait, my dad's calling me. I have to go. We can talk tomorrow. Can you pick me up?" The phone went dead before Evie could respond.

"Spacey," Evie muttered, tossing the cell phone beside her. She pulled the journal away from her chest to stare at the cover. Whether from the spaghetti or the guilt, indigestion began to rear its ugly head. She wasn't sure, but she figured that stealing someone's diary was much higher on life's bad totem pole than stealing a candy bar. She lay on her stomach and pulled the journal in front of her. Resting her head on her hands, she took a deep breath and opened it.

April 29, 1893

Today was rather exhilarating! I met a college friend of Nabs. Even though he was a rather frustrating man, I have to admit, it was the most exciting thing to happen in a long time. I can still picture the encounter with him as if it were happening at this very moment.

It was the night of the ball. Laughter and music drifted through the large doors to the main ballroom as I hid in my usual spot. Tucked into the bay window across from the rather tall gold-rimmed double doors, I tried to stay as silent as I could, waiting for the moment I would have to walk in and have them announce my arrival. As always, my mother had outdone herself with my latest gown. The large poofs of white fabric covering my arms made me feel like one of those carnival attractions that come into town every summer. I pulled the blue cornflower sash around my waist and tried to breathe through the tight corset while scrunched into the small alcove. However, nothing could ruin my excitement this evening. Master Senoy had finally acquired a printed copy of Dominico Angelo's 'Ecole des Armes.' The brilliance of this expert swordsman's words cradled within my arms was enough to keep me away from the Welcome Celebration Ball altogether.

"Dominico Angelo," Just saying his name causes shivers down my spine.

His expert fencing is what caught my attention, but his love story is what held me in rapture. According to rumors, Dominico caught the eye of the beautiful actress Margaret Woffington, who presented him with a bouquet of roses before his first fencing match. Dominico attached the roses to his jacket and went on to win every match, with the roses remaining unscathed, just like his love for Margaret. Although, like all fanciful stories, he never ended up with her. He married some other woman, if my memory serves me correctly. However, it begs the question: why should it be that way? If only we could find our one true love. Either way, I knew I did not have the option of missing the ball. Why I was the ultimate prize, was I not? As I wrapped one of my mother's love sonnets around the book, I turned the page engrossed in the specific instruction. That is when Lord Ninny (whose real name I shall disclose later, but I think it suits him perfectly), a friend of Nab's, decided to introduce himself.

"You poor dear," Lord Ninny said. "I promise it cannot be all that bad inside. Surely, there are many young gentlemen to go around with no need to be a wallflower."

I looked up from my book and stared at the strong hand stretched out before me.

"Come," he added, "Let me write my name on your dance card."

This is the part where I looked right into the most brilliant brown eyes I had ever seen. I quickly lowered my gaze, and the book I was holding fell from my lap onto the floor. "Oh, pardon me. I was just..." Stammering, I tried to regain my composure. That was when his words finally sunk in. Wallflower? To think he thought I was a wallflower. Regardless if it was true, how should he know? I had never met him before. Suppressing the heat rushing into my face, I tried to push myself higher in the small, confined space.

"I will have you know, sir, that my dance card is always full. Most men are unable to secure a spot on it." For effect, I slid off the windowsill to pick up my book, but of course, as fate would have it, I ended up tripping on my gown instead. Drat, my Mother's incessant preoccupation with multiple petticoats! The large hands quickly grabbed my shoulders and easily brought me back upright.

"It must be your witty charm and not your gracefulness on the dance floor that keep the young bucks coming back for more," he responded. His smile was blinding.

"Thank you," I replied tightly. If only I had a sword. I would easily wipe that smirk off his handsome face... And to my utmost chagrin, he was the most handsome man I had ever seen. His dark, brooding eyes were enough to lose oneself in, not to mention the dark, wavy locks pulled back into a low ponytail. His size was all-consuming, not an ounce of fat but pure muscle, which was uncommon for a Lord of leisure. His broad shoulders all but blocked out the adjacent entrance to the ballroom. His hands radiated extreme heat into my shoulders as a severe tingling began to riot in my stomach. The surprise must have crept into my face because I suddenly heard his laughter breaking into my uncomfortable thoughts.

He gracefully bent down to pick up my forgotten book. A smile spread across his face as I watched him read the cover of the love sonnet.

The color red flashed before me. I tried to yank the book out of his grasp. "I was just-"

"Oh, I have a pretty good idea of what you were just doing. I never understood the attraction women have to this nonsense." He waved his hand in the air, then seemed to remember where he was and tilted his head forward. "I do not believe we have been properly introduced. My name is Lord Wyndham. I am a guest of Lord Nab. He has invited me for a week of leisure and, of course, the games. I suggest we forget this little indiscretion of ours."

Indiscretion? Of all things male! He reminded me of a peacock.

"You are the first Lady I have had the pleasure to meet. Clandestine as it is, perhaps you could help me?" He looked around for any other guests, and seeing none, he leaned in closer.

My heart skipped a beat.

"Lord Nab, along with the rest of my family, seems to be very intent that I marry soon. He insists that I meet his sister. It sounds as if she is already a spinster if you ask me. I dare say that must mean she was not blessed with her mother's good looks. What a pity. I must steer clear of her at all costs."

"Sir!" I gasped as my mother rounded the corner.

"Evelyn!" my mother exclaimed. "There you are! Where have you been? I swear that one of these days, you will send me to an early grave!"

Lord Wyndham turned around and tilted his head to my mother in surprise. "Ah, Duchess March, how good to see you again. You are as beautiful as ever. Why, that must mean this is Lady Evelyn." He turned back to me and had the audacity to wink.

I stood up straight to meet the laughter in his intense gaze. "It is Lady March to you, sir," I said firmly. Grateful for my mother's intrusion, I touched her shoulder. "Sorry to worry you, but poor Lord Wyndham was having difficulty finding the ballroom. It seems with his advanced years, his eyesight is not what it used to be." I gave him a brief, feign look of sympathy.

Lord Wyndham's laughter echoed through the large hall, causing the pounding in my head to increase. "Touché, Lady March. Have no fear, Duchess. Your gracious daughter was just telling me how best to woo my future wife. She was providing me examples from her lovely book here," he said with yet another wink, laying down the gauntlet.

"Evelyn! What are you doing reading books out here? You will never find a husband if you continue to read that foolishness!" My mother's cheeks turned a very attractive pink hue. She could even make embarrassment look good. In her late thirties, she was as beautiful as the princess I used to think she was. She was still considered a

rare beauty with silver-blond hair and unusual green eyes. She did not last one month on the marriage mart before Father snatched her up. It was too bad that I inherited my father's dark looks. At least that is what Mother always says.

"Oh, but Duchess March," Lord Wyndham interrupted, "Dominico Angelo's poems of love have given me true inspiration. For hath Lady Evelyn not been here at this moment, I do not know if I would have been prepared." He held out both arms and smiled at my mother. "Please allow me the honor of escorting you both into the ball. I shall be the envy of all."

My mother had forgotten all about my indiscretion and took hold of Lord Wyndham's arm. If Master Angelo had been here, I dare say he would have challenged this fool to a duel. To think Dominico, one of the best swordsmen in the country, would ever stoop to writing such drivel. That was when the proverbial hammer hit me right between the eyes. He had said Dominico Angelo's poems. He had seen through my disguise of the love poetry to the fencing manual. Touché Lord Wyndham. Taking his arm, I realized that I was going to have to stay away from this exceptionally aggravating Lord. Far, far away.

****

3. SPELLBOUND

Upon hearing the opening strings to a Minuet, the defined edges of Evelyn's exorbitant era faded into Evie's present suffocating nightmare.

Evie suddenly found herself in the familiar yet unsettling forest from her previous dream. Without the cover of darkness to hide the frightening images around her, the instinct to run hit her in the gut, causing her heartbeat to triple. Urging her feet to move, she pitched forward into hard, cracked dirt. Distinct high-pitched screeches echoed above as she looked up into thousands of tiny yellow eyes. She rubbed the scrapes burning on her hands and tried to stand. Once more, she found herself wearing a dress that belonged to the 19th century. She gazed at the delicate pink frock, pulling on the long petticoats inhibiting her escape. A light breeze lifted the dirt-stained ruffles along her collarbone as a cool drop of sweat dipped into the cleft between her breasts, giving credence to her current reality. She grabbed the bottom of the dress and began to rip. With each echoing slash of the ancient frock, a new wave of excitement rippled through the congregation of owls hovering above. After freeing herself from the bindings, she peered again into the forest brush. Unseen until now, a smoke screen of blue embers burned in the distance, begging her forward. With the flames leaping towards her, a familiar warmth seeped into her chest. In the bright, hot core floated a sword spinning with the hum of a nearby lullaby. The musical tones buzzed in her veins, inviting a sense of peace that her body seemed to crave desperately. A voice mixed in with the lyrical sound caused a slight pressure on her right temple.

"Well, Evie," the voice murmured. "We finally meet."

Evie slowly turned her gaze towards the sweet voice. Standing beside the sword, just out of the burning flames, was the most beautiful woman she had ever seen. Her shimmering golden hair flowed in the breeze as moonlight danced on its tips. Her blue eyes, deep as the sea, were rimmed with a dark color that called out to any lost soul, trapping them within its romantic vividness. She wore a gossamer white gown that played along the edges of her lush curves, providing the necessary contrast to her full red lips. As Evie reached out to the goddess, the musical rhythm began again.

"You do not have to run from me," the goddess urged. "You can trust me."

The comforting words washed over Evie, offering relief to her strained muscles. As she opened her parched mouth to speak, an eerie screech escaped her dry lips.

"Evie, wake up," a voice urged, breaking into the dream. "Are you okay?"

Evie gasped and clutched her throat, watching the goddess crumble into the darkness.

"Evie, wake up!" the voice repeated.

Evie tried to reach out and save the apparition, but it had already disappeared, leaving nothing behind. A lightness descended over her cheekbones as she opened her eyes and focused on the dark hair tickling the bridge of her nose. She relaxed into the rocking motion.

"Just breathe, Evie," her mom said. "It's going to be okay."

"Mom?" Evie whispered.

"Yes, sweetie. You were dreaming," her mom ran her fingers through Evie's hair and leaned away to examine her face. "You look like you've seen a ghost. What were you dreaming about?"

Struggling to hold on to the last fragment of her vague memory, Evie could sense the details of the vision gradually slipping away. "I think it was something about a sword," she muttered nervously, biting her lower lip. "Or perhaps it was about a woman." She wiped the beads of sweat from her forehead, still trying to recall the elusive memory.

"It must've been some dream. You scared me half to death."

"Why, what happened?" Evie started to pull away from the comforting grasp and could feel the heat of embarrassment in her cheeks.

"I heard a loud screech," her mom replied. "I almost thought you were strangling Sheba."

"Oh my gosh, I'm so sorry," Evie said, sliding away from her mom and pulling on the lace trim hanging from one of her yellow bed pillows.

"There's nothing to be sorry about. I'm just a little concerned. Did you sleep at all last night?" her mom asked, her frown deepening. "You still have your clothes on, and the bed's still made."

"I'm not sure," Evie muttered, catching Sheba's bright orange fluff out of the corner of her eye. She picked up the pudgy cat and moved to her desk chair. As she rubbed Sheba's white belly, she tried to remember the final images of the dream.

"You're not sure?" her mom asked, looking confused. "Were you reading last night?"

Evie felt a chill slide up her back. "What are you talking about?"

Her mom picked up the journal and flipped through the pages. Evie grabbed the book, causing Sheba to drop to the floor. The cat hissed and swished out of the room, ignoring Evie's scowl.

"Sorry, Sheba," Evie apologized before opening the first page of the diary. It was blank. She nibbled on her thumbnail.

"Is everything okay?" her mom asked. "You aren't acting like yourself. Are you starting a diary?"

Evie tried to hide her disappointment and replied, "Yeah, I was reading last night." As she leafed through the rest of the pages, a weight started to press on the back of her head. The entire book was blank.

Her mom touched her knee. "What's wrong?"

Evie was at a loss for words. She closed the book and nervously brushed her hand across the crude stone on the front cover, causing a static ripple of sensation to spread through her fingertips. "Nothing... I'm fine," she managed to say, struggling to keep her voice steady. She casually dropped the book on her desk. "And your right. I am thinking about starting a journal." She was surprised that the lie had flowed so easily out of her mouth and prayed that her mom wouldn't notice her wince.

"I used to have a diary," her mom said as she got off the bed. "I'll have to pull it out for you sometime." She walked towards the door but turned back to Evie. "Are you sure you're okay? You know you can talk to me about anything, right?"

"I know. I'm fine." Evie pushed herself out of the chair, grabbed her robe from her closet, and continued, "I promise. It just took me a second to wake up. Lana gave me the journal yesterday, and she has a matching one." The lies continued to grow. Next, she'd be telling her mom she was getting an "A" in History.

"Alright, by the way, I'm off today if you wanna take the car," her mom offered.

"Great! Thanks, Mom! Lana'll be excited." Glancing at the clock, Evie brushed past her mom and headed to the bathroom. "I'm gonna be late." She paused in the doorway of the small bathroom and turned around to look at her mom. "I really am sorry."

"Don't worry about it. That's what moms are for. I'm just worried that-" Before her mom could finish her thought, Evie's phone began to ring.

"That's probably Lana," Evie smiled, running back into her room to pick up the cell phone.

"That girl calls earlier and earlier," her mom murmured, shaking her head as she headed downstairs.

Evie looked at her reflection in the dresser mirror and answered the call. "Hey, Lana."

"Hey! Sorry about the hang-up yesterday."

"Don't worry about it," Evie sighed, rubbing her hand over a pimple starting to sprout on her forehead. "I have the car today." She considered telling Lana about the dream.

"Great! What are you wearing?"

Evie looked down at her shirt from yesterday and shrugged. "What do you think I'm wearing?"

"Evie!" Lana yelled. "You're killing me!"

"Do you wanna ride or not?"

"Yes,"

"Then see you in thirty." Evie dropped the phone on the dresser and tried to squeeze the pimple with both fingers.

Evie found it difficult to focus during her morning classes. Instead of paying attention to the parallel line segments in Geometry, she found herself studying the star-shaped doodles she had drawn unconsciously. She was so distracted that she almost gave up and went to the nurse's office. However, fate finally intervened and gave her a reprieve. When she walked into her final class before lunch, she saw the teacher, Mr. Moore, bent over numerous papers on his desk with his bald head. She sat at the back of the classroom, remembering what Lana had told her about him. Mr. Moore was known for despising change and never deviating from his 2005 syllabus. His class had become legendary and was the most popular among the jock scene. Since his tests never changed from year to year, it was the easiest class to purchase an "A" in. According to Lana, everyone loved Mr. Moore, and he hated everyone. Thankfully, he had a soft touch when it came to muddling through a reading of Shakespeare's, "Romeo and Juliet."

"Alright, class, quiet down," Mr. Moore grumbled as he pushed his round glasses further up his nose. "Since your homework was to start 'Romeo and Juliet,' we'll watch the first couple scenes of the 1968 movie adaptation this morning. Next class, we'll discuss the text and the differences." With a click of the remote on his desk, he

started the movie and returned his attention to the papers
in front of him.

After a student in the room turned off the lights, Evie pulled out her notebook. She felt her shoulders relax for the first time that day, already knowing the tragic love story by heart. Henry Mancini's 'Love Theme' swept over the dark room, silencing even the smallest murmurs. She was finally free to wander through the murkiness of the previous day.

The diary had to be a dream. There was no other conclusion. All the stress from the first day of school had caused her mind to create a rabbit hole of tricks in a book of blank pages. A dream that quickly turned into a nightmare.

She took a deep breath and looked down at her shaky hands. Black ink scribbles covered her red spiral notebook, forming an oddly shaped star with only four spokes. The sparks of light shooting from the insides of each triangular shape were slightly familiar. As the period bell startled her, she quickly pulled the notebook into her chest and grabbed her book bag. It was the same pattern etched into the stone on the diary. The hairs on the back of her neck tingled.

"Don't forget to come prepared next class." Mr. Moore said, not even bothering to look up from his papers. He opened his desk drawer and pulled out a soda.

Evie headed to her locker and could feel the red spiral notebook burning a hole through her chest.

"Whatcha holding so tight?" Lana asked, snatching the notebook out of Evie's hands. "A cheat sheet to everything Shakespeare?"

"Like I would need one of those." Rolling her eyes, Evie tried to grab the book.

"Good point." Lana smiled.

"Just give it back. There's nothing to see."

"Not so fast, Van Gough." Lana pointed to one of Evie's crude stars on the front cover. "What's this?"

"Nothing."

"It doesn't look like nothing," Lana said, pulling the book further out of Evie's grasp.

"Just some symbol I found. I thought it was pretty."

"Pretty?" Lana asked, wrinkling her nose. "You can be so strange sometimes."

Evie grabbed the notebook and shoved it into her locker.

"What's up with you anyway?" Lana continued. "All morning, you've been in la-la land! I waved to you on your way to Geometry, and you just stared past me like you didn't see me."

"Sorry," Evie apologized. "I just keep thinking about that weird dream I had last night."

"Oh yeah, I forgot about that," Lana said as she yanked open the cafeteria doors and waved Evie through. "What was it about anyway?"

"To be honest, I don't remember. It must've been pretty scary, though, 'cause my mom came running in. Apparently, I'd been screaming."

"Wow, that sounds kinda serious." Lana stopped in the lunch line and debated getting the french fries. She grabbed the greasy container and looked back to Evie. "Are you okay?"

"Yeah, I guess. Maybe I just need more sleep."

"Or, take my advice and stop gaming. Besides, it's so unattractive."

Evie frowned at Lana and picked up a plate of salad. "Whatever. Didn't you have some new plan or something you wanted to tell me about?" Suddenly, a pair of sweaty hands covered her eyes.

"Guess who?" came the familiar voice.

"Sweaty hands? Hmm...must be Seth." Laughing, Evie pulled Seth's palms off her face.

"I do not have sweaty hands," he said before wiping them on his jeans.

"Yes, you do," Lana said, paying the lunch lady. "Now, leave us alone."

"Care if I join?" Seth asked.

"Yes!" Lana shouted. "We have important stuff to talk about."

"Oh, that sounds serious," Seth replied. "Like what?"

"None of your business!" Lana hissed, pushing Evie towards the table.

"Wait!" Seth exclaimed, touching Evie's arm. "You never called last night."

"Oh man, I'm sorry." Evie shrugged. "I got caught up in stuff."

"No problem. How about tonight?" Seth asked.

"Can't you get the hint?" Lana interrupted. "She isn't interested."

Seth turned to Lana with a frown. "Was I talking to you?"

Lana stopped in the middle of the crowded lunch room to stare at Seth. "When are you gonna get a clue?"

"And what am I supposed to get a clue about?" Seth sneered.

"You're worthless," replied Lana as she swung towards the cafeteria exit.

"Lana, wait!" Evie gasped.

While rushing towards the exit, Lana slammed right into the chest of the reigning Hillstead High heartthrob.

"Whoa, slow down," Damek said, holding Lana by the arms. "You okay?"

Lana was stunned, and so was Evie. An entire congregation of butterflies started a riot in Evie's stomach.

"Oh," Lana gushed, "I'm sorry." She stared into Damek's eyes, forgetting all about the lunch tray held tightly against her chest.

Damek released Lana's arms and ran his hand through his thick hair. "You get your land legs back yet?"

"Yeah, I think so." Lana's face turned a bright red.

"Lana, right?" Damek chuckled as he picked a French fry off Lana's neck. "Good thing you didn't have ketchup."

Lana looked down at her shirt, breaking out of the trance. "Oh, man," she moaned. "This was brand new." She peeled her lunch tray away from her chest and tried not to cry.

"Oh well, guess you could start a new trend?" Damek offered.

Lana set the tray on a nearby table and frowned at the growing giggles around her."Easy for you to say," Lana griped, removing the fries from her shirt.

Damek turned towards Evie. "You're Evie, right?"

"Um, yeah." Evie stuttered, trying to regain some semblance of composure.

"I'm pretty good with names once I meet someone. Are you guys coming back to fencing?"

Lana started shaking her head. "I don't think fencing's for us."

"Are you sure?" he asked, keeping his gaze on Evie.

"Well, actually, I was thinking about giving it another try," Evie replied.

"You were?" Lana and Seth said in unison. Picking one of the fries off her shirt, Lana threw it at Seth.

"Jinx," Seth interjected, deflecting the fry with his hand.

"Shut up, Seth," Lana hissed before looking back to Evie. "Are you really thinking about going back?

"Well, yeah," Evie muttered. "I kind of enjoyed it."

"Evie, with a real sword? Now that's something I would pay to see," Seth replied, lightly touching Evie's back.

Lana gave Seth a strange look, but Evie didn't even seem to notice Seth's possessive gesture.

"I think you would look great holding a sword," Damek teased. He continued to look at Evie with an expression she could only describe as slightly goofy. His smile faded into a straight line as he searched Evie's face for some unknown question. In her mind's eye, she could see his hand begin to reach for her shoulder, chasing away the chill that had encased her entire body. The heat rose into her cheeks as his hand landed on its final destination. A static shock jolted through her shoulders just as the brief interlude was interrupted by a quick shout of Damek's name. He jerked his head to the left and scanned the busy room.

"Sounds like I'm being summoned," Damek said with a smile. "See ya tomorrow then!" He darted off towards his friends. Evie continued to stare at his back.

"Earth to Evie," Lana giggled, nudging Evie's arm.

"Hey," Evie breathed. She couldn't remember how long she'd been standing there; a mere second or an eternity?

"You okay?" Lana asked, forgetting all about the previous argument. She brushed the rest of the crumbs off her shirt and began to sing teasingly," Evie and Damek sitting in a tree-"

"Shut up, Lana," Evie snapped.

Lana folded her arms over her chest. "So, you do like him."

"Damek?" Seth interjected. "You can't be serious!"

"Why do you care?" Lana asked, pushing her finger into Seth's chest.

"Guys, stop!" Evie yelled. "I don't like Damek. I've just been spacey all day. I'm fine. Let's go eat."

"Whatever," Seth said. "Anyways, I've better things to do. Call me later, Evie." Turning away from them, Seth stormed out of the lunch room.

Lana interrupted Evie's jumbled thoughts, "You know you made him jealous, don't you?"

"I did not," Evie denied.

"Seth has a crush on you." Lana tried to adjust her rumpled shirt.

"No, he doesn't. He just wants me to see his new computer," Evie said, turning her back to Lana and heading towards their usual lunch table.

Lana grabbed her lunch tray and followed Evie. "Yeah, I bet he just wants to show you his new computer," Lana chuckled. Evie tried to smile at the pun but failed miserably. They plopped their trays on the table, and Evie glanced at the jock's table. Lana stole a tomato from Evie's plate and pointed her fork at her. "So this explains the salad today. You never get a salad." She took a bite of the tomato and leaned back. "It's okay if you like him."

"I get a salad sometimes," Evie argued.

"Stop ignoring the real issue here."

"What issue?"

"Damek," Lana replied.

"I don't like Damek," Evie grumbled.

"Well, if you do, it's okay. I've moved on. But just remember, he's heartbreak waiting to happen."

"Look who's talking! It doesn't matter anyway. I'm not interested." Evie shoved a fork full of salad into her mouth.

"Do you wanna talk about what's really bothering you?" Lana asked.

"I," pausing to swallow the lump in her throat, Evie took a deep breath. "I found a book on the bleachers yesterday."

"The bleachers?" Lana questioned.

"Yeah," Evie replied, nodding. "In the gym. When we were at fencing club."

Lana shrugged her shoulders, staring at her tray. "So? What's so creepy about that? I forget crap all the time."

Evie was confused by Lana's lack of interest and leaned in closer. "Yeah, I know, but this was someone's diary."

"Someone's diary?" Lana asked. She seemed to debate her next response and leaned in closer to Evie with a smile. "Whose was it? Oh wait, don't tell me. I bet it was that blond bimbo Damek calls a girlfriend. Sounds like something that ditz would do."

"No, it wasn't her," Evie responded, pushing her empty tray aside. "Here's the strange part - It's from a girl named Evelyn who lived in 1893."

Lana leaned over the table, placing her hand on Evie's forehead. "Like the 19th century? Are you sure you don't have a fever?"

"No. Stop it!" Evie said, lowering her voice. "Get this, that wasn't the weirdest part. When my mom found the diary this morning, it was blank."

"What do you mean?" Lana asked, confused.

"I mean, I'd read it the night before. Then, in the morning, it was blank."

"I bet it was blank the whole time. Your mind was probably playing tricks on you. Happens to me all the time."

"Maybe," Evie muttered.

Lana sighed at Evie's disappointed look. "Did you look at it again when your mom left the room?"

"No. I was kinda in a hurry."

"I would recheck it," Lana recommended. "Didn't you learn anything from all those old Nancy Drew books you have stacked in your closet?"

"I thought you didn't know who Nancy Drew was?"

Lana pulled a stray crumb off her shirt. "Don't try to change the subject. Do I get to see it?"

"Yeah, I guess," Evie decided. "It's just so weird. Every time I read the diary, I feel like I'm in it."

"Like in the actual place or something?"

"Sort of. I mean, I wasn't really there, but I could picture it. And then suddenly, the picture disappears, and I'm sucked into this horrible nightmare that I can't seem to remember," Evie explained.

Lana leaned closer to Evie. "Are you sure it wasn't your imagination? Perhaps it's just one big dream?"

"I thought that too."

"What if I came over after school today?" Lana suggested. "Maybe stay for dinner?" Her excitement was contagious.

"Um, sure. I'll ask my mom," Evie replied.

"Great! Seeing as I didn't get much to eat today, anything would be better than this," Lana complained as she frowned at her lunch tray. She then paused and turned back to Evie. "Wait, so you stole someone's diary?"

"Yeah. Is that bad?"

"Very bad!" Lana's eyes widened. "That's way worse than stealing a candy bar. There never was a quiz, was there?"

"No,"

"Dammit! Oh well. Did you notice anyone looking for it?"

"No, and we were one of the last ones to leave." Evie took a deep breath and tried to change the subject. "So, I noticed your brother wasn't here today. Is everything okay?"

Lana stared at a poster for a Leukemia fundraiser on the wall behind Evie. "Yeah," she hesitated while twisting the end of one of her red hair extensions. "Someone in the family passed away that none of us were close to...except for Blake. He went to the funeral. He should be back in a few days."

"You know you can talk to me," Evie said, sensing that her best friend was lying.

"There's nothing to talk about," Lana replied.

"How about your dad?" Evie probed further.

"Everything's fine, Evie!" Lana waved her hand dismissively. "So, how about Rick Meyer?"

"Rick Meyer?" Evie asked, confused.

"Rick Meyer...the football player...my future boyfriend."

"Oh, Lana, be serious!"

"I am!" Lana insisted. "I learned from today's run-in with Damek. I'm gonna do the same thing to Rick."

"Just run right into him?"

"Yeah!" Lana beamed. "Brilliant, isn't it?"

"Not another scheme..." Evie moaned.

"Hey, talk about schemes! At least I didn't perform larceny!"

"That's different," but before she could finish her thought, Evie realized she was heading down a slippery slope. "Alright, fine. You win. What do you want me to do?"

Lana spent the last 15 minutes of lunch explaining Evie's role in the "How to get Rick Meyer to notice me" plan. Grateful for the distraction, Evie started to feel like her old self again. She didn't think about the journal or the dream for the rest of the day.

4. Deception

Lana leaned over Evie's bed, trying to coax Sheba out from underneath. "Here, here, Kitty," Lana cooed. "I don't think your cat likes me very much."

"Well, you aren't gonna be on her good side calling her Kitty," Evie responded. "Besides, she doesn't like anybody." Evie held the magic diary with both hands. "So, are you gonna look at the diary or what?"

Lana frowned and yanked the book from Evie's hands. She touched the stone on the front cover. "I've seen better artwork from a 5-year-old."

"Really?" Evie asked, looking at the stone again. "You don't think it looks mystical or anything?"

"I'm worried about you." Shaking her head, Lana flipped it open. "Let's see what all this drama's about, shall we?" She leafed through a couple of pages and stopped in the middle of it. Looking back at Evie, she sighed. "It looks blank to me."

Evie stared at the blank pages. "I guess that confirms it. I'm crazy." Hot resentment pushed its way into her throat. She grabbed the diary from Lana and reached for her book bag.

"I'm sorry," Lana offered.

"No, it's probably a good thing. Apparently, I was blessed with a healthy imagination." With a grimace, Evie shoved the book into her bag and jumped off the bed. She started pacing in front of her dresser mirror. "I guess that means I'll have to put it back on the bleachers tomorrow."

"You want me to do it?" Lana asked. "I'm pretty good at that sort of thing."

"Nah, I'm the one that took it." Falling back onto the bed, Evie rubbed her eyes. "It shouldn't be that big of a deal. It's not like anyone wrote in it."

Lana laid down next to Evie and twirled one of Evie's curls around her finger. "How do you think you came up with a girl from the 1890s?"

"I've no freaking idea."

"Girls," Evie's mom called from the kitchen. "Dinner's ready!"

"Finally, I'm starving! Your mom makes the best stuff." Jumping from the bed, Lana opened the bedroom door.

"Really? Seems pretty plain to me," replied Evie. "Don't you eat dinner at your house?"

"Yeah, but it's not the same. It's more fend for yourself."

"Neither you nor your dad cooks?" Evie asked.

"It's complicated."

"What do you mean?"

"Don't worry about it. I'm too hungry to make any sense!" Lana bounded down the stairs but stopped abruptly on the middle landing. The smell of beef filled the house. She peered into the kitchen and saw Evie's mom placing bowls of steaming rice on the dining room table. Evie's father was already seated at the head of the table, attempting to sneak a piece of flank steak from the pan sizzling in the middle.

"Looks like my mom's pulling out all the stops for you," Evie joked. "I can't remember the last time we used the dining room table." She pushed on Lana's back. "You ok? I thought you were hungry."

"You don't know how lucky you are," Lana mumbled.

Later that evening, after Lana left, Evie found herself back on her bed. She drummed her fingers to the beat of the bass ringing in her ears as she concentrated on the clumps of dust threatening to fall off the sides of her spinning fan. She couldn't stop thinking about her best friend. Lana had completely dodged any question about her father or Blake, to the point where it became a bit uncomfortable during dinner. Even when she drove Lana home, all she wanted to talk about was Rick Meyers. Evie pulled out her earplugs and tossed her phone to the edge of the bed. It bounced off and landed on the floor. As she reached to pick it up, she noticed the blank diary peeking at her from inside her open book bag, the tip of the damn thing enticing her from the open zipper. Her heartburn promptly came back and set up residence in her chest. She slid to the floor and pulled out the diary. Heat began to spread into her palm as she grazed the front stone, and a light blue glow seeped from the rock through her fingertips. Narrowing her eyes to the tiniest slits, she held her breath and opened the book. There in front of her were the words she knew existed.

April 30, 1893

It can be so daunting being a woman.

I often daydream about the future and the changes that are already being made. I have even heard that women may be granted the right to vote in as little as a year. Can you imagine? Master Senoy once told me a story about Chevalier d'Eon, a great male spy who posed as a woman to lead a band of female spies. What would it be like to serve my country in espionage? The things I would get to see, the excitement it would bring...

Senoy acted very strangely today. All I can do is write down the events, for at this time, I do not know what to think. It all started when I headed to the gymnasium to find him. I could already hear the clash of swords from the front hall. To my chagrin, I found only Lord Wyndham and my brother. (As a side note, I do not have to worry about Lord Wyndham's fencing ability during tomorrow's tournament.)

"Touché, Lord Nab," echoed Lord Wyndham's booming voice.

"Well, well, old man, perhaps you are losing your touch. We may need to rethink your entry into the tournament tomorrow," laughed Nab. *Imagine the shock of seeing my brother Nab beat anyone! He could not fence his way out of a flour sack.*

"I will have to agree with my brother, Lord Wyndham," I said as I entered the room. "I do believe you should just enjoy the other revelries of the celebration."

"But I was told ladies enjoyed the sight of a man wielding a sword," replied Lord Wyndham.

"That is quite true," I agreed. "However, I believe it is the opposite effect if even my brother can best you."

"Alas," Lord Wyndham feigned. "I guess I am set to be a laughing stock."

I pretended to examine a fencing mask on the side table, hiding my mirth. "Oh, no worries, Lord Wyndham, I am sure you already are." At this point, Nab was already choking on his laughter.

"That is highly doubtful," preened Lord Wyndham. "Why, just this morning, Countess Meriweather told me she would champion me in the tournament."

"Hmph! I wonder what Count Meriweather would think about that?" I said, grinning at Nab and tossing the mask to the table.

"Excuse me, Lady March. Have I offended you in any way?" Lord Wyndham asked.

This is where the ground beneath me started to give way. Even the blue and red wall coverings flanking the only window in the large room became hazy. Lord Wyndham took a few steps toward me, causing those blasted butterflies to start again. I began to back away when, to my surprise, I backed right into the man I had been looking for. Drat! This was all Senoy's fault. If he would have been here, to begin with, none of this would have happened.

"Ah, Master Senoy," Lord Wyndham exclaimed. "Just the man I was looking for. Lady March was running away from me, as always, it seems."

Senoy gently placed his hands on my shoulders, instantly calming the butterflies in my stomach. "Glad I can easily accommodate, Lord Wyndham," he said, moving further into the room. "Evelyn, were you running from Lord Wyndham?"

Turning to face my mentor, a calmness spread through the heat in my cheeks, bringing back my ability to speak. "I was not running. I was looking for you."

"You fence, Lady Evelyn?" interrupted Lord Wyndham.

"Why yes, I do." I must say, I added the next bit with pure relish. "And I beat Nab every single time."

"Then I look forward to a match with you," replied Lord Wyndham.

"That would not even be a match, would it?" I asked.

"Ah, but to lose to such a beautiful woman..." Lord Wyndham grabbed my hand and bent into a regal bow, keeping his gaze steady on mine.

Right here is where everything changed. Just as I was about to give Lord Wyndham the reprimand he deserved, I made the mistake of glancing at Senoy. The words died on my lips. The expression on his face was plain fear with a mixture of something I could not quite recognize. However, it instantly vanished behind his once again calm demeanor.

Glancing between Lord Wyndham and myself, Senoy made his apologies and abruptly exited the room.

I quickly made my farewell to Nab. Feeling the butterflies descend again into my belly, I ignored Lord Wyndham and fled from the room, trailing after Senoy. Losing him in the kitchen, I sat at the prep table closest to the fire crackling in the large brick oven. I stole one of Cook's blueberry tarts from a nearby basket and let my thoughts wander. What had happened?

And on another note, how could I ever be a great spy if I cannot even trail an old man like Senoy? Let alone letting my repulsion of someone wreak havoc on my insides; so much for my duty in espionage.

****

Once again, the nineteenth-century vision blended into Evie's nightmare. The same nightmare that had her wearing a regal gown of multiple layers. Evie memorized the swirl of colors left by the enchanting dream. As she tried to focus on the last palate of red disappearing before her, an apparition materialized into the beautiful Aphrodite she had met previously. She reached out to the vision in front of her and swallowed to relieve the rawness in her throat, but as she dropped her gaze to the ground, she couldn't help but scream. Dozens of snakes lashed their tongues at her wide eyes, pinning her ripped dress to the forest floor.

"Do not worry, my dear," the goddess said in a soothing tone. "They will not hurt you."

A single tear slid down Evie's cheek and dropped into the pile of serpents, emitting a hiss among their tribal chant.

"Evie, come now," the goddess said. "No tears to be shed among our homecoming."

"I don't know what you're talking about!" Evie shouted, her hands clutching her temples, trying to force the absurdity out." This is just a dream!"

"Evie, I need you," the goddess implored. "I love you. Please do not push me away."

Evie could feel the anguish flowing from the goddess's vivid blue eyes. She realized she was willing to give this woman anything. The sword, never forgotten, continued to swirl between them, casting its blue light over the entire scene. As she reached for the sword unconsciously, Evie froze.

A voice yelled out from the darkness shaded behind the overwhelming brush. "Evie, do not give her the sword!"

Evie squinted into the dense forest, trying to place the insistent cry.

"Evie, do not listen," the goddess pleaded. "They only want to hurt you." As the goddess's words caressed the inside of her ear, the familiar male voice cried out again, "Evie, please!"

The surrounding forest seemed to be swallowed into a black hole, leaving only the enchanted sword spinning in the throes of its blue light between Evie and the blond temptress.

"You do not need them," the goddess continued, "I am your family, Evie. We are bonded, you and I."

Evie longed to be embraced by the open arms of white gossamer, feeling the goddess's golden locks feather across her cheeks. She sighed, "Who are you?"

"My dear, you know who I am. Do not worry; our time will come. You could never fail me."

The swirls of blue haze cast by the sword engulfed the vision as the woman's harmonious laughter mixed with an alarming beep coming from the edge of reason.

5. Fencing

Evie lay on her bed and gazed at the ceiling, trying to catch her breath. The harsh gasps forcing the air through her lungs collided with a consistent beep coming from her nightstand. She slammed the off button on her alarm clock, causing the diary to drop to the floor. It was just another dream or, rather, very odd nightmare. She got off the bed and rubbed her temples. Taking a calming breath, she walked over to her dresser mirror and was not surprised by the stark white image that greeted her.

"I must be going crazy." She looked at the clock and groaned at the late hour before rushing to the bathroom and tying her unruly hair into a ponytail. After changing into her standard uniform of a T-shirt and skinny jeans, she found her mother's note waiting for her on the kitchen counter.

> Took your Dad to the airport. Look forward to seeing
> you at dinner. Hope everything is ok with Lana.
>> Love you, Mom

She grabbed an apple from the fruit bowl and smiled. When Dad was gone, that meant she had a car to use. Perhaps the day was starting to look up, the nightmare escaping into yet another forgotten memory.

The day turned into a complete disaster. She spent the entire ride to school listening to Lana lecture about the finer points of doing one's hair, flunked her first "surprise" Geometry quiz, and, to top the day off, tripped right in the middle of the cafeteria, leaving her lunch at the bottom of a mop bucket. By the end of the day, all she wanted to do was go home and crawl into bed.

"Best bell ever, huh?" Lana joked as she ran into Evie after their last class of the day. She pulled on Evie's ponytail.

"No kidding," Evie mumbled.

They walked in silence to their lockers. Evie could feel Lana's gaze on her but didn't say anything. Just as Evie was about to open her locker, Lana blocked it with her hand. "Hey, are you okay? What's going on?"

"I don't know," stuttered Evie. She debated telling Lana about the strange images that had been stuck in her head. It's not every day that one dreams about a goddess begging for help.

"It's the journal, isn't it?"

"I guess," Evie replied.

"Once you return it, you'll be fine."

Evie opened her locker door and winced. "Crap! I knew I forgot something."

"No big deal. Just return it tomorrow."

"Yeah," Evie muttered. She pulled out her book bag and closed the locker. If only it were that simple.

"You know, you don't have to stay after today. It's not like you have to keep up the pretense of actually liking fencing," said Lana.

"No, I really wanna go," replied Evie.

"Suit yourself. Besides, I made other plans," said Lana, lowering her voice as she leaned in close. "I'm hanging out with Donna Mercer to watch the football team practice."

"What?" Evie asked. She stared at Lana, confused by the sudden change in topics.

"I talked to Rick Meyer today." Lana's smile quickly turned into a deep scowl as she noticed an unwanted guest waving his fingers behind Evie.

"I take it Rick Meyer must be the new crush?" Seth interrupted, making air quotes around the word 'crush.'

Lana's face took on a purple hue as the few straggles of students left in the hall turned towards the commotion. "Seriously Evie, you need to pick better friends!"

"You know that would include you, right?" Seth said with a smug look on his face. "Besides, why do you keep picking these guys you have no chance with?"

Lana ignored Seth's comment and walked away, heading towards the football field. Before Evie could intervene, Lana turned around and glared at Evie, "Call me when fencing's over. And just so you know, I'm getting a ride home from Donna."

"Lana, wait!" Evie called out. "Are you mad at me?"

"Forget it!" Lana replied, continuing down the hallway.

Evie let out a sigh and slung her book bag over her shoulder. "Seems only fitting to end the day like this."

"Bad day?" Seth asked, peering over Evie's head to watch Lana disappear around the corner. "I don't see what her problem is."

"Stop it, Seth," Evie replied. "I'm not in the mood. You hurt her feelings."

"Whatever. Anyway, that wasn't what I wanted to talk to you about." Seth shifted his focus back to Evie and lowered his voice. "Are you mad at me?"

"At the moment, yes," Evie confirmed, heading towards the gym.

"No, I don't mean about Lana. You didn't call again last night. And I get it; as Lana said, you've turned over a new leaf. That's cool. I just wanted to know."

"No, it's not like that. Things've been busy." Evie struggled to open the gym door and used her foot to push it open. "How about this Friday?"

"Maybe," Seth replied. "You're not the only one who makes plans, you know."

Evie forced a smile, grabbing Seth's arm as he turned to leave. "I promise."

Seth nodded and walked away. She let out a slow breath, two friends down, and no more to go. Suddenly, a familiar chill snaked its way up her back.

"Getting cold feet?" A familiar, deep voice rumbled behind her.

Trying to casually move her foot away from the gym door, Evie tripped over it instead.

Damek tried not to laugh at the blush creeping up Evie's face but failed miserably. "I really wanna say, 'walk much,' but you don't look like you're in the mood."

"Thanks." Evie tried her best to regain her composure, but her forced smile looked more like a grimace.

"Professor Mike's about to begin if you wanna come in and take a seat." As he grabbed the door to let another student in, his shoulder bumped her arm, sending a rush of adrenaline through her limbs. She froze.

"Hey, Damek!" shouted the incoming student, giving Damek a quick nod of the head.

"Hey, Sam," replied Damek. He ignored Evie's uncomfortable expression and followed Sam to the bleachers.

Evie regained her balance and hoped that the redness in her cheeks had faded away. She quickly looked around at the group as she walked towards the third row of bleachers. The number of students had decreased by half since the first class. Evie composed herself and smiled wryly at the few girls in the first row who were still vying for Damek's attention. Biting her lip, she couldn't help but wonder if she might be one of them.

"Welcome back, everyone!" greeted Professor Mike. As the chatter from the front row subsided, a sense of peace washed over Evie. Her mind went blank, and all she could hear was the soothing sound of the professor's voice.

"Due to the large number of beginners this year, we have decided to divide the class into two groups. One group will be for beginners and intermediate levels, which Damek will lead. I will handle the advanced level, but I will be available to help everyone. If you are a beginner, you can use the school's uniforms and equipment, which Damek will explain. However, I recommend purchasing your own equipment if you continue with the sport."

Stepping closer to the front of the bleachers, he took a deep breath. "I know the most common question is whether beginners will be able to participate in a bout this year. Generally, it is better to wait until the second year of practice." Hearing the groans ripple through the bleachers, Evie wondered what 'a bout' was. The Professor raised his hands to continue and answered her unspoken question. "However, depending on everyone's aptitude, I may make some allowances towards the end of the year for some sort of beginners' competition."

Fully engaged in the Professor's blue eyes, Evie felt an unexpected anticipation blossom in her chest.

"Well then, let us get started. Beginners to my left, advanced to my right, and please remember to wear sweats next class."

Voices echoed through the gym as everyone moved to their designated groups, but Evie remained seated, gazing at the Professor, lost in her thoughts. Suddenly, she realized that he had turned towards her.

"Well, young lady," the Professor said, "are you going to join us today or just watch?"

"Oh, sorry!" Evie exclaimed, unsure how to explain her reaction. She quickly made her way down to the gym floor.

"You look very familiar," the Professor added. "Have we met before?"

"I don't think so," replied Evie, a bit unsure herself.

"What is your name?" the Professor asked.

"Evie"

"Evie," he repeated. "What a nice name." He reached out his hand towards her cheek with his long fingers but then quickly retracted it, second-guessing the gesture. "You remind me of someone I used to know quite a long time ago."

Evie gazed at him, attempting to recollect a fleeting memory that threatened to surface. She could almost feel the lightness of his once-golden hair and the strength of his chin. However, before Evie could voice any of her confusing thoughts, the Professor briefly glanced at Damek. Evie's nerves took over, and as she attempted to say the first thing that came to mind, she found herself once again the focus of the Professor's attention. His tangible excitement, similar to hers, quickly dissipated as it seemed that perhaps she had imagined the whole brief exchange.

"It was nice to meet you, Evie," the Professor said. "Please go ahead and join the beginners." He motioned towards the small group of new students beginning to form and then smiled at another advanced student approaching him to speak.

Evie knew she'd been quickly dismissed. Making her way over to her assigned group, she peered over her shoulder for one last look at Professor Mike.

A new voice interrupted her thoughts, "Newbie too?"

Startled, Evie turned around to see the same kid who had followed her into the gym. "Oh, sorry! I'm Evie," she said apologetically.

"Sam. Nice to meet ya," he responded. Standing eye to eye with Evie, Sam was a skinny kid with black spiky hair. He had this goofy grin that made Evie want to smile. Even the slight stutter in his speech added to his laid-back personality, and Evie immediately felt a connection with him. "So, how many of these girls you think will last?" Sam asked.

Evie glanced over at the three girls huddled on the other side of him, all dressed in their tightest yoga pants. She couldn't help but let out a quick snort of amusement, thankful that something else had caught their attention. As a familiar cold breeze hit the back of her neck, she followed the girls' gazes and unconsciously held her breath. Damek was in a heated discussion with Professor Mike, causing her uneasiness to return. Damek's agitation was apparent, and she wasn't the only one taking notice. The majority of the class had stopped talking. Professor Mike quickly waved his hand in retreat, ending the brief argument. Evie could have sworn they both glanced in her direction, making her feel even more uneasy.

"Don't be telling me you're one of them too?" Sam whined, nodding to the groupies huddled in conversation.

Evie blinked, trying to clear her head. "What did you say?"

"Oh, great!" Sam replied, rolling his eyes. He smiled at Damek, who was walking towards the group. "Already getting into trouble, huh?"

"Me?" he asked, moving to the center of the group. "Never." Damek gazed at the motley crew. Evie cringed. Damek was stuck with three boys and four groupies. "All right, guys, let's start by going over the uniform." By the time Damek got through fencing jackets, foil masks, and loose pants, Evie knew she was hooked, in fencing, that is. That could be the only explanation for her avid attention to Damek's every detail.

"We don't have much time left today. Before we finish, let me go over some of the rules and etiquette," Damek said, turning towards the fencing strip. As he briefly met Evie's eyes, the cold control she had harbored during the instruction started disintegrating. He motioned for her to join him on the strip, causing heat to rush into her cheeks. She wanted to reach for him. Assessing the distance to the door, Evie tried to calm her wild imagination.

Damek wiped his hands on his jeans. "Well, strike that. Time's up anyway. On Friday, we can start going over some basic moves."

Her breath came out in one big gush, not realizing she'd been holding it. She looked at Sam and caught his scrutiny. She tried to smile.

"You okay there?" Sam asked, lightly patting her on the back.

"Yeah, I just think I might be coming down with something."

"Good thing class is over," Sam remarked as they walked towards the bleachers. He turned to give her one last look. "You sure you're okay?"

Evie nodded, "Yes, thank you." From the corner of her eye, Evie watched as one of the groupies, smearing gloss on her lips, started to make her way toward Damek.

Damek spotted the incoming intrusion and ducked in the other direction, only to find himself staring at Evie. Evie wasn't sure which he would have preferred, the groupie or her. Rubbing his finger over one of his eyebrows, he took a quick breath and said, "So, not too bad, huh?"

"Yeah, we'll see," Evie said. Her hands curled into fists at the ease of his forced nonchalance. She stared at his chest and tried to gain the courage to ask the question that choked in her throat. "Were you and the Professor talking about me?" But the unspoken words died on her lips as a mass of blond hair swung into view.

"Hey, babe!" exclaimed a cheerleader as she threw herself into Damek's arms. "Missed you today!"

Evie felt a tightness in her chest and looked up at the ceiling.

Damek pulled the slender beauty into his arms and kissed her. Then, remembering that Evie was there, he turned back towards her, keeping his arm around the beautiful blond. "This is one of the newbies," he said, nodding to Evie.

"Hey," the girl responded, immediately dismissing Evie altogether. She laced her hand through Damek's arm and pushed him towards the bleachers. "You aren't gonna believe who showed up at the football field today."

"Come on Lexi, you know I don't like gossip," Damek responded, grabbing a water bottle from his bag.

"Oh please," Lexi said, lightly slapping his chest. She fluttered her long eyelashes. "You know you like it."

Damek finished packing his fencing gear and slung his bag over his shoulder. Without so much as a goodbye, the perfect couple headed out of the gym. Evie watched the swing of Lexi's short blue skirt and tried to imagine what it would be like to be beautiful and wanted. Even Lexi's brown eyes looked more mahogany, while hers just resembled the color of mud. Life wasn't fair. Blocking out the incessant chatter of every guy's dream girl, Evie tried to listen for Damek's familiar baritone. She briefly wondered if he was the invisible voice in her dreams.

As she looked around the gym, she realized that she was the only one left. Tears welled up in her eyes. Unable to explain the onslaught of emotions, she looked up at the ceiling and willed them to stop. She reminded herself that it was far better not to be noticed. It had been her survival strategy for the last seventeen years. Moving from school to school, unknown and unremembered, there was a reason it worked. She collapsed onto the bottom bleacher and hugged her book bag against her chest. Perhaps that was what all the nightmares were about: a cold, hard memory that everything could be taken away with the flick of a black pen. Military orders, stamped with the official seal of a soldier's written commitment. Another town, another group of faces.

There was no cold, no heat, just the reminder of a very humiliating day. Angry at herself for feeling like every other average teenage girl, she headed towards the exit. Looking back into the gym, she gave one last wish for something special to happen, anything. She let the door swing shut behind her and entered the parking lot. She dropped her book bag by the car and fumbled for her keys.

"Evie," someone whispered.

Evie instantly looked up from her bag, but no one was around. Her heartbeat sped up as a tangible fear pushed away any lingering thoughts of unrequited love and hallucinogenic nightmares. She scanned the parking lot and realized she was the only one left. She clenched the keys through her fingers like a makeshift weapon and remembered the Colonel's safety speech. Reciting each step like a prayer, she checked under the car and in the back seat for potential attackers, but found nothing. As she hit the unlock button on her car, the keys slipped from her sweaty fingers.

"I get it, ok! How much more can I take?" Evie yelled, aiming her frustration at the sky. Her only answer was a light breeze. With a growl of annoyance, she bent over to pick up the keys and, once again, heard someone call out her name.

"Evie," the voice said.

Startled, Evie stood up abruptly and smacked the back of her head on something hard. A soft cry escaped her mouth as she instinctively reached for the spot where it hurt. She looked up and saw a pair of black Converses in front of her.

"Damn it, Evie, it's me!" Blake swore, holding his nose.

"Blake?!" Evie exclaimed.

Blake winced with tears in his eyes. "Remind me never to sneak up on you again."

"What the hell were you doing?" Evie yelled, surprised that her anger had loosened her tongue. "You really freaked me out!"

Blake lowered his head and pulled his faded Cubs baseball cap lower over his forehead. "Sorry Evie, I just..." Hearing a sound behind him, he darted a glance into the trees that lined the parking lot. "Why are you the last one to leave school anyway? Where's Lana?"

"Hey," Evie replied, feeling a sudden rush of nerves. "I think I'll be the one asking the questions." She realized with a start that she was speaking to Lana's good-looking brother, who now had a bright red nose to mar his surprisingly already haggard appearance.

He cracked a smile at her apparent surprise and looked around. "What's up with the yelling anyway? I thought you were the silent type."

She focused on his swollen nose and tried to calm the hysteria threatening to overtake her. "What are you doing here, Blake? I thought you were at a funeral," she asked, her voice shaking.

"Funeral?" Blake questioned. "What's my sister telling everyone?" He scanned the parking lot again, then turned back to Evie. "Look, I need you to do something for me."

The smell of metal and filth hit Evie. She tried to hide her surprise when she realized Blake looked like he hadn't showered in weeks. She covered her nose with her hand and stared at the tight brown t-shirt matted to his chest. Watching his hands move down towards his thighs, Evie gasped at the faded rust-colored spots on his jeans. "Blake, what happened?" she asked.

"Look, I know I'm a mess, but I need you to listen."

"Are you ok?"

"I don't have time for questions. Just listen," Blake said gripping her arms tightly.

"What the hell, Blake?! This isn't like you!" Struggling out of his grasp, she stumbled backward when he let go.

Blake caught her arms but quickly let go again when she was standing upright. "I'm not going to hurt you," he said, raising his hands in surrender. "I swear! I'm sorry." He took a step back, frustration causing his voice to crack. "How's Lana?"

"Haven't you seen her?"

"No," he responded. "I haven't been home."

"How come?"

"Just answer the question, Evie."

She noticed the fear in his bloodshot eyes and took a step back. Rubbing the dull ache in her arms, an overwhelming need to comfort Blake overshadowed her brief fear. "She's fine...I think. Probably mad at me."

"Good. Can you just tell her that I'm okay?"

Evie lowered her voice and forced herself to remain calm. "Blake, what's going on?"

A piercing screech cut off her words, reverberating throughout the empty lot. They both turned to see an owl perched on a low-hanging branch of an elm tree, furthest from the school. Its pointed ears and alert yellow eyes were fixed on them as it hovered over an empty bicycle rack. It was the smallest owl Evie had ever seen.

"What is that?" Evie breathed.

Blake turned around, emitting a muffled curse. "I have to go. Please tell Lana I'm okay." He then jumped into the GTO, parked in the handicapped spot, and revved the engine. As he passed by, he rolled down his window, his words hanging heavy in the air, "For what it's worth, I don't think you're crazy." Checking his rear-view mirror, he slammed on the gas, lighting up the already well-worn tires.

Evie watched as the car drove away and disappeared from view. She looked around, half-expecting to see a stereotypical mafia guy stalking toward her. Instead, she caught sight of the owl again. It briefly looked at her with intense eyes before breaking the connection with a quick blink. The owl took off and never looked back as it soared higher into the sky. Evie quickly got into her car, locked the doors, grabbed her cell phone, and called Lana.

"Lana, hey!" Evie exclaimed when Lana picked up the phone.

"Evie, I'm so sorry!" Lana said apologetically.

"No, I'm sorry. I know Seth can be irritating sometimes, but hey, I need to tell you something. I just ran into Blake."

"Blake? Are you sure?" Lana asked, surprised.

"Yeah, positive. Is everything okay with him?" Evie asked, sensing a hesitation on the other end.

"What did he say to you?"

"Not much. He wanted me to tell you that he was okay."

"Thank God!" Lana exclaimed.

"What aren't you telling me?" As the silence continued to stretch, Evie sighed. "Lana, something's really wrong with him. He looked like he hadn't showered in weeks and acted like somebody was following him."

"He had a huge fight with Dad and just took off," Lana said before pausing for a moment. "It was kind of weird. I don't even know what they were fighting about."

"Why didn't you just tell me the truth?"

"Evie," with another pause, Evie could hear a yell in the background. "Look, I can't talk about it right now. I gotta go."

"I'm coming over," Evie insisted.

"No, you aren't. I'm fine. It's not a big deal."

"But-"

"I have to go. My dad's calling me. Please," Lana begged, "Don't tell anyone. Pick me up tomorrow, yeah?"

"Yeah,"

"K, bye"

Evie heard a dull click in her ear, and the cell phone slipped from her hand into her lap. She rested her head on the steering wheel and considered driving to Lana's place.

But a sudden queasiness gripped her stomach, and she realized she needed to lie down, whether it was due to her selfishness or the flu. She lifted her head and looked out the window to see the sun setting low in the sky. It was time to head home.

6. The Games

Evie sat on the edge of her bed, staring at her phone. She couldn't shake the image of Blake's anxious eyes, so help her if this was just another one of Lana's many practical jokes. Just like when Lana snagged her note cards the day of her presentation in Speech class on "Why Recycling is Beneficial." Not that Lana didn't give them back in time, but it made her sweat all through first period. There had to be something Lana wasn't telling her. She tried to concentrate on the hangnail, painfully leaving its red mark on her thumb, and threw herself back onto the bed. Thankful that she had made it home in time for dinner; it had been a fairly uncomfortable affair. She had never needed to lie to her parents before, and she was pretty sure her mother saw right through her constant nail-biting. As she picked up her third crushed taco, she finally gave up, using her Geometry homework as an excuse.

Evie closed her eyes and let her mind wander over Evelyn's fascinating life. She pictured the front stone embedded on the journal cover and sat up, letting her legs dangle over the side of her bed. Staring at the crude artwork lying on her bedroom floor, she willed the magic to begin and urged the familiar blue haze to seep out of the tiny indentations scattered over its hard surface. It created a curtain of blue smoke that embraced the worn, cracked leather. She slipped off the bed and covered the stone with her hand. The iridescent color seeped through her fingers and disappeared, leaving a soft sheen on her skin. Whether out of fantasy or pure will, she went along with the illusion and picked up the journal. She laid it in her lap and leaned against her dresser, forgetting about the day's turmoil as she opened to the next entry.

May 1, 1893
Never under any circumstances underestimate your opponent.

The day of the tournament was a feast for the soul! The meticulously landscaped lawn had been turned into a bright-colored fair, providing every possible entertainment for its guests. Mother and Father had spared no expense. The main attraction was the Maypole, adorned with blue and white ribbons spun especially for this event. Everyone from the surrounding counties had come dressed in their best. Men were challenged to show their brawn with their prized horses on display. Women wore their finest gloves, hats, and smiles as their match-making mamas sized up the challengers for the upcoming marriage mart.

Since Mother was so busy being Hostess, Aunt Lettie was to act as my chaperone. Aunt Lettie has a horrible habit of falling asleep, which meant everything was running smoothly for my transition into Sir Moore from Asbury.

The green foyer had been turned into a male den of food, comfortable chairs, and tankards full of mead. For me, it was an experience like no other. To be allowed in the private club of men...

"Sir Moore, may I say you are looking splendid out there," said a portly older man as he grabbed another leg of turkey from the large meat platter sitting on the sideboard.

"Why thank you, Lord Ormsby," I beamed with subdued excitement about winning my last match. I was in the finals. Pulling at my jacket, I started to relax. Everything was going to plan.

"I apologize," Lord Ormsby said, "but have we met? You look rather familiar."

As I watched some turkey fat dangle from his chin, I racked my brain for a quick answer. Just as I reached for a tankard of mead, a warm hand grabbed my shoulder.

"Lord Ormsby. I see you have met my cousin from Asbury," said Master Senoy, breaking the awkward silence. I placed my tankard back onto the table and frowned at his quiet reprimand.

"I should have known he was your cousin, Master Senoy. I shall be placing my bets on this one," the Lord responded, waving his third turkey leg at me.

"Thank you, Lord Ormsby. However, I must excuse my cousin. Final preparations, you know," Senoy said, ushering me towards the exit. He waved to the man now attacking the platter of sweetbreads.

As we entered the adjacent library, I swaggered over to the pier table. "How could he fit any more food in? No wonder Lady Ormsby has taken a young paramour."

"Evelyn, we do not talk about such things," Senoy said sternly as he closed the library door.

"Oh, I am sorry. I do enjoy the freedom men have of speaking their minds," I said as I threw myself onto Mother's pink settee. I draped my leg over the edge and let out a sigh. "It is amazing the freedom that trousers offer. I should have done this ages ago!"

"Evelyn, put your leg down! You must be careful interacting with these men. One of them is bound to realize there is no Sir Moore of Asbury."

"Oh, stop worrying, Senoy. You are starting to sound like Mother." Laughing, I crouched away from his grasp and jumped over the back of the settee.

"Have you seen your final competitor?"

"Lord Wyndham? Are you jesting? You should have seen Nab beat him yesterday."

"This is a different man playing out there today. Even Nab realizes that Lord Wyndham was just being a good sport." Master Senoy rubbed his hand through his thick hair as he walked to the window. "He has strength and speed."

"Are you saying that I cannot beat him?" Surprised, I joined him at the window.

"Evelyn, you have never been confronted with someone of his skill."

"Please stop worrying and just be happy for me."

"Evelyn," with a shake of his head he gazed into the garden below, "I do not think this was a good idea."

"Do you have no faith in me Senoy?"

"That is not the right question."

"I am tired of your wordplay," I said, picking a nonexistent piece of lint off my collar. "Besides, tonight you will realize you were wrong." With no response, I gazed at his tense profile. "Is something else bothering you?"

"No, I am sure everything will turn out as it should be," he sighed.

"There you go. That is the spirit!"

A loud celebration of male voices erupted in the green foyer. My curiosity got the best of me, and leaving Senoy behind, I ran out the door. Lord Ormsby was still at the food table, pouring himself another tankard of mead, when he noticed me. He quickly raised his cup in a toast, adding in a boisterous voice, "Well, it seems, young man, that you may have met your match!"

"What do you mean, sir? Are you having a change of heart?" I asked. Out of habit, I gave him my best enchanting smile. His face turned the color of a ripe turnip.

"Oh, not at all," he stammered. "Lord Wyndham is your challenger, and compared to him, you are...well, you are just out of the nursery, my dear boy."

"I can beat him just as well as any man," I yelled a bit too loudly as my temper started to get the best of me.

"Hear, hear! You will need that young man's courage."

Senoy quickly walked up and grabbed me by the collar. "Come, let's get ready for the final match," he said a bit gruffly. I tried to pull loose with no success.

"Good luck, Master Senoy. You may have to keep that one on a leash," he said with a laugh as mead splashed all over the front of his shirt.

"On a leash??!!!" I yelled. I would have gone for his throat, but Senoy had such a tight grip on me that all I could do was follow behind. As soon as we entered the sitting room, he loosened his grasp, and I jerked away. "Why are you treating me like a child?" I asked, turning to face him.

He stood his ground and stared straight into my eyes. "When you act like a child, I shall treat you like one. Do you realize you almost broke your cover with a smile like that?"

My eyes immediately dropped to the floor. "I was perfectly fine."

"Your arrogance astounds me." His voice lowered to a whisper. When I met his gaze, I was surprised to find disappointment written on his face.

"I hate it when you treat me like a little girl!"

"You are a little girl!" he yelled.

"No, I am not. Look at me, Senoy. I am a grown woman!" The tears began to gather in my eyes as I continued. "A grown woman about to be sold to the best man in some stupid competition! Would that be happening if I were just a little girl?!"

Instead of providing me with the comfort I expected, he walked back to that blasted window. "You are right, Evelyn. You are no longer a child. I knew it was coming, I...I guess I was not ready yet."

I slowly walked up behind him and gazed at the back of the man who had become more of a father to me than my own. I wrapped my arms around him, my anger dissipating like a scolded child. I could never stay mad at Senoy. "I am sorry. I love you, Senoy."

"Evelyn..." he whispered. He continued to stare into the garden as if waiting for someone to appear. The hairs on my neck began to tingle when suddenly the door to the sitting room opened. I jumped away from Senoy, hitting my hip on the side table.

"Ouch!" I yelped.

And, of course, who else would it be but Lord Wyndham walking into the room like it was his own private study? "Oh, excuse me. I did not realize anyone was in here," he said. "You must be Sir Moore. Congratulations on your victory today! I look forward to our final match." He smiled and extended his hand towards me.

All I could focus on were the long hairs curling in his face, glistening with sweat. "Uh, you as well," I said a little too roughly, keeping my hands to myself.

Senoy turned around and offered Lord Wyndham a congratulatory smile. "If you are looking for some privacy, we were just leaving. Good luck today." He grabbed my arm and led me towards the door.

"Thank you, Master Senoy," replied Lord Wyndham, looking down on me briefly as we passed through the door. I had the strong urge to stick my tongue out but quickly decided against it. He seemed to know exactly what I wanted to do and nodded his head with a knowing smile.

****

May 1, 1893 - Continued.........

I know it is not like me to write more than once a day, however, I had nowhere else to turn.

I have been defeated. Everything Senoy said was true, and now, due to my incompetence, I have lost the sword forever, along with my freedom. It is only a matter of time before Father starts whispering in the ear of Lord Wyndham of the advantageous match he would make with me: the dowry of land, money, and jewels he would gain. I would not be surprised if, by tomorrow, the marriage contracts are signed. I wish I could explain, but my words cannot do justice. During the entire match, I held him off, and we were tied up with only one point to decide the victor. I knew I had him. In the end, I was sure my speed would beat his strength any day. However, in truth, I am sure that it was his skill that won out over my pure arrogance. (I see now, too late, why Senoy was upset with me.) As Lord Wyndham lunged towards my chest, I deflected the hit by turning to my left, only to meet the point of his sword on my right. He had adapted to my speed and, only to admit to my deeper self, was probably three moves ahead of me the entire match. I do not know if it was his skill or his lopsided grin at the end that angered me the most. What does it matter? Our stakes were never equal.

Even now, I can hear the laughs and revelry from the celebration continuing under my window. When Father presented Lord Wyndham with the sword during dinner, I thought I would be sick. It was a good thing I was still disguised as Sir Moore. For if I had been myself, I would have had a tantrum right in the middle of the dining hall. (I do feel bad about giving Aunt Lettie a sedative, but it was for the cause. With Mother thinking we were both suffering a headache, it gave a sound reason why Evelyn could not attend.) Once the toasts were over, I quickly retreated to my room using the back corridors. Seeing my distress, I knew Senoy would not be far behind.

"Come in," I said as Senoy lightly knocked on my door. "Please close the door behind you."

"Evelyn, you know I am not allowed in your chambers," replied Senoy, still standing in the doorway. "Perhaps we could walk in the front foyer instead?" He continued to look at me, waiting for my response.

"I do not need your pity, Senoy. Everyone is downstairs and already deep in their cups to care." The tears I had been holding back finally broke loose. Senoy looked down the hall, then quietly closed the door behind him. As awkward as it was for him to sit on my bed, he effortlessly pulled me into his arms.

"Evelyn, you did your best. No one else was a match for Lord Wyndham. You have not trained with someone who embodies the same skills and has learned to harness their strength."

"But Senoy, you know better than anyone that this was not just a game for me. It was my life I was fighting for."

"I think perhaps we have gone about this whole endeavor incorrectly. Have you tried to reason with your father?"

"It is no use. He will not change his mind," I said, wiping the tears from my eyes. Nestling deeper into Senoy's arms, I focused on the steady beat of his heart until my thoughts became clear. It was an internal call to battle. There was something more important than myself. "I must take action, or we will lose the sword forever. As for the marriage, I can make Lord Wyndham's life such a living hell that he would never agree to marry me."

"Perhaps I should talk to your father," Senoy said as his hand began to rub my back. His familiar hum of 'Für Elise' reached my ears.

"Hmmm...I have not heard Beethoven in a long time." The arpeggios of the melody pushed me into action. I knew I needed to do everything in my power to preserve the past. Determined, I pulled myself out of his arms and headed to my dresser. "I am going to take the sword back."

"You will do no such thing," he calmly stated as he got off the bed. He assessed my attire with one brief look. "You knew what you were going to do this whole time. I was wondering why you had not changed out of Sir Moore's attire."

"I will not allow the sword to leave our family. The responsibility of guarding the sword was supposed to be passed down to Mother and then to me. It was never meant to be in Father's hands. It is my legacy to protect the sword."

He patiently looked at me and asked, "Do you even know why you protect this sword?"

"Grandmother never had the chance to explain. However, she made me promise on her deathbed to keep a watchful eye over the sword. She never approved of Mother handing the sword over to Father. Though we all know my mother was never strong." As I paced back and forth, a plan began to form in my mind. "I cannot believe how selfish I have been. All I was thinking about was how this would affect me, completely forgetting about the promise I made to Grandmother. How thoughtless of me!" Looking at Senoy, I hoped he had the answer.

"Perhaps it is best that the sword stays with Lord Wyndham. He is rather strong and seems to have an affection for it."

"How can you say that?" I asked incredulously.

"I have seen the women in your family get hurt multiple times, all in hopes of keeping the sword safe. What has it brought them but more grief? Perhaps your mother was right to pass it on to your father. Let someone else carry the burden."

"What are you talking about?" I yelled. "I do not have time for this. Perhaps you should have told me everything a long time ago. Right now, I need to find it before Lord Wyndham returns to his room. I assume he would have put it there after dinner. At least, that's a *starting point. I..." I paused my tirade to gauge Senoy's reaction and swung my empty sword bag over my shoulder. "Senoy... please try to understand." With no response, I headed towards the door. Suddenly, he grabbed me from behind and pulled me into his chest. I tried to move, but his strength increased tenfold. His lips were mere inches from my ear, and my breath caught.*

"Evelyn, please know this. I will always support you. Perhaps I was wrong; you need the sword just as much as it needs you." His grip on me loosened, and I slowly turned around to examine his face. There was a mix of tenderness, sadness, and an unidentifiable emotion. I withdrew cautiously and made my way to the door. After opening the latch, I turned back to him, not knowing what to say. I furrowed my brow slightly before finally walking out the door.

****

May 1, 1893, 6 am
Everything has changed. In one night, nothing is as it was. I am writing everything down, in hopes of coming up with a solution. I must start at the beginning with my search for the sword. This is where the real story begins.

Silently making my way towards Lord Wyndham's room in the north corridor, I found the entire hallway deserted due to the ongoing celebrations. After receiving no response to my knock, I cautiously entered the room, quietly closing the door behind me. The candles on the side table were unlit, indicating the room was empty. The moonlight illuminated the small room, revealing the sparsely decorated, perfectly made bed. My mother specifically kept these rooms for male guests, as it was commonly believed that men did not enjoy the sight of a round cherub staring at them while they slept. I was drawn to the sword lying unprotected on the table beneath the open window. To be honest, I had never held the sword before. My father had always kept it in a glass case, believing that a woman's role was to be a good daughter and a dutiful wife when the time came. Perhaps fencing was initially my way of rebelling against his expectations. The thought of finally touching the cool steel made my fingers tingle with anticipation, and a smile formed on my lips.

As I slid my fingers over the stone inlay on the front part of the guard, I couldn't stop my hands from shaking. The craftsmanship was truly amazing. According to Senoy, the stone resembled the Mesopotamian Glyph of the Sun God Utu-Shamesh, which corresponded to the revolving sword of fire used to guard the Garden of Eden and prevent access to the Tree of Life. At that moment, I wished I had paid more attention during my history lessons. My hand traced the eight-spoke solar wheel etched into the hard stone. It always just looked like a rude imprint of a star to me, with its four bursts of light radiating out of the corners. Despite its simplicity, the glyph was truly beautiful. Suddenly, a dusty blue glow gently rippled through the streams of the glyph and sank into the tips of my fingers, leaving warmth in its wake. I could not move.

"Stupid man! How could anyone not protect something so valuable?" I whispered, not quite sure if I had said the words aloud.

"I did not know someone was planning on stealing it," came a deep male voice behind me. "Particularly while I bathed."

Startled by the voice, I whirled around into a fighting stance. Standing next to the bathing screen, in all his glory, was the naked body of Lord Wyndham. Well, partly naked. Drat! How had I not noticed the screen? A towel covered his lower half, but his chest and calves were bare. I had never seen a man without his shirt, let alone his pants. I could not take my eyes off the hard planes of his chest, glistening with wet drops illuminated by the moonlight.

"What a shame, Sir Moore. I am very disappointed in you," Lord Wyndham continued, ignoring my surprise. "You could not handle defeat, so you step down to thievery? Where is the honor in that?" Placing his hands on his waist, I watched the muscles in his chest contract.

"I... I...I did not think you would be here. Why are you not downstairs celebrating?" I stammered, suddenly remembering my disguise. I felt disappointment wash over me as I stared at the hand holding the towel.

Surprised by my willingness for it to fall, a buzz of excitement stirred in my stomach as a growing heat spread from my legs up to my cheeks.

"Look, young man, I do not have time for this. I must be off early in the morning." Slowly processing his words, I looked up to see him chuckling. "You act as if you have never seen a grown man naked before. Do not be envious. If you keep practicing your fencing skills, I have no doubt you will look like this in no time."

"I am not jealous! Just..." My words escaped me as he reached to light one of the candles, causing the towel to drop lower.

"Just leave the room, and no one will be the wiser. You are on your way to becoming a great swordsman. Do not make a rash decision that could ruin your future."

Unable to find my voice, I shook my head in silence.

"I would highly recommend you take my bargain. Stop acting like a petulant child. Otherwise, you leave me no option but to pull the servant bell." He grabbed the tassel mounted on the side wall and waited for my response.

When I heard the word "child," anger flushed through my cheeks, breaking my dazed fascination. Trying to suppress my anxious feeling, I spun around to grab the sword off the table. The sword's weight almost caused it to slip from my grip, but I managed to readjust and hoist the blade over my shoulder. "I am no child, Lord

Wyndham!" I yelled. I adjusted the painful weight pressing into my shoulder and strained to open the bedroom door.

I used my anger to push me down the corridor, through the kitchen, and out the side door to the private gardens. Seeking refuge, I ran towards the middle section of the garden lined with my mother's rose bushes. I flung myself behind the statue of Venus to catch my breath. Closing my eyes, I leaned against her cold, naked back, letting the sword's point rest on the gravel. Suddenly, I could hear the sound of crunching pebbles heading towards me. I peered around the enchanted goddess, washing her feet at the trickling fountain. The noise stopped, shifting further away. A blue glow started to seep through my fingers. When I moved my hand, I gasped in amazement. The stone had become a brilliant blue beacon, shooting its light into the sky. Whether out of fear of the stone or the coming intruder, I pushed away from the statue and ran for the bordering forest. The sword continued to weigh me down as I approached the entrance to the tall, looming trees. Stopping in front of a large fir with a gnarled side, I glanced down to find the stone black once more. I let it fall to the ground, and I doubled over. As the pain in my side subsided, I stood up to lean against the tree. A powerful arm swooped around my chest and slammed me against the tree's deformed trunk. The bark cut into my back, and I yelped in pain, closing my eyes tight.

"Oh, believe me, young man, you deserve more than a little smack against a tree," yelled the attacker. "Did you think you could just run away from me without being caught?"

Opening my eyes, I found Lord Wyndham only a breath away. I had no choice but to meet his gaze and struggled to speak. "You...you forgot your cravat..." My words came out broken and shallow, a new emotion beginning to suppress the extreme pain in my back.

"Answer me, dammit!" he yelled. "This is not a farce!"

"Stop! You are hurting me!" I tried to regain control as the fear in my voice took over.

He quickly leaned back, keeping his firm hold. "Who are you, really?"

My only response was a scream, as the pain became a fire ripping across my soft back. To my utter dismay, he yanked off my cap, and my coiled braid fell over my shoulder as the rest of my hair came tumbling down.

"Who are you?" he gasped. I could see the answer in his eyes as he stared at my hair. "Wait...no."

"What?" I asked, finally finding my voice. "Could not handle the fact that a woman almost bested you today?" Struggling against his arm, I tried to kick my feet away from the tree to get loose.

"My God...you are Nab's sister," he whispered.

"Let me go, you big oaf!" He loosened his grip but held me firm against the tree. My fear became palpable as I watched the surprise in his eyes turn to pure rage.

"What in hell were you thinking? You could have been seriously hurt today! And now you try to steal the sword? Do you realize I could easily turn you over to the constable or do something worse, were I not a gentleman?"

"You would not dare," I challenged. "I am a Lady!" He remained silent, trying to regain his composure. I realized I was going to have to change my plan of attack. I dropped my head over his arm and closed my eyes, trying to produce the tears I knew were already close to forming. "I am sorry," I whispered, "please do not say anything." I lightly grabbed his arm with my fingers, and as I expected, he let go. I suddenly fell from the tree and landed on all fours. I pushed myself onto my feet and tried to stretch, hoping to alleviate the pain.

"Are you crazy or just plain rebellious? Does your father even know?" he yelled.

"About the tournament or the sword?" I rubbed the back of my neck and winced.

"All of it?!"

"No."

"No wonder your father wants to get you married off!" He started to pace, brushing his hand through his hair.

"What are you talking about?"

"Like you do not know," he said, abruptly stopping his pacing and staring right at me. "Is that what this is all about? Poor little Duchess finds me so repulsive you developed this little farce so that I would not want to marry you? Well, I could have saved you the trouble. I already told your father I did not want to marry you."

"No, this is not about that at all," I said. "Wait, you do not want to marry me?"

"No," he replied firmly.

"Why?" I asked, surprising even myself.

"Are you serious?" he responded, rubbing the side of his jaw and leaning against the tree.

"Well..." I stuttered. It was my turn to begin pacing. "That is not what this is about." I turned back towards him and pointed to the sword. "I need that."

"The sword?" he asked. "Why not just ask your father?"

"He hates the sword and wants to be rid of it. However, I am sworn to protect it. It has been in my family for ages, and my father had no right to give it away."

He pushed himself away from the tree. "Is that so?" A smile spread across his face as a new light appeared in his eyes.

"Well...yes," I answered as I scooted further into the forest. I could hear my heartbeat pounding as he stalked closer to me. "Why are you smiling? Did you even hear what I said?"

"Not really, but does it matter? I have a better idea. We will fight for it. Sword to sword with no disguises."

"Right now, right here?"

Fondling the handle of the sword strapped to his side, he nodded his head without breaking eye contact.

"And if I win, I get the sword?" I asked.

"Correct, but if I win, you will not bother me again."

"Agreed," I said. "However, I do not have my sword with me."

"Just use the sword you so passionately protect."

"Well, I guess...It is rather heavy."

"Is that whining I detect? Do you want to do this or not?" he taunted.

"Yes!" I adjusted to the sword's weight and pointed it toward Lord Wyndham. "En garde!"

The adrenaline rush pushed us further into the dark forest as our jabs and parries ricocheted off the dense trees. The clatter of steel mixed with the howls of the woodland creatures playing spectator in the wings. My moves became less precise as the sword's weight caused my arms to shake. Gasping, I swung my blade to the right, falling wide. Lord Wyndham lunged for my middle. Deftly moving behind me, his arms pulled me against his chest like a caged animal. My breasts felt tight. His heat pressed into my back as the delicious smell of soap and male sweat assailed my senses. Feeling an aching pulse in my chest, I registered his laughter rumbling through my body.

"This is not fair! You are not allowed to touch me!" I yelled, struggling against his firm hold.

A piercing screech rippled above us. We froze as dozens of owls surrounded us, breaking into the light of the full moon; their yellow eyes urging us to continue our entertaining confrontation. As Lord Wyndham loosened his hold, I jerked forward. Both of our hands hit the guard of my sword, and a blinding heat immediately shot up my arm. In an instant, we were engulfed by a blue flame that I was unable and unwilling to fight. As my feet left the ground, a torrent of memories consumed me, fragments of another life flashing before my eyes, leaving a burning desire in the pit of my stomach. I saw a young boy running through hay fields with his friends, wielding a crude wooden sword. I felt the painful guilt of this same boy being scolded by his father for accidentally letting a horse loose from a barn. I watched as the boy grew into a young man keeping a stern eye on a professor in a college classroom full of other men.

The confusing images continued to flash by until it was quite clear that it was Lord Wyndham's childhood I was playing witness to. His emotions ripped into my heart, leaving them there for all eternity. The extreme fever devoured my body as the flames burst from my fingertips and toes. I realized I could no longer touch the ground. In that moment of vulnerability, a shadow descended, blotting out the blinding light that had enveloped us. Lord Wyndham's touch against my damp cheek served as a bittersweet reminder of our shared connection, a fleeting moment of intimacy amidst the chaos. Yet, as quickly as it had begun, the spell was broken, and we tumbled to the forest floor in a tangle of limbs. I lay utterly immobile on top of him. Even our audience of owls and wolves had vanished. Had it even happened? Feeling a bit shaky, I pushed off the man whose pride had been laid bare before me. I was unable to meet his gaze as my raw emotions threatened to break me down completely. Without a backward glance, I ran as fast as I could, leaving the family heirloom of protection behind.

"Evelyn!" Lord Wyndham called.

I could barely hear the call of my name through the sudden boom of thunder. I sprinted past the statue of Venus as cold drops of rain hit my head and splattered off the stone goddess as if to announce my arrival. The storm suddenly intensified, soaking me to the bone before I could even reach the side door of the manor. I was unaware of the water dripping off my tailored suit as I sprinted to my room. The sounds of the house beginning to wake up for the day could be heard, the slam of my door covered by the repeated claps of thunder echoing through the large house. As I fell onto my bed, my wet clothes became a cocoon, and I briefly glanced at the light show playing outside my window. I could feel myself drifting off to sleep, but a rather powerful knock suddenly jolted me back upright.

"Evelyn!" A familiar voice urgently whispered from the hall. "Are you in there?"

"Senoy!" I called out, tears running down my face as I raced to the door.

As I yanked on the latch, I froze. My surprise at the intruder left me speechless. Standing before me was a blond god dressed like a warrior about to go to bed. I could not take my eyes off his rich blond locks and bright blue eyes. And then I noticed the hard, lean muscles visible through his open white shirt. Before I could look any further, I slammed the door in his face. Sliding down the back of the door, I buried my head in my hands.

"I...I am sorry I thought you were someone else. I think you have the wrong room." My voice trembled through my tears.

"Evelyn, it is me, Senoy," the muffled voice pleaded.

"Please go away."

"Evelyn, you have to trust me. I have so much to explain. I know I should have explained sooner, but I never expected this... at least not so soon."

"If you do not leave, I will ring the bell," I threatened, my sobs growing louder.

"Evelyn, it is me," Senoy repeated. "Do you remember how you used to sneak into my bed after a nightmare when you were a little girl? I would hum 'Für

Elise' until you drifted off to sleep. Or how I taught you how to best Johnny Tucker with a sword? You have always been a bit headstrong when someone told you that you could not do something. Remember when your father made you spend the day in the barn when he found out you stopped that pig from being slaughtered? You begged me to take the pig to a better place and not tell anyone. I ended up taking it over to Mrs. Fields' and she still has it to this day." He continued to rattle on until I stood up against the door. "Please, Evelyn, open the door," he pleaded.

Cracking the door slightly, I looked into Senoy's eyes. There were no doubts, just instant trust. It was Senoy's eyes. "I...I do not know what is happening," I faltered, my voice shaking. "With the night that I have had, I actually believe..." But before I could finish, the tears came out in loud, unladylike gulps. Senoy pushed me from the door, stepped inside, and gently closed it behind him. Pulling me into his arms, we both slid to the floor. The thunder drowned out my cries as Senoy continued to rock me like a child.

"The time has come once again," he whispered.

****

7. The Bet

A rocking motion continued to press a heavy weight onto Evie's chest while a light breeze tickled the inside of her ear. Straining against non-existent bonds, she opened her eyes to complete darkness. A low melodic tune vibrated the hard surface she was lying on. A voice so sweet, Evie wondered if she was still dreaming.

"Evie, my dear, time to wake up."

Pushing up to a seated position, Evie tried to concentrate on the soft words. Gradually, three blurry masses of white materialized through the dense gloom. As her vision adjusted, the ghostly forms expanded further on each side, blazing with radiant light. She shielded her eyes from the intense illumination, and a shrill screech echoed through the vision, causing the apparitions to waver. She reached out, feeling they were somehow her only saviors in this darkness. Suddenly, a thick layer of red goo dropped onto her head and completely covered her eyes. Her scream ripped from her throat. She thrust her hands to her face, only to realize that the thick substance she thought she felt was already gone, just another trick of her imagination. As she opened her eyes once again, a light reverberation began to beat consistently against her ribcage. Light flooded the small space.

"Sheba!" Her throat contracted on the loud syllables.

She lifted her head to stare at the bright orange cat sitting on her chest and instantly let it drop back to her bedroom floor. Now acutely aware of each and every groove in the popcorn ceiling, she tried to concentrate on Sheba's repetitive purring.

The cat jumped off Evie's chest and licked her paw before crossing over the journal to disappear under the bed. Evie turned to her side and let her fingers curl around the worn edges of the leather as the squeal of water pipes groaned overhead. Reality was finally sinking back in. Tugging on her shirt from the day before, she noticed the morning light was already streaming through the closed blinds.

"Crap," she whispered.

Evie glanced at her alarm clock and leaped from the floor to open her dresser drawers. While searching for her favorite blue vintage t-shirt, she tried to distinguish between the events in her journal and her nightmares. Lost in thought, she headed to her desk and opened her laptop. She typed in the words "Screech Owl," and a preview of small images began to load on the screen just as the rush of water stopped with a loud bang. Knowing that her mother would be walking in shortly, she slammed down the laptop and dashed into the bathroom.

Evie spent yet another school day lost in her thoughts, resulting in her grades suffering and her fingers feeling the effects of her anxiety. As she made her way to her locker from her final class, someone pulled her ponytail, causing her head to jerk back. "Ow!"

"You deserved it!" Lana said, sliding up next to her.

"What the hell for?" Evie dropped her book bag and frowned. "I told you I was sorry about yesterday!"

Lana grabbed Evie's hand and examined her fingers. "Hungry much?"

Evie pulled her hand away and shoved her books into the open locker.

"What's wrong with you?" Lana asked.

"Look who's talking!" Evie narrowed her eyes, hoping Lana would give her more information about Blake—anything to make sense of her turbulent week.

"Hey, I've already told you everything I know. Blake and my Dad had a fight, and then Blake left. I haven't seen him since."

"I just don't understand why you aren't worried! He looked horrible!" Evie noticed a few concerned looks from students passing by and lowered her voice. "I hope this isn't some horrible prank of yours!"

"Are we back to that again?! I already told you no more pranks. Besides, Blake can take care of himself. Anyway, I have another bone to pick with you."

"Oh? There's more?" Evie slammed her locker closed, ignoring Lana as she headed toward the gym.

Lana quickly caught up. "Yes, there's more! I had to listen to Seth in homeroom whine about how you never call him anymore. You either need to let the guy down or freakin' call him!"

"What the hell? I told him I would hang out with him on Friday!"

"You do realize today's Friday, right?"

Evie winced.

"Seriously, I don't buy this whole story about you not getting enough sleep. You've been out of it all week." Waiting for Evie to respond, Lana sighed. "Okay, fine, I'll drop it for now. Did you bring the journal with you?"

"Oh, yeah," Evie said, letting the lie roll off her lips. "I did."

"Good! At least you can finally be rid of the stupid thing."

"Yeah…" Evie stopped to push a pencil pouch falling out of her book bag. She jiggled the broken zipper and ended up carrying the bag in her arms. "So, I didn't hear from you this afternoon. I take it you didn't run into Rick?"

"Nah, but I plan on staying after today and watching him practice again." With a tight smile, Lana continued down the hall.

"Really?" Evie ran to catch up but stumbled along the way.

"Well, at least something got your attention. You might want to tie that shoe and get a new book bag while you're at it."

"Good idea." Smiling, Evie bent down. "So, Rick again, huh?"

"The things you do for love. So, can you give me a ride after practice?"

"Sure, no problem," Guilt started to eat at Evie. Standing back up, she grabbed Lana's arm. "Look, I'm really sorry. I know I've been acting weird. Let's do something tonight, and I promise to help you with Rick." Tugging on the mass of necklaces around Lana's neck, she grinned.

"Fine," Lana said, pulling her necklaces out of Evie's grasp. She rolled her eyes. "What about Seth?"

"Oh yeah...I'll figure something out."

"Now, get your fingers out of your mouth and hurry along to sword practice like a good little girl. Wouldn't wanna be late for you-know-who." Lana pushed Evie towards the gym before heading off toward the fields.

As Evie walked into the gym, she was immediately drawn towards the commotion inside the coach's office. Due to the recent renovations, the office now had a first-floor view of all the action between the new, state-of-the-art basketball hoops, another advantage of having an upscale athletic program. While passing by the equipment closet, Evie watched the drama play out as Professor Mike and Damek stood directly in front of each other. Unable to look away, she could easily tell that Damek was yelling about something, as his cheeks had taken on a purple hue. The Professor shook his head, urging Damek to lower his voice. As Evie concentrated on the muffled voices, she stopped in surprise. A hand reached out from behind Damek to touch his shoulder. Everything around Evie slowed down as if she was watching the interaction in slow motion. Her gaze followed the offending hand up the owner's arm and landed on his face. She took an intake of breath. The hand belonged to Blake. Shaking off the suspicious feeling that they were talking about her, she realized Blake was looking straight at her.

Evie felt a light pat on her shoulder. "You eventually get used to their love spats," said a blonde girl with dark brown eyes, smiling directly at her.

"Excuse me?" Evie asked, trying to focus on the advanced student.

"Damek and Professor Mike," she said, pointing towards the office. "Rumor has it that Damek's parents are fencing fanatics. They gave the school a huge grant just to set up a fencing team for Damek. Man, what money can do, huh? Then they hired Professor Mike to teach. He's like a family friend or something." Dropping her equipment bag to the floor, the student pulled her blond hair into a tight ponytail. "Doesn't matter to me though. At least the rest of us get to learn, too. We may not be as good as Damek, but who cares, right? We get pretty close."

"Oh, right..." Evie didn't know what to say, so she tucked away the new tidbit of information.

"I'm Mary, a senior," she said, extending her hand to Evie.

"Evie. I'm a Sophomore." Shaking Mary's hand, she quickly glanced back into the office. Blake was gone.

"Well, if you need any help, just ask." Mary picked up her bag and headed to the bleachers. Evie followed slowly behind, trying to interpret the defeat she saw on Damek's face.

"Wait a sec, Mary. Did you recognize the other guy in the coach's office? Blake Cohen?"

"Blake?" Mary shook her head and looked back into the office before setting her things down on the bleachers. "I didn't see anyone else. It looks like they're all gone now." She grabbed her foil out of her bag and headed over to the advanced group.

Evie wasn't sure what to think of Blake's conversation with the Professor and Damek. Given that they belonged to different social circles, it almost guaranteed they never spoke to one another. Either way, neither seemed too happy about what Blake had to say. Feeling a bit removed from reality at the obscure moment, she tried to concentrate on the group in front of her. Heading over to the beginners, Evie called out to Sam. "Hey!"

"Hey! Glad to see you're back. Looks like you get the award for last groupie standing." Smiling, Sam winked at her. Evie noticed she was the only girl left in the small group.

Sam whistled over her head before she could come up with a good retort. "So Trace, you're the sub today? Damek get demoted?" Evie turned her attention to the advanced student walking towards them.

"Yeah, something like that," Trace replied, pointing to the office windows. "When the two of them get into it, it's best just to walk away." Trace rolled his eyes and turned to the rest of the group. "I'm Trace. I'll be your coach today."

Evie looked around the room to find Damek and the Professor nowhere to be seen. Her heart began to race with the uncanny feeling that it was her fault.

"From what I hear," Trace continued, "you've already gone over the rules, so let's get our gear and start with the proper grasp of the sword." Trace pointed towards the equipment racks, and the group scrambled to find the best jackets. There weren't many. Trace was considered the second-best fencer and also happened to be Damek's best friend. Being fairly tall and thin, he reminded Evie more of a basketball player than a fencer. After tying his long dark dreadlocks into a ponytail, he gestured for everyone to form a line.

Evie surprised herself by speaking up instead of grabbing a jacket like the rest of the small group. "Do you know what they were arguing about?" She took a step back, gaining Trace's full attention. "I mean Damek and Professor Mike."

He briefly looked her up and down. "No, not really. Why?"

"Just curious. Never mind." Feeling the humiliation spread into her cheeks, she grabbed a jacket and got in line with the rest of the students, making sure to avoid eye contact with Trace.

"Hello. My name is Inigo Montoya. You killed my father. Prepare to die," Sam said, swinging his sword in a large arc, and attempting to imitate Mandy Patinkin's character with a famous line from the movie "Princess Bride". Evie's embarrassment quickly began to fade with everyone's laughter. After saying a silent prayer of thanks to Sam, she poked her finger through a hole in her worn fencing jacket.

"Nice Sam," Trace said, pushing Sam back into line. "Like we don't hear that every year."

Evie immersed herself in the lesson, entranced by the body's form and position, blocking out all thoughts of Damek and Blake. The knots in her stomach eased and gradually disappeared, taking on a beautiful form of symmetry. She felt whole, the moves becoming graceful and second nature. Reviewing her foot placement, she finally registered the groans around her.

"Come on, Trace! When do we get to learn some actual fighting moves?" Sam whined, lunging towards Evie with his foil. She deftly moved to the left, sidestepping any intended hit. "Nice move, Evie!"

"You have to learn the concepts first," Trace interrupted. "In the next class, we can start going over the lunge."

"Sweet!" exclaimed Sam, with his usual goofy smile. He took off his jacket and headed to the bleachers. The others quickly followed. Evie placed her feet back on the en garde line and concentrated on the wall in front of her to maintain her balance. She wasn't ready to give up the peaceful calm just yet.

"Hey, you're catching on pretty quick," Trace said, rubbing his hands on a towel. "What's your name again?" He placed his foil on the equipment table.

"Evie," she replied. Before her name left her lips, a cold sensation began to prick at the hairs on the back of her neck. She felt someone behind her.

"Sounds like you're getting the hang of it," Damek's voice had turned a bit icy. It bordered on rudeness, and he noticed Evie shiver. "Cold?"

"No," Evie mumbled, taking note of the frustration in his voice. Looking up, she realized Trace had too.

"What's your deal?" Trace asked. "Professor Mike put you in a bad mood?" He threw his towel in Damek's face and sat on the first bleacher.

Damek caught the towel and made his way to the equipment table. "Something like that."

"You know, Damek, I was thinking," Trace continued. "Evie would be perfect for the bet."

"What are you talking about?" Damek asked as he straightened the foils on the table. He ran his hand over the many dings etched into the well-used blades.

"She already has the concentration. I bet she'll pick up the moves pretty quickly, too." Touching his forehead with his finger, he winked. "I've a sense for these things, you know."

"Yeah, right," Damek dismissed with a forced laugh, throwing a towel back at Trace. "Pick someone else."

"What are you guys talking about?" Evie asked.

"Come on, man!" Trace said, ignoring Evie. "It'll be perfect. I'll take Sam, and you get Evie. Besides, it's my choice, not yours."

Finally meeting Evie's gaze, Damek frowned as if he had just remembered she was there. "Trace had this brilliant idea of training two beginners for a match at the end of the semester, basically testing our teaching ability."

"I thought the Professor said no beginner matches until the end of the year?" Evie asked.

"Yeah, well, that doesn't mean we can't do it on our own time," Trace interjected, raising his eyebrows. "Besides, you owe me, Adams."

"Owe what?" Looking at Damek, Evie was confused.

"Nothing that concerns you. Just pick someone else, Trace."

His rejection coiled in Evie's stomach, tears gathering in her eyes unexpectedly.

"No way. It's too perfect," Trace responded. He grabbed his book bag and punched Damek in the shoulder. "And stop being rude. It's not your style."

Evie closed her eyes and quickly wiped the tears from her cheeks. She tightened her grasp on the foil she was still holding and pushed her shoulders back. "Did you guys stop to think that maybe I don't wanna do it?"

As he walked towards the exit, Trace looked over his shoulder at Evie. "Like you don't wanna have a chance to bout this semester and learn from one of the best?"

She was at a loss for words. A whole semester of training with Damek. Every girl's dream. That's what she wanted, right?

Understanding Evie's blatant expression, Trace smiled. "Exactly. End of the semester, Adams. See you tonight. Oh, by the way, Evie wanted to know what you and Professor Mike were arguing about." He waved his hand and walked out of the gym.

Evie stammered, "Um, well..." but Damek ignored her and started moving the foils from the table to the equipment rack. She took off the fencing jacket and contemplated giving him an out.

"Look, it's not a big deal. Just pick someone else," she said silently, hoping that he would turn around and magically say that nothing was wrong. Perhaps a day when he broke up with his hot cheerleader girlfriend and found a plain-faced nobody like her charming.

He wiped one of the blades on his sleeve. "Don't worry, I will."

She stared at her foil before surprising herself by whipping it around in the air before her. A new emotion was starting to take hold. "Look, did I do something to make you mad at me?"

He slowly turned his attention back to her. "Well, that depends. I don't really know you, do I?" Evie had the distinct impression it was a loaded question.

"What are you talking about?"

Damek glanced around the empty gym and peered into the coach's office window. No one was there.

Evie tried to read his expression. It reminded her of the crazed look Blake had in the parking lot. "Do you know Blake Cohen?"

Damek inspected a dark, skid spot on the floor and whispered, "Does the name Lilith mean anything to you?"

"What did you say?" Taking a step closer, Evie lowered her blade.

He met her gaze and repeated the name louder. "Lilith"

"Lilith?" The name rolled off her tongue easily. "No. I don't think so. Should I?"

"I didn't think so." With finality, he grabbed Evie's foil and fencing jacket. He loaded them into the equipment closet and slammed the door, pushing the wheeled contraption to the front of the office. "Look, don't worry about the bet. I'll get someone else."

"Maybe I wanna do it."

"That's just too bad, isn't it? I don't, at least not with you. It isn't a good idea."

"I don't understand. Why isn't it a good idea?" Suddenly, a tennis shoe squeaked across the gym floor.

"Hey babe," Lexi said. "Trace said you guys were finishing up." She swung between the tense pair and hugged Damek. "Is something wrong?" she asked, giving Evie a snotty look.

Damek conceded the staring contest with Evie and wrapped his arm around Lexi. "Not at all," he said, glancing back at the coach's office. He paused, realizing it was no longer empty. Professor Mike stood there watching him with his arms crossed over his chest. There was a moment of silence as they seemed to communicate some unknown message. Evie couldn't move. She tried to ignore the nausea in her stomach-patiently waiting for the floor to suck her in.

Damek kept his eyes fixed on the Professor, his voice reverberating off the walls, "Evie, the bet is on."

"Excuse me?" Evie could hardly hear her voice over the pounding in her ears.

"You heard me," Damek replied. "The bet's on, and you're the lucky one I'm gonna train." He broke the intense gaze with the Professor and turned towards Evie. "We'll start practicing on Monday after fencing class." Without waiting for a response, he grabbed Lexi's hand and headed towards the exit.

"What was that all about?" asked Lexi.

Damek ignored her question and took one final glance at the coach's office. "Oh, and by the way," he said, looking back at Evie, "Trace is having a party tonight. You should come." The Professor looked at him with disapproval, but Damek ignored it and raised his eyebrow. Evie looked at the Professor. Aware of the direct challenge, Evie was unsure how to respond.

"Trace's uncle owns this storage warehouse over by Fisher's Creek," Damek continued. "He's been trying to sell it for months. Anyway, it's completely empty, so tonight we're having a get-together."

"Oh," Evie said, confused by his sudden change in behavior. She said the first thing that came to her mind. "And it's okay with his Uncle?"

"Did you seriously just ask that?" laughed Lexi, tossing her curls over her shoulder. She caressed Damek's shoulder and sighed, "Come on, Damek. Why are you inviting her?"

"It'll be fine," Damek said. "Let's go."

Evie watched as Damek walked out of the gym and tried to ignore Lexi's whiny voice. When the gym doors shut, Evie rechecked the coach's office but found it empty. The Professor was gone. Yet again, she was the last to leave the gym. As she walked back to the bleachers for her bag, she stopped. Her mind was racing, and all the confusing events from the last thirty minutes melted away. She had been invited to a party! Willing her feet to move, she ran to her book bag and pulled out her cell phone.

"Hey, Lana! Guess what??!"

"Hey!" Lana responded. "I'm waiting in the parking lot. Are you coming?"

Evie continued to nibble on the inside of her thumb as she paced in front of the bleachers. "Yeah, guess what?!"

"You made a fool of yourself and tripped over your sword."

"Ha, Ha...No, I was invited to a party. And not just any party. One with Damek's friends!"

"Seriously? Tonight? Wait, I thought you weren't interested in him?"

"I'm not, but I've never been asked to a party before. It's over at some warehouse near Fisher's Creek."

"Trace Morgan's?" Lana asked, surprised.

"Yeah, how did you know that?" Evie stopped pacing and picked up her book bag.

"Please, give me some credit! I do know a few things about the star basketball player. Can you please get out here? I'm only getting about half of what you're saying."

"I thought I recognized him." Evie headed to the school exit. "I'm on my way. Do you wanna go?"

"A party at an abandoned warehouse? Do you really need to ask?"

"I know! I mean, it's not that big of a deal, right?"

"Funny that you say that, but don't you have a hot date with Seth?"

"What?!" Evie winced into the direct sun when she opened the school's front door.

"You promised him Friday, right?"

"Oh, crap!"

Lana waved at Evie from the car. "How ya gonna get out of this one, Ms. Popular?"

"Shut up!" Evie ended the call and hit the unlock button on the car. Shoving her book bag into the back seat, Evie tried to smile through a grimace. "I guess I'm just going to have to invite him."

"Do we have to?" moaned Lana. "I shouldn't have brought it up. He ruins everything."

"Oh, stop being so dramatic! He isn't that bad!"

"Whatever! Look who's talking. Let's go! Unlike you, I have to plan what I'm going to wear."

8. History Lesson

Evie rushed into the house, yelling a quick greeting to her mom. With thoughts of the party still causing somewhat irregular heartbeats, she bypassed the sweet smell of onions and garlic coming from the kitchen. Ignoring her mother's surprised greeting, Evie took the stairs two at a time. She flung her book bag to her bedroom floor and yanked open her accordion closet doors, staring at the clutter of clothes lying on the floor. She had nothing to wear, now feeling the sting of not listening to Lana.

Pulling out a yellow silk top from the heap, she pushed her finger through a hole in the armpit. She bent down to sift further through the mess and groaned. She was going to have to borrow something from Lana. Sitting cross-legged, she leaned against the pile of abandoned outfits and noticed a stuffed owl her dad had won for her at last year's county fair. She picked it up and pulled on the tag attached to its butt, and froze. Evelyn's journal was lying beside the open accordion door. She reached for the book, running her fingers over the dial chiseled into the front stone.

"I swear I left you on my bed this morning," Evie murmured. "I can't seem to get rid of you, can I?"

A light breeze skimmed the side of her neck as a romantic melody, slowly picked out on a child's piano, began to play in the distance. She relaxed further into the dark closet and realized she could just make out the rusty tune. As she placed the journal on her lap, the pages began to rustle through her fingers. Unable to voice her surprise, the pages abruptly stopped at the latest entry.

May 2, 1893, 9 am

Here I sit, alone in the middle of Mother's rose garden, with only my confusing thoughts for company. The statue of Venus before me reflects my own bewildered expression. Where do I go from here? I no longer have my comfortable father figure in Senoy, for he has become something more than my warring emotions can control. I feel different. Handsome, avenging guardians amid emotional turmoil that somehow hinges on me. Where do I begin? Perhaps we should start where I left off, in my room.

I was held speechless, cradled in Senoy's arms against my bedroom door, my nerves about to crack, not to mention my sanity at gazing at yet another male chest this evening. Master Senoy, my childhood teacher, and this perfect young warrior were the same. My mind could register the emotional connection, but the physical form was another matter altogether.

"Senoy, what has happened to you?" I whispered.

"Evelyn, I have something to tell you and..." pausing, he began to massage small circles into my back. "I know it will take some time for you to fully understand."

As he spoke, an unexpected sense of calm washed over me, replacing the hysteria overwhelming my senses. My eyelids grew heavy, a deep sleep threatening to take over. For the first time since running away from Lord Wyndham in the forest, I could breathe again. I could not quite remember why I was upset or confused.

"You have a destiny," Senoy said. Before he could continue, a loud bang came from the other side of the door. Senoy shoved his hand against the solid oak just as my memories of the night came flooding back.

"Evelyn, are you in there?"

"Oh no, it's Lord Wyndham," I gasped. Grabbing onto Senoy's shirt, I looked into his bright blue eyes. "I did something rather rash."

Senoy peered down at me. "Evelyn, how did you activate the stone?" His expression reflected my fear as my thoughts became jumbled.

"The what?" I asked.

"Evelyn," Lord Wyndham yelled, losing all pretense of whispering. "If you do not open this door, I will break it down!"

"Do not say anything to Lord Wyndham until we have had the chance to speak in private," Senoy said. He pulled us up from the floor. "I need to understand what happened." He hugged me quite tightly before he headed to the bedroom window. "I promise to explain everything." Opening the window with one quick jerk, he turned back around to gaze into my eyes. I would have followed him anywhere. Without any hesitation, he leaped right out of my window.

"Senoy!" I screamed. Running to the edge of the windowsill, I leaned over. My bedroom door crashed into the side of the wall, reverberating the pale blue curtains hanging from my bed. Lord Wyndham came barreling through, yanking me from behind and pulling me against his chest.

"Evelyn?!" he yelled. "What are you doing?? Get back from the window!"

"I am not going to jump, you imbecile!" I struggled to free myself from his grasp. "Let me go!"

Lord Wyndham cautiously dropped his arms.

I returned to the window and leaned over to look at the side of the house.

"Evelyn, what is going on? Was there something out there?"

I continued to stare into the empty sky. Where had Senoy gone? Surely, he would have met his death. Not one star lit the gravel path outside as I tried to scan the vines *that grew up the side of the manor, searching for any sign of Senoy.*

"I don't understand," I whispered to myself. The breeze hitting my face helped cool the intense heat radiating from my back. Slowly swinging around, I tried to meet Lord Wyndham's eyes with no success. The same strange anticipation I had felt before began to swirl in the pit of my stomach. I walked over to the door, my hands clenched into tight fists. I looked out into the hallway, and my only consolation was that most of the guests were still sleeping too soundly to hear the commotion. I closed the door with what was left of the hinges. Leaning against it, I could not move my eyes from Lord Wyndham's feet. "I...I do not know what is going on."

"Why did you yell for Master Senoy?" I could tell he was trying to regain his patience.

"I...I was scared. After what happened in the forest, I had nowhere to turn. Senoy has always been there for me."

"And you thought he would hear you from your private room?" He moved toward me.

My hands instinctively went up. "Please stay where you are." I took a step back, trying to figure out what to say. "Besides, who knows who you have already awoken."

"Me? With a screech like yours, I am quite sure you already took care of that."

Words continued to escape me. I kept imagining Senoy lying lifelessly on the rocky ground below.

Lord Wyndham's forehead relaxed. "Evelyn, I would prefer if we used our given names. Call me Adam." He stretched his hand toward me, and I focused on the calluses that lined the inside of his palm. Taking advantage of my stupor, he closed the small space between us and grazed the bottom of my chin with the rough tip of his finger. My thoughts of Senoy were forgotten as my eyes focused on Adam's firm lips. The confusing heat became unbearable, and I scooted back, hitting the bedside table behind me.

"Lord Wyndham," I said, trying to clear the lump in my throat, "I did not give you leave to use my given name."

"I do believe we are a little late for that. You started this when you attempted to steal my sword."

Unable to speak, I rubbed my hip, willing my eyes away from his lips.

"Stop stalling, Evelyn, and tell me what happened!"

"Well, which part?" I stammered.

"The whole thing, damn you!!" Taking a deep breath, he tried to recompose himself once again. "Let us start with the sword. Why do you need it?"

Amidst the confusion of the day and my current raw emotions, I tried to piece together a coherent thought. "The sword belonged to my mother. It has been passed down to the women in my family for generations. We were entrusted to keep it safe. But my mother foolishly gave it to my father, who has now done the unforgivable and given it over to a," I paused, choosing not to use the word "buffoon," and let out a deep sigh, "You."

"Why do you believe the sword needs to be protected?"

"I do not believe, I know!" Watching his eyebrows lift at my childish outburst, I dropped my eyes to the floor. "I do not know."

"So you were willing to give up your freedom or perhaps your life with this ridiculous escapade? All for a sword you know nothing about? Do you not trust your father?" He took a step back and rubbed the side of his jaw. "Or perhaps this is just childhood rebellion. I would think you are a bit old for that."

"Stop treating me like a child! I can feel its power! Are you telling me you can not?!" I rushed forward to push him aside, but my hands flew back from his chest as if singed. Memories of the forest came flooding back.

"Evelyn..." His voice was soft and gentle, almost like a caress. I found myself unable to look away from his lips, even though every fiber of my being was screaming at me to pull away. Traitor! But my body seemed to have a mind of its own, and I allowed him to pull me into a gentle embrace. I closed my eyes, savoring the warmth of his body against mine.

"Did you see or feel...what I did?" He whispered, his breath hot against my ear.

I shook my head, feeling the soft fabric of his shirt on my cheek. As his hand came to rest on the back of my neck, I knew I needed to do something. I had to think of Senoy, of my Grandmother.

Pulling out of his arms, I lifted my chin defiantly. "I do not know what you are talking about. I felt nothing."

"You are lying."

A knock on the door broke the intense silence. "Evelyn, are you well?" Senoy's voice sounded hollow, coming from the other side of the door. "Are you in there?"

"Yes, Senoy," I choked. A rush of relief flooded through my chest at his reassuring voice. However, I was unable or unwilling to pull away from Lord Wyndham's intense connection.

"I need to speak with you concerning an urgent matter. I apologize for the early hour, but please meet me in the library momentarily."

"Yes, Senoy." His footsteps quickly dissipated, and the uncomfortable silence became palpable.

Lord Wyndham took a step back. "Do not lie to me again, Evelyn. If you do not want to be honest with me, then I have no other course but to discuss the matter with your father." Turning to the door, he continued, "I do not want to cause a scene as of yet. Go find out what Master Senoy wants, then make haste to find me in the gardens.

We need to discuss what happened. I shall postpone my journey home for another day." Before opening the door, he pinned me with another stare. "Do not lie to me again. I know you are not indifferent to me."

My lip curled into a sneer, and I dropped into a slow curtsy. "As you wish, my lord."

"Until later, my dear."

"I am not your dear," I said as he smiled and closed the door behind him. Resting my hand on the closed door, I took a deep breath. There was no time to rest. I quickly removed Sir Moore's clothing and did my best to put on one of my day dresses without a lady's maid. Checking my disarray one last time in the mirror, I glanced at the discarded corset lying on the floor. I could feel Mother's disapproval. (For a lady should never be without her corset.) With one last thought of my mother's highly thought-of reputation, I quietly closed my door and headed down the back servants' stairs. I could hear the staff busy preparing the household for the stirring guests. The smell of fried ham almost tempted me to break my cover. When I reached the library, Senoy was staring into the fireplace. Making the most of my unseen moment, I examined his new form. His hair, once gray, was now golden blond, falling freely just below his muscular shoulders. His body was that of a young man in his prime for battle. As he reached down to stoke the fire, I could see the muscles ripple through his shirt. Where was the safe Father figure I used to know?

Senoy cleared his throat and turned around to meet my gaze. "Yes, I know. It is quite a transformation."

"I do not mean to stare, but it is rather amazing," I murmured. "Hard to believe, really, but I know it is you." His eyes were as blue as the bright summer sky, and the dimple in his chin was sculpted perfectly. Everything about him was intoxicating. It made me forget all about his death-defying leap from my window.

"It is only natural to be curious. I must say, I am surprised you have accepted the changes so readily."

I paused with a smile of recognition. "Senoy, I think I would recognize you anywhere, even if it meant in a different form."

"Well that as it may be, I do apologize that I never explained our current trend of events earlier. This is all my fault." Senoy gestured towards one of the many armchairs and approached the library desk. "Do you know why your grandmother asked you to protect the sword?"

It took me a few moments to realize I truly believed this young man was Senoy. Once I regained my composure, I sank into my favorite blue chair. "Not really," I finally responded. "She only said that it could be dangerous were it to fall into the wrong hands. Though, in truth, I have no idea who that would be."

"The stone inlaid in the sword's guard holds a power greater than anything we could imagine."

"Are you talking about the glyph?"

"So you did get a chance to look at it?" I could hear the pride in his voice.

"Oh yes! It is beautiful. I think that is what drew me to the sword so intently. When I saw it lying in Lord Wyndham's room, the stone seemed to call to me. Almost as if I were meant to take it. I know that sounds absurd, but..." I paused, unable to stop from yawning.

"Not absurd at all. It is as it should be," he interrupted.

"What do you mean?"

"We must start at the beginning. A history lesson, if you will," he said as he pushed himself off the desk and sat opposite me on the wooden chair. "Do you remember the stories I shared about Adam and Eve and how they were banished from the Garden of Eden?"

Staring at his dimple, I shook my head.

"Please concentrate, Evelyn."

"I am sorry. I am just so tired."

"What do you remember about the Garden of Eden?"

I tried to sit up straight and recite the childhood teachings. "God had warned Adam and Eve not to eat the apples on the Tree of Life. However, Eve was tempted by a serpent to eat the forbidden fruit, and she convinced Adam to do the same. As a result, God banished them from the garden and cursed them with a lifetime of hard labor."

"Good. I am glad to hear that you listened. With all your daydreaming, I was a bit concerned. As the story goes, God placed three angels with a flaming sword to guard the entrance of the Tree of Life, and no one was allowed to enter. It is commonly believed that the sword, along with the Garden of Eden, was lost during the Great Flood. However, contrary to what the angels made history believe, they hid the sword within the human race. They believed that there was goodness in humanity, which would ultimately keep the sword safe from harm. The angels chose a young woman named Lady Evangeline March to guard the sword and to pass it down to future female generations."

"Why her?" I interrupted.

With a ghost of a smile, a faraway look seemed to cloud his features. "Eva, or Lady Evangeline, was chosen because of her love for all humankind. Not only did she possess pure kindness, but she also had a strength not found too often in women of that era." He admired the large flames of the fire as a shadow passed over the side of his face.

"Are you feeling alright, Senoy?"

He cleared his throat before continuing, "Throughout the centuries, angels have watched over the female descendants of Lady March. However, Evangeline was the only one to sacrifice her life to protect the sword."

"What do you mean?"

"There has only been one demon that has attempted to take the sword. Apart from the original protector, Evangeline, the avenging demon has never returned."

"Demon?" I asked, confused. "I thought demons were only legends created to keep children mindful of their parents."

"Oh yes, my dear. There are many demons among us." Running his hand through his thick hair, he continued, "For centuries, the female descendants have lived rather quiet lives. The sword's history has become more legend and hearsay to the current generations. No one could blame your mother for getting rid of it. She never believed that her life was tied to a "piece of metal," as she likes to call it. Your father saw no just reason to keep it."

"I do not understand. How could the angels allow the sword to be given away?" I asked.

"There did not seem to be any harm in it. It has been quiet for centuries. Perhaps we wanted to believe that the danger was gone." He got up from his chair and began to pace. "Your grandmother warned me something was changing, but I did not want to believe it. I found comfort in my current way of life. We were starting to be at peace again. I should have believed her."

"What do you mean, we?"

He ignored my question, lost in his thoughts. "Your grandmother always knew that you would be the one."

"The one for what? You are not making any sense, Senoy."

Senoy stopped pacing and gazed into my eyes. I was mesmerized and lost my ability to speak. "Forgive me, I have started this all wrong. Evelyn, look at me," he said, spreading his arms. Suddenly, I felt a weight press on the back of my head, and a long-forgotten memory wavered on my temple.

"What are you trying to say, Senoy?"

"I think you know."

As I took a deep breath, I could not believe what my heart knew was true. I tried to ignore the ringing in my ears and whispered, "You are one of the angels." I felt like I was drowning.

"Some call me Senoy, others call me Snvi, but the most popular is Michael," he replied, taking a small reluctant bow.

"Michael, as in ArchAngel Michael, the leader of the Army of God Michael?" I could not close my mouth.

"To some extent. Time has a way of expanding on the truth."

Silently repeating the name in my head, everything seemed to become clear. He was Michael. "This is just too much," I mumbled, shaking my head.

"I know it is, but we must continue. There is little time. As I said before, there has only ever been one demon brave enough to steal the sword. Her name is Lilith. Adam's first wife."

"What do you mean 'first wife'? I thought Eve was his only wife?"

"The earliest written form of the Lilith legend comes from the 'Alphabet on Ben Sira' created by the early Mesopotamians. Lilith was created from the Earth at the same time Adam was. They began to fight because each thought they were the 'superior one.' In a burst of rage, Lilith left Adam and fled the Garden of Eden. Adam begged God to bring his love back, so God summoned me and two other angels to bring Lilith back to the Garden of Eden. When we found her, she was outraged by the direct command and would not return. We threatened to drown her in the sea, but she begged us to leave her be."

Struggling to keep my eyes open, I detected a hint of guilt in his voice.

"We finally agreed to let her live. In return, she agreed to God's curse, which was to live forever in eternity as the mother of all demons." He could tell that I was struggling to believe the tall tale. He started to pace. "She was then banished to a cave off the shores of the Red Sea. Adam became lonely and pleaded with God to create another mate for him. Eve was then created from Adam's rib bone. However, Eve was never a Lilith. Lilith and Adam had shared a love that was like no other. It is said that their passion could emit blue energy, which could be seen for miles. It was the beginning of what the romantics like to call soul mates. However, just like any passion, its extreme mate is anger. Adam never truly found that same

intense need with Eve. Oh, they grew to love each other, but it was more of a companion love. In time, Lilith also realized she had lost her one true love forever."

Senoy gazed into the burning embers of the fire and extended his hands towards the flames. "Lilith would go to any lengths to get Adam back. They say that nothing is more dangerous than a woman who has been scorned. Some believe that Lilith was the serpent that tempted Eve. Eventually, Adam and Eve passed away and entered the afterlife, but Lilith was never granted that peace."

"It sounds like fiction to me. All of this for just some love story? What are you getting at Senoy?" I asked.

"Love? Hmmm... Maybe at one time, but it has turned into something much darker. Lilith embraced the demon she was cursed to be. After Adam's death, she discovered that one could enter the afterlife by passing through the Tree of Life. However, we denied her entrance and guarded it until God decreed the mass flood. We then hid the sword with Evangeline. Quite by accident, Evangeline discovered that if two people who share some sort of ignited connection touch the sword, it emits a bright blue flame, binding their souls together for eternity. However, it can not create love where none exists. To this day, we do not understand why it does not work for just any two people, and it has only ever happened once."

He nodded his head toward me and lowered his voice. "Well, I guess it makes it twice now. The energy seems to be similar to the intense passion once shared by Lilith and Adam. When Eva, I mean Evangeline, activated the sword, the flame became a beacon for Lilith. She believed it was created for her and held her only true redemption to enter the afterlife. Fortunately, we were able to save the sword."

When he did not continue, I roused myself from my tired stupor and went to stand by him. "Are you alright, Senoy?" I asked, placing my hand on his shoulder.

He looked up at the ceiling and breathed deeply before closing his eyes. "Evangeline had to give her life. I swore that I would not let that happen again."

"What happened?"

"A story for another time," he replied curtly. He pulled away from me and headed back to the desk. "Since then, Lilith has been quiet. We assumed that she had given up. All the women in the March line were placed in arranged marriages. The chances for true love were left to the fiction in romance novels; the sword locked safely in a case. However, in the last few days of your grandmother's life, she began to feel some changes coming."

"What changes?"

"She said that there would be an event where the resources of two worlds would be combined."

"Grandmother ranted about many strange things right before she passed away. I do not think she was in *her right mind." I flopped back onto the chair and tried not to yawn.*

"So I believed as well, but you have changed everything."

"What do you mean?"

"Evelyn, you activated the stone." He slowly walked towards me. "Who did you touch the sword with?"

I could not seem to find my voice.

"Was it Lord Wyndham?" he asked softly.

"Maybe," I whispered. "Oh, I do not know..."

A war of emotions played across his face. "You and Lord Wyndham have activated the stone. I am certain of it. Which means Lilith has already seen it. She will be here shortly."

"You are jesting. This can not be real."

"I assure you it is very real."

"Wait, are you saying that Lord Wyndham is my true love? I can not even stand the man!" I exclaimed, jumping out of my chair. "Senoy, you are daft. You expect me to believe that some love-avenging demon woman is coming after the sword? Let alone that you are an angel that has been alive since the beginning of time and..." I stopped, my anger taking over. "And how can you be old one minute and young the next?"

"Angels age like humans when on earth. However, when an event requires us to fight, we return to our younger forms."

"Can you ever die?"

"I have heard stories that there is a way, but I have realized it is just a myth." He briefly looked into the fire, hiding his face from me. "God created Angels in the afterlife. These human bodies are just a facade. We live forever."

I felt as if I had been cheated on. My heart fluttered in my chest. "How dare you tell me this now!! It makes no sense! They are all lies! I fear perhaps you have contracted whatever Grandmother had. How can I believe any of this? I...I trusted you." Fighting the suspicious truth, an uncontrollable madness filled my mind, leaving no room for coherent thoughts. "You are not Senoy," I said.

Senoy moved to hug me but abruptly stopped and shook his head. A soft, flickering light emanated from his silhouette, gradually blurring my vision. "You are correct," he said. "I am no longer the Senoy you once knew but the Arch Angel that has always been your guardian. You must think about what I have said. There is so much more, but you need time to think. I will leave you alone, however, not for long, Evelyn. Lilith is on her way."

I watched the angel of deceit walk towards the door, and I could only assume the loud, agonizing cry had come from my own lips. "No! You stay here. I can not breathe. I...I need to get out of here." Running out of the library, I did not look back.

****

9. THE PARTY

Panic caved in around Evie as she watched the back of Evelyn fade into a blur of pastel colors; the idyllic land of her dreams washed away. Her body tensed. The dreams were now becoming habitual. As she opened her eyes to the darkness, a yellow glow flickered in the distance. With each step, the light became brighter as it approached her still form. This time, there was no pain. Evie focused on the beam of light and felt the woman of her dreams drawing nearer.

"Evie," said the familiar voice, "I grow weary of your teenage antics. You are not an ordinary adolescent."

Evie groped around in the darkness when she felt a soft caress brush against the side of her cheek, calming her tense muscles. She relaxed into the strange motherly gesture but then felt a blast of cold air hit her cheeks, leaving a lingering sting.

"You are acting like a confused dimwit!" the voice lashed out. "I cannot allow that."

A small whimper vibrated through Evie's teeth.

"Creating you was no small feat, and this is how you thank me? That soul of yours is just getting in the way. Necessary, but a damn nuisance. Must I do everything?"

The lulling murmur increased into a high-pitched tone, threatening to pierce Evie's eardrums. Despite the discomfort, an image of Damek wavered in her memory. She concentrated on his ghostly image and could just make out a slight movement of his lips. Every line of his face spoke of extreme pain. Who could cause such agony? She squinted her eyes and strained to hear the words the ghost seemed so desperate to convey.

She whispered the name Lilith, and then Damek's image disappeared into thin air like smoke vanishing into the atmosphere.

"Perfect, my dear. I think it is quite time we started to move things along."

Evie sat up abruptly, gasping for air as a cold shock gripped her chest. She glanced around her room and realized she had been dreaming. Wiping the sweat from her forehead, she crawled out of her closet on all fours, feeling disoriented and confused. Her mind was filled with incoherent images, and a single word hovered on the tip of her tongue. "Lilith," she murmured.

She got up from the carpet and stopped to look at the plain girl in her dresser mirror. She couldn't remember what she was supposed to be doing. Then she looked at her alarm clock and remembered that it was still Friday, and she had been invited to a party! She pulled on her ponytail holder, letting her hair fall into a tangled mess. Using her hands to comb through the knots, she cursed. At least she was able to find some sympathy reflected in the plain brown eyes staring back at her, the eyes that seemed to be shifting from their usual simplicity. Focusing on the black pupils, swirls of colors began to bleed into the whites of her eyes. Trying to shake the crazy image, she suddenly felt lightheaded.

Her hands unconsciously traced her reflection in the mirror. The rainbow of hues melted into the entire pane of glass, creating large patterns of waves rippling through the entire reflection. A featherlight breeze emanated from the pulsing waves, playing on her fingertips and softening the ragged dryness in her hands. With the question of her insanity lingering, she stood taller. A hiss erupted from the waves, turning their gentle laps into a raging storm. Giving into her hallucination, light blue smoke radiated through the howling wind, sinking into her fingertips.

"I think it is time we had a little fun," a voice laughed seductively.

Dizzy with anticipation, Evie recognized the voice from her dream. It was her—the intoxicating woman who played the lead role in her nightmares.

"Lilith," Evie whispered, but her words turned into a scream as an intense heat of flames clawed into her head. She pulled her hands from the mirror and squeezed her temples, trying to release the agony. Her eyes blinked, and the illusion spontaneously disappeared back into the recesses of the cheap plywood mirror. Evie slammed her hands against the mirror but couldn't find her voice. Suddenly, there was a knock at her door.

"Evie? Are you ok?" Her mother's muffled voice called out.

Evie concentrated on her breathing as her mom rattled the doorknob.

"What's going on?" Her mom asked again.

Evie dragged herself away from the mirror to unlock the bedroom door. "Sorry, Mom, "she said, wincing at the crack in her voice as she opened the door.

Her mother's concerned expression unexpectedly turned into a smile. "Wow, Evie. You look beautiful," her mom paused, stumbling over her words.

"What are you talking about? I look the same as always." Evie collapsed onto the edge of her bed, unconsciously feeling the inside of her wrist. She was surprised by the steady pulse that belied her extreme anxiety.

"Nice joke, sweetheart. But seriously, what was all the noise? I thought a herd of elephants were coming down the stairs."

"Noise?" Evie tried to grasp at the memory quickly slipping away. She fell back onto her bed and covered her eyes, feeling a slow uneasiness in the pit of her stomach.

"Evie, you're starting to worry me."

Evie cleared her throat and tried to act normal. "I've... I've been invited to a party."

"Really?"

"Yes, really." She uncovered her eyes and glared at her mom. "And I have nothing to wear!"

"Oh, I see." Her mom closed the bedroom door and sat down next to her. "The outfit you have on looks amazing!"

"Only a mother could love, right?" She sat up, attempting to smile. "Thanks, Mom."

"Oh, stop pretending. Where did you get that top anyway?"

"What you are talking about?" Evie glanced down at her chest. "What the...," she gasped. Her eyes widened as she stared at the tops of her breasts, filling out the light red shirt fitted to her torso. She then leaped from the bed to stare at her reflection in the mirror. Her hair was no longer a humid tangled mess, but instead, it was a stunning set of ripples of glossy light brown curls falling to her chest, illuminating the well-formed face between them. Her eyelids glistened with sparkles, drawing the observer in. Her eyes were defined with black eyeliner, highlighting the dots of green hidden in the depths of her dark browns. The red smudge on her lips gave her a pout that even she couldn't stop staring at.

"Is this the infamous outfit Lana picked out for you at the beginning of the year?" her mom asked.

"Um, yeah, I think so," she said, surprised that she couldn't even remember where she had stashed the obscene top. Lightly covering her breasts, she spied the black lace peeping over the edge. She pulled the neck of the shirt up and racked her brain for when she would have bought a racy bra.

"Lana did a great job," her mom added. "You should go shopping with her more often." She stroked the side of Evie's cheek and sighed. "The makeup makes your eyes look amazing! I might need to take some lessons from you."

"I...I can't wear this," Evie stammered.

"Why not?"

"Look at these!" Evie gasped, pointing to the large mounds in front of her. "This shirt makes them look way too big."

"Stop being ridiculous! They do no such thing. You were lucky to get that feature from your Grandmother. Besides, women pay tons of money for those things."

"It just isn't me."

"Well, you look great. But if you're uncomfortable, then change." Her mom's brow creased. "By the way, Lana called my cell while you were getting dressed. She said you didn't answer your phone. Are you sure everything's ok?"

"Yeah." Rubbing her hands over her tight-fitted jeans, Evie turned to stare at her backside in the mirror.

"What aren't you telling me?" her mom asked, getting up from the bed.

Evie turned back to her mom and tried to smile. "I swear I am fine. I'm sure it's just my nerves. I've never been to a party like this before."

"Okay, but if something's wrong, you know you can talk to me, right?" She kissed Evie on the forehead and stood back to admire her once again.

"I know, Mom," Evie said, stretching her arms out for a hug.

Her mother wrapped her in a tight embrace before letting her go. "Well, I'm headed out. I have to pick up your dad from the airport, and then we're going out to dinner."

"Ooo," Evie teased. "Date night!"

"Something like that," her mom smiled. "Remember, curfew is midnight. I'm..." she hesitated while she played with Evie's curls, "I'm glad you're getting out."

"Thanks, Mom. You make it sound like I'm a hermit. Where's the speech about not drinking and not staying out late...boys? Does any of this ring a bell?"

"I trust you. Do I need to be concerned?" Her mother narrowed her gaze. "Should I have that speech with you?"

"Mom, please!"

"Alright, have fun, and remember I love you." She headed out of the bedroom and down the stairs.

"I love you too," Evie whispered.

"How touching," a voice grated in Evie's head.

Evie turned back to her reflection in the mirror. "Stop!" Pushing against her temples, she pleaded to no one. "Please don't tell me I'm crazy...I promise not to read any more of the journal!"

"Oh, you are many things, my dear, but crazy is not one of them. You are a true goddess in my making. This is going to be so much fun." A feline laugh echoed through the bedroom as a calmness settled over Evie's subconsciousness. With a lone screech piercing the sky outside her window, a tangible submission settled on her right temple. A light jubilance spread through her body, taking over the last thread of her inner self. Evie was no longer in charge. Checking her reflection one last time with a seductive smile, she grabbed the car keys and headed out into the long-awaited night.

"WOW! Where's my best friend, and what have you done with her?" Lana exclaimed in surprise.

Evie chuckled. "I just thought it was time I started having some fun, don't you think so, Lana Cain?" As they drove away from Lana's house, Evie glimpsed at the owls, following them closely in the rear-view mirror.

Lana raised her eyebrow and made a face, "Okay, but, eh... why are you using my middle name? It's weird. Don't do it again." Looking at Evie with a glint of mischief, she pulled down the passenger visor mirror and applied more red lipstick. "I can't get over how great you look. I should've bought that top for myself. Damek won't know what hit him."

"Why settle for just one?" Evie said, keeping her gaze on the road.

"What? Seriously, stop acting so weird! Anyway, you aren't gonna believe who I saw today!" Lana continued to talk excitedly, accepting her best friend's new fiery personality. She paused only when Evie stopped the car in front of a large warehouse hidden in the backfield of Fisher's Creek. "Man, this place looks straight out of some cheesy horror movie." Pointing at the generic silver siding, Lana yanked over the rear-view mirror to check her makeup one last time.

"Maybe it is best if you stay here." Evie's voice came out bit raspy.

"Nice, Evie," Lana joked, opening the car door.

The field was completely dark, with the only light coming from a small circle of cars shining their headlights into the massive open garage. The garage was empty except for a handful of gyrating teenagers and the deep pounding of music reverberating through the hollow walls. The girls scanned the property to find the rest of the popular student body hanging in segregated groups outside. As they walked, they sidestepped a short kid suspended by his feet in the air over a keg, trying to avoid the splatter of beer gushing out of his mouth.

"Man, Evie, this is great! You gotta try a keg stand," interrupted Seth, walking out of the garage. His jaw dropped. "Wow, Evie, you look amazing!"

"Why, thank you, Seth. You look rather handsome yourself." Evie crooned. She let her eyes roam slowly over his beige sweater, two sizes too big to match his baggy jeans and then ran her hand down his arm. Lana stared at Evie as if she had grown a second head.

"Um, thanks, Evie," Seth said with a stupid grin, rubbing the back of his neck. "You wanna beer?" Handing his beer to Evie, his elbow bumped into the side of Lana. He shrugged as if just noticing that she was there, too. "Oh, sorry."

"Whatever," Lana bit out. "I can't believe I reminded Evie to invite you."

"What?" Seth asked, trying to hear over the pounding bass.

Evie's head turned abruptly to the left, her stomach lurching like a dog following a scent. She noticed a group of jocks lounging around an old, rotted oak tree and licked her lips. In the middle of the boisterous entourage was Damek.

"You okay, Evie?" asked Lana, grabbing her arm.

Evie continued to keep her eyes fixed on Damek.

"Ah, my pet, so there is our mate," a low voice murmured through Evie's lips as her eyes racked over his entire body.

Lana's hand dropped back to her side.

"Did you say something?" Seth asked, leaning closer to Evie. Lana quickly pushed him away, giving Evie a deep scowl.

Evie ignored Lana and Seth altogether and followed the trail to her prey. Damek's eyes immediately clashed with hers, taking his time to return her longing gaze. A grin broke out on his handsome face as a pink flush tinged Evie's cheeks.

"Hey Evie, I'm glad you decided to come," said Damek as he slowly walked towards her, ignoring his friends. Evie looked up into his face as her body cringed, waiting for the familiar coldness to seep in any time Damek was around, waiting for the intense heat he would leave in its wake. Nothing happened. It seemed not only did Lilith have the ability to control her speech, but the erratic hormones that inflicted her anytime she was in the jock's vicinity.

"Thank you for inviting me." Lilith's confident words flowed from her full red lips without any hesitation. Internally screaming, Evie tried to break through the possession. She could feel her heart begin to race with an intense predatory need. The lioness had gained complete control, and no one, not even her best friend, seemed to notice.

Damek broke their intimate connection and nodded towards Lana. "It's good to see you again."

Lana responded with an awkward smile.

Turning to Seth, Damek extended his hand. "And you are?"

"Oh, I'm Seth. Evie invited me," he said, shaking Damek's hand.

"The more the merrier." Turning back to Evie, Damek caught the playful expression in her eyes. "You look great by the way."

"So do you," Evie said, her eyes fixated on his chest.

"Evie, you have to see this!" interrupted Seth, pulling on Evie's arm. Damek instantly moved closer, and Evie felt Seth's hand fall from her arm. Shifting her gaze upward, she noticed the emotions playing in the depths of Damek's eyes: his dominance, a silent command to Seth. A sense of protection engulfed her senses. Confused, she tried to step back into the safety of her friends, but Lilith kept her rigidly held in place.

"You, ah, have something right here," Damek said, rubbing his thumb over the center of her chin.

A flame encompassed Evie's heart, and she couldn't breathe. The puppeteer's voice murmured inside her head, "Calm down, my sweet. Now is not the time."

Damek's thumb froze on the edge of her lower lip. The sexual pull, evident in the heat pulsating through his fingertips, left their mark tattooed on her forever. Suddenly, Damek's arm was wrenched to the side by a blond enemy in pink. Evie struggled to hold back the growl of anger unleashed in her throat as her hands curled into tight balls—the only acknowledgment of the rage embedded in the imprints left by her nails.

"So, you decided to come." Raising her eyebrows, Lexi blatantly stared at Evie's breasts. "Nice shirt. I guess you do own more than a sports bra." She looked at Damek and smiled. "We were beginning to wonder."

Evie's arms habitually rose to cover her chest as an unseen weight dragged them back down to her side, causing her chest to heave forward. A war of words aimed at Lilith exploded in her mind, but after a moment of hesitation, Lilith won. Under the demon's control, Evie grabbed Seth by the arm and pulled him in front of her. She cradled his face with her hands and gave him a full kiss on the lips. With no time to reflect on the action or witness Seth's surprise, she turned back to Lexi and licked her lips.

"By the way, you have something on your shirt," Evie said, pointing to the cheerleader's outfit. She smiled at Damek and added, "It's always a pleasure to see you." As Lilith's laughter echoed in her mind, Evie felt a brief flash of heat run down her spine. She awkwardly swung away from the couple and laced her hand through Seth's arm. She nudged him back towards the gyrating party in the garage, her anguish threatening the bile sitting in her belly. Evie forced herself to look back and saw Lana with her mouth wide open while Damek remained expressionless. Lexi, on the other hand, was beet red. Lilith had created her first web.

"Come on, Damek, I have something of my own to show you," Lexi said, yanking Damek further into the darkness of the trees.

Lana finally found the use of her legs and ran to catch up with Evie. "What the hell was that?!"

"What are you talking about?" Evie replied, bored.

"Yeah, Lana, why do you care?" smirked Seth.

"Can I talk to you alone for a sec?" Lana squeezed Evie's arm.

Evie tried to convey her inner turmoil through her eyes, but all that came out was Lilith's hateful indifference. "What for?"

"NOW," Lana said, not waiting for a response. She pulled Evie deeper into the privacy of the trees. "What the hell was that?" she whispered. "What's wrong with you?"

"I was just trying to keep things exciting. We did talk about this, did we not?" Lilith's response came out too easy. Evie was losing this battle.

"You know Seth's gonna think you like him now, right?"

A slight smile lifted the corner of Evie's mouth. "Good."

"Are you being serious? What's wrong with you?"

"Why do you care?" Evie asked a hint of sarcasm in her voice. "Does Miss Cohen have a crush on the computer geek?"

"No, of course not. That isn't the point."

"Why do you continue to fight your destiny? There is no hope for you."

Lana took a step back. "Why are you being so mean? I don't understand anything you're saying."

Evie tried to push through the compulsion and reach out to Lana, but pain ripped through her right temple. Before she could stop herself, only hurtful words came out. "He is not coming, you know. They never will."

Lana gasped as if she had been slapped. She gazed over Evie's head, keeping the tears at bay. "I don't know what you're talking about, but I'm done with whatever this is."

"Good," Evie said. "I can not waste any more of my precious time with the likes of you."

Evie had been defeated. A tear of her true identity trailed down her right cheek as the predator within her fully took control. She quickly wiped away the ridiculous show of emotion and sauntered back to Seth. Grabbing his elbow, Evie looked around and saw that Damek was staring directly at her. Her smile was pure Lilith, indicating that her transformation was complete.

After several hours, Evie began to regain consciousness. She felt her sanity slowly returning to her control. As she opened her eyes, she expected to hear the voice of her inner demon, but instead, there was complete silence. She struggled to lift her swollen eyelids and found herself lying face down in the dirt, shivering uncontrollably as the wet ground seeped into her clothes. Pushing against the soft ground, she tried to get her bearings and realized she had no memory of the previous night. Her shirt was torn at the collar, revealing more of the black lace bra that had caused her so much agony. She quickly tugged at the tear to cover herself and used her other hand to remove the leaves stuck to her neck and mouth. As she spat out the unpleasant taste of dirt, she heard hushed male voices. Crawling around a large bush, she could just make out the top of Seth's head getting into a car with another guy she vaguely recognized. Instinctively reaching out to him for help, she paused.

"Man, did you see how Evie was all over me tonight?" Seth asked, smiling at the other guy.

"Yeah, dude," the other guy said, "but seriously... she was all over everyone."

"Take that back!" yelled Seth.

"Whatever you wanna think, man. Come on, I gotta get home. My mom's gonna be pissed!" Jumping into Seth's car, they sped off towards the main road.

Evie watched the red glow of their taillights disappear.

"You awake, sleeping beauty?" The angry voice echoed behind her.

Evie turned around and found Lana sitting against a tree, staring at her. "What happened?" she whispered.

"Hmm..good question. Which part?" Lana's words grated on her nerves.

"I guess everything," Evie replied, looking down at her clothes and wiping her hands on her jeans. "What the hell happened to me?"

"So this is how you're gonna play it? Pretend like you don't even remember?"

Lana's image became blurry. "Lana, please," Evie replied, not sure what else to say. As she reached for her best friend, she noticed small moon-shaped gashes on her palms.

Lana looked into the forest, unable to meet Evie's gaze. "Where do we start, hmm? How about the part where you hang on every guy here, or even better when you played the prostitute for Seth, and oh yeah, the worst part, by far, completely ignoring your best friend." With no response from Evie, she continued, "and I can only assume you were pounding the drinks as well since Paul came to find me saying you passed out in the bushes while making out." Lana got up and pushed away from the tree. "Seriously, Evie????"

"I...I don't remember any of that, Lana," Evie said, rubbing the sore inside her mouth. She had a brief glimpse of an argument within herself.

"Don't you mean Lana Cain?"

"Huh?" Evie replied.

"Don't even remember constantly using my middle name?"

"No, I don't. I don't even think I knew your middle name. Did I?"

"Whatever. I'm done."

Evie tried to push herself off the ground, but her legs gave out. "Why the hell can't I remember what happened to me? I feel like I was beaten up from the inside."

"Probably serves you right."

The cold words shook Evie to her core. Her gaze narrowed. "The only thing I remember is getting dressed and my mom coming up to talk to me. Something about sounding like a herd of elephants."

Lana took a deep breath. "Did someone put something in your drink? Were you drugged?"

"I don't even remember drinking anything. You would think I would remember that, right?"

"Does your head hurt like you're gonna puke?"

"Nope, none of that. Just really confused."

"Look, Evie, you're not making any sense," Lana said, waving her hands. She started to pace back and forth. "The truth is, you've been acting weird since school started. First, you stopped hanging out with Seth, and now me. If you wanna end this friendship, then just do it!" Lana stopped and turned back to Evie. "Just admit it! You wanna be part of the popular crowd."

Evie felt her heart race. Losing Lana wasn't an option. She pulled herself to her feet and wiped the tears streaming down her face. "Lana, you are my best friend! I promise I'm telling the truth. It all started with that journal. If I can just..." Evie's words faltered as she saw a brief look of sadness in Lana's eyes.

"Do you hear yourself?" Lana yelled. "You're blaming your actions on some freaking book! I can't take it anymore!"

Evie pulled at a memory hanging by a thin line and grabbed Lana's arm. "Lana, it's the truth. I think it has to do with a woman named Lilith."

"A woman in this blank journal of yours?" Lana sneered.

Evie hesitated, "I'm telling you the truth!"

Lana yanked out of Evie's grasp and started up the small hill towards the parking lot. Evie followed but stumbled and fell over her own feet.

"You know," Lana said, turning back towards Evie, "you didn't even give me the chance to tell you that I talked to Blake."

"Really?" Evie asked. "You talked to Blake? What did he say?"

"Does it matter? You wouldn't care anyway." Heading back to the car, Lana stopped again and turned around. "Oh, and Rick was supposed to meet me tonight. Do you think he showed up? No! Why would he? Why would any of you care about me, right?"

Tears blurred Evie's vision as she sat on the cold ground. "Look, I don't know what's happening to me, but I can promise you this: You are my best friend. You're an amazing person. Something probably happened, and Rick couldn't come. And if that's not the reason, then it's his loss."

"Easy for you to say." Lana shook her head and leaned against the car. "Look at you. You think you're this outsider, but the truth is you belong with them."

"What are you talking about?" asked Evie as she stood up, trying to put weight on her left leg.

"Even with ponytails, t-shirts, and yes, even swollen eyelids, they want you."

"Who?"

"Seth, Damek, even my freaking brother has this weird need to protect you."

"Look who's being ridiculous now! They could care less about me!"

"Just get in the car," Lana said, shaking her head. "I'm driving." She got into the driver's seat of Evie's car.

Evie limped to the passenger side and opened the door. "Lana... You're my best friend. I love you." Falling into the seat, Evie grabbed Lana's hand. "I don't know what's happening to me."

"Yeah, I know. Some stupid blank book." Lana pushed the drive button on the dash.

"You think I'm crazy," Evie whispered.

"I think you need to see someone," Lana replied, her voice cracking. Turning onto the main road, both girls sat in silence.

Evie gazed at Lana's stony profile. "Maybe you're right."

The rest of the car ride passed in silence. Evie stared at the bright red clock blinking like a beacon in the middle of the dash. Checking her back pocket for her cell phone, she began to panic.

"Your parents called my phone when they couldn't reach you," Lana said, pulling into her driveway and putting the car in park. "And no, I don't know where it's at. I told them you lost it."

"Um, thanks," Evie said.

"They're still pretty upset, though."

"Yeah, I figured," Evie replied. She placed her hand over Lana's. "I'm really sorry."

Lana snatched her hand away and kept her gaze out the front window. "I need some time. Please just leave me alone for a while."

"Lana, don't," Evie pleaded.

"I'm sorry. But right now, I just..." Lana paused and opened the driver's door. "I hate you." She jumped out of the car and ran towards the front door of her house.

Evie watched in slow motion as the front door slammed shut. The sound of the door echoed through the trees lining the driveway. Looking up, she saw a lone screech owl perched on a branch, watching her. She could sense its order, commanding her to pull away from the house. Trying to defy the yellow eyes, she felt pressure pushing on the back of her head. She awkwardly moved into the driver seat and sped off, the speedometer shaking past the point of comfort as the owl continued to follow in the rearview mirror.

"I hate you, do you hear me?" Evie yelled into her empty car. "Leave me alone!" The owl kept its constant vigilance as she pulled into her driveway. Evie turned off the car and jumped out, the adrenaline temporarily relieving any pain. The owl landed on the roof of her house, right above the ledge of her bedroom. Tugging her shoe off, Evie threw it at the owl, hitting her bedroom window instead. The owl's screech rang in her ears as it flew down the street and out of sight. Just then, the front door jerked open, and her dad came running down the walk. As he took in her haggard appearance, his anger simmered under the surface of his apparent concern.

"What happened??!! Are you ok?" Her father asked as he touched her face and winced.

"I'm fine. I just had a fight with Lana." Evie said, trying to keep her legs straight.

"With fists?" her dad gasped.

"No! I just..." Fatigue rattled her body. "I'm so glad you're home, Dad. I need to lie down. I promise to tell you everything." Placing her arm around his shoulders, he gently lifted her. As soon as they reached the front door, Evie was sound asleep.

10. The Museum

The physical pain had finally subsided, leaving only the hurtful memory of Lana's words in its wake. As she drifted off to sleep, her dreams were consumed by darkness while the odd aroma of tea filled her senses. Although her body had relaxed into a deep sleep, the nightmare lurked just beneath the surface.

The predator was back. "You have done well, my dear."

Evie tried to struggle against the hum in her ear, but even in repose, the temptress lurked.

"Oh, do not worry, child," Lilith said. "We are once again buried safely in the recesses of your dreams."

Evie swallowed hard, trying to push past the lump in her throat. "What have you done?" she choked out.

"What had to be done. Surely, you have a better question than that."

A salty breeze caressed Evie's hair. Succumbing to the enchantment, she took a deep breath. A vision of Lana materialized in her mind, pushing the demon's voice further away. With her best friend lying next to her, Evie smiled. She rolled onto her right side as she tried to grab

Lana's hand. Unable to quite reach it, she shuddered. Lana's once energetic blue eyes turned a deep shade of red.

"Who are you?" Evie asked.

"Your ignorance is making you weak," Lilith snapped, her tone sharp. Then softening, she sighed, "You must relax. Do not worry. In time, you will gain all the knowledge and power you will need."

Evie could feel the demon's voice flow through her veins, the familiar pressure keeping vigilance on the back of her head. She could not see the woman, but without moving a muscle, Evie concentrated all her attention on the severe pain. "You will never take over my body again. Do you hear me?"

"Ah...there is a hint of my goddess. I was beginning to think all my work was for naught. Anything you wish, my dear," Lilith said, pausing on a sigh. "I have missed you so."

Evie was speechless, her mind racing with thoughts. Was the voice simply a part of herself that she could easily control?

"It is time for you to wake up, my dear. We do have our purpose. Until next time, love."

Evie's ears were still ringing with the word "love" as she opened her eyes, squinting in the bright sunlight streaming through her white bedroom blinds. She threw her bedspread over her head, trying to forget the embarrassing conversation with her parents the night before. They were shocked that something so adolescent had happened to her. Had she really passed out in her father's arms? The guilt was churning her stomach. She knew she had to make things right.

A loud ringing echoed through her room, causing her to cover her ears instinctively. After a moment, she realized it was just her cell phone on the nightstand, causing the old wooden surface to vibrate. Her heart skipped a beat as she knew it had to be Lana.

"Hey!" Evie gushed. "I'm so glad you called. I'm so sorry!"

"Um, okay," a male voice responded.

Surprised, Evie bit her lower lip. "Uh, who's this?"

"Damek. Though apologies are probably in order, don't you think?" Evie could hear the sneer in his voice.

"Excuse me?" she asked.

"Never mind. I was calling for another reason."

"Another reason? Wait...YOU are calling ME?"

"Well, yeah...I mean, after last night," he stuttered, then paused for a second. Evie could hear muffled voices on the other end. "Anyway, I was calling to see if you wanted to practice today."

"What?" Evie asked, confused.

"Practice...for the competition at the end of the semester?"

Evie scratched her head, trying to figure out if she was still dreaming. "I thought we were meeting on Monday after school?"

"I told you I'm pretty competitive. Anyway, I have time this morning. You should come over."

"Come over where...exactly?"

"To my house."

Unsure how to respond, Evie thought she heard more muffled voices. "Is someone with you?" she asked.

"No. Look, can you come or what?" His words came out brisk.

"Um, yeah, I guess."

"Be here around eleven. I have something at two."

"Okay," she responded, nervously biting her fingernail. Glancing at her clock, she quickly checked her outfit. She only had an hour to get ready and get to his house on time. She didn't need to bother asking for directions as everyone knew where Damek lived.

"See you then," he added.

The line went dead before Evie could respond. She vaguely remembered losing her cell phone at the party last night and being grounded when she got home. As she gazed at her phone, she wondered if someone had found it and dropped it off. Confused and unable to think straight, she placed it on the nightstand and rubbed her temples. Evie was pretty sure being grounded meant no trips to boys' houses. Pushing herself to the side of the bed, she assessed the rest of her body. Everything appeared normal, except for the unease in her stomach that had persisted since the night before. Bringing her palms to her face, she examined the imprints that her nails had made.

"Lilith," the name came out like a curse.

She felt a renewed sense of purpose as her heart beat faster. Hadn't Damek mentioned something about the name Lilith? She knew she had to find a way to sneak out of her house to investigate. For her, it was a matter of crazy versus sane. She carefully stepped over the creaky floorboards in her room, trying her best not to make any noise. Opening her bedroom door, she winced at the high-pitched squeal coming from the hinges. She could only hear the consistent ticking of the Cuckoo clock her dad had brought back from Denmark. As she made her way down the stairs, she was surprised at how quiet it was for a Saturday - especially after last night's commotion. She braced herself for the disappointment she expected to see on her parent's faces, but when she peered around the corner, she only saw a single note lying on the counter island.

We went to visit your grandmother. Should be back after lunch. Remember you are grounded. Call if you need anything.

Love you, Dad

She whispered a silent prayer to the ceiling as she raced back upstairs, feeling her stomach lurch. She had to make sure she was home again before her parents ever noticed she'd left. It was the first time she had outright disobeyed them. Massaging the cramp on her left side, she went to her bedroom to change. She quickly put on a white tank top with a pair of grey stretch pants and pulled her hair into a ponytail. Grabbing her shoes, she headed back down to the kitchen. She stared at her parents' note and took a deep breath before crumpling it and tossing it into the trash. As she did, she swore she heard faint laughter. Hastily trying to slip on her shoes, her fingers fumbled with the laces, causing her to lose her balance. She regained her footing and bolted out of the front door.

As Evie drove up the gravel lane to Damek's house, she felt like she was stepping into a parallel reality where cars and technology didn't exist. She hesitated at the entrance, mesmerized by the black wrought iron gates securing the entrance to the vast property. Her attention was quickly caught by a red cardinal sitting in the open mouth of one of the stone lions flanking the gates. The sight made her smile; simplicity in the jaws of terror. Her grip loosened on the steering wheel. The lions reminded her of a much more grotesque version of the pair in front of the New York City Public Library, which she had visited in seventh Grade. A snapshot came into view of her best friend Brittany and herself, smiling in front of the library, making a pack to be friends forever and trusting each other with their utmost desires and secrets, and then learning the hard way that when one moves away, it is easy to forget the promises that were once made. However, time had a way of finding new friends to share secrets with, and Evie wondered what had happened to Brittany. A picture of

Lana came into view. Even Lana, who was pretty computer illiterate, could handle an online social network, something she was constantly pressuring Evie to do. She smiled at the memory of Lana's words, "How would anyone find out if you were single or attached?" She sucked her lower lip into her teeth. What Evie heard was, "Why aren't you catching up with all those friends you left behind? The friends you promised never to forget?" She tried to push the thought away as the indigestion quickly made its way up her throat. Shaking her head to clear her thoughts, she concentrated on the task at hand.

Damek's house was known for its obscure location and large size. The four-acre estate sat twenty miles outside of town. Forgoing the ease of a central location, Damek's parents reveled in snubbing the advancements of the 21st century. Most locals referred to the Adam's place as a museum, though in other circles, an insane asylum. However, regardless of what people thought about it, everyone knew where it was and held a certain reverence for it. After all, old money spoke volumes.

As she made her way down the fenced-in lane, the abundance of foliage was nothing short of breathtaking. The time and care were apparent in the disordered beauty of the plants breaching through the gaps of the crude oak posts. A blanket of gardens wrapped the home in its fragrant embrace, with flowers of every shape and color lining the entrance. Trees as old as the land itself blocked the magnificence from prying eyes. Even the birds and other creatures living in its comfort knew they'd found an oasis in the middle of suburbia.

Applying pressure to the car break, the sight of a feminine statue caught her eye, triggering a sense of deja vu. It was situated in the middle of an English rose garden, nestled in pink and apricot blooms. The statue resembled the goddess of Venus, tending her weary feet at a long-ago dried-up fountain. Evie tried to recollect a faint memory of another Venus statue but felt the memory quickly fade away as she rolled down the car window. A strong scent of tea assailed her senses, and the incoming breeze rattled old school papers in the back seat. She knew the house was about to make its grand entrance.

Following the slight left turn in the lane, there it stood, straight out of the 19th century. The house showcased its high window peaks and pointed turrets, reminding Evie of her latest romance novel forgotten underneath her bed. She memorized the numerous chimneys towering over the fortress of grey stone, waiting for the beautiful princess to lean out the high window. It was a castle hidden within the folds of an English manor, just waiting for the handsome knight to leap from his brilliant white steed and climb the Ivy to his lover's window; the English Ivy, now an integral part of the entire home. Evie pulled into the roundabout drive and parked the car next to one of the square bushes, inundated with little yellow flowers poking their heads out of the green fauna. She got out of the car and stared at the large, plain black door. She knew she could do this. Before her foot even hit the first step, the door opened. Standing at the entrance was the beautiful princess, her sandy blond hair pulled back into a braid and her dark blue eyes gently assessing Evie. Dressed in a light yellow muslin top and beige khakis, the princess extended her hand in greeting. It had to be Damek's mom.

"Hello, you must be Evie. I have heard so much about you. Come in, please." The slight British accent surprised Evie, especially since Damek didn't even have a hint of the lyrical tone. "I am Damek's mom, Mrs. Adams."

Evie smiled and quickly looked around the entrance hall. Glass cases lined the front room, packed with nicknacks of all sorts, mainly of the fencing and documentation variety. A deep red rug flanked by gold trim ran the length of the hall, inviting the guests to enter its core. "You have a beautiful home," Evie said softly.

"Oh, thank you! I know it can be a bit eccentric, but we do love playing up to our creepy personas."

"Excuse me?" Evie asked.

"Oh, you know, the 'Addams Family'?" she said, smiling at Evie's confusion. "I guess I'm finally starting to show my age." She closed the front door and led Evie down the hall. Evie tried to keep up as Damek's mother jumped from one topic to the next, talking excitedly about the various historical artifacts they passed. After pointing out one of her favorites, she paused and turned back to Evie.

"Well, enough of my boring nonsense for one day. Damek is in the gym. He has been practicing all morning."

Evie moved her gaze from a battered suit of armor back to Mrs. Adams.

"It seems the devil's in him when he gets like this," she added. "Just like his father."

"What do you mean?" Evie asked, unable to concentrate on Damek's mother due to the overwhelming display of artifacts in the house, leaving no vacant wall in sight.

"He's just dedicated, that's all," she said, turning down yet another long hall. "You must have Damek show you around the house sometime. It's fashioned after my ancestral home in England."

"I didn't mean to gawk. It's just you have so many things."

"Damek's father and I are avid collectors," Mrs. Adams responded, stopping at yet another entrance to a small room that led to another hallway. She cleared her throat. "Damek tells me you have never fenced before."

"That's correct," Evie said, ogling a strange African tribal mask. She scuffed her toe against the edge of a lion-printed throw rug, trying to examine the picture in further detail.

"He seems to think highly of you."

Evie lifted her head abruptly. "What do you mean?"

"Well," she paused, "I guess he thinks you will do very well."

"Oh, well, he's just being nice," Evie stammered, unable to make eye contact.

Mrs. Adams quickly acknowledged her statement and turned down the deep green hallway that branched off to the right of the small room. Swords lined the confined space.

"Our collection began with just swords and anything related to fencing. However, over the years, our interests have expanded." Damek's mom continued to point out a few artifacts of interest as they made their way to the gym. They stopped before a closed door, and Evie heard a low vibration from behind the hard oak. The door was a memento from the past, and Evie admired the artwork above the entryway before freezing in surprise.

"Who's that?" Evie blurted out, pointing to a gold framed picture hanging above the door.

"That is Michael," Mrs. Adams said. "One of the Archangels."

Evie was left speechless as she stared in amazement. All at once, a mixture of emotions flooded her mind, making it hard to speak. Here in faded splendor was Michael. The angel of her dreams, or rather Evelyn's. Here was the warrior buried in the pages of her fictional heroine's deepest thoughts. Despite his faded splendor, he still embodied everything she had ever imagined him to be.

Uncomfortable with Evie's silence, Mrs. Adams continued, "Michael is the leader of God's Army. In this picture, he is guarding us against evil. See how he is stepping on Satan's back with his spear aiming between the devil's wings? Brilliant really. It has always been my favorite."

"It's... It's beautiful," Evie stuttered. She looked up to see a sword hanging above the worn print with its leather-wrapped handgrip and solid metal guard. Evie felt a familiar pull towards it. It had an antique metal finish that triggered a glimmer of recognition in the back of her mind. The guard was ornate, with a dragon curled around it, protecting a large gap. "I've seen that sword before," she said, surprised.

"I highly doubt you have seen that particular sword," replied Mrs. Adams, looking up at the weapon. "This sword has been in my family for ages. Notice the empty gap in the guard? It once held a beautifully sculpted piece of artwork - a stone engraved with a star."

"A stone?" whispered Evie.

"Why yes. It was believed to possess magical powers. Though-"

"What kind of powers," Evie interrupted.

"Oh, I am not quite sure. Our research has led us to many dead ends. I've only ever seen it in pictures."

Evie bit her thumbnail, thinking about the small crude stone nestled in the journal under her bed. "Do you know what happened to the stone?"

"We believe that robbers might have stolen it at some point or another. Like Michael, it has always been one of my favorites, and I do think the two complement each other, don't you?" Returning her focus to Evie, she continued, "Have your parents ever tried fencing?"

Surprised by the strange question, Evie's concentration faltered. "Um, no...I mean, I'm pretty sure they haven't," she replied, feeling a bit awkward. "My father is military. We move a lot."

With a sigh, Mrs. Adams gazed at Evie, "You remind me of someone I once saw in a picture."

"Excuse me?" Evie asked, jolted out of her thoughts.

"Oh, never mind. I tend to get engrossed in my research, and I've already taken up too much of your time." Mrs. Adams turned back towards the main house and nodded to the closed door. "Damek is in there. You two have fun."

With one last glance at the avenging Archangel, Evie swung back around to thank Damek's mom but found she had already left the narrow hall. Turning back to the door, she grabbed the knob and pushed.

Music swept into the hall with a mix of rock, accented with the strings from a trio of cellos. Its noxious melody enchanted Evie, and she forgot all about Michael and the stone. The gym was large, similar in size to a basketball court, and in the center was the fencing strip. Damek's sword moved quickly, and Evie could picture the vibrations bouncing off the metal with each sweep. She was mesmerized by his footwork, jabs, parries, and lunges. The electric guitar intensified the hits of each point taken. She admired Damek's body rather than the moves, feeling her lips for any sign of drool. He had given in to the fight, holding off an invisible enemy at the gate. His dark, brooding look was enough to scare any demon away. Evie chuckled, realizing that was precisely what she was looking for.

Damek leaned forward into a lunge, his eyes locking onto Evie's. Suddenly, he rose back up and retrieved a small controller from his white fencing knickers, causing the music to stop. He remained motionless on the line while Evie attempted to regain her composure.

"Um, hey. You look great," Evie said, stumbling over her words. "I mean fencing, you know." Tugging on her tank top, she smoothed her ponytail back. "You're, ah, mom, let me in."

"You wanna talk about last night?" Damek asked rather abruptly.

She avoided his intense stare and focused on his white shirt instead. "What do you mean?"

"Hmm, Okay. Let me rephrase it for you. What the hell was last night about?"

The edge in his voice brought Evie's hands to her hips. Making eye contact, a red hue colored her cheeks. "Why do you care?"

"Just answer the question."

She wanted to tell him the truth. However, her pride urged her to take him down a peg or two. "I don't know. I was just having some fun."

"Is that all you're gonna say about it?"

"Yeah"

"Fine. Then there's nothing more to talk about. Let's practice." Damek turned his back to her. He knew something. She was sure of it.

"Wait a sec," Evie said. "Do you remember when you asked me about Lilith?"

"What did you say?" Damek asked, still keeping his back turned to her.

"Lilith," Evie repeated.

Turning around, he stared at her again. "What about her?"

"Who is she?"

"Why do you care?" Repeating her words, he smiled.

"I'm just curious, that's all."

"In this case, curiosity is a dangerous thing," Damek warned, grabbing a foil off the table and pointing to a fencing jacket. "That should fit; it's my mom's." He moved to the fencing strip and waited.

She felt like a scolded child as she struggled to pull the jacket over her shirt. The music began to blare around them, making it difficult to focus. A cold smile spread across Damek's lips, and Evie wanted to scream as she lifted the extra foil off the table. Taking her position on the fencing strip, she gripped the unfamiliar sword, worried that she wouldn't hear Damek's instructions over the loud bass.

"En garde," Damek whispered.

Evie heard his icy tone clearly over the whine of the cello strings. He swiftly whipped his blade around, catching her off guard. She clumsily blocked the attack, causing the blades to provide their own dull clack to the rhythm surrounding them.

"What the hell was that?" she yelled, her adrenaline pumping loudly in her ears.

"Instincts," Damek replied, watching her like a hawk.

She stepped back and raised her hands in a forfeit. She could recite the lines of the body, but that was as far as her skills went. Damek bent his knee and lunged towards her. She instantly gripped the sword, bringing it up in front of her face to block the attack. She grunted as she backed away from the intended hit.

"You're crazy!" Evie cried out. "What's your deal?" She left the fencing strip and placed her foil on the side table. As she tried to take off her jacket, she could feel Damek coming up behind her. The music stopped abruptly. Caught in his web, she could feel his warm breath graze the back of her ear.

"We're not done yet," he growled.

Evie turned around. "Yes, we are. I can't do this." Realizing how close he was, she leaned back. "You haven't taught me any moves yet."

"Trust me," he replied. "Just go with it. I think we'll both be pleasantly surprised." He walked back to the fencing strip. "Otherwise, just leave now. You aren't worth my time."

Upon hearing the challenge, Evie felt a sudden rush of controlled fear. She quickly grabbed her foil and walked over to the fencing line, glaring at her opponent. "En garde!" she shouted. The music picked up where it had left off as the two fencers began their match.

Damek made a sudden move to attack. Evie reacted quickly by swinging her blade down to the left, successfully deflecting the hit. After returning to her starting position, Damek waited for the next move. Evie attempted to mimic his previous movement by bending her right knee and lunging forward. Although her technique was impressive, Damek effortlessly blocked it with a light tap.

Evie focused all her attention on the swords as the gym around her faded. A slight tingle ran down her arms as she stood up and lunged at her opponent, aiming for his chest. Damek blocked the attack by swinging his foil upwards, causing both blades to clash. Evie felt a burning sensation seep into her legs as he pulled her in closer, their breaths mingling as one.

The next hour was spent retreating, lunging, spinning, and grunting. With Damek in the lead, he jumped forward and lunged. Evie could feel her arms shaking from the strain of the intense workout. Swinging her sword in a rather clumsy semicircle, she deflected the attack. A brilliant blue spark flashed out of the swords as they connected, causing Evie's foil to career out of her hand, landing on the hard floor. Damek galloped back in retreat, and the music suddenly stopped. They continued to stare at each other, with only the sound of their labored breathing. An intense heat engulfed the distance. Pulling the neckline of her jacket, Evie tried to push away the suffocating feeling of giddiness.

"How the hell did that happen? There's no way a spark could have-" Unable to finish his thought, Damek rubbed the sweat from his forehead. "I think that's enough for today."

Evie stood frozen in a fighting stance, torn between her opponent and the sword on the floor.

Damek shifted back into position. "Evie, I said enough. I'm exhausted." Watching her, he didn't move.

Taking a deep breath, Evie tried to ease off the intense concentration. Relaxing her shoulders, she crumpled into a seated position.

Damek fell to the floor, continuing to keep a wary eye on her. "Hmm, no lessons, my ass," he mumbled, laying his sword on the floor.

Evie raised her head, pondering his words. "But I haven't. Believe what you want." She then looked at the foil. "I suppose nothing should surprise me these days," she said, more to herself.

"What's that supposed to mean?" Damek shot back.

"Nothing," Evie said honestly, "Look, that wasn't me at the party."

"Oh, we're back to that again. I thought you didn't wanna talk about it," said Damek as he grabbed his sword and stood up.

"Damek, you need to tell me what you know about Lilith."

"Not until you tell me why you wanna know."

"Well, I think-" Evie said, suddenly interrupted by an exaggerated clap echoing through the gym. She turned around to see Lexi walking towards Damek with a towel. The blonde tossed her hair over her shoulder and winked at Evie, a gesture she was beginning to despise. Looking at Lexi's low top and cut-off jean shorts, Evie grumbled at her own sweaty white tank stuck to her midriff.

"Miss me?" Lexi asked, planting a sultry kiss on Damek's lips. She recoiled, running her hand over his sweaty shirt. "You need a shower, babe, and we literally need to leave here in like, 10 minutes."

Damek grabbed the towel from Lexi and wiped his face.

"So," said Lexi, crossing her arms, "someone had a good time last night."

Before Evie could answer, Damek lightly tugged on Lexi's long hair. "Shut it, Lexi," he commented, placing his sword back on the table.

"Hey!" Lexi replied, smiling at Evie. "What's wrong with having a good time, right? So, which one of those guys did you end up with anyway?"

Evie tried to think of a witty answer. Again, she felt like the outcast, the unpopular geek who couldn't open her mouth to answer a question.

Damek threw the towel he had been using on the table. "I said drop it, Lexi." He refused to look at Evie. "Just leave the jacket and foil on the table. I'm running late. You can find your way out."

Picking up the forgotten sword, Evie grasped it tightly. "Wait," she said, feeling that familiar rush of adrenaline, "we haven't finished our conversation yet."

"Yes, we have," Damek said firmly, as he walked to the door. "Lexi, meet me in the kitchen. My mom'll probably be in there."

Evie lowered her eyes into slits, swung the sword around, and lunged. "Coward."

He didn't turn around.

"You know he doesn't like you that way, right?" Lexi said, placing her hands on her hips.

Keeping a tight hold on the sword, Evie turned around. "Excuse me?"

"Look, let's stop pretending. I know you like him. I'm just trying to save you some heartache."

"I highly doubt you know what I like," Evie snapped.

"Please!" With a wave of her hand, Lexi flicked one of her curls off her shoulder. "It's so obvious. I see it happen all the time."

"Last time I checked, we weren't friends," Evie exclaimed as she slammed the foil onto the table. She grabbed her stuff and headed out of the gym. A chill raised the hairs on the back of her neck as she walked through the door - a feeling she was getting quite used to. Glancing over her shoulder, she noticed the picture of the Archangel staring at her as if daring her to stay. It was time to get out of this strange maze of a house. "Adam's family, my ass," she mumbled.

Driving out of the past and turning onto the street of the present, Evie picked up her cell phone and dialed Lana. After ten attempts with no answer, Evie decided to call the house phone.

"Hello," said a man's voice on the other end.

"Hi. Mr. Cohen. It's Evie. Is Lana there?"

"She isn't feeling well," replied Mr. Cohen, with a slight stammer.

"Do you mind if I stop by and see her?"

"Not now, Evie. She's sleeping, and she needs her rest. She'll see you Monday."

"Um, will she need a ride?"

"I don't think so."

"Okay...You sure she doesn't need anything?"

"Look, Evie, I appreciate your concern, but I have to go." The stern voice on the other end abruptly ended the call.

Her eyes began to cloud over. Jerking the steering wheel to the right, she turned on Dogwood Street towards Lana's house. She needed to see her. Something wasn't right. As she approached a traffic light, she watched it turn green in the distance and pushed down on the accelerator, determined to get there as fast as possible. Suddenly, a figure darted out in front of the car, and she slammed on the brakes, the car's pedal stuttering and jerking before finally squealing to a sudden stop. Catching her breath, she saw Blake approaching the passenger side door with a wide grin. She unlocked the doors, and Blake quickly hopped in.

"Blake?! Are you crazy??" Evie yelled, "I almost ran you over!" She checked the rearview mirror to find the road deserted.

"Nah," Blake responded, "you did great!"

Evie tried to calm her racing heart and took the time to assess Blake's attire. This time, he looked pretty clean. His v-neck green button-down shirt and dark jeans looked brand new, and his hair was still wet from a recent shower. Taking a deep breath, the smell of pine assailed her senses. She scooted closer to her window and tried to mask her sweaty aroma.

"So," Blake chuckled, "I hear you're a master at the sword already?"

"Huh?" Evie asked, forgetting about her grubby attire. "Where did you hear that?"

"Damek. I just talked to him, and he said you'd been there. Sounds like you're a natural."

"I, uh, didn't realize you and Damek were friends."

"We aren't."

Evie widened her gaze, waiting for Blake to elaborate. "So, that's it? That's all you're gonna say? How'd you find me anyway? I didn't even-"

"Evie," Blake interrupted, "I don't have much time. I need you to stay away from Damek."

"Why?"

"Because it's dangerous."

"What?"

"I'm being serious. I need you to stay away from him."

Evie suddenly had an epiphany. She rolled her eyes and hit her hand against the steering wheel. "Oh, I get it. He couldn't just tell me himself? He needed some lackey to do it for him? I didn't realize you had sunk that low, Blake."

"That's not it at all," Blake laughed.

"Sure it isn't."

"Look, he said you were asking some questions. Just leave it alone." He paused, then leaned in closer and took Evie's hand, causing her heart to skip a beat. The feeling was a bit uncomfortable and exciting at the same time. "I also need you to stop reading that journal. Just go put it back where you found it."

"Huh?" Evie gasped. "How did you know about the journal? Did Lana tell you?"

"Um...yeah, she did." He quickly changed the subject and moved his hand to her knee. "And don't worry about Lana. She'll be fine. Just give her some space. I promise everything will go back to the way it was."

Evie couldn't stop staring at his fingers, though she didn't believe him. Could he feel the butterflies in her stomach? "Blake," Evie pleaded.

He craned his neck to look through the back window and quickly turned around with a wild look in his eyes. "I gotta go. Please just do as I said. Return the journal."

"But," as Blake's eyes gently caressed her lips, a sudden warmth spread through her body, and the words she wanted to say died in her throat.

"You've been so good for Lana," he continued, "I can't begin to thank-" but a shrill screech cut off the rest of his words. Blake and Evie jolted in their seats and peered out of the front windshield. Evie gasped. Another owl was sitting on the car hood, its piercing eyes fixated on them.

Blake jumped out of the car, a mischievous grin spreading across his face. "Who's ready for a shower now?" he teased before slamming the car door shut and racing towards a cluster of trees.

Evie still had so many questions. She tried to open her car door but forgot about her seat belt. Struggling to unlock the belt from its latch, another low screech caught her attention. The owl's yellow eyes bored into hers one last time before it rose from its perch on the car and headed in Blake's direction. She watched until it disappeared into the distance, lost in thoughts about Blake. As she ran her hand along her lower lip, she could still feel the intensity of his gaze. She smiled, reminiscing about the first time they met during a sleepover at Lana's. He had stopped in the doorway of Lana's room to tell Lana he was going out for the night. At the time, Evie thought he was the most handsome guy she'd ever met. She could still remember what he was wearing: dark blue jeans and a plain black T-shirt. Blake was never much into labels. His dark black hair was cut short and spiked up in the front. He ignored her; in fact, she was pretty sure he hadn't even noticed her. Why would he? All she had to offer was a bulky T-shirt and sweats.

She shook her head, letting go of the memory. At least it was confirmed that Blake was talking to Damek and knew something about the journal. He must know who Lilith is. Why were the owls following him, too? Taking a deep breath, she grimaced at the smell of her shirt. She turned back around to look at the empty street in front of her and checked the clock. "Crap," she muttered, as there were only thirty minutes left before her parents would be back. Pressing on the gas, she headed in the only direction she could...home.

ii. First Kiss

After a long, hot shower, Evie returned to her room, drying her hair with a towel. The weight of Blake's words lingered in her mind. Maybe he was right. If she could only get rid of the journal, everything would return to normal. She spotted the journal lying closed on the floor. It seemed innocent enough, but ever since she found the small book, her entire world had been turned upside down. It was time to take it back. She picked it up off the floor and touched the front stone one last time. The cold, hard surface left its usual soft residue on her fingertips.

"Goodbye, Evelyn," she whispered, but as the words left her lips, the familiar blue smoke began to seep out of the closed pages. She dropped the book to the floor and considered running downstairs to talk to her parents. But there was something off about their muffled voices, and the anticipation that once hummed in her throat turned into dread. She cracked her knuckles, the sound echoing in the room. Grabbing her phone off her nightstand, she stared at Lana's name in her favorite contacts, hoping to calm the gnawing need in her stomach. She began to pace, the unease growing stronger.

Perhaps she could take one last look. She could handle it. She was strong. Throwing the phone on the bed, she turned around to look at her reflection in the mirror. Her plain brown eyes stared back at her with no signs of indecency, smoke, or waves. Everything was going to be okay. She pulled her hair into a messy bun and picked up the journal. Suddenly, a loud clap of thunder rattled the room, causing the pages of the journal to rapidly flip open before her, urging her closer. Looking at the page, she saw a familiar conversation hovering over the brown-tinted paper. Her heart began to race, anticipating the words she knew would soothe her extreme need. But need for what? Her knees buckled as she collapsed onto the floor. Cradling the book in her lap, she gave in to the final impulse and read the first sentence. Her shoulders relaxed.

May 3, 1893 noon
Three significant things have happened to me today, and I am not quite sure which order they should be in.

1.   *I met my first demon.*
2.   *I learned that Angels do exist.*
3.   *(And the least important or most important)...I had my first kiss.*

As always, I will relay the details that led me to the above facts. However, I fear that everything is about to change.

After leaving Senoy alone in the library, I found myself wandering the halls, not quite sure where to go. My thoughts were scattered, and nothing made sense. As I leaned against one of the walls to hold myself upright, I was startled to find I had made it to the dining room. A serving maid stopped to curtsy to me, and I did my best to smile back at her.

Fortunately, our housekeeper, Ms. Cooper, shooed the young maid towards the hall. "My Lady, we are about to clear breakfast if you would like to eat something. Pardon me for saying Miss, but you do not look well at all. Perhaps you should lay down a bit." She checked my forehead for any signs of fever and escorted me out of the room. "I will have Cecilia bring up some tea and make the necessary excuses to your mother."

Bless Ms. Cooper. She did not give me a chance to argue. I must remember to surprise her with a gift. As I headed up the stairs to my bedroom, I was stopped again.

"Evelyn! I was wondering where you were at breakfast. Everything alright?" asked a familiar male voice.

Turning around to make my apologies, I found Nab standing next to the most beautiful woman I had ever seen. She was a true goddess. I honestly believe my jaw dropped...whether from astonishment or sleep deprivation, I do not know. "Oh, I do apologize. I guess I overslept," I replied.

"Oh, right, just like everyone else. The price of having too much fun, eh? I do hope you have managed to get some rest." (Just like a man not to notice.) "Allow me to make introductions." With a gesture, he directed his attention towards the enchanting figure before him; his voice filled with reverence as he spoke her name, "Evelyn, may I present Miss Lilith Magdolyn."

Her long, flowing golden hair feathered over her petite frame, glistening with flecks of gold encased in the twirling locks. Her blue eyes were as calm as an ocean, beckoning any passerby to dip their toe in. Her lips reminded me of bright red roses waiting to be savored. As my gaze traced the shape of her form, I could not help but notice the dress straining against the curves beneath. I started to pull at my modest collar, feeling the heat rise in my cheeks. Beside me, Nab's hands trembled with eager anticipation as he hastened to complete the introduction.

"She is a cousin of Lord Pratley's, one of my buddies from Cambridge," Nab explained. "She is going to be spending a few days with us."

Meeting the new lady's lingering gaze, I felt the exhaustion lift from my body and leave a light giddiness in its wake. I had the strangest urge to giggle. "Have we met before? I apologize for my rudeness, but you seem so..." my voice caught as my gaze continued to revel in the apparition before me.

"Familiar?" interrupted Miss Magdolyn. "I feel the same way. Please call me Lilith. I know we shall be very *close." Her words flowed like a melody as she laid her hand on my arm.*

"Lilith?" I said, confused. The L's rolled off my tongue.

"Why yes. My father gave it to me," she replied, her smile not quite reaching her eyes.

I felt a strong urge to run outside through the gardens and smell the fragrant bouquets. Clearing my throat, I tried to concentrate. "Please call me Evelyn. Welcome to our home. I look forward to seeing you at the rest of the festivities." I covered her soft hand with mine.

"Miss Magdolyn will be attending the ball tonight," Nab said. "I have asked Lord Wyndham to escort her, as to my utmost sadness, I have already agreed to escort Lady Braxton. I hope you will help her feel welcomed."

With a subtle nod, I looked at Lilith and smiled, reflecting the joy bursting inside me. "But, of course, it will be my pleasure."

"Thank you, Lady Evelyn. I look forward to this evening," Lilith replied graciously, dipping her head in acknowledgment before returning her hand to the crook of Nab's arm. "Now, Lord March, where is this painting you mentioned I simply must see?"

As I watched them walk towards the gallery, my smile faded, and I suddenly felt cold. I rubbed my arms, trying to make sense of the sudden loss and exhaustion that had overcome me. I pushed myself towards my bedroom and hastily shut the door behind me. My breaths became large gasps, and my body felt like it had run for miles. As sleep started to take over, a pounding noise began to splinter in my head.

"Oh, please leave. I need some rest," I called out.

"Beg your pardon, My Lady, but Master Senoy needs to speak with you right away. He says it is urgent. He requests your presence in the library."

"Cecilia, did you actually see Senoy?" I asked curiously, opening the bedroom door.

"Why no, My Lady. Mr. Hops, the ground's keeper, relayed the message. However, he said it was very important. Why, should I have?"

"No, no. I will go to the library shortly. Thank you."

After the maid curtsied and left, I walked back into my room and caught a glimpse of my reflection in the mirror. I frowned at the dark circles under my tired eyes. Feeling exhausted, I made my way back to the library.

The comforting tempo of 'Für Elise' drifted into the hall. Leaning against the sturdy frame of the doorway, I steeled myself, summoning the courage to confront my fencing master, who now magically appeared much younger.

"Are you going to come in or fall asleep right there?" asked Senoy, his youthful voice sounding strange to me.

"I am supposed to be asleep in my bed. What is so urgent that you could not give me the time I requested?" I was not quite sure if my words came out coherently.

"Evelyn, please come in," he urged, wrapping his strong arms around me and guiding me to a nearby chair. "I am sorry," he said. "I know you are tired, but this can not wait." My eyelids started to close as his voice mingled with the melodic chords of the tune still playing in the background. "Do you believe me now?" he whispered.

"Hmm? Are you creating that music?" I mumbled, my words barely audible.

"Evelyn, what are you rambling about? Wake up!" he said urgently. "Lilith has arrived."

Try as I might, I could not open my eyes.

"I do believe you just met her with your brother," Senoy added.

"The goddess, yes," I replied, not sure if I spoke the words aloud.

"Yes, Lilith has always been a very beautiful woman," he commented. "But with that beauty comes extreme danger. She is no goddess, Evelyn. She is the Mother of all demons. She can easily charm you into giving her anything she desires."

"Hmm..." I murmured, slowly drifting off to sleep.

"Evelyn, wake up!"

"She was so familiar," I mused.

"I am not surprised. You are a descendent of Evangeline."

Struggling to gather my wits, I sat up straight and rubbed my eyes. "What does that mean?"

His gaze bore into mine. "You were born for this, Evelyn."

"Back to that again? It is too much, Senoy! I do not believe any of it," I protested, feeling the stress and tiredness taking over me as I fell to the side of the chair. Senoy quickly rushed to my side and began rubbing my back.

Quietly and perhaps more to himself than to me, he whispered, "Evelyn, I cannot promise this will end well, but I can tell you this is what you were born for. We have been guardians to every sword protector through the centuries. A change is coming, and I can only hope that it will choose our side."

"A-hem..." The sudden interruption caused Senoy to withdraw his hand immediately.

"Did I interrupt something?" Lord Wyndham asked, leaning against the open door frame with a casual demeanor that belied the tension he radiated.

"Ah, Lord Wyndham. Just the person I wanted to see," said Senoy, quickly moving away from my chair and walking towards the door.

"I do not believe we have met, sir." Lord Wyndham responded.

"Well, actually, we have. But for now, you can call me Michael." Extending his hand towards Lord Wyndham, he gave up on any pretenses.

"Excuse me?" Lord Wyndham's blank face showed no emotion.

"I believe you were looking for Evelyn? Perhaps regarding the incident with the sword and activating the eye?" Senoy added.

"How did you know about that? Did she tell you?" Looking back at me, he seemed to assess my entire body in one glance.

"No. Evelyn was coming to me for the same answers you seek."

"Senoy, please!" I yelled as I desperately tried to stop what was about to happen.

Lord Wyndham looked from Senoy to Evelyn. "Senoy?" he asked. "Is that not the name of your fencing master?" He pushed away from the door frame and stood up to his full height, his question more of a threat.

I could not let Lord Wyndham privy to Senoy's wild tale. Pushing up from the chair, I tried to regain some semblance of balance. "Senoy, what if the sword made a mistake?"

"There are no mistakes," he replied smoothly.

"Senoy, please!" I cried. "He is an outsider."

Searching my eyes, Senoy lowered his voice. "Is he, Evelyn?"

"If you do not step away from her, sir, I will not be responsible for what happens," Lord Wyndham warned.

With a tight smile, Senoy nodded toward Lord Wyndham and stepped out of my arms. Embarrassment washed over me, and I could feel the heat moving into my cheeks. Bright, hot anger shot through my body, giving me the brief energy I needed for this ridiculous encounter. I marched straight to the source of all my problems.

"You have no control over me!" I shouted. "I hate you! None of this would have happened if it had not been for you!" I tried pushing Lord Wyndham against the door, but the stupid clod was like a brick wall that did not move. Defeated, I fled into the hallway. I felt like a coward running away, but everything was spinning out of my control.

Tears blurred my vision as I ran through the back halls. I had no idea where I was headed. All I wanted was to get away, but I could hear someone following closely behind. I picked up my pace and stumbled as I tried to turn down yet another dark hallway. Collapsing against the wall to steady my fall, something or someone grabbed my arms and completely lifted me off the floor as if I were a child. I was gently turned around, and my back came to rest against the side wall, my feet unable to touch the ground. I allowed myself to relax, the tense silence enveloping us both. As my eyes adjusted to the darkness, I realized I must have headed to the wine cellar. Panic began to take hold as I tried to make out who was in front of me.

Lord Wyndham's face came into view as my eyes adjusted to the darkness. "Evelyn, stop pushing against me. I am not going to hurt you."

"Then put me down!" I yelled into his face.

"And risk you running off again? I think not."

"What do you want from me?"

"I mean something," he said in a commanding tone, his eyes filled with anger.

"Excuse me? You are making no sense."

"Stop acting like a child."

"I am not a child!" I snapped. There was that stupid word again. Why did everyone continue to call me that?

"No...you are right. You are no child."

His lips came crashing down on mine. My mind was telling me to struggle, but my body was screaming for more. The taste of salt and brandy, mixed with an unbearable longing, surged through my entire body, setting it aflame. As Lord Wyndham's grip began to loosen, my traitorous arms instinctively wound themselves around his neck, seeking support and drawing us even closer. His hands, rough and commanding, delved into my hair, igniting a fierce passion that left me gasping for air. I could not get enough.

"I beg your pardon. It seems I am the intruder now," a male voice interrupted. "Lord Wyndham, I believe you should let Lady March down."

Senoy's voice broke through the haze of bliss as reality came crashing down around me, his tone sharp and unfamiliar. As I slid down the wall, I stumbled forward, but Lord Wyndham caught me by the arm and looked at me with a lopsided grin.

"Please let me go," I stuttered.

"Whatever you wish, Lady March," he said, holding me up and rubbing my arm with his thumb. I yanked it out of his grasp.

"Come," said Senoy sharply. "It is time we all talked."

"Please, after you, my lady," Lord Wyndham gracefully bowed, gesturing for me to pass. I hurried to catch up with Senoy, keeping my gaze fixed on his back. The intense warmth emanating from behind was like a beacon, urging me to turn back and surrender myself to the flames of passion once more.

"By the way," Lord Wyndham added, "I assume you are going to explain how you found the fountain of youth, Master Senoy?"

"How did you know?" I gasped, turning around.

"Well, I still do not believe it, but I assume that is what you are going to tell me," Lord Wyndham replied, the desire in his eyes still burning bright. I swiftly turned back around, feeling the scorching intensity of his gaze searing through me.

"Come," Senoy beckoned. "I will tell you everything."

Upon entering the library, I quickly settled into an armchair, leaving Lord Wyndham no choice but to take the sofa himself. However, the lingering heat between us made no difference where I sat. I could feel his every move. As I continued to shift uncomfortably, Lord Wyndham calmly turned to Senoy for answers. Master Senoy proceeded to recount the sword's entire history, as he had explained it to me earlier.

"So you will have me believe that you are Michael the Archangel, Evie is the sword's guardian, and Lilith, Adam's first wife, is here to steal the sword to enter the afterlife?" Lord Wyndham asked.

"I understand it is a lot of information, but yes, that is the truth," Master Senoy replied.

"And how do I fit into this...tale?"

"Believe me, sir, it is no tale," Master Senoy sighed, shaking his head. "You activated the eye of the sword with Evelyn."

Lord Wyndham paused as if thinking about his next words carefully. "What is the eye, and what does that mean?"

"The eye is the stone inlaid in the guard of the sword. It is where the sword derives its powers. It is activated when two soulmates touch the stone at the same time."

"And that is why I saw and felt...everything about Evelyn?" Lord Wyndham rubbed his jaw with a faraway look in his eyes. I knew he was trying to find the words to describe the unexplainable.

"Yes"

"I do not know quite how to respond. It is too unbelievable."

"See," I spat, finally finding my voice, "I told you he would not understand."

"Evelyn, you are still trying to grasp the truth yourself while he is just learning of it." Senoy gestured to both of us as he walked towards the fireplace. "It is very rare when two halves of a whole meet. In our lifetime, our world has grown so large that most people never even come across their soulmate. However, the female descendants of Evangeline, who guard the sword, have always been fortunate enough to meet their soulmate in their lifetime."

"Does that mean Lilith tries to obtain the stone every time there is a new guardian?" I asked.

"This is the change I was talking about. No other guardian has ever realized that they have met their soulmate. They never had the chance to touch the sword, and throughout history, many of them were in arranged marriages, which, of course, were not to their soulmate.

The only guardian who ever fought Lilith was the original, Evangeline."

"She met her soulmate?" I asked.

"Yes, but there must have been a mistake. However, as it was, they both were able to activate the sword, not understanding the power, much like you did."

"Ha, so the sword can make a mistake!" I added with a hint of excitement.

"Not this time, Evelyn."

"Could they be together as long as they do not touch the stone at the same time?" Lord Wyndham asked.

"In theory, but it would eventually happen," Senoy responded with a wave of his hand. "The sword calls to the pair."

"What happened?" I asked, turning to Senoy. "I mean to Evangeline?"

"You must understand that this was the first time, as protectors, we found true power hidden in the stone. It was our first and only time dealing with Lilith after her curse. We underestimated how the curse had turned her into a true demon devoid of any goodness. Although we were able to push Lilith back to the Red Sea, we lost Evangeline in the process..." pausing, he took a slow breath and continued, "Evangeline died protecting the sword, and her soulmate never laid eyes on her again. Since then, the protectors have lived on Earth, stationed in various parts of the world. The rest of them should be arriving soon."

"Is that the answer then?" I asked.

"What do you mean?" Master Senoy replied.

"Should Lord Wyndham leave and never be seen again?"

"N o w , w a i t a s e c o n d ," Lord Wyndham interrupted, jumping to his feet.

Senoy extended his hand to halt him. "No, my dear. I would not do that to you. Furthermore, now that the stone has been activated, Lilith will stop at nothing to obtain it. We must prevent this from happening to future generations. I believe the answer lies in the combined strength of both of you and the stone."

"Look," said Lord Wyndham, "I am not entirely sure how much of this I believe. However, I do know that when I touched the stone with Evelyn, she became a..." he trailed off, struggling to find the right words.

"A part of you?" asked Senoy.

"Perhaps..." grunted Lord Wyndham. "All I know is that something strange happened. I can not leave her here defenseless if what you say is true."

"I am not defenseless!" I yelled. "I have Senoy. He is all I need."

"Evelyn, you are mine," Lord Wyndham declared possessively, surprising even himself.

"How dare you! You have no control over me," I seethed, my tone rising with each word, "and must I remind you, I did not give you leave to use my given name!" Turning back to Senoy, I hugged my chest, trying to control the raw intensity that made me want to lash out. "How could you think this brute is my soulmate?"

"You can think what you want, my dear," Lord Wyndham replied, his tone unyielding, "but I am not leaving."

Ignoring Lord Wyndham, I stared in disbelief at Senoy. "How can you just stand there?"

"It is not my place to interfere. What would you have me do?" Senoy asked.

Turning away from them both, I headed to the window, my gaze vacant, not really seeing the flowers in the garden below. "Senoy, you have been my mentor, my friend," I murmured, "and this is how you treat me?" Suddenly, I felt his presence behind me, his arms enveloping me in a comforting embrace.

"Evelyn, I am your friend. But most of all, I am your protector."

"I think..." Lord Wyndham interjected.

"Not now!" Senoy said firmly. "We need to get to work." Leaving me by the window, Senoy headed to one of the long reading tables across from the sofa.

Swinging around, I assessed the two warriors in front of me. "Senoy, I will do as you say. I have trusted you my entire life," I declared, the heat of my words matching my determination. "However, both of you will understand this. I do not care what some stupid stone says. It does not rule my life or my emotions." Fixing my gaze unwaveringly on Lord Wyndham, I continued,

"There will never be anything between you and I. Do you understand me?" I kept the words as calm as I could, though I had the uncanny feeling my words belied my true feelings, daring him to challenge my resolve.

"We shall see," Lord Wyndham responded. He did not move. The uncomfortable heat rose between us.

"I understand you have both met Lilith," Senoy asked, breaking the unbearable silence.

"Why yes," Lord Wyndham acknowledged with a slight nod. "Such a beautiful creature. I believe I am to be the lady's escort for the ball this evening." As he let his finger glide across the back of the sofa, a smile curved his lips, though it lacked warmth, revealing a small dimple on his right cheek. "You know Evelyn, it would be wise to take some lessons in lady-like behavior from her."

"It is Lady March, Lord Wyndham!" I screamed, unable to do anything but stomp my foot.

"I'm sorry, Lord Wyndham," Senoy interjected, stepping away from the table. "But that is exactly what Lilith wants you to believe. She has the ability to enchant anyone and everything. Her beauty and charm will draw you in. And only once she has what she needs will you see the true ugliness within. She can transport herself and other demons through mirrors. She can bring the storms under her full control. The screech owl and serpent are her apostles and will do anything to uphold her commands. She will stop at nothing to obtain the stone's power to enter the afterlife, including taking another's

life. We must not give her what she wants. Otherwise, humankind will no longer exist. At least not in the way we know it."

I struggled to concentrate on Senoy's description of Lilith. My mind began to wander. Here I was being lectured on a potential war I was supposedly born to be in, and all I could think about was the two very different men standing before me. They were undeniably handsome, yet with each, a different emotion stirred within me. One brought unease and uncertainty, while the other offered comfort and consistency. Could an angel even be with a human? Did Senoy have wings like the angels in my childhood books?

"Evelyn," Senoy interrupted, "are you paying attention?"

Lord Wyndham's lips curved into a subtle smirk as I realized I had been inadvertently fixated on his mouth. Slowly, I lifted my gaze to meet his eyes—laughter and something stronger that I had no words for radiated the distance between us.

"Yes, my lady. You should pay attention," Lord Wyndham remarked, his smile widening slightly. "One can only wonder what has gained it otherwise."

Startled, I blinked rapidly and turned towards Senoy, a flush creeping up my cheeks.

"Please focus," Senoy urged. "This is very important."

A chuckle escaped Lord Wyndham's lips, laden with undeniable charm. "Oh, I do believe the lady was very focused," he said before sitting on the sofa.

As sleep began to take over, I ignored the lout's ridiculous comment. "Senoy," I groaned, "I am so tired." Although I knew I was whining, I did not care. "Besides, what is the harm in allowing Lilith to enter the afterlife? If her only desire is to reunite with Adam, why is that such a bad thing?"

"Evelyn, have you not been listening?" Senoy asked. "The afterlife does not exist in the way Lilith believes it does. She still believes in the passionate love that once prospered in the Garden of Eden. That no longer exists, at least not in the way she thinks it does. Her anger, resentment, and longing for an eternal love that no longer exists have become a curse and have destroyed any goodness she once had. Lilith has become more demon than human. Over the centuries, she has proven her sinister abilities with her demon spawn, and should she enter the afterlife, she will destroy us all."

"Such a tragic love story," I sighed.

"Leave it to the female to find the love story," remarked Lord Wyndham, propping up his legs on the footrest.

Why did I constantly feel the urge to stick my tongue out at him? Perhaps I was still a child.

"Lilith's goodness was shattered centuries ago, replaced by emptiness and deceit. She will use your emotions to get what she wants, so be prepared."

"What is expected of us?" Lord Wyndham asked.

"With an impending battle on the horizon," Senoy began, "it is imperative that both of you join forces. Your combined strength holds the key to our success. Lilith is aware that you have both activated the stone but remains ignorant of the extent of your understanding. She will continue her deception until she is ready to strike. Like us, she grapples with how to wield this power. Remember, despite your differences, cooperation is essential. While my brothers and I will shoulder the brunt of the battle, history has shown that it takes more than sheer force to vanquish her permanently. If only we knew what that 'something' was."

"So much from a beautiful, timid creature..." Lord Wyndham mused.

"Timid she is not," Senoy countered. "You will see for yourselves tonight."

"What did you mean by 'my brothers'?" Evelyn asked.

A mischievous grin appeared on Senoy's face as he tilted his head, sensing the arrival of a new guest. "Ah, I believe you are about to make their acquaintance."

I had never seen Senoy's face light up so brightly. Following his gaze, I could not help but gasp in awe as three more warriors entered the library with an *air of familiarity as if they had been there many times before.*

"Well, brother, I see we are a bit late for the history lesson," remarked the towering blond man. Senoy walked over, and they exchanged fierce hugs and pats on the back. A younger man, possibly in his teens, watched the scene with a type of reverence.

"It has been a long time, ol' man," Senoy laughed.

I stood there mesmerized as the three youthful gods exchanged greetings. All three in their prime for battle. Hard to believe the tale of angels. Each one more beautiful than the next. To Senoy's right stood a man with the same golden blond hair and piercing blue eyes, so alike that they could easily be mistaken for siblings. However, where Senoy's features were more fierce, the other exuded a softer demeanor. Come to think of it, if I had not known Senoy, one look from him could strike fear in any person. On Senoy's left stood another figure, handsome in a darker, more rugged way. His hair was a rich, raven black, and his eyes were deep-set, almost mirroring the hue of his hair. He reminded me of the wild dogs that prowled over the moors at night. He bore a scar on his right cheek, which I was surprised to find only enhanced his elegance. As my gaze wandered, our eyes met, and I found myself drawn into his intense stare.

"My god, it is Evangeline. How did you do it?" The dark-haired man turned to Senoy, his expression a mix of astonishment and disbelief.

"No, this is Evelyn. She is a descendent of Evangeline's," Senoy clarified.

"The resemblance is uncanny. None of the others have..." the dark-haired man trailed off, his thoughts left unfinished.

"I know," Senoy interjected, cutting off any further discussion with a wave of his hand. He then turned his attention to the young man standing on the outskirts, extending his hand in greeting. "And you must be the new recruit?" Senoy shook hands with the newcomer before nodding toward the dark-haired warrior. "I hope Gabriel is not working you too hard."

"No, sir. I am deeply honored. I have been eagerly anticipating this meeting," the young man replied with a respectful bow.

Senoy gently tapped the young man on the shoulder, encouraging him to rise. "And what is your name, young one?" he inquired.

"Galiel, sir."

"We can dispense with the formalities. Please call me Michael."

It was too much for me. Senoy, now Michael, stood before me as the Archangel, leading this small army of angels sent from the heavens.

"I am sorry to interrupt this reunion, but can someone please explain what is happening?" I managed to ask, my voice cracking slightly higher than I expected.

All four gods turned their attention to me, and I fought the urge to cringe back. Even the younger one carried a commanding elegance, his light brown curls framing his green eyes, adding to his undeniable allure.

Grasping the dark-haired warrior's shoulder, Senoy beamed. "My apologies, let me make the introductions. Evelyn, Lord Wyndham, this is Gabriel." Gesturing towards the blond man, he continued, "And this is Uriel." I could sense Senoy's pride swelling at the mere mention of his brothers' names. Was it jealousy that caused my frown to deepen? Ignoring my brief reaction, Senoy motioned to the youngest angel. "And as you heard, this is Gabriel's new apprentice, Galiel."

"Senoy, this is all too much," I murmured, feeling overwhelming nausea creeping up my throat as the men's voices grew louder.

"Senoy? It's been ages since I've heard you called that," remarked Gabriel as Senoy quickly moved to my side, offering support. Leaning against him, I felt my mind begin to cloud over.

"Oh, forgive me," I murmured, feeling my words slurring together. "I suppose I should start calling you Michael now. Nothing is quite the same, is it?" A gentle stroke passed over my back, accompanied by deep, rumbling laughter that seemed to echo in the encroaching

darkness. Finally, I succumbed to sleep, uncertain what I would awaken to.

****

12. Best Friends

Blackness reigned; the dream escaping into an exhausted heap.

"Lana, Lana, Lana," Evie's voice echoed, the name rolling off her tongue like a chant keeping her grounded. White feathers embraced her through the darkness, blurring her vision and sticking to her clothing; their downy softness providing a comforting embrace amid the uncertainty. As she reached out to touch the vision, she could see strands of black hair entwined in the bright plumes. Grasping one of the raven locks, it curled around her middle finger.

"Enough of this!" The demon's voice echoed through the idyllic dream. "That girl will always have the mark of sin. Hear me now, Evie; her jealousy will always win out. Hers is a destiny tainted by the soul of Cain, destined to endure anguish echoing through every lifetime. Put Lana from your mind. We have work to do. The time has come."

"I don't understand you," screamed Evie. "Who is Cain?" She couldn't quite grasp the delusional dream. Lana's murky image ripped apart into a scattering of mist, briefly illuminating the darkness. "Just leave me alone, demon!"

"Is that what you think I am, Daughter of Mine? A demon? I believe it is time we do a bit of catching up."

Drowning out the witch's voice, Evie continued her mantra. "Lana, Lana, Lana..."

"Evie?" A male voice interrupted, breaking into the chaotic nightmare. Blinding streams of fluorescent light began to seep in, pushing the hallucination further into the receding darkness.

Evie opened her eyes and lifted her head. A foggy image struggled to take shape. Concentrating on the two circles in front of her, a pair of glasses sitting precariously on the edge of someone's nose came into view.

"Evie," the man's voice, unmistakably Mr. Sadler's, pierced through her drowsy haze once more. "Wake up."

Blinking away the remnants of sleep, Evie slowly regained awareness, the familiar sound of students snickering around her making her cheeks flush.

"Glad to see you decided to join us again. If I were you, Ms. March, I would be more concerned about not flunking Geometry than catching up on your Z's." Mr. Sadler walked back to his desk and looked up at the clock hanging above the classroom door.

Evie followed his gaze, trying to register the large numbers. Saved by the bell, she dropped her head back into her hands. She tried to ignore the laughter around her, but at some point, she even considered joining in. She could add laughing stock to her long list of Sophomore complaints.

Peering down at the open math book in front of her, she was reminded of the night before. It was the first time in a while that she had woken up without any nightmares after reading Evelyn's journal. Everything appeared to be normal again, or so she thought. Even her Dad woke her up with his usual two-minute good morning speech before heading out the door. Well, normal minus the guilty reminder that she was grounded for two weeks and the fact that Sheba completely ignored her. Even the ride to school was rather mundane. Since her father was back from his trip, she no longer had the car to use. Boarding the bus was like starting the year all over again, before Lana had ever entered her life.

Daydreaming, she looked closer at the open geometry book in front of her. Apparently, her dreams were not limited to her bedroom anymore. Boldly written over the illustrations of obtuse angles was the name Lilith. She recognized her own slanted letters. She slammed the book shut and shoved it into her book bag, half scared that Lilith may choose that moment to leap out of her math book. She looked up to meet Mr. Sadler's concerned gaze.

"Is everything ok, Evie?" Mr. Sadler asked, pushing his thumbs against the middle of a pencil.

"Yes," Evie said, urging the pencil to snap. She cleared her throat and could tell he was uncomfortable. "I'm really sorry about falling asleep. I promise it won't happen again. Rough night, I guess." Pulling the book bag onto her shoulder, she started to head out the door.

"See that it doesn't. Next time, I may not be so lenient. By the way, you were mumbling something about Lana." Evie could feel the familiar flush creeping up her face as she turned around. "I know you and Ms. Cohen are good friends. Would you mind giving her the assignment for this week?" he asked.

"Sure, no problem," she said as she walked out into the hallway, heading towards her locker. "If she'll even speak to me," she murmured under her breath. It was lunchtime, and there was no Lana. She wanted to throw up. Fumbling with the lock, she tried to take a deep breath.

"Hey Evie," Seth said, coming up behind her and lightly squeezing her waist.

"Oh, hey, Seth," she replied as she finally managed to open her locker. She slowly turned around to face her shame.

"So, Friday night? Great, huh?" Seth's smile was blinding.

"Yeah...great...look, Seth, I wanna apologize for how I acted," Evie said, her arms folding over her chest as she leaned against her locker.

"Is that why you've been ignoring me all morning?" Seth's fingers brushed a strand of Evie's hair behind her ear, his expression softening. "Don't worry about it!" Leaning in closer, he paused, his eyes searching hers for reassurance.

She pushed against his chest. "No. I wasn't myself. I'm not sure why I acted that way, but it wasn't real." She bit her lower lip. "Do you understand?"

"So does that mean you don't wanna hang out again this Friday?" he asked, lowering his gaze to concentrate on her lower lip.

"Um, well, maybe." Evie tried to push further into her open locker.

He grazed the bottom of her chin with his hand and then suddenly received an abrupt smack on the back of his head. "Ouch!" he exclaimed, startled by the unexpected blow.

"There you are," interrupted Blake with a crooked grin. "I've been looking everywhere for you."

"Hey man," Seth growled. "What was that for?" He rubbed the back of his head.

"Blake," Evie interrupted. "What are you doing here?"

"Oh, come on, bro," Blake said, nodding towards Seth. "It was just a little tap. And hey," he turned to Evie with a smile, "I do go to school here."

"Yeah, but..." Evie started, but Blake didn't let her finish.

Cutting her off, Blake turned back to Seth. "By the way, I'm Blake."

"Yeah, I know who you are," Seth responded. "Lana's brother. Never seen you in the sophomore hall before."

"Never had a reason to be," Blake replied casually. Turning back to Evie, he leaned against the adjacent locker. "Did I?"

"What?" Seth asked before Evie could.

"Come on, kid," Blake said, brushing off Seth's question. "We need to talk." Without waiting for a response, he seized Evie's arm, catching her off guard.

Seth reacted instinctively, grabbing Blake's shoulder.

"I wouldn't do that," Blake warned, his tone low but threatening.

"Seth," Evie intervened, "It's okay. I'll talk to you later."

"Are you sure?" Seth asked.

"Yeah, positive."

Blake took advantage of the brief win and gestured to Evie to start walking. She quickly headed for the end of the hall, determined not to glance over her shoulder, fully aware of Blake's presence trailing close behind and Seth's watchful gaze.

Silently congratulating herself on keeping her cool, she turned the corner. "What was that all about?"

Blake shrugged his shoulders. "You look like you needed some help."

"No, that's not what I mean." She stopped in the middle of the hall and put her hands on her hips. "I can handle Seth just fine, thank you."

"Yeah, it looked like you were doing a bang-up job," Blake retorted, leaning against the wall, his eyes sweeping over her.

Evie had the strangest feeling he was looking for something. "What are you doing here, Blake?"

"Going to school like every other normal kid."

"Stop lying and tell me the truth. I'm tired of all the cryptic messages. Where's Lana?"

"Wow, Evie. I'm surprised. Where's the shy girl I used to know?"

Evie's heart fluttered slightly at the sound of her name, but she maintained eye contact. "Stop trying to stall Blake."

"Lana's fine. She'll be back in school soon enough." He pushed away from the wall and ran his hand through his hair. Evie was starting to recognize the nervous trait.

"And what about you?" Evie asked. "Why are you here?"

"Perhaps I've found a reason to turn to the good side. Abandon my rebellious ways and stay in school," he responded, leaning in so close that Evie could feel the heat emanating from his body.

"Too bad the real world doesn't work that way," Evie murmured, her voice barely audible.

With a low chuckle, Blake withdrew slightly, but the intensity in his eyes only seemed to grow. "I'm glad you're starting to realize that. You're gonna need it."

"What are you talking about?"

"Look, I'm just keeping an eye on you. I know the dreams are getting worse. I told you to get rid of the journal. This is my last warning. If you keep reading, there's no turning back. She's coming for you."

"Are you talking about Lilith?" Evie's heart beat faster.

"So you are starting to remember what you read. I knew it." Looking behind him, Blake became lost in thought.

"Sort of. She's pretty hard to forget," Evie admitted. Trying to gain his attention, Evie moved to his side, waving her hand in front of his face. "What aren't you telling me? What does she want from me?"

Placing his hands on her shoulders, Evie could feel the tension in his fingers. "You need to get rid of the book as soon as you get home. I would recommend leaving school now, but wouldn't want you picking up my nasty habits."

"Why? What's gonna happen? It's not real, right?" Evie implored, searching his eyes for clues.

"Nothing will happen if you get rid of the book."

"Is it real, Blake?" she pressed. When he didn't answer, she raised her voice. "You're not being fair. You obviously know something."

Looking over Evie's head, Blake frowned. Evie glanced around and realized she had gained the attention of the surrounding students. She didn't care. They already thought the worst of her.

Blake grasped her hand hard, an urgency in his touch. "I have to go. Just get rid of the journal," he insisted. He strolled down the hall like he had no care in the world. Just before he reached the doors to the courtyard, he swung back around and winked at her.

She needed to scream. Evie made a beeline for the girl's bathroom, her steps unsteady as she stumbled through the doorway. Gripping onto the sides of one of the sinks, she stared into the bathroom mirror. All day long, she had endured the stares and whispered remarks that seemed to follow her every move. More than once, she thought she caught the word "slut" muttered under someone's breath as she passed by. And now, after Blake's public display of affection, she might as well have a scarlet letter "A" emblazoned on her chest, just like Hester Prynne in "The Scarlet Letter." Once considered a nobody, she was quickly climbing the social ladder two steps at a time.

Forcing another breath, she recognized the dull pressure fluttering in her chest. It was the same weight that hit every time she felt the need to move on—the need to move to the next town with the next set of friends. Once you got in thick, the move was always hanging right around the corner; No need for any tearful goodbyes. Rubbing her eyes, she held the tears at bay. How long did the Colonel say they would be here? She looked up at the ceiling for an answer that never came. What would Lana do? She needed Lana.

Squeezing her eyes shut, Evie felt a breeze tickle the loose strands of hair hanging over her vision. With a hesitant exhale, she reluctantly opened her eyes. A wisp of blue smoke wafted across her nose, thickening as it seeped around the edges of the mirror, suffocating the air around her. Evie's heart raced with a sudden wave of fear. Lilith was coming. Suppressing the urge to scream, she used her hands to feel her way out of the nightmare. She shoved the bathroom door open with a spasm of coughs and ignored the stares of the few students lingering in the hall.

She needed to get some answers. Heading towards the front of the school to find Blake, she ventured to the stoners underneath the field bleachers. They hadn't seen him. Her only hope was to make Lana understand. With a determined grin, she squared her shoulders. Whether out of determination or sheer panic, there was no time like the present to become a delinquent.

She followed a couple of the other students into the parking lot. With an open lunch policy, she knew it wouldn't be a problem to sneak around the corner to the local bus stop. She had never ridden any form of public transportation apart from the school bus. Briefly wondering what her parents would think, she waited impatiently for the bus to arrive, tapping her foot against the sign pole in anticipation- the beat slowly becoming a chant urging the bus to appear. When the bus finally arrived, she hastily inserted her money and slumped into the nearest seat, avoiding eye contact with the other passengers. Ignoring the idle chatter of two elderly women behind her and their pointed stares, she focused on the stained seat before her until she reached the stop closest to Lana's house.

As she made her way through the quiet neighborhood, Evie regarded the crows sitting on the tall lamp posts flanking every other house. She was just grateful they didn't have wide yellow eyes and pointy little ears. However, as she approached Lana's driveway, her steps faltered. The front yard was a chaotic mess, the grass towering over two feet high, strewn with discarded fast food wrappers and empty soda cans. How had she not noticed the mess? Was Lana right? Had she not been paying attention to anyone but herself?

She ran the rest of the way up the drive and repeatedly pushed the doorbell. With no answer, she tried banging on the door. She knew Lana had to be home. Looking around the side of the house, she judged how safe it would be to walk in the high grass. Pictures of snakes dancing around her made her grimace. She pushed the recent nightmare aside and trampled through the wet ground. She swatted at the long blades of grass tickling her legs. Lana's room was the first window on the back of the modest one-story house. She banged on the window and could hear movement inside. She banged harder.

"Go away!" came the muffled voice inside.

"Lana, it's me," Evie whispered, trying to avoid drawing attention from the neighbors.

"I know. I said go away!" Lana yelled again.

Tension pounded behind Evie's eyes. Something snapped inside her. Banging with both of her fists against the dirty pane, she screamed. "If you don't open this window, I'm gonna break it."

The curtain was jerked open abruptly, revealing Lana's agonizing face staring back at her. A large bruise circled her left eye with another dark mark on the edge of her chin. A gasp escaped Evie as she took in Lana's appearance, her gaze widening in shock at the short, edgy black hair framing the prominent cheekbones, her once-long black locks lost to the blunt edge of kitchen shears.

"Lana, what happened?"

"Just go away!" Lana scowled, retreating into the dark room.

"I'm not going anywhere! Open the window!" Evie could feel tears gathering in her eyes.

"I'm fine. I just tripped and hit the edge of my dresser. I don't feel good. Just go away." Lana disappeared even further into the shadows.

"Look, Lana, I'm not leaving. Open the window, or I'll find something to break it."

"Fine!" exclaimed Lana as she unlocked the latch and attempted to open the window. The window made a squealing sound due to misuse and neglect, but Lana persisted until it finally gave in. Evie climbed through the bug-encrusted ledge and tried to clean the dirt and grime from her clothes. She shuffled her feet back and forth, unsure of where to begin.

"Can you please tell me what happened?" Evie finally asked.

Lana dropped to the edge of her bed and stared into her lap.

"Please," Evie begged again. She gently sat beside Lana, reaching out for her hand.

Lana pulled away and retreated into the tangled mess of sheets. "Like you care..."

"How can you say that?"

"That's funny. You haven't listened to a word I've said since school started," Lana shot back.

"That's not true! I've asked you what's been going on. You just tell me not to worry about it. It's not like I haven't tried."

"We just don't fit anymore," Lana retorted.

"That's BS. Look, if you don't tell me what happened, I'll tell my mom about your face," Evie blurted out, instantly regretting the empty threat as soon as the words left her lips.

Lana met Evie's gaze, a heavy silence settling between them. After a moment, she sighed and rose from the bed, her movements slow and deliberate. "When I got home Friday night after the party, it was late. I was so upset over our fight that I completely forgot to sneak in through my window." Looking up at the ceiling, she muttered under her breath. "Not that I've had much reason to do that lately." With a shake of her head, she refocused on Evie. "You know what the funny thing is, though? He wouldn't even have remembered I'd gone out if he hadn't seen me." Lost in the brief thought, she quickly recovered. "Anyway, I came through the front door to find him completely blitzed."

"Who?" Evie asked, trying to follow Lana's story. "Your Dad?"

Lana's expression hardened, her arms folding defensively across her chest. "It was my fault. I should've known better."

Evie jumped up from the bed. "You're Dad hit you?"

"Not on purpose!" Lana's voice rose, her fingers grabbing one of her many tacky necklaces on her dresser. "Like I said, it was my fault."

"No, it's not!" Evie countered. "We're teenagers. That's what we're supposed to do! We break curfews."

Lana's fingers trembled as she fiddled with the silver wing hanging from her necklace. "Anyway, he was pretty upset..."

"We need to tell someone. You can come and stay with me."

"And then what?" Lana asked. "They take my dad away? He's the only one I have left! It only started after Blake left, and he feels horrible about it. My dad's had so much pain. What my mom did..." Her voice trailed off, her eyes welling with tears. "Look, he says it won't happen again."

"Lana, listen to yourself. Nothing makes beating your kid right."

Lana got off the bed, folding her arms in front of her. "I didn't say that's what happened! You just don't understand. I have a method for handling it." Taking a few steps to the bedroom door, she whirled around and threw her hands in the air. "I was just so upset with you on Friday. It's all your fault."

"What? Do you really believe that? That it's my fault?" Evie's voice cracked as she stumbled backward toward the window, tears finally breaking free.

"Look, I'm not dense. I know he needs help, and I'm trying to help him. But Evie, he's all I have. Please don't have him taken away from me..." Lana's voice softened, her eyes locking with Evie's, devoid of tears despite the weight of her words.

Evie shook her head. "I don't know what you want me to do."

"Just forget about it," Lana said, turning away from Evie to look at her reflection in the dresser mirror. She ran her fingers through her short hair. "I can handle it."

Stepping up behind Lana, Evie studied the bruises on her friend's skin in the reflection. She winced at the sight. "Apparently, you can't."

"Eh, like you're one to talk," Lana shot back, her gaze piercing through Evie's reflection in the mirror. "You can't even handle yourself right now. One minute you're Miss High and Mighty, and the next, you're the town slut."

The haze of tears clouded Evie's vision. "Wow, that hurt," she whispered, swiping at the wetness on her cheek.

"Good. You need to know how I feel. I thought you were my best friend."

"I am... I've tried explaining what has been happening to me, but you don't wanna listen."

"Oh right, the journal." Lana suddenly pushed away from the dresser, backing into Evie with a fierce jerk.

"Ouch!" Evie winced, rubbing her chest. She knew Lana had meant for it to hurt. Perhaps she deserved it.

"You know what the worst part of all this is? I was actually jealous of you."

"Jealous?" Lilith's words echoed in Evie's ears.

"You have everything. Great parents, good grades, the handsome jock of the school drooling after you...everything just comes so easy for you. It's not fair."

"Oh yeah? Well, you'll be happy to know that I'm officially crazy. I keep having nightmares and painful visions that are just getting worse. Owls seem to follow me everywhere I go, and to top it off, I'm now grounded. I had to sneak out of my house over the weekend."

"Oh, no! Sweet little Evie was grounded? Can't be out past ten o'clock? Spare me!" Lana's mocking tone sent a chill down Evie's spine. She felt her chest constricting, her breath catching in her throat as she struggled to hold back tears.

"You know," Lana continued, "you're just like all those stupid teeny bopper flicks we laugh about where the nerdy girl ends up being beautiful and getting the most popular guy in school and always saying, no way that could happen in real life. Well, the thing is, that's you. And what makes it even worse is you don't even know it! You could have made friends with anyone when you moved here last year. You only chose me because I was the first one to talk to you. You can easily slip right into the crowd you want to be in so badly. I'm letting you! Just go! You were made to be in that world. I was just being selfish."

"Is that really what you think?" Evie responded. "Do you realize I have moved around every two years of my life and never had a best friend? I found it wasn't worth putting in the effort to become close to anyone because I would just have to turn around and leave. You were the only person I met who came into my life and wouldn't take no for an answer. You barged your way in, and I hate to tell you, but I am not letting you go. You mean too much. I need you."

The weight of Evie's words hung in the air, punctuated only by Lana's softened expression. Before either could speak further, Lana's curiosity broke the silence. "So, what happened on Friday?"

"I don't know... I'm terrified, Lana. I swear I'm not making this up. That journal... it's like it's cursed or something. I can't seem to get rid of it."

"We're back to that book again."

"But that's the problem! I swear! There's this woman or demon named Lilith. Blake keeps warning me about her."

"You saw Blake again?"

"Yeah, he keeps appearing and disappearing, telling me to get rid of the journal and to stay away from Damek. And then he shows up at school today like he never left."

"He was at school?" Lana asked, retreating into her own thoughts.

"Yeah," Evie responded, waving her hand to get Lana's attention. "What's going on, Lana? What aren't you telling me?"

"Funny. Now you even have Blake following you around."

"Stop this!" Evie yelled. "Did you hear anything I said? What's going on with Blake? You can at least tell me that."

"After a huge blowout with Dad, he split. I only saw him briefly before the party on Friday. He just wanted to make sure I was okay. He wouldn't tell me where he was staying."

Evie had the uncanny feeling Lana was lying.

"Anyway, the other day, I was looking around his bedroom for any sign of where he would've gone, and I noticed a couple of strands of blond hair on his pillow. They were a little odd, though. I mean, they were so blond that they looked more like doll hair than real hair. Shiny like. I assumed he split with that bleach-blond bimbo he was dating. I heard him talking to her a few times. These walls are pretty thin."

"Blake's dating someone?" Evie furrowed her brow.

"Nice, Evie. That's what you would hear. Why do you care anyway?"

Ashamed of her train of thought, Evie tried to change the subject. "Wait. He just left you here alone with your Dad, knowing what could happen?"

"Look, you'll never understand," Lana said, shaking her head.

"You're probably right, but something needs to change," Evie insisted.

"Everything's fine. I am who I am, and you are who you are. Please just leave," Lana said, rising from the bed and crossing over to the open window.

"How can you say that?" Evie's voice cracked.

"Because I am. You'll be fine. You always are, right?"

"Please, Lana," Evie pleaded softly, feeling lost for words. The news of Blake threw her off guard. He was dating someone.

"Just go," Lana said, gesturing towards the open window.

Focusing back on Lana, Evie scratched the back of her head. The guilt washed through her. How dare she think of a boy at a time like this. Lana was right. She wasn't worth being a best friend. "Are you coming back to school?"

"I haven't added 'dropout' to my list yet. Now, please, just go. It's almost five o'clock, and my Dad will be home soon."

Surprised by how quickly the afternoon had slipped away, Evie glanced at Lana one last time, realizing she really did need to go. If she didn't get home soon, her parents would start worrying, especially after being grounded. As she climbed out the window, a brief image of Damek flashed before her. Her head ached with a reprimand of sorts. She had missed fencing practice, including her session with Damek.

"Crap!" Evie muttered as she hit the ground with a thud, the mud seeping around her shoes and soaking the hems of her jeans. As soon as her fingers left the windowsill, the window crashed down with the click of the latch. It felt like the end of something. It was time to get rid of the journal once and for all.

13. Normal

November came and went. With the cold weather blowing in, the nightmares, Lilith, the owls, and Lana disappeared. After that faithful fight in October, Evie immediately went home and buried the journal deep in the recesses of her closet. The deep corners that actually ate the contents and were never seen again. She couldn't quite bring herself to return it to school. It had become a tangible figment of her imagination rather than a real object.

She continued her campaign of calling Lana every day. Even with no answer, she felt closer just keeping her best friend informed of the daily Hillcrest gossip over voicemail. It had become routine. With Lana gone, Blake returned to school on a regular basis. He was passing around the rumor that Lana had mono. In High School, the kissing disease was always bound to improve one's social ranking. Since then, he continued to bring all her work home. Blake became what Evie liked to call, 'The Shadow.' No matter where she went, Evie could feel his presence not far behind; especially after fencing practice. It had become a ritual of sorts. Walking her to her car or driving her home, he always asked the same questions. Had anything happened with Damek, had she had any more nightmares, blah, blah, blah? After a month of the third degree, she thought he would finally give up. He never did. Hearing some of the romantic rumors surrounding the two of them, she tried to break the ice. However, each time she tried to get closer to him, he would push her away with one of his flippant remarks. He was determined just to annoy her. It was enough to drive a person, or at least a sixteen-year-old hormonal girl, crazy.

Damek continued to work with her on fencing. Nothing was ever brought up about the tension at his house and he never invited her there again, nor anywhere for that matter. If it didn't have to do with fencing, they didn't talk. In fact, he pretty much ignored her if she happened to see him in the halls. However, their weekly fencing practices were her favorite part of the week, minus his cold shoulder. She had fallen in love. In love with a sword that is. The weapon of choice acting like an anchor to her inner reality. The stronghold to her emotions. When held, she became the backbone of her own faith. She was a natural. Her entire surroundings disappeared the moment she stepped onto the fencing strip with the grip held tight in her hand. Her only soundtrack was the squeal of tennis shoes on the gym floor and the dull clack of the practice foils echoing off the padded walls. She was ashamed that she couldn't direct the same determination into her everyday life. She had surpassed all the beginners and was starting to give the advanced fencers a run for their money.

Many of them stuck around after practice just to see Evie get fairly close to beating Damek. Even her parents were excited. With her grades dramatically improving, Evie woke up one weekend to her very own fencing jacket and three-weapon mask sitting on her dresser. The next weekend she found a Foil Belgian Pistol Grip laying against her bed. She was pretty sure her father was buttering her up. Just this morning she found a college flyer about the Air Force Academy sitting on the kitchen counter. An image of the Women's Fencing Team printed on the front; Top notch according to the brief sales pitch. Her mother encouraged the fencing as well, but seem to know that something else was wrong. Evie did her best to ignore her worried looks over the dinner table.

Her days had become mundane once again. New gossip surpassed her days as a 'floozy' and life went on. Even the owls and smoke-filled mirrors no longer made an appearance. Sitting in the lunch room, Evie looked around the room at the normal groups. Everything was back to normal. It was as if she was able to put a cork in whatever battle was imminent. A cork keeping her life on pause. Sitting alone in the school cafeteria munching on her apple she wondered if Lana was ever going to come back. Letting her gaze wander over to the jock table for the umpteenth time, looking for the familiar blond hair, she realized she had become the social group of one, well, make that two.

"Hey, Evie" Sitting down across the table from Evie, Seth placed a candy cane on her tray. "Tis the season..."

"Nice, Seth." Picking up the candy with her fingers she struggled with the wrapper.

"You know, it's been kinda nice having Lana out. I mean, you know, so we can hang out more." Pulling the candy out of Evie's hand he tore open the small bit of plastic. "Everything ok between the two of you?"

"Yeah, things are fine." Evie stammered. Reaching for the candy, she plopped the small cane into her mouth. Sitting with Seth was becoming her regular lunchtime routine. In the beginning, his friends would sit with them, but slowly they all started to sit at other tables leaving only Seth behind.

"So, any plans for New Year's?" he asked, biting into his hamburger.

"Hadn't thought about it." Evie glanced over her shoulder to where Damek and Lexi were sitting. Strike that-Damek was sitting, and Lexi was conveniently propped on his lap. Looking back at Seth, she caught the wrinkle on his forehead. She took a bite of her apple. "I mean, it's not even Christmas yet," she mumbled.

Ignoring her comment, Seth dropped his burger on his plate and wiped his hands. "You interested in doing something? I mean, unless that is you aren't doing anything with Damek or whoever..." Making it obvious, Seth rolled his eyes toward the jock table. "I don't know why you continue fencing. You know he isn't into you, right?"

Evie picked up one of the fries on his tray and threw it in his face. "That's not why I'm fencing!" Getting the reaction she wanted she returned his smile. "Besides, I'm actually good at it."

"Yeah, I know. I've heard."

"Why do you even continue to hang out with me? No one else does. Even my own best friend fake's mono because she doesn't wanna see me."

"That's not true. It's just, well, after that night of Trace's party..." Swirling one of his fries in ketchup, he became silent.

"Yeah, I know. I'm the new school slut. Maybe I should make it official and try out for the cheerleading squad."

"Nice Evie. You know if you need any help in that department," Seth joked.

"I was kidding. Besides, I thought that gossip was old news."

"It is." Looking back into her eyes, Seth shrugged his shoulders. "Look, you just need to make a choice. You're sitting in limbo. You either need to join that group you keep staring at or..."

"You sound like Lana," Evie interrupted.

"Well, she's probably right," Seth agreed, raising his voice. "You need to start being yourself again. What happened to the fun Evie?"

"I don't know..." Evie sighed.

"You need to start doing the things you used to. Believe me, I've known Lana way before you showed up. She'll be fine and back as soon as you know it. Everything will go back to the way it was."

"Why do you dislike Lana so much anyway?"

"It's complicated." He pushed his lunch tray away from him.

"Try me."

"Lana and I go way back. All the way back to Kindergarten."

"Really? That's cool." Shoving her elbows onto the table, Evie propped her head in her hands.

"Yeah, not so much. We used to play tag on the playground. Back then, my mom used to put me in these stupid jeans that were way too big- probably hand-me-downs from my brother. Anyway, Lana thought it was funny to pull my pants down whenever she would tag me. She was always taller and much faster than me."

"Seriously? That's it," laughed Evie. "And that's why you guys are mortal enemies?"

"Hey! Getting your pants pulled down by a girl in front of everyone is pretty damaging to a kid's reputation."

"Hmmm...interesting..." Evie tried not to smile.

"Enough with all the drama. So are you coming over to my place for New Year's or not? My parents are having a party and I was gonna invite a few people."

"Um, yeah, I guess." A high-pitched laugh coming from the jock table caught Evie's attention. Looking over her right shoulder, she found Damek staring at her. With a wrinkle in his brow, he seemed to be trying to figure out an unanswered question. His gaze caused an excited flutter in her stomach. She couldn't look away. Feeling the slight burn in her eyelids, she blinked. The connection was lost and Damek rejoined his friends' boisterous conversation. Slapping Trace on the back, Damek tipped his head up to the ceiling and laughed. Lexi playfully pulled on one of his curly blond locks hanging over his left eye. Evie's fist clenched into a tight ball. Trying to relax her fingers, she slowly turned back to Seth.

Seth crossed his arms on the table. "So your fencing competition is tomorrow, right?"

Evie took a quick drink of water. She tried to focus on what Seth was saying, rather than the brief interlude with Damek. She had probably imagined the whole thing. Slowly screwing the top back on the water bottle, she took a breath. "Yeah, it is. Time has gone by fast. I can't believe the end of the semester is almost here."

"You ready?"

"I think so. I don't know how to explain it. I just feel so...free when I'm fencing." A picture of a sword surrounded by a dull blue light flashed in her mind.

"Sounds interesting." Standing up with his tray, Seth glanced at the exit. "I have to get going."

Surprised by his disinterest, Evie grabbed her tray and stood up. "Wait. What's wrong?"

"Nothing. I just need to see Ryan before the period bell rings." Walking over to the garbage can he placed his tray on top.

"Seth, wait," Evie said, following close behind. "I'm sorry."

"Don't worry about it. Just don't forget about New Year's, Ok?"

"Looking forward to it." She threw her apple in the garbage and swung back around to walk out with Seth, only to find him heading out of the cafeteria. She wondered why she couldn't like someone like Seth, a guy that thought the world of her. Enough so, that he even gave up hanging out with his friends to be with her. Perhaps that was her problem; the next step she needed to get her life back to normal - asking Seth out. She waited for him to turn and wave, planning to give him one of her brightest smiles. He never turned around.

Gazing around the rest of the cafeteria, she realized that Seth was right. She needed to get involved and figure out what she wanted. Her current plan of doing nothing wasn't working out so well. It was time to make her social life a priority. Taking one glance in Damek's direction almost choked her. Lexi was heading out as well and giving Damek a pretty sultry goodbye kiss. Evie picked up the pace to the exit. Outside of the cafeteria, another long lunch table was covered with a white cloth. Paper snowflakes hung down from the sides, creating a makeshift winter wonderland. Evie recognized the two girls sitting behind the table as some of Lexi's friends. Above their heads hung a green banner calling to the student masses in large red ink.

Sign up to decorate your Class Hall for the holidays!
The best hall wins $100 for their Class Activity Fund!

She could hear Seth's voice in her head. She walked up to the table before she lost her courage.

The brunette turned to Evie and smiled. "Would you like to sign up? What year are you?"

"Sophomore."

After handing Evie the list, the brunette turned back to her blond friend and continued her animated conversation about some freshmen girl puking in the bathroom.

"Thanks," scribbling her name into the third spot on the list she heard someone walk up behind her.

"Hey, Lexi," the brunette smiled, looking past Evie.

Evie cringed, silently repeating her new priority. She looked up from the list and smiled at the one person she hated the most. "Hi, Lexi."

"Um, hey," Lexi said, excusing Evie with a brief look. She turned back to her friends and picked up the junior list. "We are so gonna win this year!"

Straightening her blue and gold cheerleader top, the blond behind the table gestured to the rest of the papers on it. "So far, we have the most volunteers."

"Of course we do." Placing the list back on the table, Lexi winked. "I have to go girls. Keep up the good work." Ignoring Evie, she flipped her hair over her shoulder and headed down the hall.

"Aw, now isn't that sweet?" interrupted a new voice.

Evie straightened her back, recognizing Blake's usual sneer.

"Signing up to help your classmates. Now that is what I call getting involved."

"Shut up," Evie pushed her book bag further up her shoulder and tried to get away from the table as fast as possible. Blake grabbed her arm.

"I was just kidding. Stop being so sensitive."

Before Evie could respond, a giggle came from the table. "Hey, Blake."

"Hey, Heather," Blake responded with one of those annoying boyish head bobs.

Evie tugged harder.

"We're so glad you're back," Heather smiled.

"Thanks. See you in Chem." As Evie watched the blond girl hit Heather in the arm, she tried to overhear their whispers. She could just make out a few words.

"Heather, stop. He's a stoner." The blond girl curled her upper lip and briefly met Blake's gaze. He gave a lazy wink and started pulling Evie down the hall. "Come on let's go. History, right?"

"Um, yeah." She yanked her arm out of his grasp and frowned. "Stalk much?"

"Now come on. You know you'd miss me."

She couldn't believe that just four months ago she could barely say two words to the guy. What had she been thinking? He was a total mess. "Don't you have more important things to do?" she asked, picking up her pace down the hall.

"Like what?"

"Oh, I don't know. Getting high or," nodding her head back toward the girls at the winter table, she continued, "perhaps hang out with one of them?"

Blake took a second to respond because he couldn't stop laughing. "I have too much going on right now to think about girls."

"What about the blond bimbo I heard about?"

"Blond bimbo?"

"Yeah," Evie said, stopping in front of him. "The last time I talked to Lana, she said you were seeing some blond."

"That's right. I forgot about that. Lana told me you came over. I wouldn't recommend doing that again. I just might have to up my surveillance routine."

With a grunt of frustration, Evie started walking again. "You didn't answer my question."

Blake easily caught up. "About what?"

"The blond bimbo."

"Oh, yeah. Why are you so concerned about my love life anyway?"

"Hey, if you're gonna drill me on my daily activities then I should be able to do the same in return."

"Fair enough," he responded, pushing her to the side of the hall. He pulled a forgotten pencil out of her ponytail and handed it to her. "To be honest, I've no clue what you're talking about."

"Think harder, please. Lana said she found some blond hair on your pillow."

"She did, did she?"

"Would you just answer the question?"

"I just don't think you can handle the truth quite yet." With a wink, he gestured toward her history class. "This is you. Later."

Evie bite her lower lip and watched Blake duck into the adjacent restroom. Fighting the urge to stomp her feet, she swung around and headed into Ms. Langston's room. She wondered if Blake was actually going to class or just hiding out in the bathroom stalls until he could easily make his way to the bleachers with the rest of the potheads.

"Jerk," Evie whispered, dropping into her usual chair and pulling her notebook out of her bag.

When the last bell finally rang, Evie thought the day would never end. She made a beeline for her locker and couldn't wait to get to the gym. Her favorite part of the week was finally here. Pulling her books out of her bag, she paused at a drawing sketched on the front of her geometry book- a crude picture of a rose with the name Lilith entwined at the stem. Grabbing a pen from her bag, she scribbled over the image and shoved the book into her locker. She chanted the word "normal" in her head and grabbed her fencing gear.

Entering the gym, she made her usual perusal of the room looking for Damek and Professor Mike. Nothing out of the ordinary had happened since she got rid of the journal, but like everything else, it had become routine. Placing her bag on the bleachers, she caught Damek's attention talking to a group of beginners. It was now or never. With a smile, she waved at him. Surprised, he made an awkward motion with his hand that Evie could only assume was his attempt at a return wave. Securing her vest, she picked up her foil and headed over to the group starting to form in the middle of the gym.

"Hey, Evie!" said Sam, knocking into the side of her. "Think today's the day you beat Damek? We've started a bet and my money's on you."

"I would've thought you'd be betting against me?" laughed Evie. "Remember you and I have a match tomorrow night?"

"Eh, who are we kidding? You know you're gonna win." Bending down to tie his shoe, he looked back up at Evie. "But it won't be so bad if you beat Damek as well. Then I have an excuse. How could I beat someone that had already beaten the best of the best? Right?"

"Gotcha. So the sooner I beat Damek the better."

"You got it." Standing back up, he straightened his worn-out fencing vest.

"I'll see what I can do." Evie hadn't felt this light-hearted in a while. Her laugh even caught Damek's attention. He was standing next to the professor and motioned for her to join them. She smiled, knowing nothing could ruin this part of the day. She stopped in front of Damek and turned to Professor Mike. "Hi."

"Hey," Damek interrupted. "You're in a good mood."

"I am, aren't I? I kinda feel giddy. You know there's a bet that I will beat you today."

He stared at Evie like she had two heads. "I guess that's better than all the sulking you've been doing."

She shrugged her shoulders and widened her smile. "I haven't been sulking."

"Evie," interrupted Professor Mike, "I was hoping to speak with you for a second if you don't mind."

"Sure, no problem."

Damek gave her a confused look and headed over to the beginners. "Join us when you're done," he said.

"Yes, sir." Evie responded, accidentally giving Damek her practiced salute.

Professor Mike smiled at Evie and asked, "I assume Damek has been a good teacher?"

"Sometimes," Evie responded too quickly. "I mean, yes, he has."

With a slight pause, the Professor moved his right hand toward Evie. His fingers made a slow roundabout before resting on his chin. "I wanted to commend you on your skills. It seems you are picking up the sport fairly quickly."

Not realizing that she took a slight step back, Evie quirked a smile. "Thank you. It grounds me. It's hard to explain."

"No, I could not agree more. I have been watching you. You immerse yourself in it completely, just like someone else I once knew." He cleared his throat and lingered on his last statement before continuing. "I look forward to moving you into the advanced group soon, if not by the end of the semester."

"Wow, thank you!"

"By the way, I know about the competition."

"Oh," surprised by his admission, Evie wasn't sure how to respond.

"Do not worry. I am not upset. Besides, it seems to be drawing a lot of interest from prospective students. I just wanted to make sure that you were comfortable."

"Oh, yeah. I'm fine." Keeping her full attention on the Professor, she began to sense his awkwardness, almost akin to the strange attraction she felt around Damek. She shook the crazy thought aside and glided her tongue over the raw skin on the inside of her cheek.

"I also heard from Damek's mother that you stopped by their house."

"Um, yeah I did." Her teeth bit down on her cheek again.

"Sorry, I do not mean to sound like I am giving you the third degree. I am just curious, is all. I have known Damek's mother since she was a little girl."

"Oh,"

"She mentioned that you were interested in some of their collectibles. Mainly a portrait of Michael the Archangel?"

Shifting uncomfortably, Evie tried to picture the worn print. "Well, everything was pretty cool. I, just, well..." She didn't know what to say and found herself concentrating on the Professor's chin.

"The picture has always been one of my favorites as well. By the way, one of the advanced students said they lost some sort of personal book. You did not happen to find anything, did you? I asked the rest of the class the day you were out."

"Um..." The butterflies started again. She couldn't think. "No, I didn't see anything."

"Hmm... Are you sure?"

"No. I'm sorry."

The Professor was lost in thought and gazed at Evie before scanning the rest of the students. He focused on the advanced group and turned back toward Evie with a light smile. "Maybe he just forgot where he put it. In any case, I'm excited for the upcoming match."

A million questions swirled in Evie's mind. Did he say the owner was a guy? Should she ask him who? Was it Damek? Instead, she said, "Oh, you're coming?"

"I would not miss it. It has created quite a buzz. I would not be surprised if the whole school showed up."

She suddenly felt nauseous. Why did she have to lie about the book?

"Are you ok?" Professor Mike asked, lightly placing his hand on her shoulder. "You do not look so good."

A soothing warmth seeped into her belly.

The Professor quickly pulled his hand away and examined her expression closely.

Evie took a deep breath and contemplated heading to the bathroom. "No, I'll be fine."

"I better let you get back to practice. I will be rooting for you," he said with a slight nod of his head. He reached his hand out briefly, but then quickly pulled it back to his side.

Evie watched the Professor head to the advanced students and tried to concentrate back on her sword. After a few deep breaths, her pulse slowed down.

The practice continued as normal, with Evie playing guinea pig to the attacks Damek was instructing. The only difference was that Damek seemed happy to see her again. He joked and was once again the carefree Damek that she remembered from the first class. As the last student was finishing their assigned movement, Trace walked up and swiped over the top of Damek's blade with his own.

"Hey man, I can't stay after today for practice, so you guys have the gym to yourselves," Trace said, scanning the growing crowd on the bleachers. "Oh yeah, I forgot you guys have quite the following now." He punched Damek in the arm and grabbed his duffel bag. "Good Luck and don't forget to lock up."

Damek ignored Trace's comment and pointed Evie to the fencing line. "So, you think you can beat me, huh?" With a grin, he got into position. "Let's give them a show then."

"You aren't gonna make this easy are you?"

"Too bad you can't carry around a sword everywhere you go. I like this Evie much better."

"What are you talking about? You don't know me."

"Doesn't matter," he responded quickly.

"Wait you guys," Sam interrupted still wearing his gear. "How about you guys do a match of four points? I'll judge."

"Why don't you practice against her instead?" Damek asked.

"No way! I have money riding on this one."

"Ah, I see how it is."

"Good," Sam smiled, pointing to the fencing strip. "Now get into positions please." He turned to the group of students on the bleachers and gave a quick two thumbs up. A few of them cheered.

Evie dragged her feet to the en garde line, unable to forget Damek's last words. She moved into position and found herself focusing on his feet.

"Alright everyone," Sam yelled towards the audience, "It's go time!"

After bowing quickly to Damek, Evie shoved her mask over her head and whispered, "I do matter."

"Did you say something, Evie?" Sam asked.

"No." Determined to prove Damek wrong, she yelled, "En garde."

She could feel Damek's intensity radiating across the small line. She placed her left arm up behind her and moved into position. Everything around her disappeared as she pointed her sword at an angle- anticipation hanging in the air. In her subconscious, she couldn't shake the image of Damek's house, causing everything else to blur. The only things she could focus on were the swords and the sound of a violin's strings keeping time with a pounding bass.

Giving Damek the first attack he took a quick gallop forward extending his foil. Turning his weapon aside with a quick whack, she tried a direct hit to his chest only to feel her blade forced down low. She knew he was smiling. She could feel it. Straightening his sword he beaconed to her. Lunging she went for the attack, only to miss her mark completely. The next three points made her look like a complete idiot. Even taking a break to switch sides, hadn't changed the momentum. This was Damek's game to win. She stared at the mask in front of her and tried to forget who was beneath it. Suddenly, lightning flashed before her eyes and a woman with flowing blonde hair appeared suspended in the space between them.

"Not now," Evie whispered, knowing she was the only one who could see her.   She could feel the disappointment in the stands. Every student there was praying that someone would finally beat the best of the best. A weight pressed against her chest. The witch's words echoed in her ear as the vision dissipated, "You can do this, my sweet."

Evie envisioned Damek's sandy hair and relaxed smile as she tried to assess his next move. Suddenly, an unknown force caused her shoes to slide toward him, sending a shock down her legs. She lunged forward, but Damek swiftly blocked her sword, causing her to recoil. With a surge of adrenaline, she tried again but was met with another jarring hit from his foil. Evie felt like a scolded child as she tensed up in response.

Damek took advantage of her position and charged ahead, colliding with the center of her sword. A jolt of shock traveled down the foil, causing her arms to shake. He let out a loud laugh and moved his weapon in a quick circle. Evie could see her own failure in slow motion. Tumbling forward, she took his final hit to her side.

Damek bent over her back, making sure not to touch her. "Did you really think you could beat me?"

"Out to prove something?" she gasped not moving a muscle.

"No. I was just expecting more." He stood back up and examined the grip on his blade. "I love being right."

"What are you talking about?" Evie asked, standing up to rub a brief cramp in her side.

"Nothing."

Sam walked up to Evie and slapped her on the back. "Don't take it too hard. No one's ever beaten Damek. Besides, you held him off longer than anyone else has." He headed toward the bleachers and handed a ten-dollar bill to one of the advanced students.

"Yeah, Evie," Damek teased. "Don't take it too hard." He reached for a bottle of water out of his gym bag and tossed it to Evie.

She managed to catch the bottle and remained sprawled on the floor as the rest of the students quickly filed out of the gym.

Damek stored the last of the fencing equipment in the closet and secured it with a jiggling lock. "Are you just gonna sit there all night?" He grabbed his duffle bag off the bleachers and swung it over his shoulder.

"Sorry," Evie said. "I was just thinking about stuff."

"That sounds dangerous," Damek smirked.

Evie pushed off the cold floor and stood up. "I, uh, never really apologized for Trace's party."

"What are you talking about?"

"I could tell that you were pretty pissed. Anyway, I just wanted to say I'm sorry." Taking a deep breath, she continued, "To be honest, I don't even remember what happened. Even my best friend isn't talking to me."

"What do you mean you don't remember what happened?"

"I don't remember even being at the party. One minute I was in my room getting dressed and the next I woke up in the bushes with Lana yelling at me." She paused and grabbed her stuff off the bleachers. "But that's not the point..."

"You're telling me that you don't remember being at the party and that's not the point...?"

"No! I...Look, I just wanted to apologize."

Damek gazed at her silently for a moment before letting out a sigh. "No, I'm sorry. I had no right to be mad at you. It just didn't seem like you." His eyes shifted downwards towards the floor. "Not that I know you well, since we just met, but something felt off." He stepped closer to her, his eyes locking onto her bowed head. "Do you think someone might have slipped something into your drink?"

"To be honest, it's a long..." she paused, recalling his previous question about Lilith a few days ago.

"Long what?" Damek prompted.

"Do you remember asking me about Lilith?" Evie asked, lifting her head.

He fumbled with one of the straps on his duffel. "I don't know what you're talking about."

"I think you do."

"We need to get going. It's getting late."

"Please, Damek..." encouraged by his silence, she continued, "I've been having these nightmares...or, at least I was. They've seemed to stop recently. But there is always a woman named Lilith in them."

"It was just a dream?" he asked, running his hand through his hair.

"Yes,"

"And you don't have them anymore?"

"No, but I think it's because..."

"Well that's good," he quickly added.

"Maybe, but why did you ask me about Lilith?"

"Hmm," he thought, "I don't remember. But come on. We need to get going. I have a date with Lexi tonight." He started to head to the gym doors.

"No, stop! You aren't talking your way out of this one. I know what you said."

"Just drop it."

"No," she said, running to block the exit.

"Think you can hold me here?" he challenged with a cocky grin.

Evie bit her lip, starting to lose her courage. "I need to know, Damek."

As he placed his hands on her shoulders, he suddenly stopped and held his breath. He looked into her eyes, hoping to find a clue or an answer, but his smile faded.

Evie noticed her own uneasy feelings reflected back at her. A shiver ran down her spine and gathered in her thighs, while heat followed closely behind. She struggled to catch her breath and couldn't seem to shake off the overwhelming sensation.

"Do you feel that?" she whispered.

Shaking his head, he yanked his hands off her shoulders and began to pace.

"Do you know what it is?" she asked.

"How naive are you?" Damek bit out.

"Oh, shut up! I know what attraction is. I've met enough guys to understand the butterflies in my stomach."

Anger contorted his face as he made a beeline for her. Out of fear, Evie stumbled backward.

"How many guys have you known?" The edge in his voice was foreign.

She could feel the cushion of the padded wall against her back.

"Stop," Evie cried, holding up her hands to her chest and gesturing for him to step back.

Damek shook his head. "I'm sorry, Evie." He turned towards the empty coach's office. "I have to go."

"Wait, that's it?" she asked.

"What do want from me? One minute you're teasing me and the next you're pushing me away. I don't have time for this. Grab your stuff. I need to lock up."

"Coward," Evie whispered.

"What did you call me?"

"Nothing. Just forget it." Heading to the exit, she gasped when Damek's hands dug into her upper arms as he spun her around. She lost all thought.

"Is this what you want?" He leaned in close, his hand delicately brushing against her cheek, bringing his face within an inch of her lips.

"Yes," her assent was barely audible, but it was all Damek needed. His lips took hers in a rabid hunger that wrapped a cold hand around her heart and squeezed. His tongue demanded entrance as her lips parted on their own accord. Evie's body humming with contentment, regardless of the vulgarity of the punishment. Wrapping her arms around his neck, liquid heat pumped through her veins, urging her for more. The internal fire turned into a damn inferno, as her hips thrust forward, causing a slight whimper. Just as she started to understand the innate rhythm, the source of the heat was ripped away. Registering the loss, confusion set in. She tried to focus on Damek bent over with his hands on his knees when she remembered to breathe.

Looking at the floor, he cleared his throat. "I'm sorry,"

"No...it was," fascinated, Evie tried to put the intense feelings into a coherent thought.

"Something that can't happen again," Damek interjected.

"Why not?"

"It just can't. You don't understand." Lifting his head, he became distracted by something in the coach's office. His features became hard. "Because I said so. I don't like you that way." He quickly bent down to grab the bag he had dropped during their brief encounter.

Evie could feel the tears gathering in her eyes. "What's wrong with me?" She looked into the coach's office and saw nothing but her distorted image.

"It's not you, it's me," he sneered, looking her straight in the eyes.

She tried to hide the tears. She was suffocating.

"By the way," Damek added, "that was our last practice. See you tomorrow night." He headed towards the exit, lifting the back of his hand in a brief farewell as if nothing had happened.

She wanted to jump out of her skin. An uncomfortable twist in her stomach had her racing to reach the exit first. She turned back towards Damek and looked him straight in the eyes. "I thought you were different, but I was wrong. You are just like every other jock. I wouldn't want to tarnish your reputation. Go back to your beautiful air-headed cheerleader."

He met her stare with a subtle twitch of his eye-his smile sardonic as he added, "At least we see eye to eye." Then, he saluted her by touching his finger to his forehead.

She ran out of the gym, tears blurring her vision. Suddenly, she heard a loud bang echoing through the school hall. She skidded to a halt and leaned against a locker. Everything was eerily silent. The hairs on the back of her neck began to rise when she realized she couldn't even hear the old air ducts making their usual clanking sound. Damek's anger was something she knew she didn't want to see. She fled from the school and jumped into her car. The goosebumps continued their reign down her arms and over her legs. Thanking her lucky stars that she had the car today, she revved up the engine and pulled out of the parking lot.

She blasted the heat and turned on the radio. Sounds of her father's favorite Beethoven classics flooded the car. The first flutters of 'Für Elise' had her biting her lower lip, as she pushed herself up in the seat to look at her reflection in the rear-view mirror. She had finally experienced her first kiss. Of course, Damek hadn't felt a thing. How could he? Watching the road ahead she wondered if the kiss had been meant to scare and punish her. But for what? The force behind the seemingly gentle touch made her heart race. Who knows what she would have done if Damek had not pushed her away? It had to be just a normal reaction to a first kiss, but why did her body seem to have a different opinion?

She pulled up to the house as the front porch lights came on. With winter here, the days seemed to be getting shorter. Dragging her bag out of the car, she glanced at the tree at the end of the drive. A common practice these days. Still, no owls to speak of. Nothing but bare branches. Walking into the house, only the comforting sounds of the cuckoo clock greeted her.

"Mom?" Evie called into the empty kitchen. The message light on the house phone was blinking its red hazy hue over the center island. After turning on the lights, she hit the message button on the house phone. Her mom's cheerful voice filled the room.

"Hey, Evie. Your Dad surprised me for our Anniversary. We're headed out to dinner. Not sure where yet, as your father says it would ruin the surprise. Anyway, I tried reaching you on your cell phone. Please call when you get this. It makes me nervous when you don't answer your phone. Love you!"

"Crap!" Evie said, hitting her hand against the counter. She knew she had forgotten something. Picking up the phone she quickly dialed her mom's cell number.

"Hey, Mom. Sorry, I didn't pick up! Happy Anniversary!"

"Hey, baby!" her mom responded, "You had me worried!"

Evie tried to keep her emotions at bay. "I was practicing at the gym. I'm home now."

"Everything ok? You sound a little off."

"No, I'm fine." Evie squeezed the bridge of her nose. So much for her acting abilities.

"You sure?"

"Yeah, promise. I'm just tired."

"Take it easy tonight. You've been pretty busy lately."

"No, I will. Just gonna finish up some homework. Enjoy yourselves. Tell Dad I love him."

"Will do. Love you! See you in a bit."

"Love you too Mom."

Evie hung up the phone and opened the fridge. She stared at the leftover meatloaf and carton of milk. Smiling, she remembered how her mother used to tell her that a glass of milk could cure any problem. Too bad that didn't seem to work once you were over the age of ten. She opted for a bag of apple slices and slowly made her way up to her room. She dropped her bag on the floor and stared at the small space. She felt different. Her fingernail dug into the middle of her lower lip. She put the empty snack bag on her dresser just before the tears took over. She smashed her face into her pillow when a high-pitch-rattling noise caught her attention. Turning her head slightly to the side, she gasped and jumped off the bed. Her closet doors were shaking on the hinges. Just when she grabbed a small pink stapler off her desk to use as her only weapon, the rattling stopped. A blue smoke drifted through the breaks in the accordion doors, carrying the sweet smell of roses in its wake.

"Come on!" she yelled, "Come and get me! I'm not scared anymore!"

The smoke evaporated into thin air, leaving nothing of its existence behind. She walked over to the closet, holding her weapon higher, and yanked the doors open. Nothing looked out of place, except for perhaps the red top on the floor. She bent over to pick up the painful reminder of Trace's party when she noticed the journal laying underneath the flimsy material. The journal she had abandoned to the monster in the closet. Not even he wanted it. She had missed the worn leather binding holding the enchanted contents. Even without the book, her life seemed to be one disaster after the next. The stapler fell from her fingers as she grazed the front stone. The expected silky dew sunk into her fingertips.

Embracing the obsession, she pulled the book into her lap. The familiar craving gnawed at her insides, leaving her no choice but to flip to the next entry. Just the first sentence instantly relaxed the beast she had residing inside.

14. Diary Gossip

May 4, 1893

Tonight, I write from inside a damp cave hidden from the enemy. With the light of a crackling fire and surrounded by an army of five, we prepare for battle. The smell of burnt wood penetrates the small space and suffocates my senses. I can hardly describe what has happened over the last few days. Only the sounds of the incoming waves help to keep me grounded. The same sea I used to visit as a child. If only everything were so simple again. I have missed you. So accustomed to communicating my thoughts and wishes, it felt rather strange not to talk to you. You have become my anchor. I only hope that I will be able to finish my story. I shall start in the past with my brief meeting with the Demoness herself.

I opened my eyes and gazed at the gilded gold trim decorating the top of my four-poster bed. Everything was always better after a good rest. A slight smile spread across my lips.

"I am sorry, My lady. Did I wake you?" interrupted my maid Cecilia. She poured water from a pitcher into a glass on my nightstand. I tried to gain my bearings as I sat up in bed.

"I am not sure. How long have I been sleeping?"

"Only for a few hours, Miss. We need to start getting ready for the ball."

Confused, I glanced around my room, hoping to find any recollection of how I made it to my bed. "Cecilia, how did I get here? If I remember correctly, I was in the library last."

"Yes, Miss. You fell asleep. Lord Wyndham brought you to your room, and I ensured you were comfortably settled in. He was concerned that you had not been getting enough sleep. How are you feeling now?" she inquired, placing her hand on my forehead.

"Much better, thank you," I responded, pushing her away. I lifted my legs off the side of the bed and concentrated on a crease in my top skirt. "Did you say Lord Wyndham carried me?"

"Yes, My Lady. Though, I would not let him stay in here like he wanted. You were only asleep for an hour, and he had already asked about you." She paused and continued, "Handsome fellow, he is miss."

I pushed off the bed and grabbed the glass of water. I tried to change the subject. "Did you see Master Senoy?"

"*No, Miss,*" *she said with a look of disappointment.*

A Lady is never supposed to indulge in gossip. For once, I was adhering to that rule of etiquette. "Thank you, Cecilia. I think I will take a quick walk in the garden to clear my head."

"Do not be too long. Your mother picked out a new gown for you, and we must make you look your best."

"Lovely," I grimaced, "I will be back shortly."

I headed out the garden's side door, ensuring not to pass by the library. It had become the den of choice for the new band of Gods trying to test my patience. I needed to sort out my feelings. The last thing I remembered was being surrounded by angels. To my human eyes, it was merely the best male specimens creation had to offer. Their bodies readied for battle, and their faces that of the most abominable rakes. I felt tricked by the one person I held most dear. Master Senoy was like a father. Why did it feel like a different kind of love was beginning to surpass that fatherly emotion? Could an archangel even love a human? A picture of black hair and dark-looking eyes stole my attention. A God in his own right, but definitely no angel. Lord Wyndham was the epitome of every match-making mama in perhaps the country. Mother and Father would be ecstatic over such a match, as it would be the talk of the ton. Raising my arm to block out the sun, I realized I had made my way back to Venus. I pondered her stoned perfection, immersing my complaints in the water trickling from her worn feet. The pungent smell of the best English Tea wafted through my senses. I had finally found peace.

"Ah," a musical voice whispered in my ear, "the Daughter of Heaven and Sea."

My breath caught. Nab's goddess's overly bright blue eyes were staring at me like a lion assessing its prey. It seemed she was staring into my soul with a look of pure relish dripping from her blood-stained lips. Pure fear raced through my body as my heart tried to pump out of my ribcage. Her blond hair glistened like millions of needles about to launch right at me. Everything about her told me to run as fast as possible, for death was imminent.

"Oh, pardon me," the lioness continued, "I did not mean to scare you."

The fear racing through my body instantly retreated as an invisible haze wrapped around my body, creating a warm cocoon. I was no longer afraid, for the loveliest creature I had ever seen stood before me.

"I was just thinking how brilliant it would be to see you, Miss Evelyn, when, to my luck, you appear right here admiring my favorite goddess."

"Yes, this does happen to be my favorite spot in the garden." Remembering my manners, I gestured to the house behind me. "Are you enjoying your stay so far, Miss Magdolyn? I know Nab is very excited to have you here."

"Please call me Lilith. There is no room for formalities between friends. Your home is beautiful. I must admit, I am a bit jealous. It seems that there are beautiful men everywhere here. You must have the pick of the litter."

"I am sure I do not know what you mean."

"Why of a marriageable sort. Nab told me you were in the market for a husband."

"Sometimes I wish I would have been born a man," I sighed.

"Ah, you are not looking forward to the impending nuptials. Mother and Father afraid their only daughter will become a spinster?"

"If they would just realize I can handle myself perfectly well."

"Yes, if only you were born at another time." Lilith smiled as she pulled a leaf from a nearby rose bush. She touched the bottom of Venus's feet, letting the water trickle over her long fingers.

I knew there was something about Lilith I was supposed to remember, but all thoughts seemed to be drifting from my head one by one.

"Did you know the Romans worshipped Venus as the Goddess of Fertility?" A light laugh tinkled through her mouth as she smiled. "She always did have charm and sensuality."

"Yes, I associated her with Aphrodite, correct?"

"Hmmm...yes. Always different names for the same deities." Slowly walking away from the statue, she sat beside me. Lightly placing my hand in hers, she caressed my open palm. "Are you looking forward to the ball this evening?"

A giddiness danced along my veins with each stroke of her soft fingers. "Very much so." I scooted closer.

"Sadly, your brother is unable to escort me tonight but, in his place, has asked a gentleman named Lord Wyndham. Have you met him?"

The giddiness briefly halted at the spoken name but immediately picked up its beat as her caresses moved up my arm. "Yes, and I am afraid he is quite insufferable."

"In my experience, the insufferable ones are the most fun."

Feeling the brief loll in her tenderness, I gently pulled my arm out of her grasp. "Pardon me for asking, but are you a good friend of my brother's?" I asked.

"Oh, you know how men can be. We met a few times at my parent's house. My mother enjoys a good party for as little money as we have. My brother would always show up late, with Nab in tow. During our last outing, he insisted that I call him Nab and visit him at his beautiful estate." Looking around, she waved her hand at the gardens.

"Pardon me again for my rudeness, but do you have a tendre for my brother?" Her laughter filled the garden. My senses became acute as the laughter chased the nearby birds from their nests. Not one harmonious chirp permeated the deafening silence.

"I am not setting my cap on anyone at the moment, perhaps ever. You see, I have already reached my spinsterhood. It gives me the luxury, or I guess you could say the defiance, to finally experience life." Her eyes twinkled as I became enthralled again with the blue swirls.

"Would not that cause people to gossip?"

"Let them. As women, we have only a few weapons in our possession, and a few of them can be quite powerful. One just needs to learn how to use them." Letting her fingers run through her lengthy hair, she winked at me.

"I can see the attraction my brother has. You are lovely." Staring at the gold flecks in her hair, I tried to stomp down the urge to follow her hands through the glossiness.

"Thank you, Evelyn. I have been blessed, you could say," she smiled, taking my hand and intertwining her fingers with mine. "I do so look forward to more of these talks. Please, you must tell me. Are you interested in anyone in particular?"

"I..." my mind became blank. A wall had quickly constructed itself around my consciousness—a barrier prohibiting any coherent thought.

"I know we just met, but I hope you will learn you can confide in me." Placing her other hand on my cheek, she continued to look into my eyes. The swirls in their depths became yellow the deeper I searched. Breaking the contact, she briefly sniffed the air and quickly looked over her shoulder towards the manor.

"Why I do believe Lord Wyndham has headed this direction. He is quite handsome. I must say I am looking forward to being on his arm tonight. He seems quite virile, does he not?" Tension started to push on my right temple. Lifting my hand to massage it, I looked to where Lord Wyndham stood.

"I thought you said you were not interested in marriage?"

"Getting married and having a bit of fun are two different things, my dear."

"You mean to have an affair with Lord Wyndham?" I asked, the tension moving to the other side of my head.

"Have you heard the stories about him? I hear he has a string of women all pining after him. I heard that is why he decided to join your brother here. He was trying to detangle himself from a scandal concerning a soldier's wife. Let the gossip die down before returning to town."

The pounding in my head turned into a full orchestra.

"I am sorry. Have I distressed you?" she asked.

"No, I just seem to be developing a pounding headache," I gasped.

"Then you must go back this very instant and lie down. I can not have you missing the ball tonight."

Helping me to my feet, Lilith ushered me toward the side entrance.

"It looks like Lord Wyndham is keeping a close eye on us. Are you sure you are not interested in him?"

"No, of course not. Please feel free to pursue him." I walked back towards the house and turned to meet Lord Wyndham's gaze. A question held in his eyes, and I was uncertain if I was supposed to answer.

Continuing to lead me through the side of the garden, Lilith leaned in closer to my ear. "Nab told me yesterday that you are somewhat of a goddess with a sword?"

Breaking my connection with Lord Wyndham, I turned back to her. "I would not say goddess, but I can hold my own."

"Is it true you entered the recent May Fair match as a boy and almost won?" Her excitement became contagious as pride filled my chest.

" Well, yes, but how did you know about that?"

"Oh, you know, men. Never can keep a secret." Patting my hand, she seemed to be trying to cover her blunder. Had Nab told her everything? If it got out, Father would be a laughing stock.

"Do not worry. I will not tell anyone. We should fence sometime. I love a good match."

The fearful thoughts drifted from my mind as fast as they had appeared. "You fence?" I asked, trying to remember what I had been worried about.

"Do not all adventurous ladies?" Reaching the side
door, Lilith pulled away from my arm. *"Until tonight,
Evelyn. I must get ready."* Looking over her shoulder into
the gardens, she quickly leaned close to whisper. *"One
must look their best to snag a lion."* Winking at me, she
turned and headed back into the garden.

"I look forward to it." With heavy feet, I returned
up the stairs to my room.

The lightheaded feeling encompassing my body
rapidly drained through my toes, leaving a cold fear
crashing over my head. The memories from the previous
day flooded back. I quickly closed the door to my room
and ran to the chamber pot, feeling sick and unable to
stop dry heaving. I could not understand what had
happened. Was it a run-in with Lilith the demon or the
stunningly beautiful Miss of the Land that left me feeling
this way?

****

May 4, 1893 (continued) - Evening of the Ball

The bright music and lingering laughter from the
ballroom made me halt at the opened entrance. Standing
up straight, I squared my shoulders, ready for the
onslaught I knew would begin when I walked through
those doors. My hair lay in perfect ringlets, highlighted
with a green satin ribbon matching the dark green
brocade of Mother's latest creation. The newest trend in

fashion did not leave much to the imagination, especially when it came to the bosom. Even the front lacing was designed to draw more attention to the presentation. I can only assume my mother aimed to entice the tournament winner, an assumed betrothal waiting in the wings. Mother and Father will be so disappointed once they discover that the great Lord Wyndham has no such plans! Or did his recent actions suggest otherwise?

If only it were that easy. My life before the tournament had become a fairytale destined for the pages of this notebook. Childish antics have given way to a destiny I did not know of until the very eve of the war. My anger boiled back to the top as I centered all my will against the one person I had decided to detest the most. The angel of deceit. The one I knew my entire life. It was all Senoy's fault and no one else's. Perhaps my mother had been the smartest of all. Subduing all thoughts, I raised my head and entered through the high, majestic doors.

"Lady Evelyn March," came the booming voice from the steward standing on my right.

Silence fell over the crowd as everyone turned their attention to the new arrival. With a few nods and smiles, the buzz of gossip permeating the room regained strength. My mother had outdone herself this time. Candles blazed brightly on every chandelier. Tables of food, tending towards the exotic, graced the side corridor. The doors leading to the balcony were opened, allowing the fresh scent of Mother's prize-winning roses to waft through the opulent room. It felt like a romantic getaway in the heart of the manor. Every male in the near vicinity was giving me a once over, appreciating the view Mother had created. As I approached the refreshment table, my eye caught the only gentleman in the room who had not taken notice of my entrance. Tucked away into a small alcove beside the garden terrace door, Lord Wyndham sat enthralled by only one. Holding Lilith's hand, he leaned closer to whisper in her ear. I could hear her laughter from across the room. I felt my chest constrict.

"There you are," Nab said, walking up to me with a concerned look. "Lady Magdolyn mentioned you were not feeling well."

"No, I am fine. I was just a bit tired."

"Glad to hear it. Mother is on the warpath. Must put on your best tonight, ol' gal." Lifting his drink, he offered one of his bright smiles.

"You make me feel like a horse sometimes."

"You would be best in show." Turning towards the drink table, Nab motioned for a young man to join us.

"Evelyn, allow me to introduce the Duke of Pemberly."

"So nice to meet you." Dropping a slight curtsy, I extended my hand towards the young man, not much taller than me. However, handsome in face and fortune, as his title dictated, he was bound to be a very eligible prize indeed, if I said so myself. A few of the young ladies

just out of the nursery had taken notice and were peering over their open fans.

"The pleasure is all mine." Grasping my hand in his, he bent his head forward.

"Henry, or excuse me, the Duke, is a friend from school. I apologize, but the title is rather fresh. The late Duke, his father, recently passed away."

"I am sorry for your loss," I responded, a bit distracted.

"Please, no need to worry your pretty little head. We were expecting it. I am sure the cantankerous old man is happy to be in the ground." Giving me a wink, I tried to smile. Even now, when I try to describe his looks, I can not quite remember. A pair of dark eyes caught my attention.

"Oh, my," glancing at Nab, I felt the hairs on my neck rise.

"Good Evening, Duke, Lord and Lady March." Giving a slight nod of his head, Lord Wyndham moved into my view, letting his gaze blatantly settle on my chest. "You are looking quite splendid tonight, My Lady."

"Thank you, Lord Wyndham. I was surprised you noticed, being that your attention has been held by someone else this evening." Looking at the small alcove, I tried to hide my grimace.

"Ah," replied Lord Wyndham with the cock of his eyebrow. "One can only hope you were missing me."

"I was doing no such thing. However, if you are looking for someplace private, I would recommend somewhere else than the middle of a packed ballroom."

"Evelyn!" Nab grabbed my arm once more and squeezed.

"I am sorry. I have not been getting enough sleep lately." Looking back to Lord Pemberly, I smiled. "I do apologize for my rudeness. It has been nice to meet you."

"You as well, Lady March. I hope you have room left on your dance card for me." Letting his gaze skim over my bosom, he reached for the small card hanging from my wrist.

"But of course. I look forward to it."

"Too bad you already have a partner for the supper dance." Lord Wyndham said with a dark look in his eyes. I noticed his name had been scrawled in place when I opened the decorative card. I recognized the print before I realized it was to be a waltz.

"I believe your mother felt we should be better acquainted." Lord Wyndham continued to look at me with determination.

Turning away from him, I returned my attention to the Duke of Pemberly. "Do you mind joining me for a refreshment?"

"I would love to." Surprised by my boldness, the Duke extended his arm. Reaching for the distraction, the Duke led the way to the refreshment table. With a slight look over his shoulder, he nodded to Lord Wyndham. "It

was a pleasure to make your acquaintance, Lord Wyndham."

"Likewise," Lord Wyndham said, watching as we headed to the refreshments.

Taking a glass of lemonade from the Duke, I noticed my mother barreling from the open terrace.

"Evelyn, there you are. Where have you been? Have you seen Lord Wyndham yet?" she gushed, looking around the large crush. She continued, not waiting for my response, "I have outdone myself this time. It will be the talk of the season."

"Lemonade, Lady March?" asked Lord Pemberly, handing a glass to my mother.

"Oh my, where are my manners? I did not see you there, Lord Pemberly, or is it Duke of Pemberly now? I was so sorry to hear about your father." She took a quick sip of the offered glass, too anxious to let her guard down.

"You would be the only one."

"I am sure that is not true. Please enjoy yourself." Looking at me, she smiled and gave me a little nudge. I could already see the wheels turning in her head. Any Duke would do.

Turning back towards the punchbowl, a collective gasp from the surrounding ladies made us swing around, looking for the cause of such a heartfelt uproar. I caught the sight before the entrance, and my jaw dropped. Standing between the doors were my angels dressed in their finest. Even without wings, I am sure the other *ladies thought the same thing. Blinking twice, I tried to let the unease in my stomach settle. They were not my angels. They were the bearers of deceit. Focusing my scrutiny on the leader, I realized he was staring straight at me. The black suit brought out the brightest of his golden locks, pulled back into a low ponytail with a black silk ribbon. His blue eyes clashed with my thoughts, leaving nothing in return. Ignoring him completely, I once again turned towards the Duke. Just as he was about to say something, a frown wrinkled his forehead.*

"It seems we are fated to be interrupted at every turn." With a nod, the Duke of Pemberly looked over my head. A light touch rested on my shoulder. I knew who it was before he even spoke.

"Excuse me, sir, but do we know you?" asked the Duke.

"I am sorry. Please allow me to introduce myself. I am Sir Brighton. I am a family friend of Lady March's mother." Dipping his head, Senoy gave a slight bow to the Duke. I tried to hide my surprise at the fake name.

"It seems you have caused quite a stir with your friends." The Duke responded.

Senoy and I glanced behind to see Gabriel and Uriel blending into the crowd. Galiel, still in awe by the luxury, lingered by one of the many rose creations Mother had created.

"I dare say the matchmaking mommas will not be able to leave you alone." The Duke continued.

"Yes, we tend to do that. I apologize, but do you mind if I steal Lady March away for a second?" Senoy asked the Duke.

"If that is what Lady March wishes."

"Thank you for the lemonade, and I look forward to our dance." Nodding my head, I took Senoy's arm as he led me to the garden terrace. I could feel strong muscle through the folds of his finery. A slow heat radiated through my hand.

"Evelyn, please do not be mad at me." He continued to lead me outside onto the terrace.

"How could you tell?" I asked.

"I am sure everyone could tell. Your eyes are practically daggers right now." Stopping at the railing, he turned to look at me. Taking a step back, I looked up at his perfectly sculpted face.

"What do you want from me? Wait, do not answer that. I want you to leave." Breaking eye contact, I looked into the darkness of the garden below.

"Evelyn, you must understand I did everything to protect you and the sword."

"By not telling me anything?" Admiring the moonlight gleaming off my favorite statue in the middle of the garden, I took Senoy's silence as a forfeit. "What do I mean to you?"

"I am not sure I understand what you mean." His response came out slow.

Turning back to him, I could only look at his chest. "It is a simple question. What do I mean to you? What am I to you?"

"Ah..." Grabbing my hand, he laid it against the focus of my interest. I could feel his heart beating through the folds of tailored fabric. "I tend to forget how young you are. Evelyn, what we have is a bond. A bond created centuries before you were born. I am still the same teacher and confidant you grew up. I am here to protect, instruct, and watch over you in times of need. Especially when it concerns the sword." Grazing his hand over my cheek, I pulled away.

"That almost sounds rehearsed, Senoy."

"Please, Evelyn."

"So you will leave me?" I asked.

"Eventually..." tipping my chin up to look into his face, he searched my eyes.

"I do not understand. These feelings..." I whispered.

"They are feelings a child would have for a father. I promise you they are not what you are thinking. It is just the surprise of seeing my new form. Besides, you are meant for your soulmate."

"Do not tell me how I should feel!" Pushing away from his chest, I took a step back. "You pretend to understand exactly how I feel but know nothing. I am not some puppet created solely for its master."

"In a way, you have been. Divinity created you for a specific destiny. And should you choose to run away from it, you will only end up in ruins." Turning away from me, he looked up to the heavens. "You understand nothing, Evelyn. For generations, I have fought the battles asked of me. For centuries, I have had to watch the female children of Evangeline's grow old and die just waiting for Lilith to reappear." Anger seeped into his voice as he swung around to face me again. "Do not tell me I do not understand destiny. We are all created for some purpose. Evelyn, look at me. I am an archangel. I am the commander of God's army. It is my duty and destiny to protect."

"So what?" I yelled back into his face. "Does that mean you can not feel anything?"

His eyes became bright. "Of course, I feel. We all feel Evelyn. It is one of the most beautiful gifts we have received." Pausing, he looked into the distance. "However, it is my duty to continue protecting our gifts."

"Who do I look like?" I asked after a brief pause, surprising myself.

"Excuse me?" he looked back at me, confused.

"I remember before I fainted that Gabriel thought I was someone else."

Taking a deep breath, Senoy ran his hands through his hair. "You look like Evangeline. Not exactly, but you have many of her characteristics. I could have left you when you were young and come back if Lilith showed up. The older you became, the more you reminded me of her. I did not have the strength to leave."

"Did you have feelings for her?" My question came out in a whisper. I did not know if I wanted to hear the answer.

"Sometimes I think you are her." Lost in his thoughts, he shook his head. "Evangeline has been the only human to fight Lilith, and she lost her life. Leaving her only child left in the world alone."

"She was not alone. She had you." Resting my hand on his arm in comfort, he pulled away.

"Among the rest of her family." I could see the anger flashing in his eyes. "Generations have passed in complete silence. Then, when you were born, I could feel a change. The older you became, the more I started to worry. Something is different this time. I believe Lilith has been planning, and you are not the only pawn in her twisted game." Banging his hands onto the terrace railing, he dropped his head. "If only I could figure out what she has done. For all my gifts, I am unable to foresee our future." His back became tense. Standing up straighter, he slowly turned towards the ballroom entrance. Confused, I followed his gaze.

"Hello, Evelyn. It seems we both have prize catches on our arms this evening. We shall be the envy of all." The snake had captured her prey. Lord Wyndham led Lilith onto the now suffocating terrace.

Senoy nodded to Lilith. His face was void of all emotion. "I do not believe we have had the pleasure of meeting."

"Oh, Michael, has it ever been out of pleasure? Though I must say, this is a first for us." She raised her arm to encompass the entire manor and smiled dazzlingly. Lord Wyndham grasped her arm a little tighter. "I was surprised to hear the name Senoy again. Michael has a much more romantic ring to it. Senoy conjures up too many bad memories." Shaking her head, I noticed her shiver.

"Enough with the formalities. What are you up to, Lilith?" Senoy's gaze bored into the statuesque beauty.

I could see the hate emanating between them. I never realized how tall Lilith was. She was able to make direct eye contact with Michael. Sharing the same blond locks and deep blue eyes, they could have passed for siblings. Was there more to the story than Senoy was letting on?

"Now, why would I tell you that? Where would the fun be?" Letting her laughter sizzle, she returned Lord Wyndham's ardent gaze. Laying her hand on my shoulder, she looked back to Senoy, curling her upper lip, "Do you like my gift, Michael?"

"What are you talking about?" Senoy's voice was tight.

"Why Evelyn, of course. Remind you of anyone?"

"I knew you had something to do with this. What have you done?" Michael lunged for Lilith. Lord Wyndham immediately moved in front of her, blocking Michael. Lilith's high-pitched laugh began to draw notice from the ballroom.

"Do we have a problem?" Lord Wyndham demanded. Even with Lord Wyndham's strength, he would have been no match for Senoy.

Stepping back, Senoy lifted his hands in defeat. "My apologies, Lord Wyndham."

Feeling a strange caress against my right temple, I turned towards Lord Wyndham. He was looking straight at me. Was it pleading I recognized in his eyes? Senoy seemed to notice this as well.

Making a quick nod to Lord Wyndham, Senoy grabbed my arm and started towing me back into the ballroom. I did everything possible to keep up and not trip over my skirts.

"I knew she had done something." Mumbling, Senoy continued to push us through the crowd. Gabriel, Uriel, and Galiel quickly fell into pursuit behind him. The general was taking control of his troops. Heading towards the entrance, I pulled against his rough grasp.

"Wait, what about Lord Wyndham?"

"I thought you did not care?" he asked, pushing me out the door.

"Well, I do not, but..."

"He will be fine, Evelyn. Lilith is not going to do anything to him. She needs him."

Making our way out of the ballroom, I tried to gather my wits. Gabriel and Uriel followed as Michael pulled me into my father's office two doorways from the ballroom. Galiel quietly shut the door behind them.

Gabriel was the first to speak. "What did she say, Michael?"

"She gestured to Evelyn and asked if I liked my gift." Realizing he was still holding onto my arm, he quickly let go and began to pace.

"Do you think she is Evangeline?" Uriel asked, leaning against the wall.

"Will you stop talking about me like I am not here?!" Looking back to Senoy, I searched his face. "What happened? And why did she seem so different?"

"What do you mean?"

"She was not the same person I met in the garden today. The woman in the garden was all goodness and nothing but gracious."

"She had no power over you this evening. I was shielding you from the haze she creates over the mind. Tonight, you met the real Lilith."

"What about Lord Wyndham?" I asked.

"It was better to leave him under her spell. He was safer that way. I promise." Ignoring my confusion, Senoy looked back at Uriel. "I do not know what to believe now."

"What should we do?" Uriel responded. His nonchalance scared me. I started to pace.

"Evelyn, sit down!" Senoy's voice whipped like a command. I froze, standing in front of my father's desk.

"Senoy, you are scaring me." Backing away from the warriors, I hit the side of the solid oak.

"Would you stop being so clumsy! How do you expect to fight the greatest Demon that ever lived when," unable to complete his threat, he focused on my lips. "There is only one way to find out."

"Find out what?" I choked. Closing the gap, he stood only a foot away, his intense gaze locking onto mine as I glanced upward. His head began to descend towards me, the air thick with anticipation.

A chair's legs squealed in protest, causing Michael to lose concentration. Gabriel slammed into the side of Senoy, knocking him several feet toward the window.

"Sorry, old friend. She is not Evangeline." Gabriel's voice held a threat of its own.

"Gabriel, how do you know?" The anguish in Senoy's words made my stomach churn. He raised his hand and made a circular motion with his fingers toward the dark angel.

Trying to reach for Senoy again, Gabriel struggled against invisible bonds, a manifestation of Senoy's power, holding him in place. Unable to move, Gabriel turned his thunderous look towards Uriel, who continued to lean against the wall unperturbed.

"Are you just going to stand there?" Gabriel demanded. Uriel remained silent, keeping his blank expression focused on me.

Senoy strode back towards me with an intensity that crackled in the air. Skidding around to the other side of the desk, I picked up the only weapon I saw: a quill pen. I was afraid, an emotion contradicting his mere presence in my life. Before I could take a breath, he was standing beside me. I could feel hot tears stream down the side of my cheek. Turning to his face, I let the pen drop from my hands.

"Senoy," I begged, "please stop." I realized I could not fulfill whatever he was seeking. It was a perplexing feeling not intended for me. A strange light entered his eyes. Voices outside the hall became louder as they paused outside the closed door.

"I am sure I saw her." Recognizing my mother's muffled voice, I sighed in relief.

"I have to go," I stuttered. Lowering his head, Senoy dismissed me with a wave of his hand. Quickly moving towards the door, I paused. Galiel stepped away from the door while Gabriel stretched his arms and legs, I assume, indicating he could move again. The troops watched my every move while the leader glared at the floor. I headed into the hall and closed the door. Hearing a slight click behind me, I wondered if it was my sanity or just the turn of the lock.

"There you are, my dear," my mother said with a concerned look. *"Where have you been? Oh, never mind. We do not have time. We must get you back inside. The waltz is about to start."*

I was grateful for my mother's intrusion.

Returning to the ballroom, she immediately scanned the dance floor for Lord Wyndham. "I just saw him talking with your brother's friend, who is a delightful young lady. Let us hope Lord Wyndham is not easily tempted. After all, you two are practically engaged. You stay here while I go check the card room."

As my mother headed towards the next room, I spied a tuff of golden blond hair disappearing through the exit door next to the refreshment table. My mother always unlocked it in case we needed a breather, hidden from all but family. Sneaking through the secret exit, I recognized the melodious voice coming from the back servants' hall.

"I can not wait to see this massive sword of yours, Lord Wyndham."

The sound of Lilith's voice made me feel uncomfortable. I hurried my steps and considered going back to get Senoy, as I had no protection against her abilities. But what if I arrived too late? I was not sure which scared me more, the demon or the angel.

"Please call me Adam." Lord Wyndham replied.

My breathing became shallow and rapid. I leaned against the wall, trying to control my frustration. I saw the couple ascend the back stairs towards Lord

Wyndham's room, and then I heard a lock clicking. Without thinking, I followed behind and knocked on the door.

"Lord Wyndham, are you inside? Have you forgotten about our dance? If you do not come down right now, I'll be the laughingstock of the ball." I knocked on the door again and heard some faint voices. I leaned in closer and was startled to see the door slightly ajar. Lilith's eyes met mine through the crack, and she was laughing.

"I believe you have caught Lord Wyndham at a rather inopportune time. Perhaps the Duke of Pemberly would be a suitable alternative?" Her voice was gentle and soothing. I tried to push against the haze penetrating my senses.

"I apologize, but Lord Wyndham promised me." As I opened the door wider, I caught a glimpse of Lord Wyndham sitting on the bed without his jacket. His sword lay untouched on the bedside table. Turning back to Lilith, I saw that her dress had slipped off her left shoulder. With one more tug, it would fall off completely. "I think it is best for you to leave now, Lilith."

With a sigh, she turned back to Lord Wyndham. "Do not fret, my love. We can continue this another time."

She touched my cheek as she turned back to me and pushed through the door. Pleasure shot straight down to my toes. I leaned further into her hand.

"Be careful, young one. I believe I have much more experience in what a man needs."

I found myself unable to speak as she walked down the hallway, running her finger along the side of the wall. I did not know where she was going, but I did not care. She sang the most beautiful melody I had ever heard. Lulled into a brief comfort, I watched her disappear around the corner. The trance lifted, and I was left once more with the painful memories. Assessing my body for any damage, I pushed against the bedroom door and halted in front of Lord Wyndham, still sitting on the edge of the bed.

"Evelyn, is that you?" Lord Wyndham asked, a bit confused. "Where did Lilith go?"

"What did you think you were doing?" My question came out more like a yell.

"I am not sure." Peering down at his open cravat, he grinned. "From the looks of it, I was about to have fun with a beautiful woman. At least that was before you so rudely interrupted." Pulling off his cravat, he tossed it to the desk.

"Put that back on right now!" I stared at the tuff of hair over his open shirt, and my voice cracked. "Did you feel the change the moment she left the room?"

Lord Wyndham's smile slowly faded, and he rubbed the back of his neck. "Yes, I did. It is as if she can control our emotions and make us feel however she wants."

Turning towards the sword, I walked over to ensure everything remained intact. It was.

"It was a strange experience," Lord Wyndham continued, "I found myself reacting to Lilith according to her wishes. However, when I heard your voice from beyond the door, a voice inside me began to rebel. Unfortunately, I was unable to act on those thoughts."

"You realize she just wants the sword?"

"Among other things." He wiped his hands on his pants and stood up from the bed, looking at me with raised eyebrows. "Do I detect a little jealousy?" he asked, a playful smile on his lips.

"Will you please stop and be serious." I am ashamed to admit my curiosity got the best of me, and I could not help but ask, "What type of other things?"

"Do you really want to know my sweet Evelyn?" Moving towards me, I realized what he meant.

"Please stay where you are, and do not call me that!" I gasped.

With a sigh of resignation, he sat at the side table, examining the sword.

"Something is happening, Lord Wyndham," I whispered.

"I think we can drop the formalities now. You are in my room. Call me Adam."

"I thought you said Lilith could call you Adam." I taunted.

"I thought you were not jealous?" he shot back, looking straight at me.

I looked at the sword. "Something has happened to Master Senoy. You probably do not remember, but something passed between him and Lilith on the terrace. He scares me. I feel I do not know him anymore."

"No, I saw. I could not do anything. One part of me wanted to pick you up and get the hell out of there, but a stronger part kept me at Lilith's side. She is a charmer." Closing his eyes, he rubbed his temples. Reopening them, he lightly ran his hand over the stone on the sword. "Perhaps we should touch the sword again?"

"Do you not remember what Senoy told us? Who knows what would happen?"

"Perhaps he does not know what is best anymore. Be honest. Did it scare you in the forest?"

"Yes, in a way. But I was surprised more than scared. It felt like I knew I would never be alone." The memory made me shiver.

"I do not understand how something that feels comforting could be bad. Senoy has never experienced its power." He looked out of the open window as if contemplating something. When he turned back to me, I could sense the intensity in his gaze. "I'll be honest with you, Evelyn. I desire you."

"Now I am scared. Nothing is what I thought." I stared at him again, feeling like a trapped animal.

"Evelyn, I promise never to hurt you. Please do not be afraid of me." Getting up from the desk, he moved *towards me with his hands up in front of his chest. "How about we just start with that dance you owe me?"*

"I do not owe you anything."

"Oh, I think you do." Pulling me forward into his arms, he gently waltzed me around the room. I could feel the weight of his hand pushing on the small of my back. The light breeze from the window and the intense body heat made me feel exotic. As our legs touched with each move, a fresh new wave of excitement took hold, and the butterflies erupted in my stomach. I could think of nothing else except wrapping my arms around his neck. Bringing my thoughts into action, he looked at me with a question in his eyes. I must have said yes because his lips descended onto mine. I could not get enough. As my hands thrust into his hair, pulling him closer, his mouth nipped a trail along the side of my neck. Before I knew it, Adam lifted me off the floor. Finding myself on the table's edge, I instinctively wrapped my legs around his waist. As the passionate embrace grew stronger, I felt something cold seep through the seat of my gown. I gasped from the coldness, and Adam automatically went to move the sword. His hand slid between my bottom and the blade as a blue light exploded. The blue haze seeped into our bodies, leaving no crevice unseen.

Holding onto Adam now more out of fear than desire, the mist blanketed my mind, leaving a warm exhilaration. Once again, memories of random images flooded my mind as if I had been a part of each one. I saw a young boy being scolded by his father for hiding in a tree all day and the same boy joking with his friends at school about his first kiss. Then, I saw a man training with a sword on the field, holding his own among men twice his size. As the images became clearer, I realized it was Adam. I had known it would be him. Tears cascaded down my face as a picture of Adam laughing with my brother emerged. He had known who I was from the moment we met in front of the ballroom. It had all been a pretense to pretend he did not recognize me.

As the events continued, the blue sparkle on the fringes turned white hot. Suddenly, a gust of wind brought wet needles that sizzled and pierced my warm skin. A strong force tugged on my arm, creating a dull ache I was unable to fight. I was not ready to leave.

Finding my voice, I yelped in pain. "Leave me alone!" The pain burned down my shoulder and torso as the force intensified.

"Evelyn, let go of the sword!" a deep voice called from the darkness. I could not see who it was, nor did I want to listen.

"If you do not let go of the sword, I will have to cause you more pain."

With one final, agonizing tug, I was wrenched away, hurtling backward into the darkness. The blinding light vanished with a deafening clang, leaving me disoriented and reeling as I collided with yet another solid form. I knew in my heart it was Senoy. I buried my face against the familiar warmth of his chest, the rain continuing to pelt my body. As rain mingled with my tears, I felt a softness brush against my fingertips. Delving deeper into its plush folds, I glanced up at Senoy, only to be confronted by a breathtaking sight. Two majestic wings unfurled behind him, their iridescent white plumage radiating with an otherworldly glow. The sight triggered a memory - I had seen it before, the familiar light brown patch on the left, the way they quivered when I rubbed them. Their wingspan reached far and wide, touching the sides of the small bedroom walls. With a dawning realization, I cast my gaze around, taking in the surreal scene unfolding before me. The wall where the window once stood was gone. The night sky peeking back at me.

Senoy engulfed my hands in his. "You act as if you have never seen an angel before." Pulling me closer, he began to rub my back.

"Michael, we need to go, now!" Uriel's urgent voice sliced through the chaos, as he deftly slid the magical sword into a satchel fastened securely to his back. "She will be here any moment!"

I glanced over to see Gabriel and Uriel restraining Adam with their shimmering wings that were almost blinding to look at. Tears streamed down my face despite wiping my eyes as I struggled to comprehend the situation. I gazed up at the hole in the ceiling, rain pelting my skin relentlessly. As I tried to catch my breath, my attention returned to Senoy amidst the wreckage of the room. A loud clap of thunder shattered the silence, causing the remains of the room to quake. Despite feeling disoriented, I sensed the angels were enveloping Adam and me in a protective circle of warmth with their merciful wings.

"What happened?" I yelled.

"The sword was causing a centrifugal force we could not penetrate," Senoy responded. "The only way to get in was through the window." He squinted into the wreckage, "Well, what is left of it. Sometimes, we forget our own strength. Come! There is no time. Lilith is on her way. Grab onto me." Senoy wrapped me back into his chest.

"Let her go!" Adam roared, fighting against Gabriel and Uriel's grasp.

"Adam, I am not going to hurt her," Senoy said. "We need to get out of here before Lilith returns." Motioning to Gabriel, the angel relaxed his hold on Adam.

"What are those?" Adam demanded, trying to reach for Gabriel's wings.

Gabriel moved to pin Adam's arms to his side. "We need to leave right now," he demanded. "We can explain later. Hold on!" Adam continued to struggle against the firm grip. "We can do this the easy way or the hard way."

"What is the hard way?" Adam asked.

"I knock you out," Gabriel said, amused. *"I have been wanting to do that since we met."* With one last struggle, Adam became lax.

"Now!" yelled Senoy as I felt myself lift off the floor. A flash of lightning clashed before me as I screamed and closed my eyes tight. Burying my head in Senoy's shoulder, a warmth spread through my entire body, keeping the storm's chill a breath away as we launched into the dark night.

****

15. Final Nightmare

"Evie," Lilith's voice echoed, "The time has come. Everything we have prepared for." The demon's voice haunted her at every turn as she ran through the pouring rain. She wiped the stinging wetness from her eyes when she suddenly realized she was back in the depths of her dark forest, the one that haunted her nightmares. Gathering her courage, she screamed.

"Leave me alone! I know who you are, demon! I won't help you!"

"But my dear, you were designed specifically to do just that."

"What are you talking about?" Evie's voice wavered.

"You did not think your lovely mother and father were your real parents, did you?"

Hearing the demon's voice, Evie narrowed her eyes in suspicion. "You're lying! You would tell me anything to get what you want."

"And pray tell me, my dear goddess, what do I want?"

Evie was at a loss for words. Memories that had long been buried suddenly resurfaced. A recognizable chant, which had been drilled into her subconscious, echoed through her mind. "To be with your love again. To receive your forgiveness." Repeating the phrase caused fresh tears to stream down her face.

"Brilliant," Lilith smiled.

Evie peered down at her open palms, unsure of what she was searching for. Her gaze widened at her usual Renaissance attire that engulfed her with multiple skirts, an unwelcome accessory to her surreal experience. Her arms fell limply to her sides as she gave up, letting her knees sink into the soft black soil. The stench of rust stung her nose as she surveyed the scene around her in panic. Blood stained the front white panel of the luxurious fabric, anchoring her to the ground and causing her to gasp. As she ran her fingers over the silk laces interwoven on the front torso of the dress, her breath caught in her throat. She recognized the pattern. It was Evelyn's ball gown. She frantically tugged at the stained skirt.

"What game are you playing?" She wondered aloud. "Is Evelyn even real?"

"What do you think?" Lilith breathed. "The connection only grows stronger."

A loud voice emerged from the darkness hidden behind the trees. "Evie! Run! Don't listen to her! Just run!"

The last word bounced off the high-pitched screeches ringing through the misty air. Scanning the trees, Evie's hands balled into fists. Thousands of yellow eyes glared at her from the branches overhead, Lilith's minions playing spectator to her show.

"Damek, is that you?" Evie called, keeping her gaze on the owls.

"Yes, my darling," the demon's melodic voice rang. "Call for Damek." Lilith emerged through the thick foliage, her lucid blue eyes revealing an unsettling truth. She whirled her finger in a tight circle, causing the storm to minimize into a small funnel, spinning on the outskirts of the open field, waiting for a command to unleash its fury. Inside the haven of the open meadow, Lilith reached her arms out to Evie and smiled. "Daughter of mine, I have waited so long."

"Don't listen to her, Evie! Run!" Damek's voice was becoming a mere whisper.

A warm breeze rolled over the sides of Evie's neck, creating an embrace she was unwilling to fight. The full moon lifted above the clouds through the darkness, gracing its brilliant light over the entire wood. Not one animal sighed in comfort over the glimmering mirage. Glaring back at the demon in disguise, Evie cleared her throat.

"What do you want from me?" Evie yelled.

A cold wave of emotion enveloped her mind as a vivid picture of her dining room table popped into her subconscious. It was a table filled with take-out Chinese and two loving parents, someone else's parents. As she clung to the memory, a thick blackness descended over her thoughts, and pain shot through her chest, causing her to drop to the ground. Blinking her eyes over the sudden emptiness, Evie noticed that Lilith's attention had shifted from her to the thick barrier of trees. The sudden coldness sent shivers down her spine as the goddess focused on her new prey. Lilith raised her hands in defense, her face twisted with anger as she tried to keep her opponent at bay.

"Evie! I can't hold her much longer! Run!"

An irritating smugness buzzed in Evie's ears – one she knew too well. "Blake? Is that you?" Her heart skipped a beat.

"Silence!" Lilith screamed. She taunted the cyclone just inches from her body, whipping up the branches in its grasp.

Evie strained to identify the voice over the wind whipping through the broken limbs. The owls launched from their stations, suffocating the moonlight in their claws as they swirled above the trees, shrouding everything in darkness.

Lilith raised her arms in defense and tilted her head towards Evie. "How gallant of Damek, trying to save you."

"But that sounded like Blake," Evie stuttered.

"No! Damek is your soulmate!"

"Stop lying! I know Blake's voice."

"Do not be ridiculous. Why would that boy enter your dreams? He has another destiny to fulfill. A promise made long ago." She threatened the storm closer, emphasizing the word "boy" with disdain.

"Run, Evie, Run!"

Evie immediately recognized Blake's voice. She pushed off the ground and did exactly what he told her to. She ran. Lilith's scream ripped through the forest floor as the cyclone shot a brilliant spark of lightning at the intruder behind the trees. A male yelp of pain accompanied the storm as it unleashed its power into the realm of the nightmare. Hearing the tortured cry, Evie swung around back to Lilith. Her once blue eyes, now dark red pupils of deception, pierced through the darkness, reaching for her. Her golden locks glistened with millions of tiny needles waiting to strike, and her blood-stained lips, full and wet, stretched into a predatory smile. Evie did not wait. She forced herself to run faster, picking up her skirts to jump over the roots that were pulling from the ground in protest. As she ducked her head to avoid the flying dirt and debris, a bulky tree root, aged with disease, maliciously wrapped around her ankle and yanked her back to the forest floor. Brilliant shots of fireworks exploded into the back of her head, and the diary took over.

May 4, 1893 Afternoon

After a forced nap of repose on the hard dirt floor, I find I am unable to sleep. My mind is consumed with thoughts of the impending battle. I can sense Adam's discreet looks across the open fire. He wants to escape, but I am hesitant to provide him with the opportunity. My heart will not let me. I must continue my story before Lilith arrives. I fear that this may be my final entry. Let me begin with the tale of our fearful flight through the storm.

As the salty air whipped through my hair, I felt the water seep into my slippers when I landed softly on the cold sand. Waves lapped over the hem of my dress, though I did not care. I had just experienced the most extraordinary ride through the heavens. An adventure I was sure never to forget. When the storm finally subsided, I pulled my face away from the warm comfort of Senoy's chest. Only the low rumbles of thunder in the distance remained. As I looked up into my angel's eyes, I found him examining the contours of my face as if searching for traces of the being he once loved.

"Where are we, Senoy?" I asked, drawing his attention back to the present.

"Not too far from home, just over the dunes to the sea." Pointing into the darkness on the left, he adverted his eyes from my face. "Just over there is the cave you once played in as a child. Always meant to be a safe haven if needed."

Before I could respond, a loud thump accompanied a large body falling to the ground. With nothing but sand to break the fall, Adam lay sprawled on the wet surf, trying to catch his breath.   Gabriel (with a slight smile) landed gracefully next to Uriel and Galiel. Their wings emitting an iridescent glow that illuminated the *incoming waves, which I once thought were guarded by millions of fairies to keep the sea creatures at bay. As I took a moment to admire the multitude of feathers gracing their wings, I noticed that both Gabriel and Uriel had numerous brown patches embellishing the white folds of their velvety wings. Examining closer, one of Uriel's brown spots was black. One had to wonder if the colors were of any significance. Galiel's seemed to be pure white. Was that because he was new? Peering over my shoulder to Senoy, only his right wing carried any sign of imperfection. One small brown patch. Opening my mouth to ask what the colors meant, my thought was interrupted and altogether forgotten.*

"You could have given me some warning," Adam grumbled, rubbing his left thigh.

"I could have," replied Gabriel with a smirk.

"Gabriel, leave Adam alone. He is going to need all his strength." Turning towards the cave, the leader began to head into the darkness with his troop of angels following behind, their wings providing the beacon to find our way. I could feel the hairs on the back of my neck creep up as I turned towards Adam. He continued to lie in the sand, staring at me.

"Get up, will you? All we need is for you to die of a fever. This mess is all your fault, you know. Only a dance, you said!" I began pacing as my initial awe faded and anger boiled to the surface. Adam did not respond. As the

silence stretched, I dropped to my knees before him and felt his forehead.

"Do you want me to get up?" he asked, staying perfectly still. I thought I heard resignation in his voice.

"What do you mean? Of course, I want you to get up."

"Evelyn..," he paused, searching my eyes, "do you want me here? I can easily find my way back and be gone for good."

"That is all you are going to say?" I yelled, pushing his chest further into the sand.

He grabbed my arms and pulled me closer. "What do you want from me?" he asked. "Do you want me to tell you that I ache for you? That the feeling of your life flashing through me has made me question my whole existence? That no matter what unearthly presence threatens us, I will conquer it for you? Is that what you want to hear?"

"I..." pausing out of fear, I continued to stare into his eyes. Using my hands to push off his chest, he simply let me go. "I do not know what I want," I sighed, looking into the sky. Was this even his fight?

"Evelyn," Adam sighed, "I can not compete with that."

Without looking, I knew what he meant. "Nor can I," I whispered, glancing at the eerie glow in the distance.

Adam pulled himself to his feet. Standing beside me, we both looked into the stars, awaiting an answer. He glanced at me once more, then turned towards the flickering lights. With a brief touch to my back, he headed towards the cave. Had he found his answer?

As I followed him, I felt a sense of guilt churning in my stomach. A campfire blazed in the center of the cavern. Rubbing my arms, I became entranced by the bright flames, creating shadows of past descendants frolicking on the den's rigid walls. Perhaps one of them was Evangeline looking over us. Like a cocoon, the warmth surrounded me in comfort. The first few flutters of 'Für Elise' teased my senses. I am sure Senoy was creating this fantasy of peace, but I did not care. I welcomed it. Sitting by the fire, I watched Senoy tend to the flames with a long stick, his gaze fixed on the red-hot blaze.

"Nice work, Uriel," Gabriel said, breaking the silence. "Just like riding a bike, eh, old man." Hitting Uriel on the back, Gabriel sat next to Senoy and stretched his legs. Galiel sat beside him while Uriel stood behind Senoy, unsure if for comfort or command. Adam sat across from the warriors, lost in thought as he gazed into the fire. The wings had disappeared, and just the magnificence of the celestial warriors was left. Yes, Adam was right. Neither of us could compete.

Senoy's voice caught me off guard as I admired Gabriel's back for any sign of where the wings resided when not in use.

"Evelyn, can you please tell us what you felt when you and Adam touched the sword?"

"Oh, of course," I responded, gathering my thoughts. I remembered the intense need that had encompassed my body during the interaction. From Senoy's rather stressed look, I can only assume my face had turned beet red. "I felt..," pausing to find the right word, I glanced at Adam, "whole. I could see random images of Adam's entire life flash by me; however, it was like I had been there for each one. I was able to feel the emotions he was going through." As I gazed into the flickering flames, I found the courage to go on. "The longer we stayed bound to the light, a stronger emotion took hold of my body."

With a nod of his head, Senoy asked the same question of Adam.

Adam's gaze lingered over the shadows before he met Senoy's unwavering stare. "Evelyn pretty much said it all. Our connection was so strong that I lost my sense of self. Very strange, really. Then, of course, there was the extreme lust coursing through the both of us." He cleared his throat, whether out of his embarrassment or mine, I was not sure. "I felt a power that had no fear attached to it." They continued to stare at each other in silence. A brief understanding seemed to pass between man and Angel as the flame's constant crackle was the only sound keeping beat with the precipice of war.

"Michael, sound familiar, no?" It was only the second time I had heard Uriel speak. His accent broke into the tense silence. I was drawn to its peacefulness and moved closer to where he stood guard by Senoy's side.

"Hmmm...you are correct, Uriel." Snapping out of his reverie, Senoy glanced between Adam and me. He noticed an unspoken question lingering in the air and directed his gaze towards Adam. "I know what you are thinking. You have no choice in the matter. The stone," taking a deep breath, he nodded in my direction, "and Evelyn has selected you. If you want her to live, you must stay and fight."

"My decision was already made." Adam kept his gaze fixed on Senoy.

"Good," Senoy said. He then began to outline the plan to the group. His commanding presence made me completely forget any questions I had about the past. "We have come to believe only the two who have activated the stone can truly defeat Lilith," Senoy continued, "when the sword is activated, it is difficult to maintain awareness of your surroundings. Everything will revolve around the object of your desire. The challenge lies in controlling and directing this power towards Lilith."

"How do we do that?" asked Adam. "When it happens, we have no control."

"I do not know the answer to that. The last time the stone was activated, we were only able to send Lilith back to where she came from. The power of the sword was unknown to all of us, including Lilith."

"Who did Evangeline activate the stone with?" I asked.

Senoy forged ahead, ignoring my question. "Leaving Evangeline alone, I attacked Lilith without using the sword's power. After I recovered from one of the demon's attacks, I realized my mistake too late," he paused, throwing a stick into the fire. "Evangeline lay dead on the ground. The magic had ended, and all Lilith had left was a normal sword. She will not make that mistake again." Taking a deep breath, he continued, "We drove Lilith back to the Red Sea and safeguarded the sword until the next guardian came of age. Evangeline had a daughter from her late husband."

"Evangeline had been married?" I asked, surprised.

"Why yes. What made you think she was not? She was of age."

"Well, I thought with finding her soulmate, the father would naturally be-."

"This is not a fairy tale, Evelyn." Senoy interrupted abruptly. "Evangeline was very young when her parents arranged her marriage. She was blessed to have been able to have a child."

"Then who was her soulmate?"

"Michael," Uriel interrupted, "We must hurry. I can sense her getting closer."

"Remember," Senoy added, "The stone inlaid in the sword is the only entrance Lilith has for entering the afterlife. She has learned that she needs the two of you to activate it, but none of us know how. Do not underestimate her, for I think she has found a way. I am certain of it." Senoy stood up and rubbed the back of his neck. "I do not understand why I can not foresee her next move!"

"Michael, she is a demon," Uriel said calmly.

"I know, Uriel, but something is wrong. I should be able to see something."

"I say we have the two love birds here activate the sword," Gabriel interjected, "And then bind Lilith in the light. If that does not work, we will exile her to the Red Sea again."

"And give her another chance in the future?" Senoy asked. "It leaves too much to chance."

"What other option do we have, Michael?" Gabriel asked.

"Gabriel is right," Uriel said. "We must continue as planned. We fight until she has no more strength left." He placed his hand on Senoy's back and continued, "This is not your fault, Michael."

I felt like one of those spectators at the Globe Theater watching the main plot of a play unfold. A plot that put me directly in the middle. "I am tired of all the secrecy," I yelled. "What are you not telling us?"

Uriel and Gabriel looked silently at Senoy while Adam remained passive, staring into the fire. Galiel had moved to the side wall, continuing his silent watch. I could not take it anymore.

"Is anyone going to answer me?" Spinning around, I yelled at Adam's back. "Why are you not doing anything? Do you not care that we are mere puppets in this god's feud?"

"Evelyn, enough!" Senoy growled.

I threw my hands up in frustration and turned back to Senoy. "Oh my, the Great One is actually speaking to me!" But Senoy continued to ignore me, just like a father who ignores a child's tantrum. He immediately began barking orders like the seasoned general that he was.

"We will begin training at once. Lilith is strong and has many powers under her control. This battle will be unlike any other you have ever seen before. She can manipulate the wind and weather to do her bidding. The screech owls obey her every command, and the serpents are her allies. She will lure you into her trust, only to shred you into pieces. Despite her attractive appearance, she has become a creature of darkness that cannot die. She will entice you with her white roses and poppies but leave you with the marks of her vicious wings and sharp talons. I can only teach you the weapons that are available to mere mortals. However, unlike the messengers of God," a disgusted tone seeped into his voice, "you possess something that we apparently do not comprehend: true love."

"This is impossible," I whispered, shaking my head.

"This is the consequence." Looking straight at me, I saw a shadow pass over his bright blue eyes.

"Are you blaming me?" I choked. I felt shame creep over my cheeks. "You are blaming me!"

"I told you not to touch the sword!" Senoy's voice cracked like a whip.

The little patience I had left broke. "Lilith was seducing Adam just to get the sword. What would have happened if she had taken it?"

"You played right into her hand," Senoy responded, "She has no power without the two of you."

Adrenaline surged into my legs as I lunged towards him. He caught me in his arms as I beat against his chest. He did not move an inch but continued to hold me firmly.

"How dare you?!" I yelled, "If you want to point fingers, you should look at yourself. You had my entire life to prepare me!"

He slowly let me go. After a moment, he seemed to get taller and looked down on me with his intense gaze. "I never expected you to be so easy," he whispered, his words reverberating off the walls and blending with the snapping of the tinder.

Adam lunged at Senoy, but Uriel and Gabriel restrained him, awaiting the next command.

"Let me go," challenged Adam, "Let the bastard defend himself!" He pulled against their stronghold but was no match for God's men.

I was motionless. My heart was crushed; the pain too much to bear. I willed my legs to run as fast as they could out of the suffocating den. My knees collapsed into the cold sand as I tried to catch my breath. I knew he was not far behind.

Senoy placed his hands on my shoulders as he spoke, "Sometimes I forget how young you are." Pulling me up, he yanked me into his embrace. Abandoning all my anger like a child would for a father, I buried my face into his chest.

"No, you were right, Senoy," I said through the folds of his dress jacket. "I am ashamed of myself."

"Evelyn," Senoy sighed, "I am sorry. You had no more choice than any of us. The sword calls to our hearts. It understands us better than we do. I let my anger and confusion..." Not knowing what else to say, he sighed and continued to rub my back.

"I do not understand," I whispered.

"This is all my fault. You have done nothing wrong."

"Senoy," I asked, "what if we held the sword?" I looked up into his bright blue eyes. He held my intense gaze for a moment before slowly turning his attention towards the sea.

"Evelyn...I once thought," He paused when he seemed to remember where he was and who he was talking to. Taking a step back, he placed his hands on my upper arms and changed tactics, "You are meant to be with Lord Wyndham. Deep down, you know that. I truly never thought this would happen again. Something is different."

"You keep saying that. What is different?" I asked.

A sudden cry pierced the stillness of the night, interrupting Senoy's thoughts. The screech sent chills down my spine as I scanned the darkness for the intruder.

"Is she here?" I asked, my voice cracking.

"She is getting close. We need to start training now. We do not have much time." He turned towards me and looked into my eyes. "I promise to tell you all when the time is right." I sensed a haunted sadness that I could not place. He took my hand and led me back into the fight. He had once again become the divine guardian he was destined to be. We continued to train into the afternoon of the next day.

Tired, defeated, and anxious, we sit around the campfire, each involved in our own thoughts. This is where I now sit describing the events of the day, dear journal. I am only thankful that Senoy remembered how fond of you I am and brought it with him. I have decided to leave the past in the past, for I can see that something or someone must have hurt Senoy deeply. I only wish he felt comfortable enough to confide in me. For now, I understand. He will always only be a mentor and guardian—one who will forever be ingrained in my heart.

A partnership has grown between Adam and me. I still do not know if I love him, but I do trust him. What is love anyway? I have not had the chance to even think about the confusing emotion. When not fighting against each other, Adam and I have become quite strong. With his strength and my quickness, we may just have a chance to beat her. I am scared. I believe Adam has heard my thoughts. He has cleaned the same sword twice.

"Why has Lilith not shown up yet?" Adam yelled, pounding his fist against the cave wall. "I would have assumed she would have found us by now!"

"Patience," Uriel said. "Now is the time to save your strength. She is biding her time and preparing for the battle. She will soon be sending her messengers. It does not take her long." He wiped the blade of his sword, admiring the glimmer of its reflection.

From the distance, a low screech echoed through the cave. We all turned towards the entrance with a mix of fear and determination.

"The time has come," Senoy said, pulling out his sword. "She will be here shortly."

****

16. Awakening

Evie gazed at the curvy line marking the end of the journal entry, the usual sign of another nightmare. She closed her eyes and waited, but nothing happened. Trying to visualize the demon herself, Evie strained to listen for any indication of Lilith's impending melodic voice. She urged the darkness to appear, but her only companion was the rapid beating of her heart, keeping half-time with the upstairs Cuckoo clock. Opening her eyes, she frantically flipped through the remaining blank pages.

"That's it?" She yelled. "Show me the rest!"

Tears streamed down her face as she flipped through the journal. With each turn of the page, the previous entry disappeared until nothing but blank pages were left.

"Are you serious?!" She yelled, throwing the blank book across her room. "What am I supposed to do now?"

She flung herself onto the bed, burying her frustration into the small pillows scattered across the top. As she lay there, something tickled her upper arm. Pulling her head out of her brief cocoon, she saw two yellow eyes staring back at her. She smiled as she reached out to cover

Sheba's head with her hand and scratched the back of the cat's tiny left ear, which was the only scrawny part of the potbellied feline. Sheba moved away from Evie and stared at the bedroom door while Evie groaned at the thumping noise coming up the stairs. "Mom and Dad must be back from dinner already."

Evie tried to shoo Sheba off the bed, but the cat easily dodged her and settled into a ball in the middle. "What's got into you?"

"Evie?" Her mom asked, jiggling the locked door handle. "Is everything okay?"

"Yeah, Mom," she lied effortlessly, "I was reading a book and didn't like the ending." Opening the door, she stooped down to pick up the journal. Her mother's disapproving look prompted her to grab her book bag. But when she tried to open it, the zipper wouldn't budge. She pulled on the cheap silver attachment with all her might, and it finally gave way with a loud rip. She quickly stuffed the book inside and flung the bag against the side of her dresser in frustration.

"That bad, huh?" her mom asked, leaning against the door jamb.

"Yeah, something like that," she grumbled. "So, how was dinner? You guys are back kinda early, aren't ya?"

Evie's mom pushed away from the door and shook her head. "I knew something was wrong. I told your father to stop pushing, but he..."

"Mom," Evie interrupted, "what are you talking about?"

"Evie, it's morning already. When we got home last night, your bedroom door was locked, and your lights were off. We assumed you were sleeping."

Evie ran her hands through her hair and pulled open the blinds, revealing the icy dew covering the yellow grass outside. "It's morning already?"

"Did you get any sleep?"

Lost in thought, Evie responded in a monotone voice. "Yeah, I think so." Evie turned from the window, rubbing her eyes. "Really, I'm fine. I'm just waking up."

"I thought you said you were reading?"

"I fell asleep reading," she said, throwing her hands in the air. "Just leave it, Mom."

"I'll be so glad when we're past this teenage angst stage."

Evie quickly kissed her mom's cheek and smiled, grateful her mom was dropping the issue. "Thank you," she said.

"Are you sure your father isn't pushing you too hard? He's so excited about your fencing."

Evie avoided eye contact and swiftly headed to her dresser mirror to assess the damage. "No, not at all. I promise."

"On the plus side, you look well-rested, and you're early for once," her mother said, glancing at her watch. "You have at least half an hour before you need to leave. By the way, you can take the car today. Your dad went to work early, and he'll pick me up later to look at some samples in Stapleton for the store."

"Nice! Thanks!"

"Oh! And don't worry, we will be there tonight to cheer you on."

"Tonight?"

"Your fencing competition? That's tonight, right?" Evie's mom asked.

"Oh, yeah," Evie said, trying to hide her surprise.

"How about afterward we go out to dinner?"

"Sounds great, thanks."

"I'll see you downstairs," Evie's mother paused at the bedroom door, "Oh, and break a leg!" She laughed and continued down the stairs.

"Knowing my luck, I actually will."

Evie had a strange feeling as she drove into the school parking lot. Perhaps just lingering doubts from the morning. The cold wind whipped through her heavy jacket as she walked to the front entrance. No, she mused, something was definitely off. She felt like she was missing something. Looking around at the students, she tried to make her way through the crowds in the lobby. The excited chatter about snow had everyone praying for the day off, including the teachers. Finally making it to her hall, she noticed her locker was slightly ajar. Slowly pulling it open, a small white note fell to the floor. She realized what was wrong. She hadn't run into Blake after fencing practice yesterday. She hadn't even given him a thought after her run-in with Damek. Suddenly, she felt a cramp on her side. As she picked up the note, she recognized the scribbled handwriting.

Evie-

You've made your decision. I can't change destiny.

Blake

She read the brief letter over and over again, feeling confused. What did Blake mean? Had he seen the kiss? There was no way. She stuffed the letter into her bag and picked up her other books. She tasted fresh blood on her lower lip. Shoving her heavy coat into her locker, she slammed the door and headed to first period. Making her usual right turn to Ms. Lancaster's class, she opened her mouth to give Blake an earful.

"Hey, Evie," Seth asked as he pushed away from the wall beside her homeroom. "Catching bugs?"

Closing her mouth, Evie glanced down the hall. No Blake.

"Sorry," Evie replied. "Didn't get much sleep last night."

"I hear ya. Mid-Terms are gonna kill me!" Seth joked.

"Oh, yeah, right," Evie responded, lost in thought as she walked into class. Before entering, she turned back to

Seth and asked, "Hey, did you happen to see Blake this morning?"

"Cohen? No," Seth replied. "Not that I would be looking for him, though."

Seth followed Evie into the class, and she momentarily forgot about Blake. "Wait. Why aren't you going to your class?"

"Can't a friend just stop by and say 'hi'?"

"Um, yeah, I guess."

"Good. See you at lunch." He flashed a grin over Evie's head. "Looks like you'll be having some fun this morning."

Evie turned around towards the chalkboard and groaned. She could hear Seth laughing as he walked out of the room. The two most dreaded words for every student were written in hot pink: "POP QUIZ." Chewing on a hangnail, Evie felt the words might as well have said: "GUILTY." In her mind, she replayed the kiss from Damek yet again. She dropped into her seat and rubbed her eyes, trying to erase the vision.

Blake was absent from school that day. The morning had been a disaster. She failed the English quiz, and constant muscle spasms played havoc in her stomach. While waiting for the lunch bell, she forced herself into the Junior hall. Scanning the crowd for any signs of Blake, Evie recognized a high-pitched voice behind her. Ducking behind an open classroom door, a large poster board hit her from behind and snagged on the side of her book bag's zipper, which had now become the bane of her existence. Books and pencils went flying to the floor, making her the center of attention. Evie crouched down to the floor to avoid any further embarrassment, keeping her face averted.

"Please don't let her see me," Evie whispered to the floor.

A guy in thick-rimmed glasses offered to help, but all she could see were the bright white tennis shoes standing in front of her.

Lexi's voice echoed through the entire hall, "He isn't here, Evie."

Evie dropped her head lower and grumbled. After taking a deep breath, she picked up her last book and met Lexi's smug smile. "Do you know where he is?"

"Finishing up a project in History. However, he told me this morning that he was looking forward to this stupid contest being over."

Surprised, Evie stood up and held her book bag tight against her chest. "Oh, you mean Damek."

"No use pretending that isn't who you were looking for in the Junior hall. I've already told you he isn't interested."

"For your information, I wasn't looking for Damek." Evie snapped.

As the giggles around her grew louder, a surge of anxiety swept into her legs. Her ability to speak was lost. She turned away from Lexi and started walking aimlessly, not knowing where she was headed. Eventually, she ended up in front of the school. She pushed on the front double doors and paused under the awning. Nobody was around. The cold weather had driven all the students into the cafeteria. Even the ones that usually weren't brave enough to handle the social scrutiny. She held her book bag close to her chest to keep warm and caught sight of the usual potheads suffering the cold to make their way towards the outside track. Not one of them had the dark black hair she was looking for. Sighing with frustration, she headed back into the school and made her way to the lunchroom.

As she suspected, the place was packed. A few kids had even decided to try to meld into the side walls, hoping no one would notice them. She was surprised to find Seth surrounded by his friends. Perhaps the cold weather had provided a needed truce among friends. Or maybe her days as the rumored 'hussy' were finally done. She looked over at the jock table before sitting down, as she usually did, but wasn't surprised to see that Damek was missing. So was Lexi. Pushing aside the twinge of anxiety, she walked over to Seth.

"Hey," Seth said, scooting over on the bench to make room. "Place to be today, huh?"

"Yeah, thanks for saving me a spot." Evie sat down and tried to smile at the rest of the small motley crew. Pulling a peanut butter and jelly sandwich out of her bag, she decided to forget about Blake. After all, she had finally achieved what she had wanted all along. He was no longer following her around like a shadow. Her stomach rumbled.

"Have you seen that new redhead in Ms. Sadler's class?" Mike, a rather large Sophomore with bedhead, asked Seth, nudging his arm with his elbow.

"No, I must've missed her," Seth replied, shrugging his shoulders at Evie.

"Oh man, you have to check her out." Agreed Tom, taking a huge bite of his apple.

Evie smiled. Tom was the kind of guy who thought all girls were into him. It was a shame he was too shy to act on it. He had that cute, goofy look that some girls found adorable. Trying to fit in, Evie playfully punched Seth's arm. "Yeah, Seth. Wasn't that the girl you were checking out so thoroughly the other day?"

"Huh?" Seth asked.

"You know," Evie continued, "The one bent down at her locker."

"Oh yeah." Pretending to be uncomfortable, Seth winked at her. "You weren't supposed to see that."

"Doesn't matter. I got first dibs." Mike chimed in, finishing the rest of his hamburger in one bite. "So, Evie, what's the latest with Lana? Heard she got mono or something? Must've been a pretty severe case. She's been gone awhile.

"Yeah. Who's she been kissing?" Tom asked, juice dribbling down his chin and onto the table. At least he was trying to include her.

"Probably that football player. The one she was so gaga over," laughed Mike.

"Stop it, guys!" said Seth, crushing the empty soda can he was holding. Everyone stared at the can.

"What's your problem?" Mike asked.

"I haven't heard from her," Evie said, quickly changing the subject. "Anyway, anything going on this weekend?" Just as curious about Seth's reaction, she tried to keep her gaze on Tom.

"Not sure. But hey, I know what I'm doing tonight. Big competition in the gym, right?" Tom asked, throwing his apple core on Seth's lunch tray.

Mike pointed at Evie. "My money's on you, babe. Can't wait to see Sam go down! He's always been a cocky SOB."

Laughing, the boys continued to gossip about the day. Seth had calmed down and quickly joined right back in. Evie only half-listened, thinking about the upcoming competition. All thoughts of Blake settled in the back of her mind. She knew she could beat Sam, but in front of the entire school was an entirely different matter. Her palms started to itch. Leaving the boys, she said her goodbyes and dropped her empty paper bag into the trash can. Looking back at Seth on her way out, he gave her a brief smile. Though small, the encouragement settled the annoying pull lingering in her stomach.

Throughout the day, Evie constantly received stares, giggles, and random pats on the back. Even her Spanish teacher, Ms. Reyes, was getting into the competitive spirit. As she was packing up to leave her final class of the day, Ms. Reyes promised to cheer on her favorite student from the stands. Evie's face turned a pale shade of green. She made a beeline for the bathroom, where she splashed water over her face and tried to calm herself down. After checking the mirror for any signs of smoke, she found none. It was time. Walking back to her locker, the excited buzz of students resonated through the halls as they stole a glance at Damek's apprentice. Pulling out her fencing bag, Evie was surprised to find Lexi standing right behind her.

"Good luck," the blonde said, crossing her arms in front of her.

"Thanks," Evie replied.

"Hey, Lexi, are you coming? I wanna grab a seat in the front row," interrupted the redhead Evie recognized from the volunteer table. Tapping Lexi on the shoulder, she nodded at Evie. It made Evie think about Blake.

"Don't worry about it, Heather," replied Lexi. "Damek will save us a seat." Without another glance, both girls spun around and sauntered down the hall. Evie swore she heard their giggles about her humiliating trip down the Junior hall. Closing her locker, she straightened her shoulders and headed to the gym. As she watched the kids funnel through the double doors, Evie knew the place was packed. The cookie she had eaten in Spanish threatened to come back up. Veering off to the side door of the girls' locker room, she froze.

"Hey," a familiar voice said. It was the best sound in the entire world. "Look, don't say anything; just let me talk."

Evie remained still, afraid her best friend would bolt if she made any sudden movements. She silently prayed that the black hair and blue eyes were not just another figment of her overactive imagination,

"I was jealous, okay," Lana admitted.

Evie tentatively took a step.

"No, don't come any closer. This is hard enough," Lana said, taking a step back. "You don't understand what I go through, and to be honest, I'm glad you don't. That's what makes us friends. I don't have the family or lifestyle that you have. You were totally right to say that you have issues of your own, and I get that...but in a way, I've always felt that you had no right to complain. When my mom left us, all I had was my dad and brother. For a while, we were fine, but then things started to change." She rubbed her forehead and surveyed the small alcove. "Things were getting pretty hard, and then I met you. You were...normal. Normal, and you liked me...you got me. I was always jealous of you but loved you at the same time. I've never had a best friend." Lana dropped her gaze towards the floor, trying to create a hole in the tiled floor with her foot. "Then, all of a sudden, you found something more important than me. And to be honest, I don't even know what it was or still is. You just sort of checked out of our friendship. I mean we were together, but you just weren't there." She took a deep breath and lifted her head to meet Evie's gaze once again. "Then my brother left, and heaven knows where he went, which just leaves me and my dad. I needed you, and that night of Trace's party was the last straw. You were becoming one of them," Lana said, putting air quotes around the word 'them.' "The thing is, I realized that no matter what, I need you. I'm not ready to let you go without a fight."

Evie was stunned. She didn't know what to say.

Lana twisted the blue feather hanging from her necklace. "You can talk now," she urged.

"A fight??" Evie gushed, finding her voice. "It was all my fault! I've been horrible and was so involved with what was going on with me that I didn't listen to you. I mean really listen. I thought I could fix it, but I can't. I need you just as much as you need me. So much has happened these past few months, and I haven't been able to share them with the one person I care the most about." Biting her lower lip, Evie hesitated. "And I'm sorry about Seth. I didn't realize."

"What are you talking about?" Lana asked, tears gathering in the deep groves beneath her eyes.

"I think you know," Evie replied. "He feels something for you too. I can tell. You're just so hard to read sometimes. I wanna help you, but you continue to push me away. I guess I thought you didn't need anybody, including me."

"I..." Lana choked. "There's nothing between me and Seth."

Evie gave up on words and dropped her bags to close the distance between them. Throwing her arms around her best friend, the word "Sorry" became a muted chorus. Evie squeezed her friend tightly, almost afraid it wasn't real.

Lana eventually pulled away and whispered, "There's something else I need to tell you." Clearing her throat, she continued, "I've been going back and forth on whether or not to tell you." She forced herself to meet Evie's gaze while fidgeting with her beaded necklace. "I," taking another brief pause, she rushed the rest of her confession. "I'm the one who put the journal on the bleachers."

"What?" Evie breathed. "Why?"

"Blake asked me to."

"Blake? But he's the one that's been telling me to get rid of it."

Lana shook her head and sighed, "I don't know what to tell you. He didn't tell me anything about it. It was blank, so what harm did I think it would cause? He made me promise not to say anything and pretend I'd never seen it."

"That makes no sense! Why would he do that? How could he," Before Evie could continue, a cold breeze slid up her back and wrapped around her neck like a hand threatening to cut off her windpipe. She was no longer scared. She knew "he" was behind her.

"Hey, Damek," Evie said, not bothering to turn around.

"Hey," hesitating, Damek paused. "Sorry to interrupt. Good to see you again," he nodded towards Lana before returning to Evie. "You about ready? The Professor put your gear in the girl's locker room. He even found some white knickers for you."

Ignoring Damek, Evie searched Lana's face. "I don't know if I can do this."

"Of course, you can. That's what I love about you," Lana smiled. "We can continue our conversation later. Everything's gonna be fine."

With a deep breath and a pat on the back from Lana, Evie turned around to confront Damek.

Staring at the wall, lost in thought, he shoved his hands into his jean pockets.

"You know, we can just cancel the whole thing if you want," Evie said, trying to get his attention.

"Not an option," Damek replied curtly, finally meeting her gaze

"You could be nicer. This was your idea, wasn't it?" asked Lana, placing her hands on her hips.

Ignoring the interruption, Damek moved closer to Evie. "I'm sorry Evie. Really. No matter what you think."

Heat radiated the distance despite his cold words. Evie felt an intense thirst replace the cold whip coiled around her neck. She wanted to pull him towards her, but instead, she stepped back and rolled her shoulders. "Whatever." She slid past Lana and swung around towards the locker room.

"Wait," Damek interrupted, "your book bag." He lifted it off the floor, causing the cursed bag to spill its contents everywhere. He swore under his breath as he bent to pick it up.

"Seriously, where's this finesse that everyone's always talking about?" Smirked Lana as she bent down to help Damek.

He tried to shove the books back into the bag but paused when he reached Evie's journal. He slowly lifted the worn leather cover, eyeing the top stone.

"You gonna smell it or put it back in the bag?" Lana asked.

"How did you get this?" Damek responded.

"What are you talking about?" Evie clipped, still angry about his last comment.

"How did you get this journal?" Damek asked, turning to Evie. His words were casual, but the heat in his eyes said something else entirely.

Realizing what it was, Evie looked at Lana, who kept her head averted to the floor, fascinated with one of the fallen pencils. Biting her inside cheek, Evie reached for the book. "How do you know about the journal?"

Damek pulled the journal closer to his chest. "It belongs to my family. I've been looking for it everywhere. I thought I'd lost it."

"Oh," Evie replied, surprised. "I," realizing that Lana was not going to offer any information, Evie tried to keep her growing irritation aimed at Damek. "I found it in the gym on the first day of fencing class."

"You're lying."

"No, I'm not," she whispered, unable to move her gaze away from his accusing tone.

"I never brought the journal to school," Damek raised his voice. "Do you know how much crap I've had to face because of you? My parents are upset, and Professor Mike won't get off my back!"

"I swear, Damek! I found it that first day," Evie pleaded, tears forming in her eyes.

"Last time I saw the thing, it was in my room," Damek continued. "Are you really that obsessed with me that you would sneak into my room and take something?"

"What the hell are you talking about?" Lana yelled, finally coming to stand next to Evie. "For your information," she began, but Damek interrupted her, ignoring her completely.

"The day you came over to practice. That was when you did it, right?"

"Damek, I promise you. I did not sneak into your room. The journal was lying on the bleachers after that first class. Now I admit, I was wrong to take it then, but nobody ever said anything."

He pulled the book from his chest and momentarily examined the stone. Evie wasn't sure if he was even looking at it. She could almost see his brain processing the details. He lifted his head and looked at Lana. "You had something to do with this, didn't you? I've heard the stories. Once a descendent of Cain, always a descendent of Cain, right? And here I thought we could make our own destiny."

"Don't tell me you believe all that phony destiny stuff Blake is always harping about?!" Lana yelled.

"If the shoe fits," Damek sneered.

"Get over yourself, Damek Adams. Besides, Blake gave it to me. I don't know anything about it."

"Like I'm gonna believe you. Once a liar, always a liar."

"What are you guys talking about?" Evie yelled, unable to understand the tense exchange.

"Forget it. It doesn't matter. This settles everything. I don't intend to let some silly prophecy rule my life." Ignoring the girls, Damek waved the journal in the air as if it understood his every word.

"Wait! I thought everything was already settled. Remember? You've made it pretty clear that I'm just a nobody," Evie cried, feeling an urgency to alleviate the tension.

"At least you got something right. You are a nobody." Enunciating every word, Damek's posture hardened.

Evie's heart sank. "You know what, Damek? You can go to hell and take that damned journal with you. It was the stupidest love story I ever read!" She spun on her heels and headed towards the locker room.

"You read it?" Damek gasped.

Evie turned around and threw her hands in the air. "Oh no! She read it! The world as we know it is going to come to an end. To be honest, I'm glad to be rid of it. It has caused me nothing but trouble."

"You read it," Damek whispered again, looking past Evie's shoulder into the distance.

"Would you stop saying that?" Evie screeched. "I have a competition to get ready for." She quickly gathered the rest of her books and shoved them into her book bag before running into the locker room. She threw the bag to the floor and sank onto the nearest bench, dropping her head into her hands. She squeezed her eyes tightly shut until she saw bright, tiny stars explode behind her lids.

"Well, it seems you've made a nice mess of things while I've been gone." Dropping next to Evie, Lana started to rub her back, sliding Evie's forgotten fencing bag next to her. "I can't believe I ever liked him."

Dipping away from Lana, Evie flinched. "Whatever, Lana. You seemed to know exactly what he was talking about."

"Not really." Lana shifted on the bench. "I promise!"

"I don't believe you."

"I don't really know that much," admitted Lana. "Blake was talking about some strange destiny stuff before he disappeared. I remember him saying the name Cain, but that was about it. I wish I'd paid more attention."

Evie examined the red welts lining her finger beds.

Lana slipped off the bench and knelt before Evie, breaking the silence. She took hold of Evie's hands and made eye contact. "Please believe me. I am telling you the honest-to-God truth. Besides Cain being my middle name, I know nothing about it. I don't even know why my mom chose that stupid name!"

Evie looked into Lana's eyes, desperately trying to figure out the truth. "I don't know what to believe anymore. I wanna trust you. I just thought the journal was meant for me...like it was calling to me. I know it sounds crazy, but... turns out it's all a lie. It was never meant for me. It belongs to Damek." She pulled her hands away from Lana. "I don't know if I can handle this."

Lana grabbed her by the shoulders and gave her a firm shake. "Evie Bennett, stop this right now! You have everything you need right here," she emphasized, poking her in the chest. "I don't believe in all this destiny, mumbo jumbo. We make our own destiny. Stop feeling sorry for yourself and get back into the game. You never needed some silly book, or me, or some boy to make you great. You did this all on your own, Evie. You have amazing strength, and it's time you started using it."

"Now that was the worst pep talk I've ever heard," Evie laughed through her tears. "Please don't tell me you got that from some cheesy teeny-bopper rerun."

"Hey, whatever works, babe," Lana said as she helped them both to their feet. "After the competition, we'll find Blake and sort everything out. I'll make him talk. But for now, forget about Damek. It's Evie's time to shine. Evie, the warrior princess!" Lana spread her feet apart in a fighting stance and gestured between the two names with her hands.

Evie pushed Lana's arms down and quickly grabbed the white knickers and jacket lying on the opposite bench.

"What?" Lana laughed. "I think it has potential." Glancing down at the white pants, her grin disappeared. "I can't believe that's what they wear. You look like you should be admitted to an insane asylum."

Evie snapped her front vest and reached for the rest of her gear while ignoring Lana's comment.

Lana frowned. "I guess I pictured The Warrior Princess wearing something like leather or maybe even some spikes," she said, tugging Evie's hair. "You look like a giant marshmallow."

Evie grabbed the mesh mask from her bag, exhaling deeply before turning back to Lana. "I will always need you."

"Eh, I know." Shrugging her shoulders, Lana grinned.

"That reminds me. I thought Blake was back home and bringing you your homework."

"No, he hasn't been back at all. Ms. Jackson in the front office has been sending me my assignments." Lana noticed the confusion on Evie's face. "Why, what happened?"

Evie shook her head as the audience chanted her name in the gym. "Let's talk later; we need to go."

Heading to the gym, Lana yelled over the loud chatter. "Remember, Warrior Princess!"

As Evie stepped out of the locker room and into the gym, the entire crowd stood up. Every bleacher was full, well, at least the first ten rows were. It felt like she was standing in the center of Yankee Stadium. Evie took a moment to catch her breath and considered the possibility of leaving before anyone noticed.

"Ready?" Trace asked, catching her before she could bolt.

Evie shook her head, unable to respond. She followed Trace to the fencing line and scanned the bleachers, spotting her parents already greeting Lana from the middle section. Seth and his friends sat behind them, engrossed in their own conversation. She waved at her mom and clutched the foil's grip, glancing at the fencing strip. Sam was in place at the en-guard line, waiting for her, and he winked at her with a goofy grin. She relaxed her shoulders and took her place at the line, finally letting her gaze wander over to Damek. With the journal tucked under his arm, Damek sat on the first bench next to Lexi, whispering something in her ear. She laughed and playfully pushed him away before pointing in Evie's direction and smiling. Damek turned around, staring at the middle of the fencing strip.

Evie pulled her mask over her face and waited for the call to start. The end of the semester was finally here, and everything led up to this one small high school competition. It wasn't her adventure to begin with, but it was time to say goodbye. As Damek turned back to the crowd, waving his hands, Evie noticed Professor Mike sitting beside Lexi. A familiar zing crept into her mind as she admired his strong chin. Warm energy ran up her arms as he glanced back at her with that same faraway look that was becoming a habit.

"Quiet, everyone! We're about to start," Damek announced, and the whispers in the gym died down. "As you all know, Trace and I selected a beginning fencer to train for this competition. We have been working all semester. Trace selected Sam," the audience erupted in applause, interrupting Damek's speech. "And I selected Evie," he continued once the noise had subsided. "This is a dry bout, so Trace will referee. That means we won't be using an electronic system to keep score. The first one to reach five points wins."

"Let's begin," Trace said, facing the competitors.

Evie broke the confusing connection with Professor Mike and quickly dropped into a salute to Sam, then Trace, and then to the crowd. Her concentration immediately honed on the sword in front of her. Blackness surrounded her vision as silence prevailed over her senses. Counting her breaths, she realized she was the first to speak. "En garde!"

Evie quickly positioned herself into a defensive stance as Sam lightly grazed her sword with his before lunging forward for his first hit. With a twist of her wrist, she quickly swung his blade to the side, only to have her counterattack miss, her attention sliding between the Professor and then settling on Damek. With each parry, Damek's last words haunted her every move. His distractions were becoming a problem. How dare he accuse her of being a liar! So many questions were racing through her mind. Was he the one meant to read the journal? Was that why the end was blank to her? He seemed to know Lilith, as the demon constantly mentioned him. She moved back to the en-guard line, but her thoughts were still preventing her from scoring any points. Losing was not an option, at least not to Sam.

She pushed Damek out of her mind and extended her arm, focusing on the simplicity of her movement. Like a predator closing in on its prey, she could hear Sam's shoes squealing as he moved. She had him. Whipping her foil in a tight arc, she made her first point. Celebration rippled through the floor.

Making her way back to the line, Evie became lost in the moment. The students, the gym, and even Sam became secondary objects. The sword was the star of the show. Concentrating on the glint of the metal, she gave one brief thought to the imaginary goddess that was no longer hers. The demon; now another man's burden.

With a reverberating grunt, Sam lunged for Evie, only to have a twist of her wrist create a dull clack of deflection. A rapid cadence of clinking, protests, and near misses kept the crowd on the edge of their seats. Their low buzz of adulation keeping tempo with the unusual pair. Feeling Sam's arms begin to shake as their swords collided, Evie knew it was time for the final score.

"Goodbye, Lilith," Evie gritted through her teeth.

Taking advantage of Sam's habit of touching her sword before each attack, she moved her blade far right. Like any trained dog, he went for the bait. Deftly slipping beneath his weapon, she went straight for his chest. The slight touch reverberated up her arm. Shouts of excitement bounced off the padded walls.

Evie was unable to move and kept her gaze trained on Sam. He stepped back in defeat and pulled off his mask. The sweat dripping from the small spikes of hair falling over his forehead singularly glistened in her direction. She moved forward.

Sam panted, "Whoa, there! You already won."

Evie shifted her weight.

"Touché," Trace said, walking up to Evie with a pat on the back.

Registering her name, she relaxed. Keeping her sword lowered, Evie scanned the cheering crowd. She had won.

"Nice work, Damek. You created your perfect opponent. Can't wait to see that match!" Trace chuckled, looking towards Damek.

"Not happening," Damek replied. He turned to Trace and extended his hand, "Time to pay up."

Evie breathed a sigh of relief; she had won.

"Yeah, yeah, yeah," Trace said as he placed a hundred-dollar bill into Damek's hand. He grabbed Sam's foil and laughed, "Come on, man, you never stood a chance."

Sam shook Evie's hand and bowed, prompting cheers. "Congratulations, Evie."

"Thanks," Evie shouted over the noise. "You did great, too." Scanning the bleachers, she shook her head at her mom, waving hysterically, and her father, whose tight smile threatened to break into a full grin. Lana was already making her way down to the last bleacher. As Evie headed over to meet her best friend, she paused when she felt the familiar cold wrap around her. Turning around to face Damek's glare, she lifted her shoulders.

"You did a great job. You're amazing, for a beginner fencer," Damek allowed. He glanced at the journal in his hands and then looked back at her, "However, from now on, I want you to stay away from me. Do you understand?"

Evie stepped back, gasping as his words hit her like a blast of icy wind. As she stumbled back, she accidentally stepped on something soft and was pushed forward straight into Damek. Instinctively raising her hands in front of her, she felt a cold stone thrust into her palm as a crack of white light ripped through her consciousness.

The lightning scorched to the tips of her toes as a bright blue light blurred her vision. She struggled to hold onto reality as her surroundings faded into darkness. Random flashes of events began to break into her thoughts, creating a surreal experience. In one of them, she saw a young boy sitting in a room surrounded by strange artifacts while an adult sitting across from him drilled him with facts that made no sense to her. She almost recognized the pair and tried to understand the meaning behind the teacher's quick references to gods. Suddenly, the memory morphed into a different scene altogether, where the same young boy was winning his first fencing competition as his parents watched from the sidelines. The same familiarity washed over her as she realized that it was Damek. As he grew older, the scene flashed bright white, signifying his transition into adolescence. As she continued to watch, another image appeared of Damek's parents urging him to join them on their usual excavations, only to have him yell in protest. A sudden depiction of Damek's first day at Hillstead High wavered into view. He walked in with his head held high as a ripple of female appreciation washed over him. Evie witnessed Professor Mike starting the fencing program so that he could watch over Damek.

Evie sensed her heartbeat merging with another while the images danced into her soul, leaving indelible marks. As the rhythm increased, a pulling sensation surged into her legs, causing her intake of breath to be engulfed by the intense light. The sheer magnitude of force increased to its highest point, causing the alter existence to drop away, leaving nothing but confusion. Blinking instantly, she met Damek's gaze, breathless.

The excitement among the student body continued, held back by a distant barrier. Evie followed Damek's lead as he lowered his head. Her gaze fell to the floor, and a sense of dread gathered in her eyes. She urged the tears not to drop and stared at the cracked, worn leather lying between them on the ground. The stone, the addiction to her new reality, absorbed every last bit of the faded blue magic. As Evie took a deep breath, not realizing she had been holding it, a high-pitched voice exploded in her right temple.

"Damek!" Lexi exclaimed, pulling on his left shoulder. "That was amazing! I didn't realize fencing could be so intense. The guys were practically drooling over Evie. Can you imagine if that was me? You've got to teach me!"

Evie's heart ached as Lexi pulled Damek further away from her. Mimicking her agony, a clap of thunder rippled through the gym, causing a brief silence in the crowd. The pounding of rain tripped on its heels, bouncing about the school halls. She felt like a trapped animal.

"Oh, crap! Of course, it would start to rain when we're leaving," Lexi complained.

"Hey, did you notice anything weird?" Damek asked, pushing Lexi away to take a breath.

"Weird? Like what?" Smoothing one of his stray hairs back in place, she wound her hand through his arm.

"Um, I don't know. Just out of the norm, I guess." Grappling for the right words, he turned towards Evie with a slight frown.

"Not really. Well, I guess I could be a little jealous. I mean, seriously, the competition was awesome! But then again, it's just her," Lexi said, nodding in Evie's direction without even looking at her. Before Evie could say a word, Damek hugged Lexi tightly.

The color red flooded Evie's vision, causing her to freeze in place. She wondered if Damek had felt anything as he clung to Lexi for dear life. Losing sight of everything around her, she focused on the one being who cared about her no matter what, the one person who would carry her out of the emotional rubble. Pushing past Damek and Lexi, Evie approached the bleachers and stopped at the bottom bench. She found her.

Lana stared at Evie with a mixture of surprise and resentment in her eyes. Evie stumbled backward, feeling the bile rising in her throat. She was sure that Lana had seen the crazy interlude and it hadn't been a dream. Lana had witnessed her brief trip down the blue smoke rabbit hole. So why was her best friend in the whole wide world glaring at her in disgust?

A single tear ran down Evie's cheek as she realized she was losing the battle. "This doesn't make sense," she whispered.

Evie dropped her foil to the ground and fled. Her mother's voice echoed behind her as she pushed her legs to go as fast as they could. She soon found herself at the school entrance and yanked on the doors. Suddenly, a bright fluorescent crack of lightning lit up the front courtyard. Rain pounded her head as she sprinted past the first row of parked cars, unable to stop shaking. She skidded into a large puddle, sliding on her backside.

"Evie!" Someone yelled, breaking through the pain threatening to squeeze her chest.

She tried to wipe the constant downpour from her face when she heard a high-pitched squeal ringing in her left ear. She covered her head. An agonizing cry ripped from her throat as severe pain surged through her body.

17. The Gift

Evie rubbed her raw throat and tried to lift herself out of the puddle. The pain quickly dissipated, and instead of the blissful comfort she expected from death, all she felt was dampness. She peered down into the murkiness of the water beneath her. It was no longer rain but rich black soil, mud sticking to every part of her body. Squishing the cold dirt through her fingers, she suppressed a giggle. She wondered if she was delirious, but she enjoyed the feeling nonetheless. As she continued concentrating on the repetitive motion, she suddenly heard a brief scuffle from her right. Darkness surrounded her, and her eyes could not make out any signs of life. A real fear began to press down on her rib cage.

"Evie, it's Blake," she heard in a whisper. She closed her eyes, willing the nightmare to end and pulling the familiar voice closer.

"Evie, this isn't a dream. Open your eyes."

"Wake up," Evie repeated, lying on the forest floor and conjuring an image of a handsome dark-haired boy as she lifted her hand.

"Evie, open your eyes!" Blake yelled, jolting her with a static shock. She saw Blake's face next to hers and whispered his name.

"Can you sit up?" Blake asked as he helped Evie into a sitting position. He quickly examined her body for injuries. "Evie, I need you to concentrate. You activated the stone."

"What?" Blinking, Evie tried to focus.

"The stone. Remember the journal?"

"Yeah, but what does that have to do with anything? Are you real?" She ran her hand over his cheek and smiled, feeling light-headed.

"Yes, I'm real. Evie, I need you to wake up," he said, brushing her hand away and squeezing her arm. "The dreams were real. You and Damek touched the stone in the journal."

Evie shook her head in disbelief as she stood up and tried to push Blake away. "I didn't touch the stone. That was all a dream. Evelyn activated the stone in the sword. It was just a story." Looking around, she noticed her black stained fencing costume and asked, "Where are we?"

Blake stood up next to her and took hold of her arm, causing Evie to cringe back instinctively. "Evie, it wasn't your imagination," he said. "You were meant to find the journal. Lilith had her demons steal it out of the sword centuries ago and plant it in Evelyn's journal. She's been planning this ever since her last failed attempt into the afterlife."

"D-demons? Afterlife? Blake, I'm so confused," Evie stammered.

Blake's impatience was apparent as he replied. "Evie, think! You know all this. It was in the journal."

Evie bit her lower lip, feeling certain she must be dreaming again. She remembered vividly how Damek had taken the journal away from her, recognizing that she had stolen something that didn't belong to her. Ignoring Blake, she looked up into the sky and yelled. "How dare you? I don't have the journal anymore! Wake up!" Pinching her arm, she closed her eyes again.

"Evie, stop!" Blake grabbed her arms and squeezed hard. "This isn't a dream. This is real. We don't have much time."

"Ouch!" Evie opened her eyes and found Blake still standing in front of her.

Shaking his head, Blake started to pace. "I tried to tell the Professor, but he didn't believe me."

"Professor Mike?" Evie whispered, running her hands over the once beautiful white pants. Evie's breath started coming in quick gasps as she crouched back to the ground for fear of falling over.

"Alright, Evie. Enough is enough," Blake yelled pulling her up. Evie tried to push him away, but Blake turned her around and held her from behind. He drew her closer to his chest, and she shivered as his lips brushed near her ear. "Everything written in that journal is true," he said. "All the characters were real; Lilith has been planning this for centuries. I'm beginning to think that you were created specifically for her plan."

"What are you talking about?" Evie asked, trying to understand the internal conflict her body was experiencing at Blake's nearness. The lightheadedness was returning.

"Just listen!" commanded Blake. "You can't faint on me! I need you!" He held Evie tightly as he spoke. "Lilith needed the sword's guardian and his soulmate to activate the stone. It's the only way for her to enter the afterlife. Lilith planted the stone in a modern location, a book. She knew that with time, her legend would become just some folktale buried in the depths of a library. Lilith is the mother of all evil, and you must remember what you read, Evie. Her demonic children have been idolized in haunted tales of ghosts, vampires, werewolves, and all those other Halloween monsters. It's all true. She has to be stopped. She is the true evil that spreads through us all."

Evie listened attentively, becoming limp in Blake's arms. He loosened his grip and explained further, "She somehow found a way to... create you," he paused, letting his chin graze the top of Evie's head, "or at least I think she did. She needed to create a soulmate for Damek that she could control."

"Damek?" The mere mention of his name caused a fresh wave of nausea to wash over Evie.

"Yes, Damek. I don't know how Lilith did it. I didn't think it was possible." Blake turned Evie around in his arms and searched her face for any recognition. "Evie,

Damek is the current guardian of the sword. Lilith created you to be his soulmate. However, unlike any other demon she has made," touching her cheek, he continued, "you seem to have an actual soul." Blake couldn't help but add with a slight smirk, "I guess it makes sense that a soulmate needs to have a soul."

Evie began to shiver. Catching himself, Blake loosened his grip and said, "Professor Mike is an Archangel who was sent to protect the guardian and guard the afterlife against Lilith."

"Michael," Evie mumbled.

"Yes. Everything you read is true, Evie. I don't know how much was in there, but I can only assume you know."

"Why didn't you wait for me?" she whispered.

"What?" Blake asked, confused.

"Where were you the other day after fencing practice?"

"You had made your choice, Evie."

"So you did see the kiss. I thought so. Blake, I...," unable to finish, she focused on the black waves of Blake's hair. It reminded her of a turbulent sea making its presence known in the dead of night.

"Don't. It's the way things are meant to be," Blake responded, void of any emotion.

Losing her train of thought, Evie paused. "Wait. I thought the sword's guardian was always a woman?"

"Damek's mom was unable to have any more kids after him. The sex didn't seem to matter. He took on the same responsibilities. However, I believe there was some concern that his gender would not provide the same power over the stone," Blake explained, his eyes peering into the darkness. "But I think we've put that concern to rest."

"What do you mean?" Evie asked.

"Well, you both activated the stone," Blake replied.

Everything became clear as Evie thought about Damek's last words in the gym. She pulled away from Blake's grasp. "He knew I was supposed to be his soulmate, didn't he? That's why he was trying to stay away."

"Not exactly. I suggested it to him, but he didn't believe me."

Evie looked down at the ground and rubbed her lower lip with her tongue. "Yeah, why would he? Look at me."

Blake's eyes heated up as he gazed at her. He didn't move. "I am."

Evie met his steadfast gaze and stepped back; her heart skipped a beat. That had only ever happened once before. She was confused and shook her head.

"We need to go," Blake said as he grabbed a duffel bag lying in the dirt. "We don't have much time. I won't let Lilith ruin my family again." He quickly turned back to her, his eyes piercing through hers. "Or you."

As she felt the heat rise within her, it was different from any heat she had ever experienced before. Her body was familiar with Damek's cold demeanor, followed by intense passion, and it reacted accordingly. It knew what to do and craved him. But with Blake, it was different. Her body was confused, unsure how to respond to this new sensation. She began to think about what he had said and asked, "What did Lilith do to you and Lana?"

"It's a long story and we need to get going."

"I'm not going anywhere until you tell me. Lana said you gave her the journal."

Taking a breath, Blake adjusted the large black bag over his shoulder. "Do you believe in reincarnation?"

"Never thought about it."

"It's believed by some that everyone has a soul that undergoes reincarnation. Some believe this is a way to make ourselves better in each life, while others think it's simply a fate to relive our mistakes repeatedly, creating a sort of hell on earth. Across generations, Lilith has found both me and Lana, the souls that parallel Cain and Abel's intro of jealousy and greed to all humanity." He paused, waiting to see if Evie was following his story.

"Sorry. You've lost me."

"Lilith believes Lana and I are the reincarnated descendants of Cain and Abel."

"What?! That's ridiculous! Biblical characters? Who even knows if they really existed?"

"Well, Lilith exists, and so does the Archangel Michael. Doesn't seem so far-fetched to me anymore."

Evie shifted her weight, feeling a sense of familiarity with the story. "If I remember correctly, Cain and Abel were Adam and Eve's kids, right?" Not waiting for an answer, she continued, "Cain is the one who killed Abel out of jealousy. Something about God favoring Abel over Cain. Hmm... so, who's who in this crazy scenario?"

"I am Abel, and Lana is Cain," Blake said matter of factly.

"That's why Lilith kept saying Lana's jealousy would always ruin her."

"So, you have talked to the Demoness," Blake accused.

"Only in my dreams," Evie replied.

"That's probably the only way she can communicate with you."

"What do you mean?" Evie asked, still confused.

"Lilith created you, Evie." Blake smiled and looked off into the darkness of the trees, "But somehow, she was able to add a soul. How ironic...A demon with a soul. Something I doubt she even remembers she once had."

"I am not a demon."

Blake continued to stare into the distance.

Evie took a step closer to Blake and raised her voice. "Blake, look at me! I am not a demon! Do you hear me?" Her hysteria was creeping up into her throat.

Blake met her gaze, trying to make a decision. He combed his hand through his hair, lost in a battle within himself. Finally, he gave up and yanked Evie back into his arms. "I don't know what you are, Evie. It makes no sense," he said.

Evie leaned into his embrace. "I am not a demon," she whispered into his chest.

"You are not a demon," Blake breathed, "I won't let you be."

Evie wondered if she had just imagined his last words. She grazed his shoulder with her hand, surprised to find a large shoulder strap. She slowly slid out of his arms, trying to control her emotions.

"What's in the bag?" she asked.

"Everything in my power to stop Lilith," he said, lost in thought as he stared at her for a few seconds. "We don't have much time left, and there's something else I need to tell you. Lilith wanted me to make sure you went through the portal at this exact time."

"Portal?" Evie asked.

"Yes. The portal was a mirror. It's one of Lilith's many powers. She can travel through mirrors, whether it be time or location. She had me find a large enough mirror for you to run through, which you did when you ran out of the school and into the parking lot."

"That's ridiculous. It's impossible to go through mirrors," Evie commented with a bit of uncertainty.

"That's what I thought. At least for humans."

"I see," Evie contemplated. "So you thought I would make it through, and you wouldn't. Seeing as I'm a demon and all."

"I admit, I'm surprised it worked."

Evie folded her arms over her chest, feeling a slight chill sting her shoulders. "See, that just proves that either I'm not a demon or you're one too!"

Blake paused as he looked into the distance. Curious, Evie turned to see what had caught his attention. Suddenly, Blake voiced his thoughts, "Amazing how she knew the exact moment you both would touch the stone. How the hell did she plan something like that?" Turning back towards Evie, Blake shifted his weight and pulled his bag tighter over his shoulder. "Lilith needed you here at this exact moment. I don't know where we are, but wherever it is, she's close, and she wasn't counting on me following you through."

"Why are you here anyway?" Evie asked, holding her arms tightly around her while stepping back. "Why did you help her? And how can I be sure you're not lying to me?"

"She used compulsion, Evie," Blake explained. "She can easily control our minds, and men are the weakest and easiest for her. Plus, she's pretty persuasive. But I won't let her hurt Lana again."

"Lana? Do you really believe in this Cain and Abel crap?"

Blake threw his arms wide and raised his voice. "Evie, look around you! How can you ask that?" He did not give her a chance to answer, "When I wasn't under her control, I tried to warn you and watch out for you. But none of it worked. It just made you want to do it more. Perhaps if I hadn't said anything..."

"Perhaps if you hadn't been so cryptic and just told me outright." Evie snapped.

"You're right. I should have."

"Why you, Blake?" Evie whispered. "I mean, I get the whole biblical tale, but couldn't she have used someone I already hate, like Lexi? I'm sure she has to be the descendent of some villain."

"Easy," pausing, he laughed, "she knew you liked me."

Evie's cheeks flushed as she averted her gaze. "No, I don't."

Blake grunted before continuing. "It doesn't matter now, does it? It didn't last. You found your soulmate."

The information was too much at once. Running her hands through her hair, Evie tried to focus on one question at a time. "I take it Lana knows all about this? That would explain why,"

"No. Lana doesn't know anything." Blake interrupted her tersely.

"But, I thought..."

"No. I convinced her to plant the journal. Other than that, Lana knows nothing." Blake looked up and turned away from Evie.

"Blake," Evie paused, rubbing her arms as goosebumps began to form. "Lana saw."

"Saw what?" he asked, turning back to Evie.

"When Damek and I touched the stone," Evie replied. "Nobody else seemed to notice, but Lana did. She saw the magic."

Blake raised an eyebrow, clearly skeptical. "What do you mean?"

Evie continued, struggling to find the right words. "After we touched the stone, no one seemed to notice. It was like it didn't happen. But when I looked at Lana, I could tell she had seen it." Pausing, Evie caught a movement from her right. She looked into the woods and continued, "You know, the magic. Lana saw everything. And well, I don't know. She," pausing again, Evie looked back at Blake, "She was mad at me."

"Impossible..." Blake replied in disbelief.

"I'm not lying, Blake!" Evie yelled. "She's my best friend. I think I can read her pretty well, and what I saw was hate."

Blake shook his head when a loud screech echoed above. They instinctively ducked their heads and looked up into the dark sky, but nothing could be seen. Not a single star twinkled above them. Blake threw his duffel bag to the ground and quickly rummaged through it until he found his hunting rifle.

Evie stared at the artillery, threatening to fall out of the bag. "Do you even know how to use those?" she asked.

"Yes. I can use all of them if need be," Blake replied as he closed the bag.

Evie kept searching for the owl she knew was hovering above when a musical voice called out from the dense trees, humming possessively along her body.

"Evie," the musical voice called out, "enough with this high school melodrama. It's time."

"Evie, it's her. We have to run." Blake said, pushing her away from the direction of the voice.
They started running, but Evie quickly grew tired and pulled away from Blake, doubling over to catch her breath.

"Where are we going?" she asked.

"I don't know," Blake replied, letting his duffle bag fall to the ground. "I just know we wanna be far from her as possible."

"Blake," came the familiar voice, its hum continuing its melodic tune in Evie's veins. "You have been playing behind my back. Tsk Tsk."

"I won't let you have her!" Blake yelled into the darkness. "Run, Evie!" Grabbing her arm, Blake used all his strength to push Evie further into the forest.

"Evie, make him stop." The musical lilt became a droll command whispered into the crevices of her brain. "We are one. Do not let him take you away from me." With a cry, the lull in her voice became a high-pitched squeal. "Please, Evie, they are hurting me!"

The agonizing pain emanating through the voice hit Evie's body in one big sweep. Convulsing, she jerked out of Blake's hold. "I have to go. She's in pain!"

"No, Evie, you can't!" Blake pulled her forward, gritting his teeth.

A cold wave washed over Evie's body as a steel grip took the reins out of her conscious control. Shivering, she pushed Blake to the ground, surprised by her own strength. She met his confused stare and said, "Blake, I'm sorry. I have to go."

With a quick turn, she darted into the darkness of the trees, not knowing where her path would lead her. She could hear Blake running behind her, the tree branches crackling and protesting under his feet. Her speed caught her by surprise as she skillfully maneuvered past obstacles without a second glance. Her heart raced with anticipation as the familiar sense of competition began to set in. Her breathing came naturally, giving her body the necessary air to perform. Yellow eyes peered at her from the darkness, accompanied by a piercing screech that echoed through the forest, announcing her arrival. Looking up, she beheld the most beautiful sight she had ever seen - a bright full moon surrounded by thousands of screech owls, her proverbial companions enlisted in every dream. Whispers filled her subconscious, unfamiliar voices filled with pain and suffering. When she emerged from the trees, she came to a complete stop, the giddiness from the run draining out of her body as the scene before her reflected those of her nightmares.

18. Final Decision

Evie felt a strange connection to the host of characters all staring at her. The familiarity tugged on the hairs at the back of her neck as one word sprung to her lips, "Angels."
Evie was drawn in by a tall, well-built man, or rather a Greek God, standing within ten feet of her. He had bright blue eyes that appeared to be assessing her every move. The God's body was sculpted out of human marble, and he wore his long blond locks pulled back into a satin black ribbon. A few strands of his hair were loose, dancing in the wind. Evie felt a tingling in her fingers and an urge to touch the smooth ripples of muscle flanking the sides of his bare chest. It was as if she had felt them before. At the man's broad shoulders, a brilliant white light emanated from his back.

As she widened her gaze, the truth dawned on her. It wasn't just any light but wings made of the finest feathers of God himself, creating a power so strong that it commanded reverence.

Overwhelmed, Evie dropped to her knees. She recognized the small brown patch inlaid on his left wing as she looked up and finally dared to meet his gaze. He looked at her with familiar and confusing passion, the same eyes that had haunted her in countless forgotten dreams.

Evie felt uncomfortable and quickly broke the intimate connection to assess the rest of the group. Three more warrior angels were perched on a rock above the entrance to a cave, holding their swords and waiting for the next command. She recognized them from Evelyn's journal - Gabriel, Uriel, and Galiel. As she continued to observe, she saw a young couple lying on the ground in front of the cave. Light reflected off the jewels thread into the bodice of the young woman's gown. Upon closer inspection, Evie realized that it was the same dress she had worn in her nightmares, the weight that had been her constant companion. It was Evelyn. It couldn't be anyone else, which meant that beside her was Lord Wyndham, Evelyn's soulmate, ablaze in his beautifully ripped gentleman finery.

As she gasped for air, she realized she knew every moment that had led to this final scene. She had finally reached the last chapter of Evelyn's beloved journal. And now, here she was, a real-life character, leaping right into the pages of the epic battle that marked the tale's ending. Perhaps Lana had been right all along. Her fencing outfit would be perfect for her impending stay at the local insane asylum.

Breaking the silence, the blond warrior turned to the open field. "Lilith, what have you done?"

Evie was entranced by the man's clear voice.

"Michael…" Lilith purred. "How do you like her? My best yet, no?"

Evie's attention shifted from Michael to the creature before her, the same nightmare that had haunted her many times before. "It's you," she whispered, her words barely audible over the cool breeze. Her utterance made her the focus of the next chapter in this blank text. How would Evelyn describe her? Would she ever get the chance?

"Evie, my darling," Lilith said. "When will you see that this is not a dream or the ramblings of some insipid little girl?" She sneered at the word "girl" and stepped further into the clearing. "Besides, you are the heroine of this story." Lilith opened her arms and beckoned Evie closer. "Come, my dear. I have been waiting for you."

Evie was taken aback by the stunning beauty of the blond goddess, whose golden locks and deep blue eyes left Evie feeling humbled. She couldn't tell if Lilith was a goddess or a demon. As she rose to approach Lilith, trying to understand her fear, she suddenly halted, hearing the rustling of leaves behind her. While she was still trying to comprehend what was happening, she felt a strong tug on her arm.

"Lilith," Blake yelled. "You can't have her!" He pulled Evie towards him and stood in front of her protectively. "I won't let you!"

"Blake, stop!" Evie protested.

The demon let out a soft coo of satisfaction. "Finally, my daughter has found her voice."

Evie pushed Blake aside and walked toward the center of the clearing. Everyone else remained silent. "Lilith," she said. "You...are Lilith." The words echoed in her mind, as the silence stretched. Evie struggled to compose herself. "How is this possible?" she finally managed to utter.

"Lilith," Michael commanded, interrupting the private scene.

Evie turned her attention back to the blond God, startled by his familiar voice. Lilith's laughter surrounded the small field.

"I will ask this once more," the God continued, "what have you done?"

"Ah, Michael," Lilith responded, picking some leaves from her white translucent gown. "I have been so looking forward to this moment." She approached the archangel slowly. "This new one positively surpasses Evangeline's modest looks." She stopped in front of him and smiled. "It has been quite amusing for me to watch you suffer through each of these Evangeline look-a-likes, my poor strong Angel. I had no idea how much of a romantic you were." She attempted to touch a lock of Michael's hair, but he leaned back. "All this pent-up passion," she said, "perhaps things could have been different between us."

"Stop this charade!" Michael commanded, his words hanging heavily in the humid air.

Lilith glided closer to Evie, her touch grazing the bottom of her apprentice's chin. The warm gesture sent shivers down Evie's spine. ”Poor Michael," Lilith sneered, her smile predatory. "Always yearning for something you can never have."

Michael instantly seized Lilith around the neck, his grip unyielding as Evie was swiftly pulled back into Blake's arms, the shock of the surprise attack barely registering. Milky white wings shot out of Lilith's back, playing second fiddler to the brightness emanating from Michael's; her delicate shoes tearing at the seams as large talons burst through the soft material, grabbing Michael's arms and legs. The site of angel and beast brought Evie back to her knees, the sheer magnitude of their fight overwhelming. Above, the owls took flight, their vigilant gaze scanning the darkening skies, while serpents of all sizes slithered from the depths of the forest, a sinister army summoned by Lilith's anguished cries. The weight of Lilith's commands pressed against Evie's chest, a discomfort coursing through her veins.

"Evie," Blake pleaded in her ear. "This is our chance. Let's get out of here."

"I don't think I can," Evie said.

"What do you mean?" he asked.

Evie could feel the anticipation of joining the attack. "I can feel Lilith calling to me."

"I thought you said you weren't a demon?" Blake accused.

"I'm not!" Evie yelled, trying to fight the unease.

"Then let's get out of here. We need to head back to the portal." Grabbing Evie by the arm, Blake pushed her into the darkness of the woods. Suddenly, a blood-curdling scream ripped through the forest, causing Evie to come to a dead stop.

"Something's wrong," Evie cried, turning back towards the clearing. "That was Evelyn."

"It doesn't matter," Blake insisted. "We need to keep moving."

"But you don't understand, Blake. I have to help her! For some reason, Evelyn entrusted me with her journal, not Damek."

"Evelyn didn't give you anything, Evie." Blake tried to reason. "Lilith stole it and made sure you got it! Damek was supposed to have it, not you!"

"No!" Evie shook her head, trying to block out Blake's voice. "I don't care what you say! Evelyn trusted me. Me...just some nobody who's never been good at anything! I don't understand any of this, I don't. But Evelyn chose me, and I can't just run away!"

She felt Blake's hands relax, allowing her to step away. She could hardly see his face through the tears streaming down her face. Without further thought, she turned back and raced into the open field.

Lilith, her wings covered in bright red, stood before the cave, licking the blood from her hands. Her eyes matched the color of the deadly stain. It reminded Evie of a lion satisfied with its latest kill. The metallic smell hit Evie in the gut as she glanced behind Lilith, where Michael, the leader of God's army, lay in a pool of his own blood. Nobody moved. Suddenly, another aching scream pierced their ears, and Evie turned her head towards the wretched sound. Evie's storybook heroine, Evelyn, lunged off the ground and ran straight at Lilith.

"How dare you!" Evelyn spat. "You...you, beast!" she exclaimed, her body trembling.

Lilith raised her blood-stained hand, fingers spread wide, and Evelyn crumpled to the ground, clutching her stomach in pain, as if Lilith's hand wielded a force of torment.

"We could have been such great friends, you and I," Lilith bemoaned. "It is cruel, really, always having a weak human guard for God's most precious gift. Or perhaps I truly am the beast I was made to be." Lifting her head to the sky, Lilith raised her voice. "Humans have the ability to encompass the true gift of love-forgiveness." The word dripped from her lips.

A chill began to spread through Evie's chest.

Evelyn tried to look at Lilith through the intense bouts of pain. "You are the devil!"

"Am I Evelyn? Am I the devil? Forgiveness was denied to me. My love was ripped away from me and replaced with this," Lilith said, spreading her arms wide. "This! The mother of all deceit!"

"You were the one that chose your cursed freedom over love!" Evelyn yelled. "You made your choice!"

Lord Wyndham snapped out of the trance he was in and rushed to Evelyn's side. He fell to his knees and covered her trembling body.

"Perhaps you are right," Lilith breathed, a faraway look in her eyes.

Evie felt a gnawing sensation in her gut. A bright flash of white darted above her head as she looked up, and the ground shook beneath her feet. Gabriel and Uriel landed behind Lilith, swords raised to face the incoming beast.

Lilith's eyes met Evie's over the clearing, and she let her long-ago sadness radiate towards her protégé. An extreme pulling sensation rose in Evie's throat as if she was being commanded to do something, but she didn't know what. All she felt was confused and helpless.

Hearing the commotion, Blake tugged Evie's shoulder as Lilith's battle cry pierced the night.

With a slash of Lilith's talons, Gabriel and Uriel stepped back. Taking advantage of the hesitation, Lilith escaped from the archangels by stretching her filthy wings and taking flight. She swooped over Evelyn, still withering from the demon's last infliction of pain, and easily pulled her out of Lord Wyndham's unrelenting arms, clawing him across the face. She swiftly ascended into the sky with Evelyn in tow while Gabriel and Uriel followed closely behind.

A piercing scream tore from Evie's lips as a burning pain seared through her shoulders.

"Evie, what's wrong?" Blake yelled, afraid to touch her.

"I don't know!" Evie screamed in agony.

Feeling a thick goo oozing down her neck, Evie tried to wipe the fowl stench. She looked at her hands, but there was nothing there. Despite the excruciating pain, she strained her eyes to see through the darkness. Lilith was still carrying Evelyn further into the night sky, followed closely by the angels who were being nipped at by the owls. Lightning cracked through the night, emphasizing Lilith's control over nature.

"Evie!" Blake pleaded. "Don't you see that she's pure evil? We need to leave now!"

Evie felt like she was hovering over her body when she realized Blake was rocking her in his arms. Taking a deep breath, she entered back into the intense pain to pull out of his comforting embrace.

"Blake!" she cried. "Don't you understand? I can't leave. I think I'm feeling what Evelyn feels. Somehow, we're linked and..." Her scream cut off the rest of her thoughts. "Lilith is killing her!"

Blake acted quickly and without hesitation. Pulling Evie to her feet, he threw her over his shoulder. "I'm sorry, Evie. But we have to go. It's for your own safety. Their fate has already been decided."

As he tried to carry her over his back, Evie struggled and pushed against the pain with all her might, causing Blake to lose his grip. She stumbled and fell on the damp forest floor, landing on her backside as the smell of blood filled her nostrils. Overwhelmed by the strange sensation, she closed her eyes and felt weightless, as though she was soaring through the air.

"Evie, my dear one," Lilith's voice whispered in her ear. "It is almost over. Her death will be our survival."

The demon's voice echoed in Evie's ear as a clear vision of the above scene left a permanent mark on her soul. As Lilith thrust one of her blood-stained, razor-sharp talons into Evelyn's stomach, she let Evie's beloved heroine go. Evelyn's screams of pain ricocheted off the boom of thunder as she plummeted to the ground in the pouring rain. Evie's stomach erupted. Throwing her arms to the ground, she threw up.

"Evie," Blake yelled. "What's wrong?"

"I don't understand what's happening," Evie gasped, wiping her mouth with her arm. "I think Lilith is causing me to see things. Evelyn is-" Evie's sentence was cut short as she began to cough uncontrollably.

"You and Lilith are connected," he said, rubbing her back." You're gonna have to fight the connection; it's your only option. Come on, we have to go." Pulling Evie to her feet, he continued, "I know you can do this!"

A cry echoed across the battlefield as Lord Wyndham, consumed by fury, charged forward into the raging storm. In the center of the field, standing guard with the awe-inspiring sword that contained the stone, Evie watched as Lord Wyndham dropped the heavy metal and opened his arms wide to catch his soulmate. Instinctively, Evie reached out, but Blake pulled her back, preventing her from following Lord Wyndham into the open field.

Blake pointed to the sky and exclaimed, "Look, Evie!" Suddenly, white wings shot out of the cave, and strong arms caught Evelyn mid-air.

"It's Michael," Evie whispered. "He's alive." The words escaped her mouth as the angel landed by Lord Wyndham. Looking at Evelyn's soulmate, the archangel laid her in his open arms.

"This is all my fault," Michael said. "Only you can save her, Lord Adam Wyndham. It has always been you."

"What do you mean?" Adam yelled. "You are the angel. What the hell are your powers good for, then? Save her!" The words tore from Adam as the rage continued to boil under his skin.

"You know what to do," Michael said as he flew into the night, heading back for the beast.

"Adam," Evelyn strained to speak, "Please make the pain stop."

"No!" screamed Evie. She yanked out of Blake's grasp and ran towards the couple.

Blake followed behind, his gun now tucked by his side.

"Evelyn," Lord Wyndham whispered, "I love you."

As Evie ran, the lovers' pulled further and further away into a dark tunnel. She was unable to reach them. She felt Blake's presence as he grabbed her from behind, pulling her out of the nightmarish funnel. The dark edges disappeared as Lilith landed in front of the huddled couple. No angels followed behind.

"Well, how touching. If only a few words of tenderness could save your true love. How silly you mortals can be." Lilith's ragged, war-torn wings pulled into her back and disappeared; her talons once again replaced by dainty, beautiful feet. "A perfectly good pair of shoes ruined again."

Lord Wyndham crouched down to lay Evelyn on the ground, and then he faced Lilith with a narrowed gaze. "Lilith...You are mine."

"Lord Wyndham," Evie yelled at the top of her lungs. "The stone!"

Lord Wyndham turned around in surprise as if seeing her for the first time.

Lilith, however, beamed. "Well done, my dear," she said, her pride radiating toward her most accomplished student.

Lord Wyndham broke out of his stupor and grasped the sword. He placed Evelyn's hand on the stone and covered it with his own. A hot blue flame burst from the crude rock, creating a bright blue beacon in the sky. The light rapidly expanded into thick blue smoke, enveloping the entire battlefield. Lilith's chilling laugh echoed amidst the fumes as the rain intensified and furiously pelted Evie's face. Suddenly, rapid gunfire exploded as Lilith's laugh turned into howls of pain.

Blake held the gun, yelling, "Run, Evie, run!" as he fired rounds of ammunition into the blue mist.

A feeling of nausea washed over Evie as she realized a block had been removed from her mind. It was as if a curtain had been lifted, allowing her free will to take over. Feeling a sense of clarity and freedom, she grabbed Blake's shoulder and yelled, "Let's go!"

They ran as fast as they could; however, Evie's original grace was gone. She stumbled over fallen tree limbs, with the thick tree branches leaving their marks on her face. She could feel the creatures of the darkness hot on their trail. As Evie heard more rapid gunfire, she looked behind her.

"That should keep them away for a bit," Blake said as he stepped in front of her and drew out a dagger.

"Where did you get that?" Evie asked.

"My bag of tricks," he sneered.

As Evie watched Blake thrashing at the protruding branches, she saw him differently. She couldn't believe this was the same brooding teenager who used to blast his music and hang out with the potheads under the bleachers. As she admired his broad back, she realized that he was not only physically strong but also mentally resilient. When had he transformed into an adult with such admirable qualities? Evie felt inspired to be like Blake, knowing it was the only way she'd make it out alive. As she focused on his arm, brandishing the small sword like a true adventurer, she accidentally slammed right into his back.

"Ok, this is the spot," Blake said, disregarding Evie's clumsiness.

"What do you mean?" Evie asked.

Blake crouched down and dug his fingers into a deep groove in the black soil. "This is where the mirror led us."

"What should we do now?"

Blake put his finger to his lips, motioning for Evie to be quiet as he stood up and stepped back into the shelter of the woods. "Someone's coming," he whispered.

Lilith emerged from the forest. "Did you think I would let you get away that easy? After all my careful planning and hard work?" The goddess smiled brightly with her full red lips.

Evie felt the familiar dull ache descend over the back of her head as she admired Lilith's flawless body, not one imperfection left by the bullets. Even the white see-through fabric of Lilith's dressing gown was unblemished. The pain softened in Evie's body, and a lightness descended over her thoughts, cushioning the rough edges. She pushed the sides of her temples with her hands and glared at the witch. "Stop this!" Evie demanded. "Let me think for myself!" It was becoming harder for her to focus as she got lost in the deep blue ridges of Lilith's commanding eyes.

"Of course, my dear." As the words left Lilith's mouth, the haziness promptly lifted from Evie's thoughts and left her lucid once more.

"That's it," Evie asked, "That's all I needed to say?"

"Have I not acted upon all your requests favorably?" Lilith smiled. "I would never do anything to hurt you, Evie." Hearing the cock of a gun, the trance was broken, and both women looked at Blake.

"Stop doing whatever you're doing to her. I won't let you have her," Blake shouted, pointing his gun at Lilith. The only sign of fear was the brief shake of his trigger finger.

"Stupid boy," Lilith said calmly. "Do you honestly think you can beat me?"

"I'll do whatever it takes. You've caused enough pain and suffering."

"Ah, still aiming to be the martyr, are we?"

"I won't be controlled, Lilith. Your words can't hurt me," Blake said firmly. "I'm nothing like Abel."

Lilith raised an eyebrow. "And do you think I'm the one controlling you?" she asked incredulously. "Excuse me, Blake Abel, but who do you think created your destiny? Was it me? I only wish I had that kind of power." Lilith's anger began to surface, her eyes flashing red.

"I'm not listening to you," Blake insisted. "Lana isn't like Cain, and I won't let anything happen to her either."

"And that is your downfall, young man. When will you ever learn."

Raising his gun higher, Blake aimed directly at Lilith's eyes and demanded, "Why Evie? Why did you have to choose her?"

"Interesting word choice," Lilith answered. "What makes you think I chose her?"   Lilith's eyes glowed as she emphasized the word 'chose.'

Blake responded by firing his gun into the demon's head. Evie dropped to the ground and covered her ears, shutting her eyes tight. She couldn't stand any more gore. She waited for the sounds of pain but was surprised by the musical laughter that filled the air.

"Did you think those man-made atrocities could kill me? Me?" Her wings began to spread from her back coated with dried blood, her talons once again overtaking the beauty of her feet. "Do you forget who I am?" she asked. "Do you truly believe that a mere human can kill the Queen of all Demons? The original form of all humanity?"

"You are nothing but a woman scorned!" Blake yelled.

Evie briefly caught a glimpse of Lilith's distant pain on the verge of breaking.

The stern command, "Enough!" yelled from the darkness, shattered the silence, and brought everyone to attention. Evie knew it could only be one being - Michael, the Leader of God's Army, who had just landed next to Blake. Michael's beautiful face had scratches that were already healing. The glow of his wings surrounded the small space and illuminated the rest of the warriors who were now clearing the trees.

"I was wondering how long it would take for you to get here," Lilith said, her steel composure back in place.

"This has gone long enough. It is time for you to go back."

"To where, Michael? My poor, lowly cave by the Red Sea to make more demons that can scour the land with more heinous crimes? Humans are so fickle." Lilith waved a finger in the air, pulling her lips into a slight pout. "Tsk, tsk, tsk..it seems someone has not done their homework." Turning to Evie, she continued, "That is how they say it, correct?"

Evie pulled on her torn vest and lowered her head as the full gaze of all four angels bore down on her, once again feeling the heat rise into her cheeks.

"So, this is it? This your new weapon?" Michael asked, walking past Gabriel to circle Evie. "You brought a girl from the future back in time. How does this benefit you?" Michael continued to look at Evie skeptically. "You expect me to believe that this naive slip of a girl will help you gain entry into the afterlife? I must commend you. She is the best Evangeline look-alike you have created so far. Shall I forsake my vows right now?"

Michael's thorough inspection caused a flutter in Evie's chest.

"Who are you?" Michael demanded of her.

Lifting her head at Michael's command, Evie met his blue eyes, memories flooding her senses.

Michael broke the intense connection and turned back to Lilith. "She isn't real," he said and then looked at Gabriel and Uriel with a silent demand. Michael accepted their brief nodes of assent.

"Oh, she is more than just some pawn," Lilith replied. "You amaze me, Michael. I would think that you, of all people, would recognize the spirit within."

Michael glared at Lilith. "Stop toying with me, demon! Do not think for one minute that you understand my pain."

"Understand your pain?" Lilith exclaimed, spreading her arms. "How dare you compare my eternal punishment to your utter drool excuse of a life. At least I fight for what I want, unlike you. What would your true love think if she could see you now?"

The glow in Michael's eyes shone brightly as he refused to answer.

"Come now, Michael. Let us not play these childish games. I know what has been driving you for so long. The need to save your one true love to forsake all else can be a powerful motivator. I can not help but wonder if you would have acted differently if given another chance. After all, your soulmate did not have to die."

"Leave Evangeline out of this!" Michael yelled, taking a threatening step closer.

With a graceful movement, Lilith stepped forward and stood nose-to-nose with Michael. "So you finally admit it," she said. "Our motives may differ, but our actions are equally flawed." Michael continued to stare at Lilith when she finally demanded, "Say it; I want to hear you say it."

Evie noticed movement and glanced at Galiel. He leaned in toward Gabriel, whispering, "What's happening?"

Gabriel continued to watch Michael closely as he responded, "Michael fell in love with Evangeline. It was he who activated the stone with her. He was her true soulmate."

"But how can that be?" Galiel asked Gabriel, with no answer; he gazed back at Michael. "What is he going to do?"

"Finally make his choice," Uriel breathed next to him.

"But that would mean..." Galiel began to speak, his voice trailing off as he contemplated the implications of what he was about to say.

"Say it, Michael!" Lilith repeated. "Denounce your love for Evangeline right now in front of us all. I dare you."

"Gabriel! Uriel! You must stop him!" shouted Galiel.

Michael turned to the heavens, breaking his connection with Lilith. "Father," he cried, "I can no longer endure this agony, for the demon speaks the truth. I cannot continue like this."

With a quick flick of her hand, Lilith sneered. "I do not think so. That is too easy - drop the theatrics."

"Shut up, Witch!" Michael spat in her face. "This is what you wanted, is it not?" He dropped to his knees and stared into the heavens. "Every time I turn, I am reminded of her. This demon will not stop haunting me." He laced his hands in prayer and closed his eyes. "I am constantly reminded that I could not save the one person I love the most. Please, Father..." Nodding his head as if responding to an unheard question, the great general of God's Army dropped his hands to the ground. "Yes, I love her more than anything else." He let his heavy burden go, and a single tear streamed down his smooth cheek.

Lilith's smile gradually transformed into an expression of utter disgust. Suddenly, a crack of iridescent light illuminated the sky with a strong gust of wind, causing even the trained warriors to flinch. Descending from the sky, a stream of light particles separated Michael and Lilith.

Michael looked up at the sky and said, "Yes, Father. This is truly what I want. If you love me, you will put me out of my misery."

"No," Galiel's cry echoed through the forest, causing the owls to erupt in anticipated excitement. With another crack of lightning, a bright white spear descended from the heavens, illuminating the scene and dispelling the last remnants of the storm.

Evie could feel the warmth on her face. "What is going on?" she whispered to Blake.

"I think we are witnessing the fall of a great angel. We are all truly lost," Blake choked, unable to look away from the scene before him.

A gust of wind whipped through the group, pelting them with dead leaves and debris as they watched the flaming spear.

"STOP!" screamed Lilith, swirling her arm, creating a tornado out of the surrounding wind. She made the funnel spin faster into a tight arc using her finger. The funnel grabbed all the nearby leaves and branches and circled God's bright spear of light, keeping it tightly intact. Following Michael's gaze upwards, Lilith exclaimed, "HA! Do you think you can fool me again, Father?" She spat on the ground, showing her disapproval of the paternal endearment, and laughed, "As you can see, I have grown quite strong. With each passing decade, my powers continue to strengthen." Her arms began to shake from the strain of holding the golden rod. "How dare you?" she continued, "Giving him the freedom he so desires from his sins. What about me? Do not I deserve the same forgiveness? What did I ever do to you?" Her attempt to step closer to the spear failed, and she faltered. "This is not over! Do you hear me?! Michael is not allowed to be relieved of his burden; I will not allow it. He will continue to feel my pain." Smiling through the strain, she raised her voice. "Perhaps seeing your favorite son continue to live in agony will teach you a lesson!"

As Lilith struggled to move the spear away from Michael, Galiel jumped in front of her.

Lilith responded with a hint of sarcasm, "How touching! The lowly apprentice wants to save his mentor. Is that it? "She narrowed her eyes and focused on the young Galiel as if just noticing him for the first time. She immediately saw through his ruse. "Oh, I know who you are. You don't fool me with this wide-eyed innocence."

Evie glanced at Gabriel and Uriel to see if they understood Lilith's surprising recognition. They seemed to be just as confused.

Michael remained crouched on the ground, unable or unwilling to provide any support.

"What would God do without his trusted scribe?" Lilith snorted. "Galiel," Lilith said, letting his name roll off her tongue. "What a quaint misnomer. I guess now would not be the appropriate time to bring attention to your real name, now would it? History is our best teacher. I think you will make a delightful addition to my plan." She smiled, looking around the tense gathering. Turning towards Blake, Lilith's lips widened to reveal her white teeth. With her arms trembling, she inched the funnel closer to him.

"He is not an Angel!" Galiel yelled. "It will kill him."

"He is of no use anymore," Lilith sneered, "it's inevitable." Lilith strained against an invisible barrier, pulling the spear closer.

Evie felt pressure around her heart as she stared at Blake. Lilith's hate fluttered into her thoughts. Still aware of her bond to the beast, she took a slight step forward.

Lilith immediately noticed her movement and asked, "What are you doing?" as her grip slackened.

"I won't let you kill Blake," Evie responded calmly.

Blake tried to pull Evie back. "Stop, Evie. She's right. I'm no longer useful. Save yourself and run!"

"Let me go!" Evie yelled. She turned to Blake and calmly repeated the phrase. "I said, let me go." Blake instantly released her and took a step back.

As Evie walked towards Lilith, a sense of calmness spread through her body, along with a strength she didn't know she possessed. She spoke firmly, "If what you're saying is true, that I am a demon, then this world doesn't have a place for me. I won't harm the people I love, and I won't help you either."

"Stop this," Lilith yelled. "It is that damn soul!"

Evie walked closer to the flaming spear, which was now beginning to take the shape of a fiery ball. Its blue core entranced her as Lilith's arms began to shake uncontrollably. Feeling a slight pressure pushing on her chest, Evie took one last glance towards Michael, who was still kneeling on the ground. She was met with his bright blue eyes, now full of wonder.

"Evangeline?" he asked.

Evie reached out to the swirling center of death, keeping her gaze fixed on the ArchAngel.

"No!" Lilith howled in pain as the spasms wracked her body from the strain.

Blake ran towards Evie, shouting as she fell to the ground. Evie shielded her eyes from the bright light and saw Blake standing over her.

"It's not your time, Evie," he said. "You're the only one who can save us. We need you." He touched his hand to her cheek and lowered his voice, "I need you."

Evie stood up and grabbed the back of his shirt. "Stop!" she cried. "This is what I was meant for!"

"No...No, you weren't."

Lilith crumpled to the ground with a high-pitched wail as the spear was too strong for her to contain. The ball of power grabbed everything in its path, heading straight for Blake and Evie. Blake quickly grasped Evie's upper arms and lifted her completely off the ground, thrusting her backward. Flames licked at Evie's forearms as another brilliant flash of fire erupted.

"No!" Evie screamed. Blackness reigned once again.

19. Another Day

"Wake up, Evie," a voice whispered. "Wake up." Amidst a gentle lullaby, a voice began to pull her out of the darkness. The searing pain gradually subsided, as if carried away by an unknown force. She felt herself slipping away, her role in the climactic ending fading into a hazy recollection.

"So this is what death is like?" she asked. The romantic music played with a broken chord, slipping in and out of the dull ache while her heart kept tempo with the tonality of the Archangel's favorite Beethoven classic.

She recognized Damek's voice breaking through the staccato of the increasing beats, calling out, "Evie? Are you there?" A shadow passed before her, flickering in and out of the melody. As she reached for her forehead, her arm was gently pulled back down. Her body reacted instinctively, feeling the cold hunger and the intense heat. Even in her final moments, her connection to Damek remained strong. As the song's last note echoed in her mind, she opened her eyes to a bright light and whispered, "God?"

"God?" Damek asked, a hint of amusement in his voice. "You did hit your head pretty hard."

"Damek?" She desperately clung to her final vision in the forest, relishing his breath on her cheek. "Am I dead?"

"Not quite, sweetheart. Welcome back."

She opened her eyes, her lips parched.

"Still think this is just some stupid love story?" he whispered. Instead of heaven or hell, she found Damek, the stone's true guardian. Her heart remained calm despite the slight shivers down her spine. She tried to focus on reality, but one thought emerged: "Blake!" she cried. The heart monitor beeped irregularly, casting a red light illuminating Damek's face.

Damek leaned in close, his eyes narrowing as he hovered above her lips. "Remember, Evie. You were created for me. You'll always be mine."

There was a brief knock on the hospital door before it started to open. Damek quickly moved to the end of the bed as Evie's monitor beeped twice.

"Evie! You're awake!" exclaimed her parents as they rushed to her bed. Her mother kissed her forehead and grabbed her hand while Evie took a deep breath.

"What happened?" Evie asked, confused.

"Just relax," her mom responded.

"Mom, please. Tell me what happened."

"You were hit by a car," her mom said, searching her face for any memory.

"What?"

"When you ran out of the school after the competition, a car skidded in the rain trying to stop and," choking down a sob, she patted Evie's hand, "it hit you."

"Hit me?" Evie looked around the room and grabbed her mother's arm. "Where's Blake?"

"Blake?" Her father interrupted. "Who's Blake?"

Frantically looking around the room, Evie met her father's confused gaze as she muttered, "Lana's brother."

"Damek, can you please go get the doctor?" Evie's father asked.

"Sure thing, Mr. March." Damek gave Evie a brief nod before heading out the door.

"Evie," her dad continued, "There was no one else at the scene, just you and the driver."

"I don't understand," Evie asked. "Why is Damek here?"

Evie's mother gently brushed away the matted hair from her daughter's face. "He's the one that found you. He said the two of you had an argument after the competition, and he followed you out of the school." Evie's father brought a chair for her mother, who tried to scoot it closer to Evie's bed. "Do you remember anything?" she asked hopefully.

"Um, yeah," Evie said. "I think so. I remember the fight, but..." Her voice trailed off as she allowed the memories to flood back. She remembered everything, including the last detail of Blake pushing her back into reality. Staring at the large bandages that encircled her lower arms, she tried to move them but couldn't.

"Do you believe you only sustained some minor scratches?" Evie's mom attempted to maintain a smile. "They're pretty deep welts, but don't worry, the doctor said that the scars will eventually fade to the point where you will hardly notice them anymore."

The hospital door opened again, and this time it was the doctor. Evie caught Damek's gaze following behind. Holding the door open, Damek motioned to someone in the hall. "Look who I found lurking outside."

Taking a cautious step into the room, Lana firmly held a disposable cup. "I wasn't lurking. I was just getting a cup of coffee."

Evie cleared her throat and winced. "I'm glad you're here."

"Couldn't let my best friend parish by hospital food, now could I?" Lana attempted to laugh, but her smile quickly turned into a worried frown.

"Well, I better be going. I'll stop by to check on you later." Damek said, pushing Lana further into the room.

Lana shrugged him off with an annoyed look and took a sip of the cold coffee.

"Wait," Evie called. "I need to talk to you." She winced at the burning sensation in her throat.

"Sweetie, I think that can wait." Evie's father said, letting his concern show in the crease of his forehead. "You need to rest."

"Don't worry, I'll be around." Turning to Evie's parents, Damek smiled. "Thanks for letting me stay. Been a crazy night."

"Of course." Evie's mom said. "We can't thank you enough."

"Sleep tight," Damek said with a wink. She knew he would be back. They would all be back.

Evie had survived but couldn't shake off the feeling that Lilith had wanted it that way; the plan had worked, no matter its intent. She needed her strength, and she needed Blake. Despite not knowing how things would end, deep down, she knew he was still alive somewhere. Suddenly, the pain in her arms pushed all thoughts away. She grabbed her right forearm and let out a moan.

Her mother's voice faded as the gentle whine of a nearby machine grew louder. "Don't worry," she said, "the pain will subside soon."

"Wait," slurred Evie, "is Blake okay?"

She tried to clear the numbness settling over her mind, unable to make out Lana's response. With every drip of the medicine entering her bloodstream, her pain eased along with her ability to speak. Questions flooded her memory, jumbling into one large mass of confusion. Did Blake take the spear? Did Michael save them all? Did God intervene? Had Lana actually witnessed the activation of the stone in the gym? Did it even matter? She was there, Lana was there.

"So many questions, my little one," the demon voice hummed in her ear. "All that matters is we have won the first battle—success to the Final Guardian. With a few scars, of course, but remember, my dear, I do not like surprises. Let us not make a habit of those in the future, shall we?"

Evie let out a moan and said, "Lana..."

"Enough nonsense! It is now time to begin your training. Our time has finally come, daughter of mine." The demon's musical laughter continued whispering in Evie's ear as she finally fell asleep.

"Rest, my dear Evangeline. Rest."

Evie knew that the last words were meant solely for her.

Evie's story continues in...

THE DEMON'S JOURNEY

Book Two in the Final Guardian Series